ON WOODWARD

JOYCE VAN HAREN

abbott press®
A DIVISION OF WRITER'S DIGEST

Abbott Press books may be ordered through booksellers or by contacting:

Abbott Press
1663 Liberty Drive
Bloomington, IN 47403
www.abbottpress.com
Phone: 1-866-697-5310

Because of the dynamic nature of the Internet, any web addresses or links contained in this book may have changed since publication and may no longer be valid. The views expressed in this work are solely those of the author and do not necessarily reflect the views of the publisher, and the publisher hereby disclaims any responsibility for them.

Any people depicted in stock imagery provided by Thinkstock are models, and such images are being used for illustrative purposes only. Certain stock imagery © Thinkstock.

ISBN: 978-1-4582-1051-7 (sc)
ISBN: 978-1-4582-1050-0 (hc)
ISBN: 978-1-4582-1049-4 (e)

Library of Congress Control Number: 2013944328

Printed in the United States of America.

Abbott Press rev. date: 3/17/2014

Dedication

To John (Jack) Van Haren, my late artist-professor husband, to my sons, Jeffrey and John Van Haren, and my late daughter Julia (Julie) Van Haren, who all encouraged me.

Also, to my granddaughters Madison and Bailey Van Haren, and to my grandson, Carter Van Haren, who said when a ten-year-old, "Gramma, wouldn't it be nice if you could see your book on the bookshelf before you die?"

And last but not least, to my dear relatives and friends and writing professors who all encouraged me, also. And to the talented writers in General Motors public relations for whom I worked and learned through osmosis more writing skills. To paraphrase a well-known saying, "What's good for General Motors is good for the country," I always said, "What was good for General Motors public relations was good for Joyce."

Cover Graphics/Art Credit: Cindy Deery

Chapter 1

Alma May Combs lay on her back near the edge of the mountain ridge, her open sketchbook at her side. The wild fescue grass was rough on her bare arms, but she didn't care: The air was fresh and clean and sweet smelling here. Facing in this easterly direction, she could almost forget that she was part of the community down in the valley behind and below her. She could gaze up at the yellow-green leaves of the huge maple fluttering in the autumn breeze and almost forget about the grimy buildings of the Independent Coal Mining Co., and that she and her family lived in one of the row-after-row of company owned shacks.

She could almost forget, too, that just two weeks ago the whistle had blown, signaling disaster. Three miners had died, but her father had escaped again. "Reckon I'm too cussed ornery to die," he'd quipped with a grim half-smile when his partners pulled him out from the rubble of timber and coal.

Alma May stretched her long overall-clad legs. To her right, she saw the reddening leaves of the sumac, and to her left, the crimson seed cones of the ear-leafed wild magnolia. The sun soothed and warmed her face and body. She was almost, as her father would say, "as happy as a possum up a 'simmon tree with a dog a mile off."

This place belonged to her. She'd told no one but her father about it. Sometimes on Sundays, his day off, they'd sneak away for a little while and climb up here. If he got the urge, he'd bring along his worn guitar. He'd pick up the instrument and sit with his back resting against the trunk of the tree, and Alma May would watch his long-fingered, graceful hands play as he sang in a clear tenor voice. Maybe he'd sing one of the old Elizabethan favorites of the region, "Lovin' Nancy" or "Hangman's Song."

She'd sketch the surrounding Kentucky foothills and the tree-lined crest of Big Black Mountain, several miles south. He'd never fail to peer over her shoulder as she worked, and say in his best art critic's voice, "Some day, Miss Alma May Combs, you're goin' to be a famous artist."

Then they'd lie on their backs and make believe that the clouds above them were really The Farm.

"See that big cloud to the right an' back a ways?" her father would say. "That's the barn. An' that medium-size cloud in front a it? That's the house."

"What's that little bit a cloud to the left, Pa?"

"Why, can't you tell, Alma May? That's the tractor, a course."

After they'd worked out in minute detail such things as where the trees would be, and how many chickens and hogs they'd buy the first year, the conversation would end with Alma May asking:

"Pa, are we really goin' to have a farm some day?"

"Sure as a skunk stinks we are, Alma May. Don't we already have a hundred an' fifty-three dollars saved for it?" After a moment, he'd add, "A course, we'd have to find a place near the mountains. Ain't never goin' to live no wheres for very long without we see mountains."

Alma May shifted her body now and thought about the mine explosion. As much as she tried, she could not push it completely from her mind. If anything ever happened to Pa, she knew she'd die, too.

She raised her head a little and nestled her hands behind it. The outline of her developing breasts under the bib of her cotton overalls repeated the outline of two foothills in the distance. She smiled at the comparison. There were so many thngs happening lately with her body and Alma didn't know the reason for them. It was all so confusing. Who could she ask? There were some things she couldn't talk to Pa about. Like the way Uncle Darcas had been looking at her lately, with that funny smile twisting his lips--it made her skin crawl and her stomach feel creepy. She ought to be able to talk to Ma about these things. Several times Alma May had tried, but her mother had looked down and cleared her throat, then quickly changed the subject. One time she'd opened the *Woman's Home Companion* magazine to a page advertising Lydia Pinkham's Vegetable Compound. She took it to her mother and asked, "Ma, what they mean by 'female weaknesses' and 'irregular and painful menstruation, inflammation and ulceration a the womb'?"

Her mother had tucked her head farther down over the washboard where she was scrubbing the overalls of Alma May's eight-year-old brother, Jimmie Lee. Her face blushed as red as Pa's red-and-white polka dotted handkerchief hanging on the line behind her. "I'll tell you when your time comes, Alma May."

Well, Alma May's time had come, more than four months ago, and her Ma still hadn't told her any—

The whistle blasted in the valley below. Alma May jumped to her feet. Forgetting about the sketchbook, forgetting about everything but her father, she ran as fast as she could--down, down toward the valley. The whistle blowing during working hours meant only one thing: someone's pa was dead. The brutal sound shouted out its cruel message: "Your Pa! Your Pa!" The black gum and beech tree branches tore at her long, copper curls and bloodied her arms. But Alma May's eyes were fixed on the scene below. Women and children, stick figures from her view above, were already pouring out of their shacks, running for the mouth of the mine. "*Oh, God, don't let anything happen to Pa!*

She had only Knee High Creek to cross now before coming to the clearing. Once across the bridge over the creek, she spotted her brother running toward the crowd gathering at the opening to the mine. "Jimmie Lee, Jimmie Lee!" she shouted.

He turned his head her way, but kept on running. Jimmie Lee had been playing on the pile of culm with some of the other miners' children and was completely covered with coal dust.

Yellow-black smoke rolled from the opening and made soft dark puffs in the sky.

She was still running as she approached the crowd. She saw the large outline of her mother. Lizzie Combs was shifting from side to side, her arms folded in front of her, cradling her sagging bosom. Alma May ran up and stood beside her. She squeezed her hand into the fold of her mother's left arm. Her mother's body felt stiff, stony. Other mothers huddled with their children, their faces pale and their arms around each other. Familiar voices around her croaked and rasped with fright, but she didn't look at the owners as they spoke:

"Methane explosion again. ..."

"Brought four bodies up already. MacDonald. Creech. Haddix. Johnson. ..."

"Sure as hell, if Clyde gets out a that hole safe this time, he ain't goin' back down there no more."

"That's what I keep sayin' about Floyd, but when it comes right down to it, how else is a body to make a livin' when he ain't knowin' nothin' else. ..."

Alma May stood in a trance. Jimmie Lee joined her and her mother. She absently read the words cut into the concrete above the opening to the mine: SAFETY THE FIRST CONSIDERATION.

Silence now from the waiting crowd as two more workers appeared at the mouth of the mine. Smoke floated eerily around them, making them seem almost like advancing specters. They carried another limp body, slowly, gently. Was it Pa? Don't let it be Pa. No, it couldn't be Pa--Pa's body is not that big. She looked into the face of the dead miner as the men carried him past her. J. T. Miller. She heard Mrs. Miller's shrill scream from somewhere to her right.

Several moments passed. Or was it hours? What did it matter? Her Pa was down there. Maybe trying to climb out. Maybe blinded. Maybe knocked unconscious. Maybe ...

Another small group of miners appeared at the opening. A few sighs of relief around her. She looked at the blackened faces of the men as they walked past her and tried to recognize them behind the coal dust. Kazmarick. Pignatelli. Howard. Papantoniou.

Several more moments passed. She saw the outline of a large, heavyset miner. He carried a body in his arms. *No, God, don't let it be Pa!* Her hand, still squeezed in her mother's folded arm, grew cold and then numb. The man carrying the body neared her. She squinted to focus on the body's face. Under the smeared coal dust she recognized her father. She tried to scream, "Pa! Pa!" but no sound came out. Alma May's knees gave way under her. She heard her mother moan, but... why did she sound so far away? Alma May felt herself sink deep, deeper, into the ground.

Chapter 2

Alma May awoke and, as always, looked up at the familiar blotches that past rains had made on the ceiling under the tin roof. That blotch way over there, above the doorway leading to the dwelling's only other room, looked like the shape of Africa in her geography book. To the right, she saw the spot that reminded her of the crest of Big Black Mountain.

She glanced over and saw that her parents' bedroom door was closed. Her mother was peeling potatoes at the sink. Alma May yawned and wondered why her mother was preparing supper so early in the day, even before she'd called her to get up and dress for school. But it must be later than she thought--the kerosene lamp on the table in back of her mother wasn't lit as it usually was in the morning. The room was bright from the sun coming in the only window.

She remembered then. Pa! In a rush, she relived the nightmare of the night before--the whistle, the smoke, the waiting. And, finally, seeing Pa being carried... She sat up suddenly in bed, tossed the patchwork quilt aside, and screamed, "Pa! Pa!"

Her mother dropped the knife and potato she was peeling to the counter. With speed not characteristic of Lizzie Combs, she wiped her hands on her apron, rushed to Alma May and sat down on the bed.

"Lay back, now, Alma May. Your Pa--he's alive. Just knocked unconscious, that's all. We thought he had the smoke inhalation, like the others."

"Pa . . . not dead . . . not dead. . . . But, but, where is he? Where's Pa? I want to see Pa!"

"He's sleepin'. Hush before you wake him. Your Pa's been sleepin' on and off since last night. The doctor-man's been here to see both a you. You're both goin' to be all right, he said."

The door opened. Jimmie Lee dumped his school books on the oilclothed table. He was out of breath from running the three-quarters of a mile from school. "The teacher said I can keep my books to take with me when we go but not to tell the other kids. What's for supper, Ma? Can I have a piece a bread an' sugar an' a glass a milk?"

"Ain't much milk left and it's for supper, but you can have a piece a--"

"What's he mean, Ma? 'When we go.'?" Alma May asked.

Her mother gave Jimmie Lee a look that said, "Be still."

"What's he mean, Ma? Tell me," Alma May insisted.

Her mother hesitated. "Your Pa wanted to tell you hisself. He ain't never going down in that mine again. Never. We're leavin', Alma May. Soon's we can--"

"Leavin'? But, but, we don't have enough money saved for The Farm yet. How can we leave and buy The Farm?"

Jimmie Lee reached for his sugar bread and took a bite. He sat down on the bed next to Alma May. "Pa says we goin' up north an' he's gettin' a factry job in Detroit City like Mister McLaughlin did an' we'll save lots a money like Mister McLaughlin did an' in a year we can come back an' buy The Farm." Jimmie Lee paused for breath. "Ain't that somethin', Alma May? We gonna live in a big city an'--"

"But, but, we ain't got no money to go to Detroit. An' we can't take the money we've been saving for The Farm, an'--"

"Your Pa says we'll have to take The Farm money," her mother said. She glanced at Alma May, then resumed peeling potatoes. "But he says it ain't like we won't get it back in a couple a weeks when he'll be makin' big money--"

"An' Alma May, guess what?" Jimmie Lee added excitedly. "We're takin' Uncle Darcas's Model T! Pa says it's cheaper drivin' than buyin' bus tickets for everybody."

"Uncle Darcas…" Alma whispered. At the mention of her uncle, a shiver crept over her body. She pulled the quilt back up over her shoulders.

"Your Uncle Darcas ain't comin' with us," her mother said. "He's going to stay here and try to save some money till your Aunt Euelly gets better. And your Pa says soon's we can, we'll send them money for train tickets, on account a he's lettin' us use his car."

"But, but ..." It was all too much for Alma May to absorb! Pa's alive. I'm alive. We're leaving. Uncle Darcas's Model T.

She lay back down and closed her eyes. Maybe if she fell asleep and woke up again things wouldn't happen so fast. The familiar pillow and quilt her mother had made for her were reassuring, comforting. Pa's all right ... Pa's alive ... Pa's alive. . . .

Chapter 3

For the next several days, Alma May and her father stayed in the house resting and recovering. Lizzie Combs washed all the clothes and the family's meager supply of linen and took the yellow curtains down from the window for washing and packing. "We'll need these in our new house 'til we can buy some more."

Her father sat at the table counting and recounting their savings. It was almost as if he believed the more he recounted the stacks of coins, the bigger they would get. "This here twenty dollars is for gas and oil," he said, fingering the first stack. "This here's for our first week's rent. I'll have a job by the time our second week's due." He straightened the second stack. "This here's ..."

On the last day, Alma May gently interrupted, "I'm goin' up to the schoolhouse an' say goodbye to Mr. McAllister, Pa."

"You do that, Alma May," her father replied, still looking down at their savings. "Ain't right you go away without you say goodbye even though we're comin' back in a year."

Alma May hurried up the road. With all the bed rest her mother had insisted she have the past few days, she felt fine. She kept her eyes straight ahead as she walked, not wanting to see the coal dust-covered windows and littered stoops of the neighbors' shacks on her left. "What's the use a washin' the windows," the miners' wives (except for her mother) would say, "when they's just as dirty the next day?"

Alma May crossed the main road, its ribbon-straight length paved with coal slag. She passed the company store and angled to the right, up the steep dirt path leading to the shabby one-room schoolhouse.

She liked going up this narrow path. Sourwood trees grew thick on either side. She felt secure under the strength of their limbs, and special surrounded by the beauty of their autumn-scarlet leaves.

Mr. McAllister sat behind his wooden oak desk at the front of the room next to an American flag and a photograph of President Hoover. School was over for the day. He was correcting third-grade arithmetic papers. Alma thought how fortunate she was to have a teacher like Mr. McAllister. After earning a teaching certificate from Pine Mountain Settlement School twenty miles west of here, he'd taught in various schools twenty-five years before coming to Mountainview two years ago. Mr. McAllister knew everything. Next to Pa, she liked talking with Mr. McAllister more than with anyone.

His normally thin, serious face crinkled with a broad smile when he saw Alma May approaching. Mr. McAllister stood up and extended his hand. "Why, hello, Alma May."

Alma May was always a little surprised and amused when he rose to his full height. Ian McAllister was built with a short trunk and long, thin legs, who looked short when sitting down, but tall and gangly when standing up. She shyly shook his hand. "Jimmie Lee told me you're leaving," he said. "I'm so glad you took the time to come and say goodbye. How are you feeling?"

"Just fine. It was just that I fainted, and Ma made me get lots a rest. We won't be gone long. Just a year an' then we'll be back an' buy that farm I told you about." Alma May hesitated. She awkwardly smoothed her hair back from her forehead. Still not knowing how to begin saying what she'd come to say, she smoothed it back again. "I, I want to thank you for all you've done for me. Takin' time after school to explain about the history an' art an'--"

"Why, Alma May, you don't have to thank me."

"... and especially for givin' me the sketchbook an' ..."

Mr. McAllister motioned for her to sit down in the chair next to him. Alma May sat down gratefully.

"I wish I could have given you many, many sketchbooks and watercolors and oils and brushes. Everything an artist needs," he said with a smile. Then his face grew serious again as he leaned forward and folded his arms on the desk. After a long moment, during which

Alma May could hear the tick, tick of the clock getting louder, he spoke again. "Alma May, someday you'll understand what I'm going to say."

Alma May shifted in the stiff chair as Mr. McAllister continued: "You're indeed fortunate. Oh, you're too young to realize it yet. But I hope someday you will. You have a special talent, a feeling for capturing beauty. If you'll take the time to develop it, you could very well be a successful artist someday. Maybe even a great one. But don't waste your gift. And learn to look deeper than what appears on the surface. All people have some sense of feeling about life, but it is the poet, the writer, the musician, the artist who bring these feelings into focus, allowing all of us to have a deeper sense of what life is about. An artist has an inner eye to see things that have not yet been realized by other people. You are special, Alma May."

Alma May shifted in her chair again and studied her scuffed brown oxfords as if she'd never seen them before.

"Oh, I'm sorry, Alma May, I'm embarrassing you, and that's not what I intended."

Alma May rose self-consciously from the chair. "Well, 'bye now, Mister McAllister. Ma's waiting for me to help her pack," she lied. She headed toward the door, stopped, spun around and ran back to him. She lowered her flaming face to his and kissed him gently on the cheek. "Thanks," she whispered and rushed back toward the door.

Once outside, she paused and glanced through the schoolhouse window. Mr. McAllister still sat behind his desk. He was looking in the direction of the door and smiling.

Alma May ran toward the path. "I'm special! I'm special!" she whispered. "Mister McAllister thinks I'm special."

There was one more thing she had to do before returning home. Almost to the town's main road, she turned sharply left and headed up the steep mountain slope toward her secret place. She avoided stepping on a Carolina box turtle, and carefully picked her way in and out of the wild grapevines and saw-briars, so that her stockings wouldn't get torn. She should've worn her denim overalls. She could hear Ma's voice scolding if she came home with runs in her stockings: "Alma May, you only got two pairs a stockin's an' you got to keep 'em nice for the city school. Reckon they don't wear no overalls there."

Alma May stopped suddenly, startled by a possum as she passed the familiar stand of pine trees on her right.

She skirted the undergrowth of wild rosebud, huckleberry, and poison ivy. After a few more minutes of picking her way through low-growing laurel and rhododendron, barren now of their summer flowers, she at last reached her maple tree near the edge of the ridge.

On the ground was her sketchbook, still there from the day of the explosion. Alma May was relieved that no animal had carried it away. She reached down and picked it up. It was in good condition, only a few wrinkles from the morning dew these past several days.

She tucked it under her arm and gazed slowly around her. She wanted to fill her eyes to overflowing. Just as her mother always preserved wild quince and huckleberries for use in the coming year, Alma May wanted to preserve the memory of wild, hazy mountain tops soaring above green and purple foothills for use in the coming year.

She turned and headed toward home.

★ ★ ★

Early the following morning, the Combses were all packed and ready to leave. A small band of men in loose bib overalls, carrying lunch pails, paused at the Combses' stoop on their way to the mine. Their faces were clean and pasty white in the dawn light. Their wives joined them as they gathered to say goodbye.

They encircled Alma May and her father to tell the latest news and good-naturedly give advice. Lizzie Combs hid behind her sunbonnet, even though the sun wouldn't be bright for several hours. She stood apart from the crowd. Alma May noticed that her mother, never one to talk much, was even more silent this morning. Her face looked paler than usual. Jimmie Lee was already behind the wooden steering wheel of his uncle's car. He tried to simulate the sound of the motor with his mouth.

"Did you hear about Papantoniou?" asked Joseph Kazmarick, a small, dark young man, whose father had died in a mine explosion a year ago.

"No, I ain't heard nothin'. Been in the house most all week. What about Papantoniou?" Chet asked.

"He's worse again. Reckon the black lung disease's goin' to get him for sure this time."

Alma May looked at her father and saw a fleeting grimace of pain cross his face. Her grandfather Combs had died of black lung disease when she was a small child. He'd worked for twenty-six years in the Harlan mines south of Mountainview.

"Sure as hell," Kazmarick said, "if a explosion don't get us, the black lung will. An' all the time, the Company telling us the coal dust is good for us 'cause it coats our lungs an' wards off colds. Shit!" He emphasized the last word by spitting on the ground.

Tall and gaunt Greenberry Howard, whose young face was already lined with deep ravines like those in the surrounding land, volunteered: "You're right smart to get out a here while's you can, Chet. Don't know how you ever saved all that cash. I ain't seen nothin' but Company scrip for three years. Reckon I owe my hide an' then some to the Company store. I'm already fifty dollars in the hole an' every week they keep adding up more an' more."

"If it wasn't for Lizzie, we'd still be in the hole, too," Chet said. "She can squeeze a nickel so tight, the buffalo moans." He glanced with admiration over at his wife. The visitors smiled and looked at Lizzie, who tucked her head down even farther and smiled her shy, almost toothless smile. "But we're not endin' up with a hundred an' fifty-three dollars like I thought. The Company charged me ten dollars for a new pick an' lamp. An' I only used 'em once an' that was the day a the explosion."

Ellie May Howard, the plump, cheerful young wife of Greenberry Howard, injected a pleasant thought: "Mebbee you can get yourself one a them porsaleen bathtubs like the super's got."

"McLaughlin's got one, too," someone in the crowd said.

"How's come McLaughlin ain't wrote us for a spell?" Ellie May asked. "I figure it's been six months or more. Leastaways it seems like that."

"You know McLaughlin never wrote all them highfalutin letters," said Buford Young, the big miner who had carried Chet from the smoking mine. "He can't write no better'n we can. He must a paid someone to write them." The crowd laughed.

"Just the same, nobody's heard from him for quite a spell," Ellie May said.

"Say, Combs, where you going to buy that there farm you're always talking about?" Young asked. "They say Bluegrass country's the best for farmin'."

"That's what they say," Chet replied, "but you know I don't never want to live nowheres for long without I see my mountains. There ain't no mountains in Bluegrass country. An' it don't have to be no fancy farm. Just somewheres we can grow enough to get by, and be our own boss." As he spoke, a soft hopeful smile lit his face, and his eyes shone.

The miners laid their lunch pails down and joined their wives in a round of handshakes and hugs for all the Combses, including flustered, red-faced Lizzie and impatient Jimmie Lee, who waited by the car door now.

Ruby Young, wife of Buford Young, approached out of breath with a steaming hot huckleberry pie wrapped in a dish towel and presented it to Lizzie. Ruby Young was a dumpy woman whose plain face became pretty when she smiled, which was often. "Fresh from the oven," she said, beaming. "Reckon it'll be just as good cold. It'll go good for tonight when you're tired a eatin' all them beans an' cornbread."

Lizzie's face grew even redder, and she began to shift her weight more.

Alma May wished her mother wasn't so shy. She was so shy, she didn't even go to the little Baptist church in Mountainview, because she'd have to talk with the members.

"But, but, you shouldn't a done this," Lizzie said to Ruby. "Ain't been a good year for huckleberries. You should a saved them for yerselfs."

"Pshaw! It'll come in handy. And you can keep the pie tin to remember me by." She shoved the pie into Lizzie's hands and kissed her on the cheek. "Good luck, now, Lizzie, and take care a yerselfs, y'hear?" The rest of the crowd echoed Ruby's farewell, and "Y'all hurry back, now."

After they had gone, Alma May helped carry out the Combses' few belongings--the box full of dishes and pots (except for the biggest pot, which her mother had filled with cold beans, and the pan in which she'd baked the corn bread for eating on the trip); the two large cardboard suitcases, which contained their winter and summer clothes and a few mementoes; Chet's guitar; the box of linen, including the quilts and worn flour sacks, and the pair of curtains. Lizzie had climbed the slope the previous day and gathered a large bunch of Life Everlasting ("awful good for colds an' shiverin'.") and mustard plant from which she'd extracted seeds for making poultices to ease chest colds, and female May apple for making tea. These she'd put in three separate bags and packed them in the linen box. Since they couldn't take the furniture with them, and none of their neighbors had money to buy it, they gave the furniture away. "We ain't leavin' it for the Independent Mining Company to sell to the next renter," Chet had said.

Jimmie Lee had already packed his seven slingshots in a shoe box and put them under the back seat of the car. He was proud of them, since he'd whittled them himself.

Alma May placed her sketchbook on the package tray in front of the Model T's rear window as Uncle Darcas approached. He was on his way home from working the night shift at the mine. Alma May cringed as he drew near. It was hard to believe that he was Pa's brother. He reminded her of a prize hog she'd seen once when she was a little girl. It was at the Breathitt County Fair, the only fair she'd ever attended. Same small, beady eyes, same flat, large-nostriled nose, same big belly. He even snorted when he laughed.

"So you're on your way," he greeted them. "You won't have no trouble with ol' Tin Lizzie here if you remember to keep plenty a water in that bottle in the trunk for the radiator in case it steams up whiles you go 'round them mountains. An' remember to keep air in the spare in case there's a flat. An' don't race the engine when it's cold or you'll ruin the pistons."

"Sure was right good a you to offer the car, Darcas," Chet said. "Soon's we get the money, we'll be sendin' those tickets for you and Euelly. I promise."

"In a couple a weeks Euelly'll be better, then we can leave. She was feeling sicker last night when I left for the mine," Uncle Darcas said, with a slight emphasis on "sicker." Everyone knew Aunt Euella had a problem with corn liquor. That was why she didn't go out of the shack sometimes for weeks. And that was why she almost always had bruises on her arms and face. Everyone knew Aunt Euella was forever falling down or bumping into things in a drunken stupor.

Yesterday afternoon Alma May and her family had gone to tell Aunt Euella goodbye. They found her lying on the lumpy cot she shared with Uncle Darcas. He was at the Company store for a few minutes. Alma

May felt a great wave of pity as she bent over to kiss her aunt goodbye. She kissed her as gently as she could. She didn't want to hurt her bruised and puffy cheeks.

"Please," Aunt Euella had whispered, her voice fading, "take me with you . . ."

"Wish we could take you, Euelly," Alma May's father said. Aunt Euella closed her eyes. After a moment, he continued. "But you'll be comin' in just a couple a weeks when you feel better. And Darcas and me'll both be makin' big money, an' . . . He stopped, seeing that she had drifted off.

Uncle Darcas shook his older brother's hand now, and patted him on the back. He gave Lizzie a quick hug and teased his brother: "Those city men are goin' to steal your woman away. Better watch her."

Lizzie blushed. Uncle Darcas shook Jimmie Lee's hand and then turned to Alma May. Alma May looked the other way.

"Give your ol' Uncle Darcas a big kiss goodbye, Alma May. My, my, ain't you gettin' big," he said, grabbing her shoulders and scanning her body.

Alma May tried to wrestle free from his grasp. "I gotta go to the privy again--"

"Go on, Alma May, kiss your Uncle Darcas goodbye," her father said. "You won't see him for a couple a weeks."

Alma May hesitated for an instant, not wanting to disobey her father. Uncle Darcas took advantage of the pause and kissed her squarely on the mouth. She squelched the urge to blow saliva in his face, and struggled free. She bolted into the back seat of the Model T.

Chet chuckled and said, "Alma May's just getting shy and sufferin' from growin' pains. She don't mean no offense to her Uncle Darcas."

A moment later Alma May and her family were seated and ready to go. Uncle Darcas circled the car and kicked the tires. He walked to the front and patted the hood and then cranked the engine. As the engine started and Chet pulled the car forward, Uncle Darcas waved goodbye. He smiled his broad, black-toothed smile, looked directly into Alma May's eyes and shouted, "See you in a couple a weeks."

Alma May reached behind for her sketchbook and held it up in front of her face.

Chapter 4

Detroit. Detroit. Detroit. The sound of the tires spinning on the pavement synchronized with the sound of the word spinning in Alma May's head. Detroit. Detroit. Were they really on their way? They must be: there was Pa in the front seat behind the steering wheel. There was Ma with her faded blue calico sunbonnet on sitting beside him. There was Jimmie Lee sitting in the back seat next to Alma May and gawking at every passing car.

Was it possible? Only six days ago she lay in bed resting and now she was halfway to a city she'd only read about in sixth grade history and in Mr. McLaughlin's letters. The thought of living anywhere but Mountainview was at once exciting and scary. What kind of a place would they find to live in? Would she got lost on her way to school? How would …

"Pa," Jimmie Lee asked, "do they really have licorice lights an' cinnamon sidewalks in Detroit?"

Chet Combs chuckled. "Now, where'd you hear that, son?"

"Alma May said so."

"I never did!" Alma May said.

"Yes, you did, Alma May!" Jimmie Lee said. "You was readin' Mister McLaughlin's letter to me a long time ago when I was seven an' you read that."

Alma May thought hard. Licorice lights and cinnamon sidewalks. Licorice lights and cinnamon sidewalks. … At last her face broke out in a smile: "Oh, I remember now. What Mister McLaughlin said was electric lights and cement sidewalks. You didn't hear me right."

Alma May and her father laughed as Jimmie Lee blushed and said, "Aw, I didn't really believe it, anyways." But Alma May suspected he wanted to half believe it when she saw his smile fade.

Her uncle's car chugged and rattled down the road, while Alma May's thoughts drifted back to yesterday.

An hour after they left Uncle Darcas standing by their shack, they ascended the corridor formed by the great purple and green walls of Pine Mountain on the left and Little and Big Black Mountains on the right. All the while they paralleled the Cumberland River. The road followed a shelf below high limestone overhangs. "Look! They look like doll houses!" Jimmie Lee had exclaimed as he pointed to the small cabins clinging to the mountain's sloping side far below.

Sometime after passing through the mining town of Jenkins, with its modern buildings and unsightly shacks, the road wound through a valley. They passed a few ragged mining settlements, almost hidden among the mountains. Alma May turned her head away from their ugliness and concentrated on the desolate and unspoiled beauty of the tree-clad mountains surrounding them. The early morning sun, splashing autumn light in the valley, intensified the yellows, reds, oranges, browns, and dark greens. She thought of Mr. McAllister and what he'd told her. Someday, someday, she would have the paints to capture this view and many more like this.

Later, after passing scenes that rose like blighted spots on the land-- small, flimsy boom-time shacks near abandoned mines with warped and disjointed tipples built alongside a once beautiful creek now littered with tin cans and refuse--they traversed the valley of the Big Sandy River and its forks, the Levisa and the Tug. "Mister McAllister said this is where the Indians used to hunt the most," Alma May said. "An' he said this is the last part a Kentucky that the settlers took away from them."

"I'm proud a you rememberin' so much from your lessons, Alma May," her father said.

Alma May looked at her mother and waited for her to agree with Pa. But Lizzie said nothing.

A little north of Pikeville, Chet pulled the car over to the side of the narrow ridge and got out.

"Where you goin', Pa?" Jimmie Lee asked. He got out, too.

"Just over here to look one more time at the mountains," his father called, walking away from the car.

"But we're still goin' to be drivin' through more mountains," Jimmie Lee said.

"But they'll be little runts a mountains, Jimmie Lee, not giant ones like these," he called back.

"I'm going to look, too," Alma May said. "You comin', Ma?"

"No. Reckon I'll just stay in the car."

Alma May frowned at the back of her mother's sunbonnet and opened the rear door.

A moment later, she stood near her father on the sandy shoulder of the road. Their eyes scanned the panorama, attempting to all at once take in the thickly timbered countryside that ranged from mountainous to hilly, the narrow, winding valleys, the waterfalls in the distance, the little cabins perched on ridges.

Jimmie Lee stood by Alma May and tossed pebbles down the mountainside, listening for the echo as they fell.

"Hush," Alma May whispered to her brother. She pointed to her father.

Chet Combs stood in silence a few yards from them. A sad but almost raptured look crossed his face. Then, finally, in a voice barely audible, as if speaking to a much-loved woman, he whispered: "I'll come back to you someday. I promise."

By that evening they were out of the mountains. They'd had no car trouble other than a flat tire near Troublesome Hollow. "A natural place to have a little trouble," Chet had said, chuckling, while be quickly changed the tire. He'd helped his brother change flats often before, so he had no difficulty.

A little later he smiled as he guided the Model T down the road, which followed the low bluffs along the curving Ohio River. He reached over and patted Lizzie on the arm. "Yep. We're lucky we ain't had no more'n a flat, drivin' all the way 'round them mountains. That's a good omen, Lizzie. Our life's goin' to be better from now on."

Chapter 5

"Where are we?" Jimmie Lee asked. He sat up in the back seat and rubbed his sleepy eyes. "How did it get dark so fast?"

"Almost there, Jimmie Lee. The man at the fillin' station back there said we just drove through Melvindale," Chet said. He stuck his head out of the window in an attempt to read the street sign. "Alma May, see if you can read the sign. The man said to turn right on Oakwood an' it'll take us right into downtown Detroit."

Alma May peered through the window, straining her eyes to see in the dark. "This is it, Pa. Oakwood."

Chet made the turn onto the wide, traffic-heavy boulevard as Alma May looked over at her brother and said, "You slept all through Columbus an' Toledo an' you missed the Michigan state line. Tried to wake you up, but you were as limp as a dead possum. You missed seein' all them big buildin's."

Jimmie Lee had checked on his sling shots several times. Then he'd fallen asleep, partly out of boredom, a little south of Columbus. The terrain had become flat and uninteresting, not hilly and unpredictable like when they first started out.

Alma May, now developing an insatiable appetite for learning as much as possible about the world outside of Mountainview, had read every word of every highway sign. Quite a few times they passed a series of cheerful jingles written with white lettering on jaunty little red signs. Several words were printed on each of the series' six signs. Alma May, amused at the cadence, read one of them out loud:

"Does your husband
Misbehave
Grunt and grumble
Rant and rave
Shoot the brute some
Burma-Shave"

Her father had chuckled but her brother had been puzzled. "Why would they shoot the brute? What's Burma-Shave?" he asked Alma May.

"Oh, you're too young to understand anything,'" she answered.

Even Lizzie, still pale and drawn and still wearing the sunbonnet, had been amused enough by the Burma-Shave signs to smile slightly. Chet looked over at his wife and patted her arm again. "Won't be long, Lizzie, an' you'll be sleepin' in a nice big bed."

By now Alma May, too, was tired and anxious to get there. They had driven steadily since a short stop at an Ohio diner; they didn't want to spend another night sleeping in the car as they had the night before, or squander fifty cents of their fast-dwindling savings on a cabin.

Oakwood Boulevard had become Fort Street now. The traffic was even heavier. Alma May saw the lights of the city's downtown section several miles northeast. A light on top of what seemed to be Detroit's tallest building blinked off and on haughtily above the lower skyscrapers. She wondered what building that could be. Her stomach felt strangely queasy. Not the same feeling as when she ate too much of Ma's sowbelly, but an unfamiliar feeling--sort of a combination of anxiety and eagerness and wonder.

She was tired no longer. She wanted to see everything, to hear everything, to smell everything. She rolled down her window, in spite of the chilly autumn breeze, and looked out. A small group of men of all ages, dressed in dirty, ragged clothes were sitting by the doorway of a closed pawnshop, its windows guarded by a steel gate. They were silently sharing a bottle of something that Alma May could not make out. A few yards farther down the street, a man sat alone on the sidewalk in front of a store window on which was painted in peeling black block letters, "Di Fabbio's Market/Fresh Produce". His right leg was stretched out in front of him, and his left leg, missing below the knee, was covered by a rolled-up pant leg secured by a safety pin. Under his dirty slouch hat he wore dark sunglasses and a frozen smile. Alma May knew why he held a white cane in the crook of one arm (She'd seen a blind woman once when she'd gone to Harlan with Pa), but she wondered why he held the tin cup in his hand.

"Pa, what does 'b-u-r-l-e-s-q-u-e' spell?" Jimmie Lee was looking out of the window at a brightly lit marquee surrounded by blinking lights. Under the sign a crowd of people, mostly men, was forming a line.

"That must be the place where Mister McLaughlin said he goes where the women dance an' sing an' wear pretty outfits an' everyone has a good time," Alma May answered for her father. Her eyes shone. "Pa, are we goin' to see Mister McLaughlin tonight?"

"No, Alma May. Let's get settled somewheres first. Don't want to drop in on a body this time a night, even though he'd be glad to see us." After a moment her father continued. "He said he found some furnished light housekeepin' rooms when he first came here. They don't cost hardly no more'n just a sleepin' room an' he said he saved money by cookin' all his meals. Figure that's what we should do."

Chet stopped for a traffic light. A slumping man who had been leaning against the traffic sign, his body like a formless sack of coal slag in a baggy, shapeless suit, suddenly stuck his wizened face through Alma May's window and croaked, "Got a nickel, little lady? Ain't had a bite to eat all day."

Alma May, frightened, stared at his face. Then, in horrified attraction, looked down at the front of his suit coat. It was encrusted with droolings and vomits. She rolled the window up as fast as she could, almost severing his nose before he turned his face away.

"You all right, baby?" Chet asked. He looked back at Alma May. "Better keep your window up."

Jimmie Lee sat with his mouth agape. His head was bent down so that be could see the creature through Alma May's window. The light turned green and her father pulled forward. Alma May saw the beggar hold out his palm to a well-dressed couple walking toward him.

She soon forgot the incident when she read the strange-sounding names on the street signs they passed: *Cabacier Street. Trumbull Avenue. Griswold Street.*

At last, they arrived at what she thought must be the downtown area. "Look at all these big buildin's, Pa! Them must be the latest styles in all them windows. They must be usin' lots a 'lectricity to make them windows so bright."

She saw a line of people waiting at a theater to buy tickets under a light-studded marquee advertising Jean Harlow in *Hell's Angels*. All those people looked so beautiful and carefree. She wished she were part of the crowd.

The jarring noises of the street competing for her attention only added to the wonder and excitement: the Klaxon horns, the shrill sound of tires squealing, the pedestrians' voices, the newsboys' chants of "Get your evening *Times!*" Threaded through all of these marvelous things was an incandescent tapestry of lights, some high and some low, some blinking and some still. And to think--they were to be a part of all this!

"Here's your licorice lights and cinnamon sidewalks, Jimmie Lee," Chet said. He turned his head around in order to see his son's face. But Jimmie Lee had his head stuck part way out of the side window, attempting to count the floors of the buildings they passed.

"Quick, Pa, turn left at this big street," Alma May said, for she had spotted what promised to be even finer buildings several blocks to the left and across the street. Chet turned left abruptly, almost colliding with a Vernor's Ginger Ale truck. The driver stuck his face out of the window and yelled, "Where the hell you think you're going!"

Alma May read the street sign as they turned the corner: *Woodward Avenue*. As her father headed aimlessly north, they passed a large department store. High up on its facade was the biggest clock she'd ever seen. It was even bigger than the clock on the wall of the Company office back home. Above the clock were letters, probably bronze, which read, "Kerns". The time is now eleven oh three, she noted.

At the next red light, Alma May read the street sign: *Grand River*. She looked in the big windows of the granite and red brick department store. Never before had she seen such beautiful things, not even in Ruby Young's Sears and Roebuck catalog. A long, gold lamé evening dress hung on the elegant mannequin. She wore matching pointed-toe pumps. Gracing her haughty shoulders was a white ermine stole. A rhinestone headband with jutting black feathers circled her tightly waved wig. Below a wide rhinestone bracelet, her hand held a sparkling cigarette holder. Could it be made of diamonds, Alma May wondered. Surrounding the mannequin were wonderful displays of other evening clothes and accessories. Alma May's eyes opened in awe. Next she noticed a plaque near the corner of the building with the engraved words: The J. L. Hudson Co.

"Look!" she said. "There's the place where Mister McLaughlin buys all his clothes!"

Throngs of passing pedestrians paused to admire the display. Someday, Alma May promised herself, I'm going to have an outfit just like that.

Chet continued to drive north for several miles until they were out of the downtown section. The buildings were farther apart now, and the pedestrians fewer. On their right they passed a marble structure of Italian Renaissance design. Its graceful terraced steps rose to the building's three-arched main entrance. Bronze reproductions of sculptures filled the recesses in the end bays of the huge building.

That must be an art place, Alma May thought. She looked up at the frieze above the big doors. Engraved there were the words, "The Detroit Institute of Arts". What a wonderful building! Alma May knew she'd be spending a lot of time there.

"We'll find us a place to stay now," Chet said. "We'll stop an' ask someone where there's some good light housekeepin' rooms." He didn't stop immediately, however, but continued driving in the same direction.

"We'll just turn left at this nice wide street here an' ask someone," Chet said uncertainly. He turned left and drove a short way before stopping on the right side of the boulevard in front of a tall building of granite and marble.

Jimmie Lee looked out of his window and pointed across the boulevard to an enormous gray limestone building of a lower, more horizontal design, with projecting wings. "Look! There's cars *right inside* a that big buildin' over there!"

Alma May saw that it was true. There were glistening new automobiles displayed behind the huge windows.

But she was more interested in seeing the building on her right and watching the tastefully dressed people going in and out of the shiny brass revolving doors.

A middle-aged, portly man walked in front of their parked car to cross the boulevard. Chet stuck his head out of the window and inquired of him, "Ah, ah, Sir, do you know where there's some light housekeepin' rooms that ain't too dear? We just got here an' …"

The man yanked his cigar out of his mouth long enough to sputter, "Nope!" He pulled his narrow-brimmed hat lower over his forehead and continued across the street.

Alma May turned her head and looked down at his black and white spats. They made a wonderful, bouncy pattern on the pavement below them as he walked. Then she looked at her mother. It had been hours since she'd noticed her. "Ma," she said, "take that sunbonnet off. Ain't nobody here with a sunbonnet like that on."

"But it's gettin' real cold, Alma May," Lizzie said in a faint voice.

Alma May gave the back of her mother's sunbonnet a resigned look and said, "It ain't cold, Ma. Just a little chilly."

She turned again to look at the building. But her view was blocked by a protruding belly covered by dark blue wool and shiny brass buttons. The owner of the belly lowered his head and said sternly to her father, "Get moving, bud. Can't you see the sign? No parking!"

Chet looked out the window and noticed the sign for the first time. He jumped out and started to crank the engine. Then be looked at the officer and asked timidly, "Say, you know where there's some light housekeepin' rooms that don't cost more'n a dollar?"

The officer's face softened and he spoke more gently this time. "Why don't you check the newspaper? Look in the ads in the back."

"Don't know why I didn't think a that." Chet patted the shrinking pile of change in his pocket. "How much does a newspaper cost? And where can I get one?"

"Three cents." He pointed to the building. "In there."

The officer allowed him to remain parked a moment longer while Chet walked inside the building and bought the newspaper. Alma May shyly asked the officer what the building was called.

"This here's the Fisher Building," he said, "and that one over there across the boulevard is the General Motors Building, You and your family ought to visit them during the day. There's lots of nice things to see. There's even a radio station in the Fisher Building."

They chatted for a moment longer, waiting for her father to return. Why, he's really nice, Alma May thought.

Chet came back and cranked the engine. He started to drive west again, with more purpose now. "We'll just find us a place to stop for soda pop an' coffee, an' I'll look at the advertisements like that policeman said." He looked over and smiled at Lizzie and patted her hand. "Lizzie, you want a cup a cof-- Why, if your hand ain't as cold as a dog's nose!"

Lizzie gave him a weak smile and slumped forward. Her head hit the metal dashboard, knocking her bonnet askew.

"Lizzie! Lizzie! What's wrong!" Chet cried. The car swerved abruptly, almost hitting a parked Checker Cab on the right, when Chet reached over with his right arm and attempted to pull her upright.

Alma May and Jimmie Lee leaned over the front seat. "Ma!" they screamed.

Chapter 6

Alma May sat on a scarred wooden chair and studied the tiny room. *So these are what light housekeeping rooms are.*

Her father paced back and forth on the worn linoleum in front of the closed bedroom door. She heard a faint rustling behind it. The doctor had been in there with her mother for what seemed like hours, but maybe was only a few minutes. *What was wrong with Ma, and why was the doctor taking so long?*

Across from her were a porcelain sink with one brass faucet and a small, linoleum-topped counter. Above the sink, two wooden cupboards painted tan. To her right, a white porcelain enamel-topped kitchen table and two unmatched chairs. Too large for the room's size, the table jutted out from the corner and partly blocked a door leading to the hall outside.

In spite of Alma May's concern over her mother, she was angry with her, too. *Why did she have to pick this time to be sick and spoil their arrival in this wonderful big city?*

She looked around again. *If these were light housekeeping rooms, why weren't they light?* A bare bulb hung on a cord from the ceiling. That was all.

Alma May's head still spun from the speed at which they had found this place. Her father had continued driving west on West Grand Boulevard, his left hand on the wheel and his right arm around Lizzie. In a high, unnatural voice, he'd whispered to his unconscious wife, "We'll get you a doctor-man, Lizzie, soon as I see someone to ask." Since driving away from the crowds pouring out of the Fisher Building, the sidewalk on their right had been empty of pedestrians.

"What'll we do, Pa, what'll we do?" Alma May had cried while her brother sat white-faced and big-eyed beside her. "There ain't nobody right here to ask. Let's go back an' ask that nice policeman!"

"I'll turn here," Chet said, turning sharply right onto a narrower street. "Maybe there'll be more people out walkin'."

Alma May glanced at the street sign. *Woodrow Wilson. Woodrow Wilson was our twenty-eighth president. Mister McAllister had made the class read about him last week (Was it only last week?)* She looked at the row of tall, narrow houses jammed together close to the street's curb. "Look, Pa! Look! There's a sign in the window! 'Light Housekeepin' Rooms'!"

Chet braked the car gently and pulled alongside the curb into the only remaining parking place. "Those rooms must a just been waitin' for us, Alma May," he said, his voice regaining a little of its usual confident tone. "Get up in front an' sit by your Ma, while I go in an' get the rooms an' call the doctor-man."

Alma May sat beside her still-unconscious mother. Chet knocked on the door of the darkened house. After what seemed like forever, the porch light flashed on and the door opened to reveal a thin, middle-aged woman in rag curlers and a bathrobe. Alma May couldn't make out what her soft-spoken father was saying, but some of the woman's shrill words drifted into the open-windowed car. "Almost midnight ... don't take in roomers at night." A pause while the woman scrutinized Chet and then looked out at the Model T. "Five dollars a week ... three in family ... limit."

Another pause while Jimmie Lee stared at the house and Alma May strained to hear her father's voice, high-pitched and anxious again: "My woman ... little sick ... needs ... bed ... two young'n's. ..."

The woman studied the car once more and hesitated for a long moment. "Well ... fifty cents more ... extra kid."

Her father bolted from the porch and ran to the car. He opened Lizzie's door, stepped up onto the running board, and gently tried to lift her out. Her heavy, helpless bulk proved too much for him. "Alma May, help me lift your Ma out."

Alma May got out of the car and hurried to where her father stood. Chet placed his hands under her mother's armpits and pulled her limp form toward him as Alma May stretched out her arms to cradle her mother's thighs. They slowly lifted Lizzie from the front seat. Before turning to carry her up the rooming house's steep steps, Alma May glanced down at the place where her mother had been sitting. Alma May gasped. There on her Uncle Darcas's upholstered front seat was a pool of fresh blood. "Pa! Look! Ma's been bleedin'!"

Her father looked down at the seat. Under the glow from the street light, Alma May saw his face whiten. "Oh, Lizzie!" he croaked.

Alma May looked back again in fascinated horror at the blood. *How pretty the red looks against the gray mohair upholstery!*

The woman shook her head and held the door open for them. She led them, their arms straining under Lizzie's motionless weight, up the steps to the vacant two rooms on the third floor.

When they laid Lizzie down on the double bed's clean sheet, the woman noticed a big bloody blotch on the back of Lizzie's dress and blood trickling down the inside of her legs. "Now, wait a minute! You said your wife was a little sick. You didn't say nothin' about her bein' about to croak. Not runnin' no hospital here. Yous are gonna hafta leave!"

Alma May gave her father a panicked glance. But Chet was calm when he said, "My woman's usually strong as an ox. She ain't never been sick before since we've been wedded. Why, she'll be on her feet an' spry as a hen in no time."

The woman stuck out her chin and Alma May noticed that the three curly gray hairs on it matched the gray tendrils escaping the rag curlers. "Sorry. Yous are gonna hafta …"

Chet swallowed, desperation clouding his bright blue eyes. "I'll pay you six dollars a week."

The woman looked slowly at Lizzie, then at Chet and Alma May, and finally at Jimmie Lee. He had followed them and stood on the other side of the bed, staring open-mouthed at a red stream of blood as it trickled down the valley-like folds of the sheet.

"Make it seven and you can have the rooms. But if she don't get no better soon …"

Chet sighed in relief.

"I'll go call a doctor," the woman said. She headed toward the hall phone.

Alma May stirred now in the chair and brushed the ringlets from her eyes. *Why doesn't the doctor open the door and tell us Ma's going to be all right? And there's Pa, still pacing in front of it. But Pa will take care of everything. After all, he always does, doesn't he?*

As if reading her thoughts, Chet stopped moving for a minute and gave Alma May a little smile. "Everythin's goin' to be all right, Alma May, you'll see."

Jimmie Lee, temporarily distracted by the novelty of living in unfamiliar surroundings, had left the room to explore the halls. He returned now and ran toward Alma May. "C'mon, Alma May, an' see somethin'!"

Alma May, glad to leave the room where anxiety hung thick as the mist over Big Black Mountain, followed her brother out. Jimmie Lee ran to a black box on the wall. "Listen, Alma May!" he said in a loud, excited voice. He lifted a cone-shaped black thing on a cord from a hook on the box's left side. He reached up and held the thing to Alma May's ear. A pleasant but bored voice said, "Number, puh-leeze."

Alma May hung the thing back on the hook. "Ain't you ever talked on a telephone before, Jimmie Lee?"

Jimmie Lee's face fell. "Have you?"

"Why, sure, I have. Lots a times, at the mine office." Alma May looked at her brother's disappointed face. "Well … not really, but I studied about telephones in social science class," she added.

His smile returned, and he galloped down the hall to show her another discovery. As he neared a partly opened door at the end of the hall, he shouted, "Watch this, Alma May!" Alma May followed him into the room, which was even smaller than the bedroom where her mother lay. She watched as he reached up and pulled a brass chain from which a porcelain knob dangled. The chain hung from a white porcelain box attached to a wall near the ceiling. Under the box and screwed to the wooden floor was an oval bowl-stool, also of white porcelain. Resting on the bowl-stool was a brown oak rim. Suddenly, Jimmie Lee let go of the chain, and swirling water emptied from the bowl and new water poured in from under the bowl's inside rim.

"Ain't that somethin'?" asked Jimmie Lee, his eyes big with wonder.

"Oh, that ain't nothin'," replied Alma May. "I used an inside privy once when I had to take a message for Pa to the super's house."

But Jimmie Lee wasn't listening. He flushed the toilet again and again, each time placing his face close to the stool to watch the pattern of the water as it swirled.

"I'm goin' back now," Alma May said, starting toward their rooms.

"But, Alma May," Jimmie Lee shouted. "I got somethin' else to show you." He ran down the hall after her.

A door on their left opened, and a baggy-eyed woman with stick-out orange hair and a cold- creamed face glared at them. "What the hell you Goddam brats doin' this time a night? Where's your mother, and hows come she ain't watchin' yous?"

Alma May glanced back and saw Jimmie Lee give a frightened look as he ran even faster after her into their rooms.

Alma May was relieved to see the bedroom door opening at last. The doctor, a tired-looking young man with a roomy paunch and a grave expression, removed a stethoscope from around his neck and folded it into his black leather bag. He motioned for Chet to join him in the bedroom. Alma May was glad that he didn't close the door this time.

The doctor pulled out a white pad of paper from his bag and wrote something on it. He tore off the top sheet of paper, handed it to her father, and said gruffly, "Get this filled right away." His voice was even gruffer as he added, "You're lucky she didn't lose any more blood. She probably would've miscarried. I don't know why you didn't drive directly to Ford Hospital."

"Hospital? Hospital? I didn't think about a hosp …"

"Be sure she takes these pills as directed. And she has to stay in bed for several days with her feet elevated."

"Elevated?"

"Elevated: Her feet have to be higher than her head so the bleeding will stop." The doctor's voice was less harsh now. Again, he wrote something on the top sheet of paper, tore it off, and handed it to Chet. "Here's my phone number. Call me if she starts bleeding again. But she should be all right tonight. I gave her a sedative." His visit finished, he put on his topcoat. But still he lingered.

Chet stared at him for a moment before he realized what the doctor was waiting for. He reached into his pocket and asked the doctor, "How much do you charge?"

"Two dollars."

Chet handed him a crumpled one-dollar bill and proceeded to count out change for the remaining dollar.

The doctor looked around the room and then at Alma May and Jimmie Lee. He handed the dollar back to Chet. "Here. You keep it. I forgot that I never charge for the first call," he said softly. He closed the door behind him.

Alma May stood with her mouth open. She knew what "miscarriage" meant. She'd overheard her mother and Aunt Euella whisper that word once after Aunt Euella had lost another baby. "Ma's, Ma's, going to have a baby?" she whispered. "A baby ..."

Jimmie Lee swallowed. Then his grin got as wide as Alma May's. "You mean, you mean ... I'm goin' to have a baby brother?

Alma May's smile disappeared. "But, but what about The Farm?"

Chet quickly reassured his daughter. "We're still goin' to get The Farm."

She hesitated. "But, it'll take money to feed the baby, an' ..."

"Now, don't you worry, Alma May. Ain't I goin' to get a job an' make big money like Mister McLaughlin?"

Alma May's smile returned. Pa would take care of everything.

Chapter 7

Alma May and Jimmie Lee walked briskly toward Pingree Elementary School, a few short blocks north of their new home. The chilly morning air nipped at their fingers and faces. Dressed in their best clothes usually reserved for Sunday, they carried Detroiter brand lined notebooks, brown penny pencils, and a sack lunch. Their father had said that they should eat lunch at school. Lizzie was feeling better today, and he knew if they came home for lunch, she'd insist on getting out of bed to make it for them. Before Chet left for work, Mrs. Pasnick, the landlady, had promised to look in on Lizzie often.

Jimmie Lee carried his favorite slingshot in the rear right pocket of his brown corduroy knickers. He reached back and pulled it out again to admire it once more. "Reckon nobody in this school's got one as good as this," he said proudly.

Because of her nervousness and the cold temperature, Alma May felt a need to pee. Too late to go back home now. If only she could run into the school and find the privy right away.

The school yard was crowded with students. The younger ones were engaged in running games, and the older ones were gathered in small and large groups. Alma May's stomach began to flutter like the withered elm leaves falling down on her and Jimmie Lee from the almost-barren branches above. She noticed that, besides jackets, all the students wore hats. Several of them glanced curiously at Alma May and Jimmie Lee as they passed.

"Yous new here?" asked a pimply-faced boy. He dragged importantly on his cigarette.

Alma May turned to answer the boy, but stopped when she saw the look he was giving her. It moved slowly up and down her body--the same look Uncle Darcas had been giving her lately. Her face turned as pink as the jacket of the girl standing next to the boy. Alma May looked straight ahead, and ran toward the school building's big double doors.

"What's the matter, Alma May?" Jimmie Lee shouted. "Wait for me!"

The halls were empty except for a tall, slim man approaching. He must be a teacher, thought Alma May. But I can't ask him--a man-- where the privy is.

The young man stopped her and said, not unkindly, "Now, you know no students are allowed in the building until the first bell rings."

"But, but . . ." Alma May's pink face turned red as she swallowed her modesty. "I have to go to the privy."

"Privy?"

"Privy. Privy." Alma May's voice got higher and desperate. "Toilet! Toilet!"

"Oh. The girls' room. It's the third door on the right down that hall. But from now on you mustn't enter ..."

Alma May ran in the direction to which he pointed, found the door marked "Girls," and entered.

She ran inside the first stall and locked the door behind her. Too late. She could not stop the gush of warm urine flooding down between her legs. She stood, frozen, with her legs apart and her head down as she helplessly watched the yellow pool forming on the black and white terrazzo floor below her. What should she do? What should she do!

A bell rang. In a minute the room would be crowded. Her soaked drawers and long brown cotton stockings were uncomfortably cold. She heard the muffled voices and footsteps in the hall outside. She must take off her drawers and stockings or else she'd smell the way Aunt Euella did when she got too drunk to care, and the way Jimmie Lee did sometimes when he played too long on the culm bank and didn't stop to use the privy.

She kicked off her wet brown oxfords and removed her stockings and drawers. She shoved her feet back into her shoes just as the door to the room opened. Alma May stood in the stall holding her soaked clothing for what seemed as long as an entire history lesson. All around her she heard the doors to the other stalls swing open and slam shut. She heard the high, carefree voices of the younger girls and the giggles of the older ones, the footsteps getting louder and quieter as the lavatory's visitors came and left. All the while, she absently read and reread the words scratched on the walls of the stall. Alma May found some comfort in their familiarity, since they were basically the same messages as on the school's outhouse back home.

Another bell rang. Finally, it was quiet. She waited a moment longer to make sure she was alone. Then she slowly opened the door to her stall and threw her soaked stockings and drawers into the big green waste receptacle. She would have to make up a story to tell her mother about the missing clothes.

As her feet squished in the wet shoes across the tile, she looked down at her bare, white legs. They look like two big noodles, she thought. She tried to pull her red plaid skirt down lower to hide them.

Jimmie Lee was waiting outside the door. "What you been doin' all that time? You been in there for hours!" He looked down at her legs. "Where's your stockin's?"

"I, I got a big run in them, an' I didn't want to wear them anymore, so I threw them away," Alma May said.

They tiptoed quietly down the hall, looking for the office. As they walked, they peeked into the filled classrooms. "Did you ever see so many kids?" exclaimed Jimmie Lee. "Know what them things are?" he asked, pointing to long, narrow steel doors enameled dark green on either side of the hall. "Them's closets. I saw the kids puttin' their lunches an' mittens an' things in them."

They found the glass door marked "Office" and walked in. The smiling, triangle-faced woman behind the high counter introduced herself as Miss Perry.

"I'm in the eighth grade an' my little brother here's in the third," Alma May said. "We're startin' school here." She pulled out their Mountainview school report cards from the pocket of her worn blue jacket.

Miss Perry looked over the cards. "Fine," she said. After some hesitation, she said they could enroll today if they promised to bring birth certificates and Wayne County health shot papers within two days. "We'll start you in the eighth and third grades here until we've had time to evaluate you."

She walked toward the door. "Follow me. I'll take you both to your homeroom classes." She glanced down at Alma May's bare legs. "Aren't your legs cold? You'll find that all the girls up north wear stockings."

Jimmie Lee's room was on the same floor. He followed Miss Perry eagerly inside without a backward glance at Alma May, who stood outside in the hall. Alma May saw him pat the back pocket of his knickers to make sure his slingshot was still there.

Alma May's room was upstairs. She followed the woman down the high-ceilinged halls hung with portraits of various presidents (The one of Hoover was the same as the one in the schoolhouse back home.) While they turned first right, then left, then right again, she compared the size of this school with the one back home. Would she ever learn the layout of this building? Would she get lost finding her classes? When she climbed the terrazzo stairs, she noticed Miss Perry's seamed rayon stockings, and was conscious again of her own bare legs.

They were at last at her homeroom door. Alma May felt her stomach flutter and her hands get clammy again. She cleared her throat.

They entered the room and Miss Perry introduced her to Miss Craig, a frail, birdlike woman with beady eyes and a beak of a nose. Miss Perry left, and Miss Craig motioned for Alma May to sit down in an empty seat in the back row. Thirty-eight pairs of eyes followed Alma May as she walked awkwardly down the aisle. Thirty-eight pairs of eyes saw her brush her hair from her flaming face. Thirty-eight pairs of eyes looked at her white noodle-legs when she pulled her skirt down again as far as it would go. Alma May sat down gratefully in the wooden desk. She hoped the eyes would focus on their lessons now that she was seated.

But Miss Craig asked Alma May to tell the class what part of Kentucky she was from.

"E-Eastern," Alma May said. She was thankful that the desk in front of her partly hid her legs. She sat with her knees close together.

"What is the name of the city you're from?" Miss Craig asked in a fluttery voice.

"M-Mountainview," she answered. She looked at the big clock on the wall to her right. *Nine oh three. When would the class be over?*

"I don't think any of us have heard of Mountainview. Where is that near?"

Alma May looked out the window and saw a little brown sparrow flitting on the ledge, bobbing its beak and pecking at the window.

"Alma May. Tell the class where Mountainview is near," Miss Craig repeated. The children tittered.

Alma May cleared her throat. "M-Mountainview is near High Splint an' Clover Fork, an' Mud Holler, an' ..." More giggles.

"Those are very picturesque-sounding names, Alma May," Miss Craig said. "Tell us, what does your father do?"

"He, he did work in the coal mines, but he ain't goin' to no more." Alma May paused, remembering something. "You must a heard a Harlan. Well, Mountainview is north a Harlan." She at last saw recognition on the faces of some of the students at the mention of Harlan.

Miss Craig bobbed her beak in a semi-circle around the classroom. "Of course! Children, remember we studied about coal mines last month. Gladys Polaski, tell the class what Harlan is noted for." She pointed her finger to a girl with greasy red hair and freckles in the front row.

"Harlan is one of the most important coal mining towns in the whole United States," Gladys Polaski replied with authority.

Alma May was glad to have attention shifted to Gladys Polaski. And she was glad to have Miss Craig resume the geography lesson after giving Alma May a textbook. For the first time, Alma May dared to glance around the room. Most of the students were looking down at their lesson, but some were still staring at her. Now it was Alma May's turn to stare, for there, *right in this classroom, right in this school*, she saw a colored girl. Back home the colored kids just never went to school with whites. The colored miners' kids had to go to that little school shack way outside of town in Nigger Holler where they lived. She scanned the room again, but found no other colored children.

The bell rang at nine-forty. The students scurried out of the room. Alma May was relieved to be the last one out. No one would be behind her to stare at her legs. Miss Craig informed her that she should go to Mr. Fostick's math class next, room 236, but that her third class, history, would be back in this same room.

Since there were only three minutes between classes, by the time she found room 236, the students were already seated. Alma May opened the door timidly and then blushed. For there, standing in front of the classroom and writing on the blackboard, was the same young nan who had directed her to the privy. Alma May hoped he wouldn't remember. But the math teacher's brown eyes lit with recognition when she approached.

"Oh, hello, there. You must be the new student I've just been told about who started this morning." He looked down at a slip of paper on his desk. Alma May saw that her name was on it. "This is Alma May Combs, class. Sit down, Alma May, and tell us about yourself." He pointed to an empty desk in the middle of the room. Alma May hurried to the desk, eager to sit down again. She pulled her knees close together once more.

"Tell the class where you're from, Alma May," Mr. Fostick said.

"N-Near Harlan," replied Alma May. The students continued to stare at her. She focused her eyes on the green metal wastebasket in the front left-hand corner of the room.

Someone in the room farted. Suddenly the room was filled with titters and snickers. The girl in front of Alma May turned around and whispered, "That's Percy Soule. He's done that before." Alma May recognized the girl as Gladys Polaski, the greasy-haired girl from homeroom.

"Poor Soule!" a loud voice from the back right corner said. The class laughed harder this time. Alma May turned around to see who was the owner of the voice. Her glance met the vulgar stare of the same pimply-faced cigarette smoker of that morning. She turned back quickly. Alma May felt sorry for Percy Soule when he blushed, but she was not sorry that attention had shifted from her to him. *Saved by a fart,* thought Alma May.

Mr. Fostick did not smile. He ordered the class to look at the board as he continued the introduction to fundamental algebra. Alma May relaxed a little and looked around. She was surprised to find two more colored students, a boy and a girl, sitting together. And there was one other thing she'd just noticed. Back home the girls sat on one side of the room and the boys on the other, but in both classes here they sat together.

Time dragged until the bell rang. Alma May stood up quickly. She wanted to get lost in the crowd of shoving students. She thought she could remember how to get back to home room. But Gladys Polaski came running behind her and insisted on showing her the way. "How come you're wearing that jacket in class and got your lunch with you? Why don't you put them in your locker?" she asked.

"Ain't got one yet," Alma May said.

"How come you're not wearing stockings?"

"My legs get too warm."

"Then how come they got goose bumps?"

Alma May felt slightly comforted being back in the same room, sitting at the same desk. Some of the students' faces began to look a little familiar. The colored girl turned around and smiled shyly at her. Alma May, not used to such a bold gesture, didn't know how to react, and quickly looked out the window.

When the bell rang for lunch hour, Alma May was one of the first out the door. She wanted to avoid Gladys Polaski. Gladys was too nosey. She rushed downstairs to the main floor, and heard several whispers around her: "New hillbilly girl ... doesn't know enough to wear stockings."

She disappeared into the crowd of students pouring out the front door into the school yard on their way home for lunch. If only she, too, could go home for lunch and never come back.

She searched the crowd for Jimmie Lee. At last she saw him standing with two boys about his own age. He held his slingshot in his left hand and a stone in his right. "It ain't hard at all," she heard him say. "All you do is put this stone in the rubber band an' pull the rubber band back an' ..."

"Aw, that looks like a sissy toy," the taller of the two boys said. "I got a Daisy BB gun at home." He said to his friend, "C'mon. We can get in that game over there if we hurry. Didja bring 'nuf marbles?" They ran off across the playground to join a group of boys already forming.

Jimmie Lee looked down at his favorite slingshot. He put it slowly back into his rear pocket.

"Jimmie Lee," Alma May said softly, "forget about them. There's lots a other kids here." She looked at his bowed head. "Where you want to eat lunch? Should we go inside with the other kids, or go over there by the slide?"

Jimmie Lee looked across the playground to where the boys had run, then down at the ground and then back across the playground. "Ain't goin' to eat no lunch," he said, and ran off toward the crowd of boys.

Alma May ambled toward the slide. She felt chilled. She leaned against the deserted slide and with cold-numbed fingers opened her sack lunch. Never had she felt so alone. She felt as forgotten as … as ungathered hickory nuts that lay rotting under the tree in the school yard back home. She thought of Mr. McAllister. *How easy it had been going to Mr. McAllister's school.* She stiffly removed the wax paper from around one of the sandwiches her father had made. "You young'n's will have a special treat today. You're gettin' coal miner's steak for lunch," he'd said proudly as he placed a generous piece of bologna between two thick slices of bread.

She wondered what her father was doing at that moment. If only she were that little sparrow there, the one that was circling that maple tree, she could fly away and join Pa wherever he was. She took a small bit of comfort in eating the sandwich he'd made.

English class was on the second floor. Gladys Polaski, the self-appointed Guide for Alma May's First Day at School, cornered her before the bell rang and escorted her there. The class was boring. Alma May had already studied *Hiawatha* back home.

Her eyes widened a little with surprise when her glance fell upon the book the girl in front of her was reading. It wasn't the same book everyone else had. And there was a plain brown wrapper around it. She leaned a little forward to read the title on the top of the page. *Lady Chatterley's Lover.*

"I'm next on the list to read that," Gladys whispered smugly. She was sitting in the row to the left of Alma May. "You read it yet?"

"N, No," whispered Alma May. "Why should I want to read it?"

"Boy, you sure are dumb! Everyone, just everyone, wants to read *Lady Chatterley's Lover.* Martha Templeton stole that copy from her mother. It's a pirated copy that Martha's aunt in New York sent. Martha's marked all the good parts. There are twenty-three kids on the list after me, but if you give Martha a quarter, you can probably get on the list, too."

Alma May did feel really dumb. She wondered what a pirated copy was and how she could get a quarter and who Martha Templeton was.

She and Gladys joined the other girls in gym class next hour. Never had she seen such a huge room, and just for playing in. And what was that long white net stretched out between two iron poles for?

"Oh, goodie! We're playing volleyball today!" Gladys said.

"Volleyball?" Alma May asked.

Gladys shook her head in disbelief. "You mean you haven't heard of volleyball, either? Boy, you sure are dumb!"

Alma May's hands began to get clammy again, and her forehead sweaty. If they had to play with a ball she might have to jump up and down and maybe she'd fall, and she didn't have drawers on, and …

She hurried across the huge glossy-floored room toward the teacher, who wore a strange-looking white outfit that had a short skirt and matching bloomers underneath. Alma May just couldn't play without drawers on. She'd have to think of some excuse.

She approached the teacher and stood behind a girl who was saying something as the teacher marked in her book with a pen.

"Can't play today, Miss Schwako. I got the curse," the girl said.

"All right, you're excused for this one day only," Miss Schwako said. She made another pen mark in the book.

The girl walked away. Alma May cleared her throat. "My, My name is Alma May Combs an' I'm from Kentucky near Harlan an' this is my first day here an' I can't play because I got the curse."

There was a long pause while Alma May looked down at her shoes, which by this time were only damp, and wondered what "the curse" meant.

"All right," the gravelly-voiced Miss Schwako said. "But up north the students are expected to participate in gym every day, even if they are menstruating. You're excused this one time. Watch from the bleachers."

Alma May sat alone in the bleachers with her knees close together and looked at the game below. Volleyball was a strange game. All that hollering and screaming and bouncing the ball around. Back home it was so easy to play "the needle's eye" in the school yard with Mr. McAllister and all the other children.

Gym class was over at last. One more class to go. She hurried out of the gymnasium to escape Gladys. Not only was Gladys nosey, but she was belittling, too. Miss Craig had told Alma May that her last class today would be art, but that tomorrow it would be sewing. *One more class, one more class.* She searched for the art room on the main floor, and stumbled upon it herself, without having to ask anyone. She entered and looked around. *If Mr. McAllister could see this! Three long rows of tables and a long counter with a sink and cupboards, and ...*

Alma May approached the pleasant-faced teacher, who wore a paint-stained pink smock. Alma May introduced herself. She was relieved that the teacher didn't present her to the class, but with a smile told her that her name was Miss Garland, and to have a seat wherever she liked.

Alma May chose a seat in a back corner. She looked around as the room filled, and recognized several students from the other classes, including the colored girl from homeroom. The girl sat down next to Alma May.

"Today is a free day," Miss Garland said to the students. "You may either continue with your Halloween drawings or draw whatever you want. Come up to the counter and get your paper and colored chalk and drawing pencils."

Alma May got up slowly from her chair and followed the other children to the counter. The colored girl turned around, smiled, and said shyly to Alma May, "What you goin' to draw?"

"I, I don't know," she replied. This was the first time she had ever spoken to a Negro, and she didn't know whether to smile back.

She waited for her turn at the supplies, and then returned to her seat. With the blank sheet of drawing paper and the colored chalk and pencils before her and beckoning to her, it didn't take her long to begin. Almost as if a force beyond her was controlling her fingers, controlling her hand, controlling her arm, she began to sketch. She was back home again. Back home and sitting near the edge of her mountain ridge, back home under her huge maple tree. The voices around her grew faint and muffled, as if spoken from a distance. She lost all sense of Detroit, of Pingree Elementary School, of the classroom, as she began to sketch her mountains, her father's mountains. She sketched swiftly and self-assuredly, filling in a stand of trees here, rubbing with her finger tips to soften a patch of undergrowth there. She was unaware of Miss Garland and a group of children who began to form a circle around her. When they spoke, she felt as if she were overhearing a remote one-way conversation:

"Gee! Where'd you ever learn to draw like that?"

"That's a swell picture! Wish I could draw half that good."

"Is that ever pretty! How come you can draw so good?"

"Alma May." A pause. "Alma May." The voice got louder. "Alma May. Tell us about your picture."

Alma May stopped drawing and looked up. "What--?" The students and Miss Garland were crowded around her.

"This is Alma May Combs, children, and this is her first day here. Alma May, where did you learn to draw like that? That's really good," Miss Garland said, her voice filled with admiration.

"I, I don't know. I just do it," Alma May said.

"What mountains are those?" a pigtailed, chubby girl on Alma May's right asked.

"That big one there's Big Black Mountain an' those little ones are the foothills, an' this here's the undergrowth near my ..."

"You can draw even better'n Purlie Washington here," a bespectacled boy on Alma May's left said, pointing to the Negro girl. The girl smiled.

Alma May glanced at the girl's drawing. It was of a colored girl with a pumpkin.

"Maybe some day soon you can help me give a lesson in drawing," suggested Miss Garland.

Alma May smiled broadly. "Ain't nothin' to drawin'. But I wouldn't mind showin' everybody."

Alma May was still smiling when she met a frowning Jimmie Lee outside of the big double doors after school.

"These kids are really dumb," he said, looking up at his sister. "None a them wanna play with my slingshot. All they wanna do is play with their dumb marbles."

Alma May walked confidently across the school yard with Jimmie Lee at her side. She smiled at some of the now familiar faces. She paid scarce attention when a loud voice on her left said, "Yous know Alma May. Then again, she May not. Yous never can tell about them hillbilly gals." The speaker laughed at his own clever wit.

The voice got even louder as Alma May and Jimmie Lee continued walking. "Yeah. Always thought them hillbilly gals dint wear no shoes. This one wears shoes but don't wear no stockings. She probably don't wear no bloomers, either. She wants to make it easy for the boys."

Alma May heard the laughter of pimple face and his buddies. Jimmie Lee bent down and picked up a large stone. In three swift motions, he yanked his slingshot out of his back pocket, placed the stone in the rubber band, and pulled it back, aiming it at the boy. He hit him squarely on the leg, sending him limping and yelling across the school yard accompanied by a loud chorus of laughter from his buddies.

Alma May smiled with admiration at her brother. "Why, Jimmie Lee, you surprise me. I didn't think you'd do a thing like that. An' to someone bigger'n you."

Jimmie Lee looked surprised, too. "I never thought I'd do that, either, but I just didn't like what he said about your bloomers."

They walked silently for a moment. Then Jimmie Lee asked, "Alma May, what's wrong with bein' a hillbilly?"

"Ma says there ain't nothin' wrong with bein' a hillbilly as long as we're clean an' don't lie or cheat or steal."

"Oh," said Jimmie Lee. After a moment be asked, "Do you think Pa would give me enough money to buy some marbles?"

"Don't know why not, soon's he gets his first paycheck. An' he's probably found a job already."

Jimmie Lee gave a little skip. They turned the corner onto their street. "Do you think you're goin' to like this school?"

Alma May smiled and her eyes danced. She would write Mr. McAllister tonight and tell him all about her wonderful art class.

Chapter 8

Lizzie Combs lay in the big double bed with her feet elevated on a quilt and her husband's pillow. She felt guilty. She wasn't up cleaning the rooms and seeing about supper. Never before had she stayed in bed so long, except when Alma May and Jimmie Lee were born, and then for only a day. She knew she should lie here all day as she'd promised Chet, but she was feeling better now, and eager to get their new home in order.

She sat up cautiously and lowered her legs to the floor. She felt dizzy and black spots danced before her. She rested for a moment until the bedroom wall and doorway stopped moving. She was glad that she didn't have to pee. In her weakened condition, it was scary steadying her huge buttocks over the chamber pot. She knew that there was a privy down the hall, but she didn't have the strength to walk that far. *Such a luxury! A privy that flushed, and inside, too!*

Lizzie rose slowly on her wobbly legs and staggered into the kitchen. She was like the newborn calves back home on the farm when she was a child. She steadied herself against the sink and looked down. *A real porcelain sink!* Lizzie raised her shaking hand and turned the faucet on. *Running water right inside the kitchen!* She slowly looked around at the big white table and wood chairs, the worn linoleum floor, the wood chair next to the narrow cot with its beautiful green flowered spread, the not one but *two* cupboards. *Oh, such a fine place Chet has found for us!* She hadn't expected such luxury.

She poured water into the chipped blue enameled teakettle she'd brought from home, and placed it on the one-burner gas hot plate. Lizzie frowned in bewilderment. She'd heard about gas burners, but had never used anything but a coal stove. Lizzie slowly turned the porcelain handle and heard a faint hissing, then smelled a sickening odor. But there was no flame. Now, what should she do? Maybe that was why the box of matches was there. She opened it and lit a match. Lifting the teakettle from the burner with her left hand, she held the match to the burner with her right hand. The unexpected loud "woof" sound as the match ignited the gas startled her so much that she almost dropped the kettle as she staggered back and then fell backward over the sink. After a moment, she regained courage enough to place the kettle timidly on the burner again. She adjusted the handle with shaking hands and thought how stupid she was. Would she ever get used to city ways? Everything moved so fast here! And the people--they talked so fast that it was a strain keeping up with their thoughts. Why, it was as if she were just starting up the slope of Big Black Mountain and they were already to the peak and down again. She felt guilty about not going with Alma May and Jimmie Lee on this, their first day of school, but secretly she felt relieved. If she had gone to school, she would have had to meet and talk with a lot of strangers.

Lizzie thought of the telephone and frowned. The idea of using it frightened her. She hoped she would never have to. But Chet had promised to call her sometimes when he started making big money and could spare the nickel.

Chet. How lucky she was that he was her man! After all these years, she had to pinch herself to make certain she wasn't dreaming. And to think, if she had not ridden over in the jolt wagon from her parents' shabby little farm in nearby Breathitt County that Sunday long ago to visit Euella, she might never have met and married Chet. Euella Bach, Lizzie's cousin twice-removed, was so pretty and rosy-cheeked and lively then. She'd had half the boys in Letcher County in love with her. But she was already promised to Darcas Combs. Darcas. So loud-like and bold compared to gentle Chet. Lizzie's heart had almost fallen out of the bodice of her flowered linsey-woolsey dress that day when she first laid eyes on Chet. Chet, with his clear blue eyes and wide white smile, could have had any girl in Letcher County. But he had chosen Lizzie Bach. Her, Lizzie Bach, with her squinty eyes and hulky body. Oh, the wonder of it all! Chet had fallen in love with her. She wasn't pretty even then. She had not trapped him, either, by sleeping with him the way she'd heard tell other wives had. Lizzie's wan face turned pink thinking about being close to Chet.

It certainly wasn't my winning ways, thought Lizzie, as she lifted the teakettle from the burner and poured boiling water into the sink for washing the few dirty dishes and cleaning off the counter. She was as shy then as she was now. She wished she could be like Chet. Folks took to Chet like ants to sugar. Why, he could talk a squirrel out of a hickory tree. She was glad that Alma May and Jimmie Lee didn't take after her, so stiff and shy around people. Like her own mother was, and her mother before her. She wished she could talk with Alma May and tell her womanly things, like she wished her mother had talked with her. And she wished she could tell Alma May how pretty she was getting, that her hair was the color of a newly minted penny, that her eyes were the color of the bluebell that grew wild on the edge of the roads back home. Oh, Alma May, I'm so glad you don't look like your Ma, Lizzie thought, as she lifted the dried dishes up to stack in the cupboard. ...

Lizzie gasped. She stopped short, frightened by the face in the hazy old looking glass next to the cupboard. Chet had hung it for shaving. The dishes almost fell from her hands. Then she realized the ugly creature she saw there was *her*. She laid the dishes down slowly in the cupboard and poked her face closer to the mirror. *My lord, it would scare a ghost!* Her face was the color of window putty. Her hair had escaped its knot and stuck out like the straw on a worn-out broom. How long had it been since she'd combed it? Her eyes, always small and squinty, were now almost hidden behind swollen lids. She turned away, eager to think of something else.

On the counter she spotted the three bags she'd packed, one filled with the Life Everlasting, one with the mustard seeds, and one with the May apple root. She placed them neatly in the back of the top cupboard. Then she poured a goodly amount of beans into the large pot she'd brought from home. She would pack the leftovers for the young'n's' lunch tomorrow. She poured cold water from the faucet almost to the top of the pot and dumped a slab of bacon and a little salt into it, then placed the pot on the gas burner and turned it down low.

Lizzie looked around the room again. Her face flushed with pleasure when her eyes lit upon the pie tin Ruby Young had given her the day they left. She picked up the tin and rubbed her hand along the edge. Dear, generous Ruby. She wished she could be friendly and outgoing like Ruby, all the time doing things for people and making them feel good.

She sighed with satisfaction. The kitchen was neat and clean now, and she was happy that Chet had found them such a clean place. She would mix up the corn bread later this afternoon. Time she tidied up the bedroom.

Her faded blue sunbonnet still dangled from the head post of the bed where Chet had hung it that first night. She picked it up and rubbed her hands over the brim. The calico material, once rough, was smooth now from years of wearing and washing. Alma May was right. Nobody wore a bonnet like this in Detroit City. Reluctantly, she opened the bottom drawer of the chiffonier and put it way in the back, hidden under Chet's B.V.D.'s.

Chet had unpacked the family's meager clothing from the two cardboard suitcases and hurriedly stuffed it in the chiffonier's drawers. After straightening the clothes, Lizzie looked in the almost-empty boxes and saw that the only things remaining to be unpacked were Chet's old guitar and the faded yellow curtains. She picked up the guitar and held it against her cheek, in her mind's eye picturing his graceful hands as they flitted up and down the strings. She placed it gently in the corner next to the chiffonier.

Did she have the strength to hang the curtains? She was getting weaker again, but if she could manage to climb up on the bed and quickly remove the curtain rod, she could then sit down on the bed and thread the rod through the pocket of the curtains while she rested.

She raised her plump right leg up onto the bed, steadying herself against the wall with her left hand as she pulled her left leg up. The room began to swim around her, but she focused her eyes on the window and yanked the rod off. *If Chet and Mrs. Pasnick knew what she was doing!* Lizzie lowered herself down to the floor again. She fell gratefully onto the bed and sat for a moment until the room stopped spinning.

While she threaded the rod through the curtain's pocket, she wondered what Chet was doing at that moment and whether he had found a job. The words of the man sitting on the stool in the Ohio diner kept returning to Lizzie, like a persistent homing pigeon perched on the edge of her brain: "This is 1930, bud. Ain't you heard there's a depression going on? Hell, they're laying them off right and left in Detroit and all over. ..." But if Chet said he would find a job, he would find one. Hadn't he always taken care of them? But now there'd be one more little mouth to feed.

She swayed again when she climbed up onto the bed, but kept her balance and slid the rod into the brackets. Exhausted, she sat heavily on the mattress's edge as she gathered enough strength to make up the bed. A moment later she had finished smoothing the clean white sheets (her Ma always said it was a mortal sin to sleep on dirty sheets) and the quilt she'd packed from home, and plumped the two pillows. Finally, she folded Alma May's and Jimmie Lee's quilts that they had tossed on the bedroom floor, and placed them on top of the chiffonier. There: Their new home was all clean and tidy now. Lizzie leaned against the doorway between the two little rooms and looked with approval from one room to the other. Oh, she was going to like their new home just fine!

She was startled by the sound of the door opening. "Mrs. Combs!" Mrs. Pasnick scolded. "What you doing outta bed? You get your ass back in there!"

Lizzie cringed. She was not used to such crude talk--and coming from a woman! "But, but I'm feelin' better now, an' ... She stopped, unable to think of another excuse, and feeling like a young'n' caught with his hand in the Company store's sugar barrel.

Mrs. Pasnick grabbed Lizzie roughly by the elbow and pulled her toward the bed.

"But, but the bed's all made, an' I'm feelin' better, an' ...."

Mrs. Pasnick stopped short. She looked around. "You mean to tell me you hung those curtains and straightened up? Shit! Your brains must be where your ass hole is! You'll be bleeding again sure as hell!"

"N, No. I'm just fine. 'Pon my honor. I'll just set for a spell at that nice big table, an' ...." Lizzie lumbered over to the table and slowly sat down, making a great effort not to weave.

Mrs. Pasnick, not waiting to be invited, sat down in the other chair.

She scolded Lizzie again, but to no avail. She finally gave up on persuading Lizzie to return to bed, and talked of other things. Lizzie smiled shyly at Mrs. Pasnick. She tried to think of something friendly and bright to say, but she was not one for small talk, even around someone as gregarious as Ruby Young. Finally, she thought of something: "I, I'm glad the place is so clean."

"Oh, us Polacks is clean people," Mrs. Pasnick said. "I cleaned the place up real good after the last renter." She looked down at the linoleum floor. "Had this here floor as shiny as a nigger's heel."

Mrs. Pasnick chatted on. How nice of her to set a spell and pass the time of day, Lizzie thought. She sat in the uncomfortable wood chair, trying to appear attentive, but feeling weaker and weaker as the minutes passed.

Now Mrs. Pasnick was leaning close to Lizzie and inquiring in a confidential voice, "How far along are you?"

"Far along?"

"How long have you had a kid in the oven?"

Lizzie looked over at the small gas oven. "I wouldn't put a kid in a ov--"

"No, I mean how many weeks pregnant are you?"

Lizzie blushed and looked down at the tabletop. "Oh. I, I'm in a family way about seven weeks, I reckon."

Mrs. Pasnick shifted in her chair and stuck her chin close to Lizzie's face. She lowered her voice as if the whole world was listening. "Now this is confidential," she began.

Lizzie stared at the three curly gray hairs on Mrs. Pasnick's chin and thought how nice of Mrs. Pasnick to be so friendly, and to even tell her something confidential. What could she tell Mrs. Pasnick that was confidential in return? Lizzie didn't know anything that was confi--

"I know someplace you can go," Mrs. Pasnick whispered.

"Go? I don't want to go no place," Lizzie said, astonished. "I'm goin' to like it here just fine." She looked around the room.

"No. I mean I know someplace where there's a doctor who'll fix you up."

"Doctor? But I already had a doctor-man, and he took care a me just fine."

Mrs. Pasnick rolled her eyes and her voice got louder. "If you ain't the d-- ! What I mean is I know a doctor who'll get rid of your baby for you and he only charges thirty-five dollars. It's all safe and easy. I know two young girls what went to him and even a married woman of about your age. He fixed 'em up fine and they came home and stayed in bed for a coupla days. They told their families they had the bad monthly cramps or something. Of course, if the cops ever found out about the doctor ..."

Lizzie sat smiling attentively at her friendly visitor, but after a moment the smile began to fade and her mouth gaped open. Her pale face grew pink and her unkempt eyebrows rose in surprise. "You, you mean I should get rid a my baby? Why, I couldn't do that!"

"Why not? It's easy. The doctor's done lotsa abortions."

"Abor, Abortions? I heard a that. That's killin'!"

"It ain't really killing if the baby ain't born yet."

"But it is! It is! I couldn't kill my own baby. Not even before the birthin'!" Lizzie jumped up. Her chair fell down behind her. She folded her arms and began shifting her weight. "I, I don't want to hear no more about killin' my poor little baby!"

Mrs. Pasnick's face had grown as pink as Lizzie's had. "All right, see if I care! Here I am, come to look in on you, just because I promised your husband I would, and I find you outta bed like a dumb ass, and I try to help you out by telling you about the doctor, and ..." She rose and jutted the three chin hairs close to Lizzie's face again.

Lizzie's voice rose. "Don't call me a dumb ass!"

"You are a dumb ass! Dumb ass, dumb ass, dumb ass! You're a dumb ass because you're having this baby and you're already so poor you ain't got a pot to piss in, and--"

"Get out! Get out! Get out a my house!" Lizzie shouted, amazed at her own courage. Lizzie's voice was even louder now. Her face had grown from pink to blotchy red.

"Your house! Your house! This ain't your house! Don't forget, you're only renting it from me! I ain't getting outta my own house! You get outta *my* house!" Mrs. Pasnick shouted, stopping only long enough to take an angry breath. "Think I wanted to rent it to you in the first place? The only reason I rented to you Goddam' dumb hillbillies was because it stood empty for three months. If you'd let me arrange for the doctor to fix you up, you'd be better off and he'd give me a little money on the side. Don't look at me that way! These days I take whatever I can get to survive, Catholic or not. And it's not really a baby yet, even if my church says it is."

"It is! It is!"

"You Goddam' dumb hillbillies come up here and think you're gonna take the jobs away from us nice people. Well, there ain't no jobs to take away, and if there was some jobs to be had, they belong to us decent people what already belongs here, and--"

"My man's as decent as any man that ever lived, an' decenter than most, an' he's goin' to find a job. Mister McLaughlin says there's lots a jobs!'"

"'Mister McLaughlin says, Mister McLaughlin says.' Well, *I* says there ain't no jobs! There ain't no jobs!" Mrs. Pasnick's saliva sprayed in Lizzie's face. "And it's getting worse! You just pack your cheap suitcases and get outta here! Ain't gonna have no Goddam' dumb hillbillies living here what ain't got no job, and what's gonna have another squalling brat to wake the other renters!" She was standing tall now, with her arms folded tightly in front of her.

Lizzie's voice was calm as she wiped Mrs. Pasnick's saliva from her face. "Reckon you don't have to worry none. I wouldn't stay in no place where the landlady wants me to kill my own young'n'."

"And you ain't getting no refund on what your husband paid in advance. You only been here three days, but I'm keeping all of the seven dollars for all my trouble." With that, Mrs. Pasnick started toward the door, then stopped suddenly and turned around. "And you owe me ninety-eight cents more for the sheet you ruined the first night you came here."

"The sheet?" Lizzie asked, confused.

"The sheet. The sheet! That was a brand new sheet. Just paid ninety-eight cents for it at Crowley's, and you ruined it by bleeding all over it. I been soaking it for three days in Roman Cleanser, and still can't get the stains out."

Lizzie walked with great deliberation to the chiffonier. She reached into the top drawer and pulled out one of the ten one-dollar bills Chet had left there. She slammed it onto Mrs. Pasnick's outstretched palm and said, "Ain't got no change."

"I'll keep the two cents for putting up with you Goddam' dumb hillbillies," Mrs. Pasnick said. She folded the dollar and stuck it down the bodice of her housedress, stomped out of the room and slammed the door behind her.

Fifteen minutes later Lizzie sat on the curb in front of the rooming house. Mrs. Pasnick's cruel words still rang in her ears. She was surrounded by the two filled suitcases, the packed boxes, and the pot of half-cooked beans. The bewildered expression on her face matched that on the faces of Alma May and Jimmie Lee as they ran toward her on their way home from school.

Chapter 9

C het Combs's legs ached and the bottoms of his feet felt like raw sowbelly. These heavy miner's shoes weren't meant for walking far, he thought, as he lifted one weary leg onto a curb on the city's east side. It was now early afternoon, and he'd been looking for work since dawn.

After kissing Alma May and Jimmie Lee goodbye, he'd left a sleeping Lizzie and, with a sack lunch in hand and a map of Detroit in his back pocket, boarded a crowded Woodward Avenue streetcar. He was on his way to the city of Highland Park, a few miles north. Chet had counted their savings again and decided against taking his brother's car. Carfare would be much less expensive than gasoline.

He knew the name of only one automobile factory--Highland Park Ford. This was the one where Tom McLaughlin had said he'd gotten a job. Chet spotted the sprawling factory, partly hidden by trees, from his window. He had gotten off at Manchester Avenue, as instructed by the conductor. At the employment office gate, he found a surly looking guard who sat in a small wooden shed behind a "No Help Wanted" sign.

A steady stream of men, young and old, shabbily dressed and well dressed, had also approached the gate from all angles, read the sign, and left. Several of them had stood for a few moments and stared at the sign, as if by doing so, they might make the words disappear.

Chet knocked on the shed's small window. The guard stopped pouring coffee from his Thermos and raised the window. "Watcha want? Can't you read? The sign says 'N-o H-e-l-p W-a-n-t-e-d'".

"But I don't understand. My friend from back home said there's lots a jobs here, just waitin' to be taken."

"Swell friend. Been no jobs open here for months." The guard paused for a moment. "Sounds like you're from the hills. No wonder you don't know nothin'."

Chet smiled while the guard continued: "Most of the operations from this plant've been moved to The Rouge, anyways, and they're not hirin', either."

"The Rouge?"

"Ford Rouge plant in Dearborn. Few miles southwest of here," the guard said, his voice less harsh. He started lowering the window to signal that the conversation was ended as Chet asked, "Well, do you know of any other place that's hirin'?"

"If I knew of a place that's hirin', don't you think I'd send my brother there? He's been outta work for six months and he's got seven kids already and another in the oven." He locked the window, waved Chet away, and resumed pouring coffee.

Chet stood there for a moment. Should he wait around and try to look up McLaughlin on his lunch hour? No. Chet was too proud. He would wait until he'd found a job and could invite him over. Besides, the morning was wearing on, and he should be getting along.

A gust of chilly wind blew leaves down on Chet. He pulled his thin jacket closer around him and lowered the brim of his cap. He took the map from his back pocket and studied it. It was all a maze of straight and crooked lines, of rectangles and squares and circles and arrows. He wished he knew the layout of the city better.

His mind was a blank. He should have thought to ask Mrs. Pasnick for a few names before leaving this morning. His glance fell finally upon a rectangle on the map that read, "Cadillac Motor Car Co." Well, that was as good as any. The big bosses of the Independent Mining Co. drove Cadillacs. He would go to Cadillac.

He took the Woodward Avenue streetcar back south and transferred onto a westbound Michigan Avenue bus.

At Cadillac, Chet was greeted by another "No help wanted" sign. The heavyset young guard suggested he catch a bus back downtown to the "Loop," then at Woodward catch a Jefferson Avenue bus going east.

"There's four or five companies all close to each other there--Chrysler, Hudson, Continental, Motor Products. Probably won't find anything, but it's worth a try."

"Thank you kindly," Chet said. He pulled out the map and studied it. Be was beginning to recognize some streets. Chet's brow furrowed in concentration. The guard took the map and marked the area he'd suggested.

Chet had gotten off the eastbound bus at Woodward Avenue. He looked in a southeasterly direction and noticed a small park. It was now almost eleven. He felt tired and very hungry. It would be good to sit for a moment and watch the people as he ate his lunch.

He walked the short distance to the park and sat down gratefully on a green iron bench. Most of the other benches were occupied, too. To his right, leaves were falling on a bronze monument ornamented with soldiers and sailors. A few yards east of the monument was a vacant chipped and dingy chair of red sandstone mounted on a pedestal.

He pulled out a bologna sandwich, a jar of cold beans, and a spoon from his sack, then eagerly started to eat. When he was halfway finished, an old Negro man in ragged clothes approached and, to Chet's amazement, sat down on the same bench where he was sitting. Chet grinned. *If the fellows back home could see this. A colored fellow having the nerve to sit down on the same bench as a white!* Chet continued to eat while he looked out from the corner of his eye at the man. The man was staring at Chet's food.

"You hungry?" Chet asked.

The man shook his head no. He threw a suspicious glance toward Chet and moved a few inches down the bench away from him.

"Here, you finish it," Chet offered. "Reckon I've ate just about all I can. I'm about to bust," he lied. He moved the food toward the man. The man looked at the sandwich and beans, then with mistrust at Chet, then at the food again. Finally, he took the food from Chet and began to devour it. Chet smiled at the man.

Meanwhile, a young man had climbed up on the empty chair-monument and in an angry voice was denouncing the President, the governor, the "captains of industry," and, Chet thought, everyone else he could think of. A crowd began to form around him. Some of the men and women in worn clothes and shoes with run-down heels listened intently, and nodded their heads in agreement as he shouted.

"I remember him from that big parade we marched in down Woodward last spring," one man said.

"Yeah, that march didn't do us no good. We still didn't get no jobs and no food," another said.

Other women in the new, smartly styled longer dresses and men in fine suits and shined shoes paused for only a moment, then shook their heads and continued walking.

"If these people would get a job and work, they wouldn't have time to waste listening to these rabble-rousers," a young man in a business suit said to his male companion as they hurried away.

"He's probably one of those young Commies," a distinguished looking middle-aged man said to his young blonde woman friend. He sneered at the speaker.

Chet was amused by it all. He sat for a few minutes more, then stood up, refreshed from his rest and skimpy lunch.

He glanced at the old Negro man again, and nodded good-bye. The man looked up at Chet and smiled. "God bless you, son," he said.

Chet gave the man his widest smile. "Take care a y'self, y'hear?"

He headed south toward Jefferson Avenue, the shouts of the young man ringing in his ears: "Five million of us out of work in this country and Hoover's not doing anything to get us jobs, Governor Green's not doing anything to get us jobs, our elected officials aren't doing anything to get us jobs. The big three car companies don't care how many of us they lay off as long as they continue to live high on the hog. I say it's about time we took matters in our own hands and …"

Chet was diverted but not discouraged by the angry young man. He was going to find a job. Things always worked out for him, didn't they?

At the next corner he passed a scraggly little girl of perhaps four or five standing with a man whom Chet took to be her father. They stood next to a small cart of shiny red apples piled in uniform rows. The girl shoved a thin and dirty arm up to Chet and cried, "Buy a pretty red apple, Mister? Only a nickel." A fleeting longing to see Alma May tore at Chet. He wondered how she and Jimmie Lee were making out on their first day of school. And he wished that he could buy lots of apples to take home to his family.

He'd already boarded the next eastbound Jefferson Avenue bus before he remembered the spoon and jar from his lunch. Lizzie would notice that they were missing. He'd have to remember to buy another spoon with his first paycheck.

He got off the bus where the guard had marked on the map. At the Chrysler plant, the now- familiar "No Help Wanted" sign awaited him. There were perhaps fifty or sixty men already in line. Undaunted, he walked the quarter of a mile east to Hudson Motor Car Co. and the neighboring Continental Motor Co. "No Help Wanted."

He decided to save the nickel bus fare and walk the mile and a half to Motor Products Co. Surely there'll be an opening here for *something*, he thought, as he approached the gate of the huge automotive parts supplier. The "No Help Wanted" sign (Someone had penciled in the words, "and that means YOU") was yellowed and smudged, as if it had been posted for months. Chet knocked on the guard's door. It swung open, and Chet asked with a hesitant smile, "Please. Maybe if I could just talk with the man doin' the hirin', he'd have somethin' I could do. I'm very good with a pick--"

"A pick? Are you kiddin'? No jobs usin' picks here." The guard slammed the door shut.

Chet turned away and walked aimlessly west on Mack Avenue, which bordered the factory's south side. Now he was getting hungry again. Did he dare spare the money and time required to eat a bite before moving on? Should he spend the nickel to call Lizzie, as he'd promised? Lizzie. How lucky he was to have a woman like Lizzie, thought Chet. So unselfish and such a hard worker. Guess there wasn't a truer or kinder woman than Lizzie. She was going to be well again real soon, with Mrs. Pasnick looking in on her. And just look at those young'n's they got--Alma May with her sweet innocence and bright ways. Lord knows where she got that way she had with her drawing and painting. And if she wasn't getting about as pretty as the moon over his Kentucky mountains. And that Jimmie Lee--just as cute as a bug's ear and smart as a whip. All that and the new baby and farm to look forward to, too. But for the first time that day, Chet was beginning to wonder if he really would find a job soon. He'd just as soon die if he couldn't work.

He spotted a diner on his right. "Hamburgers 5¢", the sign on the smoke-smudged window read. Chet patted the change in his pocket. He decided not to disturb Lizzie. She should stay in bed. But he allowed as he could spend a nickel. Should he get a hamburger or a cup of coffee?

He decided the coffee would warm him more and maybe perk up his aching legs.

Chet selected a stool at the counter, and smiled at the diner's only other customer. "Nice day, ain't it?" he said.

The man swiveled slowly on his stool and looked at Chet through watery blue eyes. "Whatsa matter, you crazy? It's cold and damp and cloudy out there." He turned his pock-marked face back to his cup of coffee and resumed staring into it.

The owner of the diner, an obese middle-aged man with a handlebar mustache, smiled at Chet and said, "Don't mind MacDonald here. He's the kind of fellow who finds something wrong with everything. If he won a Cadillac in a raffle, he'd gripe because the seats were mohair and not leather." He smiled at MacDonald.

Chet took a sip of his steaming coffee. "Been lookin' since early this mornin' for a job. Know of any place that's hirin'? I'm willin' to do anythin'."

"Oh, crap," MacDonald said. "You and about fifty thousand other people in this town looking for a job. Don't know why you hillbillies bother to come up here. Guess you don't read no newspapers down there, else you'd know there ain't jobs enough for us that lives here." He spun around on his stool and got off. "Crap!" he said. He opened the door to the diner and walked out. Chet and the owner grinned.

The owner wiped the counter and began whistling "Singin' in the Rain," while Chet asked, his tone anxious now, "Reckon I tried at seven or eight places today. Can you name some more companies around these parts?" Chet named the places where he'd been.

The man thought for a moment and replied, "Well, there's the Detroit-Michigan Stove plant and U.S. Rubber on Jefferson, but I know for a fact they're not hiring. Several fellows were in here a few minutes ago who'd just been there. Sorry. Can't think of any other …" He paused for a moment. "Only thing I can tell you is to try at Dodge Main. They seem to be hiring once in a while when nobody else is. That's just a long shot. You got to hit it lucky and be there at the right time."

"I feel lucky," Chet said. "Where's Dodge Main?" He eagerly pulled out his map.

The man drew a circle around the location, in the city of Hamtramck northwest of the diner, on the map. He gave Chet directions. Chet gulped the rest of his coffee down, gave the man a grateful handshake, and hurried out.

Half an hour later, after transferring on several crowded buses, he saw from his last bus's window a huge cluster of buildings, which appeared to be faced mostly in concrete. From the top of one, four tall smokestacks belched smoke indifferently on the railroad tracks, the smaller factories, the stores, the churches, and the narrow, crowded together frame homes that surrounded the complex. Chet noticed a lone smokestack on top of another one of the buildings. Embedded in the stack were the words, "Dodge Bros.", with the letters "Bros." faded almost out.

Chet walked north on busy Conant Avenue past a company parking lot. He'd never seen so many cars in one place. He ignored the "No Help Wanted" sign and approached the guard sitting in a booth at the gate.

Before Chet opened his mouth to speak, three other men shoved in front of him. One shouted to the guard: "I hear a man's been fired this morning! Please--I gotta have that job!"

"I need that job!" shouted another. "My wife's expecting a baby and we got no food in the house!"

"Nobody needs that job more'n me," the third said. "My wife's dead, I got five kids, and they're gonna foreclose on my house any day."

The guard shook his head. "Sorry," he said through the opening in his window. "Wish there were jobs for all of you, and I was the one to hire you. You heard wrong. There's been no firing here. There's no job opening. Sorry."

The men turned and walked away. One cursed the guard. Chet stared after them. They seemed to have aged ten years in one minute.

Chet thought he'd try a different approach with the guard. He smiled his broadest and inquired with a lilt in his voice, "How are you today? You must get bored sittin' in that little booth all day. An' bein' the kindly, nice feller you seem to be, it must hurt you somethin' awful to have to keep tellin' us there ain't no work."

"Aw, get off it," the guard said. "If I heard that line once, I heard it a million times. If there's no opening, there's no opening." The guard smiled in spite of himself.

"I'll do anythin'," Chet said. "Ain't had no experience other'n minin', but I'm willin' to learn anythin'."

"Sorry."

"Well, then, feller, take care a y'self, y'hear?" Chet walked back toward the bus stop. Maybe this was not his lucky day, after all. Where to next, he wondered. He pulled out his map again.

"Hey, you! Hey, buddy! You with the hillbilly drawl!" a voice behind him shouted. But Chet's attention was on the map as he kept on walking.

"Hey, you! Hillbilly with the map!" the voice yelled again.

Chet realized then that it must be the guard shouting at him. He turned around and ran back.

The guard whispered to Chet, "Those men were right. There's been a man fired this morning." He lowered his voice even more. "Give me half your first paycheck and the job's yours. I've been trying to get word to a buddy who needs a job, but I can't hold it much longer. It's in stamping, and it's under Standish."

"Standish?" Chet asked, excited.

"Yeah, Standish. That's the foreman. He's hell on wheels. If you can work under him, you can work under anybody. He'd just as soon fire a man as look at him, and he does--all the time. He fired the one this morning. Lucky he doesn't have the power to hire, though, or we'd have only his kind here."

"Ain't found nobody I can't get along with yet," Chet said, with a grin. "I knew this was my lucky day."

"Now, you go around to the personnel office on Joseph Campau and tell the girl I sent you. She's holding the job for my friend. Meanwhile, I'll call and say you're coming. And good luck to you. You're going to need it. And don't forget our deal." He shook Chet's hand. Chet thanked him and hurried toward the personnel office.

★   ★   ★

Half an hour later, Chet was punching his time card. To his surprise, the clock next to the time cards indicated it was already two o'clock. He'd been rushed through a routine physical. Chet had been glad that he'd changed his drawers that morning.

"Ordinarily, you would have started tomorrow morning, being it's so late in the day," confided Ed Mansfield, the tall and cheerful young personnel clerk. "But we want to get the job filled before the company decides it doesn't need to replace the man fired." Chet suspected Mansfield was more in sympathy with the workers than with the management. He was convinced of this when the man added, "The men in that department are so overworked, anyway, and it would be just that much more work to divvy up the man's load."

Chet looked around in awe while he walked alongside the energetic clerk. Never before had he been in such a huge building. And never before had he experienced such deafening noise. It vibrated the floor so much, he felt it through the soles of his shoes.

Mercury vapor lights installed in the ceiling way above and on the walls helped the skylights illuminate the jungle of machinery and humanity below. Chet could see men walking on steel-railed runways over large and small presses operated by bored-looking workers. To his left, men walked on bridges over conveyors carrying parts in dozens of little four-wheeled buggies to waiting assemblers. And everywhere, workers hurried here and there, going about their business.

Chet and Mansfield threaded through what seemed like miles and miles of mazes with strange-looking contraptions on either side operated by men with sweaty backs. Chet shouted to make himself heard over the clanks and thuds and hisses: "This is just about the biggest place I ever seen."

"Not as big as The Rouge," Mansfield shouted back, "but Chrysler keeps expanding it since they bought out Dodge Brothers two years ago. This place is like a city in itself. There're over fifty buildings here—a fire department, a private telephone system, a hospital, you name it. There are about twelve hundred cars built here in an average working day."

"Ain't never seen a workin' place as clean as this, neither," Chet said. He remembered the grimy Independent Mining Co.

"Oh, this isn't too bad for a factory, but it's not nearly as clean as The Rouge," Mansfield said over the sharp "pf-f-ft" of air hoses and the whine of drills. He kicked a Juicy Fruit gum wrapper with his toe. "You can eat off the floor there. Ol' Man Henry runs a clean ship."

"Ol' Man Henry?"

"Henry. Henry Ford. I used to work there, but I couldn't take it any longer. They run it like an army, and it's getting worse all the time. This place is more relaxed. It all depends on the foreman. Watch out for Standish. Lucky for you he's off for a couple of hours. Went to the doctor for a migraine. Otherwise, he'd be breaking you in."

Mansfield stopped a stocky little man of about forty with a clipboard in his hand who was passing them. He shouted over the noise, "Hey, Masztakowski, take this new man here to Department seven forty-nine and show him how to run the Bliss, will you? The one that O'Hara ran."

"Sure," Masztakowski said, as he made a mark on his clipboard.

Mansfield smiled at Chet. "Masztakowski's a foreman in this department, but he used to run that Bliss himself."

Mansfield left and Masztakowski continued escorting Chet. "Nothin' to runnin' one of them presses," the foreman said. He walked amazingly fast on his little legs.

Masztakowski slowed down when they approached a row of giant machines that seemed about six times taller than the men operating them. "Here we are," he said. "These men are doin' the rough stampings for Chrysler's new Plymouth car. Watch for a coupla minutes and then give it a try."

Chet watched the two workers while they lifted a sheet of steel and placed it into a space between the top part of the press and the lower part.

"See the biggest part of this ol' Bliss press? The top part?" Masztakowski asked, pointing a fat finger. "That's called the movable platen. The part on the bottom's called the fixed platen or bed.

"The die that forms the shape we need is in two halves. The upper part is clamped to the top platen with those huge "tee" bolts, an' the lower half is fixed to the bed the same way.

"When it goes up, the die opens, an' you guys put a piece of flat sheet steel in the opening, an' when the die comes together, a fender is rough-formed and partly trimmed.

"Then you open it up again and you both take out the stamped fender an' put it on a conveyor to go to the next operation.

"We got all kindsa presses--punch, pierce, trim, shear, an' so forth, but they all work just about the same way. This here press can make over two hundred tons of pressure. You get your hand caught in there, and it'll come out lookin' like a Mexican tortilla. These men are turning out more'n two thousand, seven hundred fenders a day. That's over five a minute."

Chet stood with his mouth open. His stomach began to flutter.

"Think you can do it, now?" Masztakowski asked.

"Sh, Sure. Looks like there ain't nothin' to it," Chet said. He rubbed his hands together and swallowed hard as if the press were a giant iron monster and he was preparing to fight it.

"Okay, then," Masztakowski said. He motioned for one of the men to come with him and at the same time gestured for Chet to take the man's place. Meanwhile, the top platen of the press continued lowering onto the bottom platen, even though the sheet of steel was temporarily missing.

Chet moved quickly to the proper place and he and the remaining worker together lifted a sheet of steel and placed it in the press. It was heavy, but years of using a miner's pick had prepared Chet well. Masztakowski and the released worker stood in the aisle and watched Chet for a few minutes. Then Masztakowski smiled and nodded his head as he raised his hand and formed a circle with his thumb and first finger to indicate that Chet was catching on. He turned and left with the worker.

After a few minutes, Chet's fluttering stomach relaxed a little. Just when he began to catch on to the operation, the press ground to a stop. But the noise still echoed in his ears. "What, what happened?" he asked.

"We're in luck. The whole line is down," said his partner, a tall blond man who appeared to be in his thirties. He pointed to all the presses to the right and left of theirs in the same row.

"But what do we do now?" Chet asked.

"Just stand here and relax until they fix it." He smiled at Chet, revealing bright, even teeth, and asked Chet his name and where he came from. The man liked to talk, and within three minutes Chet learned that his name was Harry Buckingham; that he'd once been a teacher of English in the Detroit public school system, but had lost his job when the system had to cut expenses; that he had always loved all women and girls whether pretty or ugly or big or small or young or old; that his wife had left him when she found him in bed with another woman; that he didn't really care because now he was having the time of his life going to Chicago every other weekend where the women and bootleg whiskey were easy to get; and that maybe sometime soon Chet would like to go with him.

Chet smiled and shook his head no. "I got all I can handle right here. I got me the best little woman in the world." He thought, then, of Lizzie, and felt guilty that he'd been too busy to think of her for the past hour or so. But he repeated to himself that she'd be all right with the landlady looking in on her. Mrs. Pasnick was turning out to be a good woman, just as he knew all along she would. Yes, everything was turning out well. Just as he knew all along it would.

"Who is this foreman feller. What's his name, Stan, Stan …?" Chet asked of Buckingham.

"Oh, you mean Standish. That bastard! Don't know what his problem is. Maybe he's got a fly up his ass. Hard to please. Lot of things he doesn't like. He doesn't like the niggers because he says they're slow and always look dirty, he doesn't like the Polacks because their names sound funny and there're too many of them around here and they bring Kowalski sausage in their lunch pails, he doesn't like the Wops because they're too religious and smell like garlic. In fact, he doesn't like any Catholics because they wear that funny cloth thing on a string around their necks. Guess the bastard doesn't like anyone who isn't just like he is. He thinks he's superior because he claims he's of English descent and related to the original New England settlers. Says he's descended from Myles Standish--you know, the military leader of the Mayflower pilgrims--" Buckingham stopped talking and broke out in a laugh. "The only reason he leaves me alone is because I've convinced him I'm descended from the family of Buckingham, who the Buckingham Palace was named after. Shit! What a joke!"

The press began to hum again, and the platen to move. "Damn! They got the line fixed! Too soon to suit me," Buckingham said, with a smile. "It must've been something wrong way down at the end."

He and Chet resumed their positions. "You'll get used to the noise," Buckingham shouted. "Don't fight it. Let yourself get into the swing of it, the rhythm of the presses. Pretty soon you'll find if you don't hear the noise, it's like dancing without music. Just don't let the rhythm lull you into carelessness."

After about a half hour of steady work, the job became almost routine. Then a loud bell rang over the rumbles and roars and screeches of the machinery. "What's that?" Chet asked.

"That's the bell for a ten-minute break. Lucky for us Standish isn't here, or we wouldn't get one. Maybe someday we'll get the union in here and he won't be able to deny us one," Buckingham said.

The presses were shut down and the area around Chet was quiet, although the machinery in other sections was still operating. "Guess those fellows don't get a break this afternoon," Buckingham said. He pointed to a section a few yards beyond them. "Come with me. We'll sit down and have a smoke." He motioned for Chet to follow him toward a corner next to a pile of defective rocker panels and a "No Spitting" sign. Once more, the noise still echoed in Chet's head.

He sat down on the concrete, leaving room for Chet, next to three other men who were already lighting up cigarettes. When Chet sat down, Buckingham pulled a pack of Lucky Strikes out of his pocket and offered one to Chet. Chet took it gratefully. Very seldom had he smoked a store-bought cigarette. He usually rolled his own from Bull Durham tobacco, but lately he didn't want to splurge on even that.

Buckingham introduced Chet to the three men and explained that he was taking O'Hara's place. "Too bad O'Hara didn't change his name," one of the men, Walter Gajewski, said as he offered his hand to Chet. "Standish doesn't like the Irish." Gajewski was a middle-aged man with round eyes, round cheeks, and a round stomach. "Says the Irish drink too much and waste too much time telling stories."

The talk turned to things that were important to Chet's new acquaintances: How the Detroit Tigers had done in the baseball season that had ended a few weeks ago, how Chevrolet was beating Ford in sales, how they envied Buckingham his freedom, how radios were getting less expensive all the time and soon everybody would own one, how great Lew Ayres was in *All Quiet on the Western Front*.

Eventually, Standish became the subject of conversation again. Joe Lombardi, a young man with a shock of dark, curly hair who sweated and smelled like a wrestler, took a long drag on his cigarette and warned Chet, "Whatever ya do, don't cross him. Around here, ya don't got no mind of your own. O'Hara forgot that for a minute this morning, and look where he is now."

"Yeah. Just remember to do whatever he tells you, no matter if you don't understand it," advised Ed Sobieski, a well-built young man whose huge, flat nose looked out of place with the rest of his face's delicate features. "One time there was a fellow got in troub-- Oh, dammit! Here comes the bastard, now!" He squashed out his cigarette. Buckingham, Lombardi, and Gajewski put out theirs, too, and jumped up. Buckingham whispered under his breath to Chet, "Put out that cigarette and get back to work, quick! And don't cross him!" He scurried with the other men back to their presses.

Chet stood up and stepped on his cigarette as he watched the foreman approach. Never before had he seen such a dignified-looking man. Standish's elegantly shaped head was covered with a dark, full head of hair streaked with silver. Deep, graceful waves started from a low-parted pompadour. His sleek body was clothed in neat gray pants with a matching vest over a white dress shirt of fine oxford cloth. In his manicured fingers he held a pencil and a pad of paper clamped to a clipboard.

Chet smiled broadly, extended his right hand, and said, "How-de-do. My name's Combs. Proud to know you."

Standish stared coldly at him with deep-set, piercing eyes and said, "I know who you are. Get back to your job."

When Chet turned to leave, the foreman shoved his right foot out in front of him. Chet fell in the aisle as Standish said, "Oh, I'm sorry." He looked down at Chet but did not offer a hand to help. "We need a sky hook for your line. Go get one right away."

Chet recovered from his fall. His foreman couldn't have meant to trip him. "Sky hook?"

"Yes. A sky hook," the foreman said pleasantly. Be flashed a white smile. "Go on over there and ask for one." He pointed to an area at the other end of the building. "If they don't have one there, go to the next building. Don't come back without one. I'll put someone else on your job while you look for it."

Chet hurried away, a bewildered look on his face. What was a sky hook?

He walked immediately to the area at which Standish had pointed and inquired of several workers where a sky hook might be. The workers responded with a blank look or a shrug of the shoulders. Several said, "We don't have one," or "Try over there." Chet was on his way to the next building, as Standish had suggested, when he abruptly stopped walking. A broad grin covered his face. So he wants a sky hook, does he? thought Chet. He stood there for a moment and then grinned wider as he got an idea. He stopped a worker who was walking toward him and inquired, "Say, feller, where can I get a hook an' a flat piece a tin or somethin' that I can cut somethin' from?"

The man thought for a moment and replied, "Try the tool cage in the next department."

Chet hurried in the direction the man had pointed, passing various bins filled with stock along the way. If he wants a sky hook, he thought, with a grin, I'll get him a sky hook.

The man in charge of the tool cage, an area separated from the machines by a wire fence, gave Chet the needed hook and flat piece of tin.

"Good. Now, you got any tin snips?" Chet asked.

The man walked over to a shelf and came back with a pair of shears used for cutting sheet metal, which he handed to Chet. He watched as Chet began to cut a design out of the sheet of tin. A worried look crossed the man's face. "Oh, Lord, don't do that! I see what you're doing now. That's Standish's old trick--to send the new man out in search of a sky hook. If you're smart, you'll just go along with him and let yourself be laughed at. He's fired men for a lot less than what you're doing."

"Oh, I can't believe he's as bad as you fellers all make him out," Chet said. He made a slit in the finished star and slipped the hook through it. "Ain't nobody in the world can't take a little joke." He held up the crude tin star attached to the hook and admired his handiwork. "Thankee kindly," he said, handing the shears to the man. He hurried back toward his press.

"No! Don't! You'll be sorry," the man yelled after Chet. He left the tool cage and started following Chet. He motioned for all the workers passing by on errands to follow him, too.

Chet hid the hook and star behind his back. He spotted Standish, who was standing in the aisle next to the press being operated by Buckingham and Chet's temporary replacement. By the time Chet reached Standish, there were about twenty men following him.

"This I gotta see," one of the men said.

"He'll be outta a job almost as fast as he got one," another said.

Standish looked at the approaching Chet, then looked at his watch, then looked again at Chet. "What took you so long?" he shouted loud enough to be heard over the noise of the presses. "And where's the sky hook? I thought I told you not to come back until you found a sky hook."

By this time, the crowd had gathered around Standish and Chet. Chet was standing in front of a maintenance man carrying a large oil filled pouring can. Standish looked slowly around at the crowd, pleased with the turnout. His finely chiseled face lit up with anticipation and his eyes gleamed. He looked at Chet and yelled again: "Where's the sky hook?"

Chet smiled at his boss, slowly moved his hand from behind his back, and presented him with the hook and star. "Seems as though this hook kind a got itself caught on a li'l ol' star."

The smile faded from Standish's face as he stared at Chet's handiwork. His hands shook with rage.

Chet was disappointed. "Oh, I was only funnin' you. I reckoned you'd appreciate a little joke."

Standish moved his lips but no sound came out. An uncomfortable hush fell over the crowd. The foreman's face grew blotchy red as he found his voice. "You bastard! Make a fool of me, will you?" He made a fist of his right hand, drew it back, then aimed it with full force at Cbet's smiling face as Chet ducked. The blow intended for Chet hit the maintenance man holding the can of oil, sending the man crashing into several men in back of him and sending the can of oil flying up in the air. Standish stumbled forward and slipped on the oil. He fell to the floor, face down. Suppressed laughter from the men broke out as the foreman turned over and tried to stand, still slipping on the oil that poured in globs from his face down his white shirt and clothes. Standish muttered something indistinguishable.

"Here it comes. He's gonna fire that poor hillbilly bastard," Buckingham's partner said.

Buckingham had been watching the entire incident, without missing a move at his press. "No," he said. "I think he'll have a little fun with him first."

Chet extended his hand to Standish. "Here, feller. Let me help you."

Standish spit oil on Chet's shoes and glared up at him through oil-drenched eyelashes. "I'11 get you, you sonofabitchin' hillbilly. Just you wait," he said, his voice low and venomous.

Chapter 10

T here. That's the best she could do with what she had to work with, Alma thought the following spring as she placed the bouquet of daffodils over the largest patch on her mother's only tablecloth. Good thing that the patch was only a little off center of the cloth. No one would notice that she was hiding it. She stepped back a few feet to admire her work. The bright yellow daffodils and the pale green cloth, along with the white napkins her mother had made with fabric from Crowley's thrift department, lent an air of springtime to the drab room.

The silverware was placed one inch from the edge of the table, with the knife and spoon to the right of the plate, and the fork to the left on the napkin, just as she'd learned in home economics class. She'd given their special guest the un-chipped plate. She and Jimmie Lee would have to share a spoon. With an extra person besides Aunt Euella and Uncle Darcas for supper, there wouldn't be enough spoons to go around. Pa never did buy Ma another spoon, like he'd promised that day he'd forgotten to get it back from the colored man in the park. Alma frowned. If Uncle Darcas and Aunt Euella didn't have to eat supper here so often, there'd be plenty of spoons to go around, even for the special guest. Oh, she had no complaint against her aunt, except that she got tired of seeing her face always covered with bruises in various stages of healing. But she still wasn't used to the looks her uncle gave her, and she hated his vulgarities. She hoped he would tone them down tonight because of her father's friend. She wondered what Mr. Buckingham would be like. Pa said he liked to talk a lot. Good. Maybe her uncle wouldn't be able to butt in very often with his dumb remarks.

"Alma May, don't forget to go downstairs and get the *Free Press* from Miss Di Inganno. It'll be too late for you to bother her after supper," her mother called from the kitchen.

Alma's forehead furrowed in annoyance. Hadn't she instructed everyone to call her Alma, just plain Alma, and *not* Alma May. Alma May sounded so hillbillyish. *And now all these chores since they moved from Mrs Pasnick's flat to this one.* First her mother had made her go out and pick dandelion greens for a side dish. "Be sure an' pick only the young'n's--them's the tenderest. The old'n's is bitter." When Alma had objected to such common fare, her mother had replied, "Your Pa says Mr. Buckingham is insistin' on a honest-to-goodness hillbilly meal."

Then she had to fold diapers for Carrie Lou, her new baby sister. Her mother had spent so much extra time cleaning and shining up the house today that she had no time to fold the baby's diapers herself. And it was bad enough that Carrie Lou was wearing diapers made from cut-up flour sacks handed down from Jimmie Lee and herself. "Ma, ain't nobody up north uses flour sacks for diapers," ahe had explained to her mother. One diaper was so worn it no longer held a patch. When Alma had balked at folding it and said it should be thrown away, her mother said, "Why, that's good for a couple more wearin's." Lizzie had added her usual phrase, which was fast becoming a household slogan: "Use it up, or fix it up, or do without."

Alma headed downstairs now toward Miss Di Inganno's flat. Her mother called after her, "An' before you go to bed tonight, I'll fix you up a nice spring tonic. You been lookin' like you got the punies lately."

Alma winced. *Not one of Ma's "nice spring tonics"--those horrible concoctions of herbs and stuff that Ma believes gets rid of winter's sluggishness. Ugh!*

She was glad to close the door behind her and escape for a few minutes from the smell of beans and sowbelly and her mother's penny-pinching and thoughts of Uncle Darcas. She paused for a moment when she reached the landing leading to the downstairs flat. She looked out the window at the little cluster of daffodils at the side of the neighbors' house. The cluster was smaller now than it had been that morning. A fleeting tinge of guilt gnawed at her. Alma had told her mother she'd found the daffodils by the side of the road near a vacant field. In truth, she'd asked Jimmie Lee to sneak over to the neighbors' yard and pick a few for a centerpiece. "They'll never miss 'em, Jimmie Lee. They got plenty." To her relief, Jimmie Lee had not balked. But Ma would kill them both if she ever found out.

As she looked at the blossoming maple tree between the Combses' yard and the neighbors', a vague feeling of melancholy, all too frequent of late, overwhelmed her. It was spring, and she should be happy. Weren't people supposed to be happy in spring? She envied the grass its greening. She envied the nesting birds their happy songs and carefree capers. She envied the tree its unabashed showing of perfect leaves and perfect blossoms.

She envied Mrs. Carlson, the lady for whom she babysat, her new spring and summer wardrobes.

The last time she'd gone to Mrs. Carlson's house, she had shown Alma her new clothes, including the stylish little afternoon dress featured at Hudson's (Mrs. Carlson never shopped at Crowley's) in the new cotton batiste material.

Now Alma looked down at her own worn blue winter skirt and white blouse. It was spring, and she, Alma, should be blossoming, too! She felt excluded from the season's freshness and gaiety. She sighed and continued downstairs. Somehow, life was easier in winter.

Actually, she didn't mind getting the newspaper the Combses shared with Miss Di Inganno. A visit to Miss Di Inganno's always offered a little excitement no matter how dull Alma's day might be. But she hoped the old lady wouldn't talk about Rudolph Valentino all the time, as she often did. What did Alma care about old silent screen stars, especially one who had been dead for five years? Alma wanted to hear about today's talking picture stars. Like Clark Gable and Jean Harlow and Norma Shearer and Joan Bennett.

The Combses had moved into the upper flat on Fifteenth Street on that awful day that Lizzie quarreled with Mrs. Pasnick. They were fortunate to find an empty flat nearby whose landlord let them move in with the promise that Chet would pay a month's rent in advance as soon as he got his first paycheck. Miss Di Inganno was already occupying the downstairs flat when they arrived. She'd at one time worked as a wardrobe mistress in Hollywood for some of the leading stars. Sometimes Alma would sit at Miss Di Inganno's kitchen table for hours while the old lady reminisced. Alma sat fascinated, her hand under her chin, as Miss Di Inganno told in her husky voice stories of her wonderful past. Several times she described the flamboyant costumes worn by Jeanette MacDonald in *The Vagabond King*. The costumes had to be especially colorful, Miss Di Inganno explained, since the movie was filmed in the new color process, Technicolor. She talked about helping dress Bebe Daniels for *Rio Rita* and Norma Shearer for *Divorce*. And Alma's eyes grew big with wonder when Miss Di Inganno related the lavish and gay parties thrown by the stars and film producers; she got to dress the stars for these, too.

Invariably, though, Miss Di Inganno would get around to talking about Valentino. "There was no one like Rudy. There never was, and there never will be. He made women swoon with nothing but that smoldering look. Clark Gable can't do that. John Gilbert could never do that. ..." She would pause and her face would grow sad and then angry. "He never really loved that Jean Acker or Natasha Rambova or Pola Negri. He loved me, me! I was the only one he could be himself with. It was only a front, for publicity, when he married Acker and Rambova. Only I knew the true Rudolph Valentino. That perfect young body, those dark and brooding eyes, that sensual mouth were all mine. He loved me, I know he did. ..."

After Valentino's death, she lost her job during studio cutbacks and married a studio prop man, Mr. Wineberg. Shortly after that, Mr. Wineberg lost his job, too, and accepted a job as a prop man in Detroit for an industrial filmmaker. They moved to the flat on 15th Street then. Mr. Wineberg died before the Combses arrived. Miss Di Inganno, who had resumed using her maiden name, seldom mentioned him. It was almost as if he'd never existed.

Alma didn't mind it one bit when Miss Di Inganno would suddenly look at her, as if she'd just noticed she was there, and say, "With that hair of yours, and that complexion, you should be a movie star." Alma would blush and change the subject, but secretly she wished the old lady would continue.

Now Alma knocked loudly on Miss Di Inganno's door. Sometimes Miss Di Inganno didn't hear her unless she knocked very hard. Alma knocked louder.

"Who is it?" Miss Di Inganno asked. Alma was always surprised at her deep, husky voice.

"It's me, Alma," she said timidly, for the voice sounded annoyed. "Come to get the paper."

Miss Di Inganno did not open the door, but said, "Come in."

Alma pushed open the door hesitantly. The room was dark except for a dimly lit kerosene lamp on the table.

"You broke the spell," Miss Di Inganno cried with a scowl.

Oh, no, thought Alma. She's playing with that Shadow Cut-Out Book again. Miss Di Inganno wore a yellowed lace dressing gown and a rotted lace mantilla. She sat at the kitchen table with the lamp in front of her. She was holding a page from the Shadow Cut-Out Book up in front of the lamp. It was a paper stencil of Rudolph Valentino. A wavy image of the movie idol dressed in costume for *The Four Horsemen of the Apocalypse* flickered on the barren white wall opposite.

"See how beautiful my Rudy is!" Miss Di Inganno said, a little over her anger. "You might as well turn on the light now. You spoiled it."

Alma turned on the harsh overhead light as Miss Di Inganno blew out the lamp's flame. She put the Valentino stencil carefully in the Shadow Cut-Out Book and took the book to her bedroom. Alma looked around. The small table was the same as always. In the center was a multi-colored plaster of Paris bust, about ten inches in height, of Rudolph Valentino as *The Sheik*. Next to it was the familiar-looking cigar box measuring about nine by six inches with a picture on the cover of Valentino in a business suit. Miss Di Inganno said it contained love letters to her from the movie idol. In front of the cigar box was a tin Beautebox made by the American Can Company. On the lid was a reproduction of a portrait of Valentino as *The Sheik*. The box had once held candy, but now contained money. Every month Miss Di Inganno took ten dollars from the box, put it in an envelope addressed to the caretaker at Hollywood Memorial Park Cemetery, and gave it to Alma to mail. It was for flowers to be placed on the crypt of Rodolfo Guglielmi Valentino on the twenty-third of each month. Valentino had died on August 23, 1926.

Opposite the kitchen's narrow wall on which Miss Di Inganno had projected the image was a wall on which publicity stills and yellowed magazine and newspaper clips were thumbtacked. Alma recognised pictures of John Barrymore, Helen Twelvetrees, Charlie Chaplin, and many more.

On the two remaining wider walls were pasted photographs and portrait reproductions of Rudolph Valentino in costumes for his most famous movies. Beside these were tacked yellowed newspaper clippings about him, covers from every magazine on which he'd appeared, and theater posters and lobby cards.

Miss Di Inganno returned from her bedroom. She was a frail, stooped figure. She's probably wearing her fanciest gown in honor of her lover, Alma thought. Alma was always a little taken aback when she saw her. Each time, Miss Di Inganno's makeup seemed a little thicker and a little more caked. Alma wondered if she ever removed the false eyelashes and old makeup, or if she just put on new makeup over the old. If she didn't have all that makeup on, thought Alma, I'll bet her face would fall apart. Or maybe be half as wide.

Miss Di Inganno reached to the top of the icebox and took down the copy of the *Detroit Free Press*. She motioned for Alma to sit down at the table.

She must not be annoyed with me anymore, Alma thought. But she shook her head and said, "I really wish I could stay an' visit, Miss Di Inganno, but Ma's expecting me back up there in a minute. We're having company tonight. Mister Buckingham--"

"Oh, you can spare a minute."

"Well. Just for a minute," Alma said. She felt a little sorry for the old lady who lived alone and had only her memories to keep her company. Alma hoped she could steer her toward talking about Clark Gable or Joan Crawford. She sat down on a massive, carved oak chair. Miss Di Inganno sat down in its matching chair next to Alma. She'd told Alma that these had once been used by Valentino in his dressing room.

"What are you serving your company for dinner?"

Alma hesitated. She knew that Miss Di Inganno would not approve. "He told Pa he wants a genuine hillbilly meal, so we're having beans and sowbelly, and dandelion greens and cornbread." As soon as she said it, she wished she'd lied.

Miss Di Inganno opened her faded blue eyes wider and made her wizened face even more wrinkled when she frowned. "Beans and cornbread. Beans and cornbread! You should treat your special guest better than that." She put her elbow on the table and rested her head on her veiny hand. Alma tried not to stare at Miss Di Inganno's bright red hair, which framed her face in corkscrew tendrils under the frayed mantilla. To Alma, her hair was the color of sumac, just like that waitress in the diner in Ohio last fall. Did she put a henna pack on it, too?

"Oh, what special treatment we got at all those parties." Miss Di Inganno's eyes shone. "Imported caviar, chocolate bonbons, little canapes, the best imported champagne--we always managed to get around the prohibition law--ten-piece orchestras, sometimes Eddy Duchin would play the piano for us. Oh, what special treatment. And I got to go because Rudy insisted on it. Sometimes he and that Rambova woman would dance for us. ..." Miss Di Inganno's voice trailed off. She sat staring into space. "He never did get over that editorial, you know."

"What editorial?" Alma asked, bewildered. No answer. After a moment, she asked again, "What editorial?"

"Why, the *Chicago Tribune* editorial, of course," Miss Di Inganno finally replied. "The one that attacked his manhood and ancestry and called him a pink powder puff." She blinked her false eyelashes in anger. "Pink powder puff! Pink powder puff! He was all man, all man! ..." Her voice trailed off again. She began once more to stare into space. "Only I knew the real Valentino. He loved me, he loved me, only me. Only I knew the real Valentino." Her voice grew louder. "They wouldn't let me near his room at the hospital where he died. I was there on the eighth floor all day, every day, until the end came. The papers all said his last words were in Italian before he slipped into a coma. The doctors couldn't understand what he was saying. They didn't know he was crying out for me. ..." Miss Di Inganno's face grew hard and bitter under the makeup and she began to clench and unclench her gnarled fist. "Oh, Rudy, to die alone with only the nurses and doctors there! If only they had let me see you! I could have saved you! I could have saved you! I could have saved ...!"

Alma got up quietly from her chair, picked up the newspaper, and tiptoed out of the room.

★   ★   ★

Chet motioned for his guest to sit at the head of the table. Doesn't the table look nice, he thought. He sat down to the right of Lizzie, who sat at the end opposite Buckingham. To Chet's right was Jimmie Lee, and Alma May next to Buckingham. Across from Chet sat Darcas and Euella. The savory aroma of beans and sowbelly and cornbread almost overpowered the harsh odor of Fels–Naptha soap, which drifted in from the kitchen. Lizzie must have scrubbed the kitchen floor again today, he thought.

"Those beans and cornbread certainly have a wonderful, tantalizing aroma, Lizzie," Buckingham said, "just as I imagined they would. You certainly are a good cook."

Lizzie flushed with pleasure, and her scrubbed, shiny face under her neatly combed hair crinkled up in a shy smile. "Th, thank you, Mr. Buckingham. But you better taste 'em first before you say that."

Chet wished his wife was just a little bit less shy and could talk easily with people other than her own family.

"Call me Harry, Lizzie. Mister Buckingham sounds so formal."

Chet thought his home had never looked neater or shinier. And he wondered why it had taken him so long to invite his friend over. Buckingham had been pestering him for a hillbilly dinner for months. He'd become good friends with Buckingham since that first day on the job.

Buckingham had told him all about his escapades in Chicago and continued to jokingly pester Chet to go with him there.

The last time the subject had come up, Buckingham shouted from across the noisy punch press: "Hey, Hillbilly, you don't know what you're missing. Some of those women know a thousand and one ways to do it. The last one insisted on hanging upside down and backwards from the footboard. Hot damn! I got in so deep, I was worried I couldn't get out. Thought I'd have to come back to Detroit and leave my ole prick there!"

Chet had only grinned at his friend's foul mouth and shook his head no. "I got just what I want at home," he said, laughing.

Buckingham shook his head in pity. "I'm telling you. You don't know what you're missing."

Since Chet had begun working at the plant, the number of men gathering at lunch time around him and Buckingham, Ed Sobieski, Joe

Lombardi, and Walter Gajewski had increased, until now there was always a crowd. The mood as they ate was relaxed and friendly, one of easygoing camaraderie. Each man was encouraged to swap stories and jokes. But most often, they wanted to hear another mountain folk tale from Chet, or about a Chicago conquest or a poem from Buckingham.

One day after Chet had finished an old story about Big Black Mountain, Joe Lombardi said, "Oh, Hillbilly, you told us that twice before, and each time you told it, it's gotten longer and fancier." The men chuckled, and after a moment Ed Sobieski asked, "Say, Hillbilly, how's come you like them mountains so much?"

Chet was still for a long moment, then answered slowly, "Reckon I never asked myself that before. I'll have to think about that a spell." He stopped chewing his beans and his face became softly pensive. Finally, he answered, "Well, the way I figure is--when I look up at them mountains, especially Big Black Mountain, or when I'm up on top a them an' look down, I feel rich inside. I feel just as important as a Independent Mining Company owner or a Walter P. Chrysler or a President Hoover. All the money in the whole wide world ain't goin' to buy a better scene than what I got. Reckon what I mean is them mountains make me feel big inside."

The men had grown silent out of respect for Chet. Finally, Walter Gajewski had pointed a fat finger at Buckingham and said, "Time for a poem from The Teacher."

"Want to hear some poetry?" Buckingham asked. He'd been smiling at Chet and listening intently to him. "Want to hear a serious poem? I'll recite a serious poem. Want to hear a dirty poem? I'll recite a dirty poem. First a little from a serious poem:

"So live, that when thy summons comes to join
The innumerable caravan, which moves
To that mysterious realm, where each shall take
His chamber in the silent halls of death,
Thou go not, like the quarry-slave at night,
Scourged to his dungeon, but, sustained and soothed
By an unfaltering trust, approach thy grave
Like one who wraps the drapery of his couch
About him, and lies down to pleasant dreams.

"Now for a dirty limerick," Buckingham continued.

> "There was a young man from Racine
> Who invented a fucking machine.
> Concave or convex
> It would fit either sex,
> With attachments for those in between
> And was perfectly simple to clean
> With a drip pot to catch all the cream
> And jerked itself off in between.
> The God-damndest thing ever seen.
> And guaranteed used by the Queen."

"Well, I didn't like the serious one, but I sure liked the dirty one," Ed Sobieski said, as they all laughed.

Now Buckingham looked at Euella, who sat next to him, and smiled. "I understand from Chet that you and your husband arrived in the city a few weeks after the Combses," he said pleasantly.

Euella looked up from her plate and glanced shyly at Buckingham with a startled smile. "Y, yes," she said. She looked immediately down at her plate again.

"Chet was saying you took the train. Was it a pleasant ride?" Buckingham asked.

Euella glanced at her husband as if to ask permission to answer.

Alma looked across the table at Aunt Euella. She was annoyed with her aunt. Doesn't Aunt Euella have any opinions of her own, even about a simple thing like that? she wondered. She looked at her aunt's bruised face. That bruise on her left cheek is a new one. Alma wondered where she fell this time.

Uncle Darcas began telling about the train ride from Louisville, and that they had found a flat not far from his brother, and that he was lucky to have gotten a job a few weeks later at Briggs making automobile bodies for Ford.

Alma stole a glance at her father's friend. Even though Mr. Buckingham and her father had driven in Buckingham's Dodge coupe right from work, Mr. Buckingham had changed first and was dressed immaculately in a stylish, perfectly fitted sport shirt and slacks. She looked over at her father.

He'd washed his hands and face and changed his shirt, but his face had a stubble of beard and his shirt looked frayed and out of style.

She felt a poke on her left thigh. Jimmie Lee, who sat on an orange crate covered with a patched sheet, was signaling Alma that it was his turn to use the spoon they shared. She took it from her plate as inconspicuously as she could and handed it to him under the tablecloth.

"Say, Jimmie Lee, I see the Tigers and the Yankees have both won four and lost two so far this season," Buckingham said. "Did you hear any scores so far today?"

"No," Jimmie Lee answered as he grabbed the spoon from Alma's hand.

"Well, maybe if The Babe hadn't been in the hospital for five days, the Yankees might have won two more from the Red Sox. Gehrig and Ruffing homered last Friday, though, and that won one game," Buckingham said.

"The Babe? Who's The Babe?" Jimmie Lee asked.

"Jimmie Lee don't know nothin' about Babe Ruth yet, Harry," Chet said. "He ain't never played no baseball back home, an' he ain't been followin' the Tigers, neither. Reckon right now he's hankerin' for more marbles. An' if he does his chores real good like he's been doin', come payday he can have a nickel for some." Chet looked at his son and smiled proudly. Jimmie Lee's eyes lit up with surprise. He grinned back at his father.

Talk got around to how glad Chet and Darcas were to be out of the mines. "We worked twelve hours a day for two-sixty a day, paid the company thirty dollars a month for a two-room shack, a dollar fifty a ton for coal, and ninety cents for a sack a flour that costs seventy-five cents in a regular store," Chet said.

"Shit!" Uncle Darcas said. "McLaughlin was smart to get out a there a long time ago." He licked his chin and wiped it with his shirt sleeve as a trickle of bean juice oozed down from his lips.

Alma winced. She hoped Mr. Buckingham hadn't noticed. Uncle Darcas's new napkin lay untouched by his plate.

"Say, how come you ain't found McLaughlin yet?" Darcas asked of his brother.

"It ain't like I ain't tried," Chet said. "My brother's talkin' about our friend from back home," he explained to Buckingham. "Soon's we got settled here, I went to McLaughlin's roomin' house on Cecilia, an' the landlady said he left there a year before to move into the Normandy Apartments. Went to the Normandy, but they said he left there an' they didn't know where he moved to. So I took a bus to Ford's in Highland Park after work the next day, an' they said he was transferred to The Rouge. Well, the next day I took another bus after work to Dearborn, an' they said he was laid off an' didn't know when he was bein' called back." A sad look crossed Chet's face. "I'm hankering to see ol' McLaughlin again."

"Well, it amazes me that you haven't been fired yet," Buckingham said, "what with that thing about the sky hook and all."

"Figure I'm tryin' my best not to get fired," Chet said. "Ain't missed one day a work, ain't been one second late. Fact is, you know I been gettin' there extra early every mornin'. Ain't been lettin' up on production, ain't--"

"He could've thought up a reason for firing you long ago. I still think he's just biding his time, waiting to get back at you really good and make a fool of you--"

"It seems kind a like you was in the privy," Uncle Darcas said, "an' he was holdin' his hand on the chain just waitin' to flush you down." He leaned his chair back and grinned, showing a mouthful of rotten teeth and half-eaten beans and sowbelly.

Uncle Darcas thinks he's so funny, Alma thought. How like him to make up something vulgar like that. And in front of Pa's high-class gentlemen friend.

"Oh, I really don't think he's as mean as all the fellers say," Chet said, "an' he's not as mean as he makes out. But he sure don't know how to relax around people. I never see him eatin' lunch with nobody."

Buckingham grinned. "I noticed that he sits and eats his lunch all alone, way on the other side of the line, with his back to us," he said. "Oh. I almost forgot. I read in yesterday's *New York Times* that last Saturday the remains of Myles Standish--remember I told you Standish claims he descended from him?--well, the remains of Myles Standish were removed from his wooden coffin and transferred to a metal casket and buried at a cemetery in Duxbury in Massachusetts. The paper said there were still traces of his iron-gray hair. Isn't that amazing? And I bet that's why Standish was a little late for work this morning. I'll bet he was present at the interment." Buckingham chuckled.

Alma looked at Buckingham and smiled in admiration. She'd never heard the word "interment" before, but thought it probably meant burial. She was impressed with this knowledgeable man who read *The New York Times,* and dressed and spoke so neatly. He spoke like Mr. McAllister and her teachers at Pingree Elementary School. So different from Uncle Darcas and her father. And Mr. Buckingham knew so many things. These past few months, she was beginning to realize that Pa didn't know everything, like she'd once thought. She would write to Mr. McAllister tonight and tell him of her father's friend.

Carrie Lou, who was lying on a blanket in a cardboard box on the floor between Uncle Darcas and her mother, began to coo. Everyone smiled. Everyone but Alma. As far as Alma was concerned, her new baby sister got too much attention. And as tiny as she was, she'd caused the family a peck of trouble. Her mother hadn't felt well all the while she was pregnant with her, and especially after that awful scene with Mrs. Pasnick. And it had been so hard on Ma when Carrie Lou was born way before she was supposed to be. Worst of all, they hadn't been able to save a single red penny for The Farm, and partly because of Carrie Lou needing extra food and all.

Uncle Darcas licked the beans off his spoon and stuck it into the sugar bowl. He filled it halfway with sugar and lowered it down into Carrie Lou's cooing mouth. Carrie Lou smacked her little pink lips and cooed even louder. "See, Carrie Lou," Uncle Darcas said. "You do nice things, an' your ol' Uncle Darcas'll give you what you want."

Alma frowned with disgust and then poked Jimmie Lee to give her back the spoon. But she began to smile shyly at Mr. Buckingham when he said, "Alma May, your father tells me that you're an artist. I'll just bet it was you who arranged the bouquet of daffodils and thought up the lovely spring color scheme for the table."

Alma May flushed with pleasure and guilt and nodded yes.

"I hear you spend hours at the art institute," Buckingham continued.

"Yes. I--"

"Alma May spends hours an' hours at the art institute," Uncle Darcas said. "She likes to go an' look at them dirty pitchures."

"Dirty pictures? What dirty pictures?" Alma's voice was indignant. Her mother and father frowned at Uncle Darcas.

"Oh, I seen them dirty pitchures. I was there onct. I seen that pitchure where all them people is dancin' an' carryin' on an' that feller is standin' sideways an' his ol' peter is standin' straight up under his britches." Uncle Darcas looked around the table and grinned as wide as he could.

Alma winced again. She felt her face flame.

"That ain't true, Darcas," Chet said. "Alma May is truly interested in art, an' she goes to see all a them pictures. Anyways, them artists ain't meanin' to be dirty when they paint them pictures. They just paint the people the way they see them."

"Oh, I know the painting you're referring to," Buckingham said. "You must mean *The Wedding Dance* by Pieter Bruegel the Elder. That's--"

"Pieter Bruegel the Elder," Uncle Darcas said. "Shit! I might a knowed with a name like Peter he'd have to paint a dirty pitchure with all them peters stickin' up!" Darcas leaned back in his chair and punctuated his wit with a loud belch. "My, oh, my! My Euelly's beans I had for lunch tastes just as good the second time as they did the first time, 'specially when they's mixed with Lizzie's." Chet frowned at Uncle Darcas.

Alma wanted to crawl under the table. Uncle Darcas had said enough of his dirty remarks, and he'd snorted his pig-like snort, and slurped and drooled and belched. If he made that other, worst-of-all body noise, she knew she'd just die. She was glad, though, that the attention was no longer on her, as Uncle Darcas rambled on. She turned her burning face away from her father's gentleman guest and whispered to Jimmie Lee, "I ain't hardly had anythin' to eat yet, an' these beans are too soupy for a fork. You give me back that spoon right now, or I'll tell Ma you sneaked to the movies an' saw *Public Enemy*, an' all the time you knowin' Ma doesn't want us seein' gangster pictures."

Jimmie Lee gave her a frightened look and handed her the spoon under the table. Meanwhile, Alma May's mind raced in an attempt to think of something to say to Mr. Buckingham that would help drown out Uncle Darcas's voice. Finally, when her uncle paused for breath, she thought of something: "Mister Buckingham, Pa says you know lots a poetry. Do you think you'd mind sayin' some for us right now?"

Uncle Darcas guffawed.

Her father swallowed. His face looked concerned. "You wouldn't, you wouldn't say one like you done the other day at work, Harry."

Buckingham smiled at Alma May and replied, "I'd be honored to recite a poem, Alma May. Is there anything in particular you'd like to hear?"

Alma shook her head and answered gratefully. "I don't remember much, except 'Hiawatha,' an' I'm a little tired a that."

"Well, let's see, now." Buckingham looked around the room. After a moment, his gaze fell upon the daffodils. "Oh, I know. Something that's very appropriate. It's by Wordsworth." The concern faded from her father's face when Mr. Buckingham began to recite in a well-modulated voice:

> "I wandered lonely as a cloud
>   That floats on high o'er vales and hills,
> When all at once I saw a crowd,--
>   A host of golden daffodils
> Beside the lake,--

Buckingham's dulcet tones were shattered by a loud blast from the seat of Uncle Darcas's chair. Carrie Lou, frightened by the noise, began to tremble and cry. Lizzie reached down to pick her up, as Darcas grinned and shouted over Buckingham's voice: "That's the latest report!"

Alma's face wrinkled in disgust. But she didn't die as she'd thought she would. Instead, she sat with her head down staring at the mounds of uneaten food on her plate. She hated her uncle. How could he be related to her kind and gentle father? She was grateful to Buckingham for continuing to recite all the while, not missing a line:

> "... had brought.
> For oft, when on my couch I lie,
>   In vacant or in pensive mood,
> They flash upon that inward eye, . . .

Darcas looked over at Alma May and grinned. He glanced down at her almost-full plate and said in a big voice, "I just noticed you an' Jimmie Lee ain't both eatin' at the same time. You both usin' the same spoon?"

> "... heart with pleasure fills,
> And dances with the daffodils."

Mr. Buckingham was finished. He smiled graciously at his audience.

Alma glared at her uncle, who grinned at her and said to Jimmie Lee, "Here, kid, use my spoon." He handed it to Jimmie Lee, and then wiped his own plate clean with his fingers. "Fingers was invented before spoons, I reckon."

The streetlights were just beginning to come on, and the night air was balmy and smelled of fresh springtime earth, when Chet walked with his friend to the Dodge coupe parked next to the curb.

"Thank you for inviting me, Chet. It's been a long time since I've had a delicious home cooked meal like that. Lizzie is truly a wonderful cook," Buckingham said.

"Thank you, Harry. Reckon she is," Chet answered. After a moment, he added, "I hope you'll excuse my brother. I don't know why he acts that way. I figure the best thing is to ignore him when be gets like that. Encourage him, an' he gets worse. Deep down he ain't a bad feller, though. Why, if it weren't for Darcas loanin' his car, me an' my family'd still be beholden to the Independent Mining Company."

"Oh, there's no need to apologize. No one has to apologize for the actions of others."

Buckingham's face grew uncharacteristically grim. He shoved his hands in his pockets and looked down at the newly sprouted grass. He was unusually silent for a long moment.

Chet had never seen his friend in such a gloomy mood before. "Say, what's the matter, feller? Too much sowbelly?" he asked. He squeezed Buckingham's arm gently.

Buckingham gave Chet a joyless smile. Finally, he spoke. "My wife. She really cared for me a lot. Same as Lizzie does for you. I didn't know until it was too late how good I had it." He combed his fingers through his neat blond hair and sighed. "We probably would've had three or four nice kids by now, like yours." He opened the door to his coupe and patted Chet on the back. "Hang on to your family, Hillbilly. You got the whole world right there. You're not missing anything."

Chet watched him step slowly into his car. He waved to Buckingham as he drove away. When Buckingham reached the end of the block, he stopped the car and stuck his head out of the window. "Hey, Hillbilly," he called with a laugh, "sure you won't change your mind about going to Chicago with me next weekend?"

Chapter 11

It was beautiful and she just had to have it. But how? Ten dollars and ninety-eight cents. It might as well be one million dollars and ninety-eight cents. Alma gazed longingly again at the dress in the window of Goldberg's Fine Clothing Store, as she'd done every afternoon after school since last Wednesday when it first appeared. She'd memorized every detail. But this Tuesday afternoon in late September was different: She was finally gathering up enough courage to ask to try it on. She was glad she was able to ditch Gladys Polaski. Gladys usually tagged along on the walk home from Northwestern High School. Alma had pretended she must stay after school and work on decorations for the Autumn Fantasy dance. It was easy fooling Gladys. She was gullible. She was also practical. She would've scoffed at Alma wanting a silk dress like this.

Alma took a deep breath, pushed her shoulders back, and opened the door to the store.

"I, I'd like to try on the dress in the window," she said in a small voice to the saleswoman, whom she knew to be Mrs. Goldberg.

"Which dress, dearie?"

"Why, the copper-colored silk one, with the little blue flowers." Alma hadn't noticed that there was any other dress in the window.

"Ah, yes, that one," Mrs. Goldberg said. "Such a bargain it is. Reduced from fourteen ninety-eight. Smart is the girl who buys that dress." Her short, fat legs wobbled in high-heeled patent leather pumps as she walked toward the window.

"Right this way, dearie," she said, directing Alma to the dressing room.

Alma's hands trembled as she laid her schoolbooks and pocketbook on the dressing room floor. She removed her old cardigan, peeled off her shabby brown pleated skirt and white middy blouse, untied her frayed brown rayon neck scarf, and pulled the beautiful creation down over her head.

"Don't look yet!" Mrs. Goldberg said, while she helped Alma button the twenty-one tiny pearl buttons down the back of the dress. "Now ... open your eyes!"

Alma opened her eyes. She couldn't believe it. She was beautiful.

"For you that dress was made!" Mrs. Goldberg said, stepping back and clapping her pudgy hands. "And the new longer length was made for you. You're tall and slender and can wear it. Ah, what I wouldn't give to be able to wear a dress like that. Me, I'm too short."

Alma could already picture her classmates' heads turn when she floated into the dance. There would be a hushed silence. Then the girls would whisper envious remarks to each other and the boys would form a line to dance with her. But most importantly, Albert Salvatore, that new boy in history class, would fall in love with her at once.

Her art teacher, Miss Galbraith, was right, Alma thought: I do have hair like the subjects in some of Botticelli's paintings. It hung in long, cascading ringlets. And this dress--it really emphasized the copper color of her hair. And the little blue flowers brought out the blue of her eyes. But the dance was only three days away. Where would she get ten dollars and ninety-eight cents?

"Those short puffed sleeves really accent your smooth arms, dearie," Mrs. Goldberg said. "And the wide sash draws attention to your tiny waist."

"Oh, I don't know. I'll have to think about it. I've just started to look," Alma said, pretending indifference.

The smile faded immediately from Mrs. Goldberg's face, making her cheeks flatten. "Such a bargain as this won't last long," she warned.

Alma closed the door to the shop behind her and walked east on McGraw toward home. The Salvation Army bread lines for the unemployed were already forming. Alma looked away quickly, not wanting to see the despair and fear in people's faces, like the expressions in some of the Daumier paintings she'd seen. She did not like those paintings. They were too depressing. And seeing similar subjects right here, in the flesh, were even more so.

She glimpsed a familiar looking face in the line. Why, that was Purlie Washington! She'd wondered last week why Purlie had missed several days of school, and then Alma had heard that the Washingtons were evicted from their home and moved into a flat with two other families. For a while, Alma was afraid that Miss Galbraith might choose Purlie to head the Autumn Fantasy Dance Decoration Committee, since Purlie was good in art, too. But she figured she probably had nothing to worry about, since colored kids were hardly ever chosen for anything special.

"Form a line on the right for rye bread and a line on the left for white," an Army worker shouted now to the gathering crowd. He's hoping to throw a little humor into the mood of depression, Alma thought. But no one smiled.

Alma continued to walk and thought again how glad she was that Gladys wasn't tagging along with her. She wanted to be free to think about the dress. And Gladys was such a bore. Her goal in life was to be a typist and work until she had a husband to support her. Such originality!

Alma didn't remember when she herself had started categorizing people as either Cottons or Silks. Cotton people were sturdy, long-wearing, and practical. Silk people were special, shiny, and impractical. Cottons budgeted their money and saved for tomorrow; for recreation they planned a picnic in a public park, and dreamed of someday owning a used Model A Ford. Silks spent their money today because tomorrow there might not be any; they stopped for an impromptu wine and cheese picnic in the woods, and dreamed of someday owning a new Model J Duesenberg. Gladys was definitely a Cotton.

Alma absently kicked a stone from side to side down the sidewalk. Then she stopped suddenly and looked around. Had anyone seen her in such a childish action? She looked down at her white anklets and patent leather T-strapped sandals. They were cracked and peeling. She would have to cover up the worn out places with black ink before the dance. And maybe her mother would let her borrow her rayon Sunday Stockings.

She knew she couldn't borrow the money from her mother. She would think the dress extravagant. Her mother was a Cotton, too.

Besides, Alma knew Lizzie had only about fifty cents saved, and that was to go toward the one frivolous thing her mother wanted: Crowley's was offering a month-long special for a dollar nineteen on the new fashion rage--a side-draped simulated pearl necklace with a rhinestone clip to match.

Her father would give Alma his last cent if he had it. She took after her father. He was a Silk.

Her mother was stretching his twenty-four dollars a week until it seemed like forty. She had supplemented the income by doing mending and alterations at home, but orders had decreased as the months went by, and now there were none. Even many of the wealthy were cutting corners to make ends meet. Every penny in the Combs household was accounted for. There was nothing left for luxuries like the silk dress.

Now Alma approached the park where Jimmie Lee played marbles every afternoon after school. He bragged that he could beat any of his buddies at the game. She knew the Silk in him liked pretty things. He kept his very favorite marbles, those made of agate--"aggies" he called them--in an empty Bull Durham tobacco pouch his father had discarded. She'd discovered it hidden deep down in the living room couch, which Jimmie Lee used as his bed. He'd traded a whole shoe box full of regular marbles for his prize aggies, the "bull's eyes" and the "mossies." She liked the unusual, beautiful mossies with the dark moss-like markings the best.

Alma enjoyed coming here. Even though the city didn't have the funds to maintain the park properly anymore, and broken pop bottles and bits of paper were littered around the untrimmed hedges, it was still an oasis in the ugly row after row of stores and imitation brick flats. If she closed her eyes halfway, sunlit dots of color shimmered softly in a constantly changing Impressionistic dance, and she was in the center of it.

She walked past the overgrown fire thorn shrubs with their orange berries, past the chicory (the blue flowers were the same color as the flowers in the dress!), past the oak trees with their golden leaves, and into the clearing where Jimmie Lee and perhaps a dozen other ten and eleven-year-old boys were shooting marbles around a ring drawn on the ground.

"Jimmie Lee, you have to come home soon. Remember how mad Mom was last night when you were late for supper?" she called to her brother. He ignored her. She called again.

"Aw, go home!" Jimmie Lee yelled.

Suddenly she got an idea about the agates. "Come here! I want to ask you something," she shouted. She waited patiently while be finished his turn. Then he reluctantly got off his knees and approached her. Wait until Mom sees him, Alma thought. Jimmie Lee was a small figure in worn navy blue corduroy knickers with patches and mud on the knees. His green plaid shirt was muddy in the front and missing two buttons from his having lain on the ground. His favorite cap, the red one with the Hire's Root Beer and Coca-Cola bottle caps stuck on it, was twisted around with the bill in the back.

"Whatcha want?" he asked impatiently.

"Would you like to make some money?"

"Sure! Who wouldn't!" His eyes and freckled, dirt-smudged face lit up.

"I'll make you a deal. There's this beautiful dress I just have to have for the dance. If you let me pawn your bull's eyes and mossies, I'll pay you back double what I get for them."

"You're crazy! No one's takin' my bull's eyes and mossies!" He folded his arms and spat on the ground. His eyes widened. "Hey! Did you find out where I hid 'em?"

"Aw, come on. It's not like you won't get them back. And just think of the profit you'll make," Alma said.

"No! Them bull's eyes and mossies are mine! Ain't nobody gonna get 'em!" he yelled over his shoulder as he ran back to his waiting buddies.

"Brat!" Alma yelled.

She continued toward home. It wasn't fair, Alma thought. Here she was, head of the Autumn Fantasy Dance Decoration Committee, and she didn't have a decent thing to wear!

To ease her frustration, she slipped into her favorite fantasy. Sometimes she was Mary Pickford and sometimes she was Jean Harlow. Today she was Jean Harlow. She was wearing a slinky silk gown and a white ermine wrap and riding down Sunset Boulevard in a long, shiny Duesenberg with that new movie idol, Clark Gable, at her side. Alma adored Clark Gable. She didn't care if he did have stick-out ears! She'd read in the *Detroit Free Press* that *Red Dust*, starring both of them, was coming to town soon. Her mother didn't approve of Jean Harlow. Alma didn't care. She was going to sneak out and see that movie.

She snapped back to the present when she stood in front of her home. Alma sighed. How ugly it was. But the two-story white clapboard flat contrasted a lot with the neglected, decaying flats and lawns on either side. Those dwellings had stood vacant many times in the past year, the tenants having moved to cheaper rent districts. Her father got three dollars a month taken off the rent because he did all the maintenance and yard work on their own flat. Just yesterday he had tidied up around the chrysanthemums lining the narrow porch, and Jimmie Lee had helped him rake the leaves.

Alma ran up onto the porch, opened the front door, raced up the stairs, and hurried into the kitchen where her mother sat feeding Carrie Lou. She stopped suddenly, staring in disbelief. Never before had she seen the kitchen in such a mess. The normally neat, immaculate linoleum counter tops were strewn with dirty pots and pans. Only the wooden Detrola radio was in its usual place next to the sink. From it came the cheerful voice of Ted Healy singing the hit, "I Found a Million Dollar Baby (in the Five and Ten Cent Store)." The Combses were proud that they still owned a radio. Many of their out-of-work acquaintances had long ago hocked theirs to pay for milk or shoes.

"What's wrong, Mom?" Alma asked self-consciously (Alma had recently ceased calling her mother "Ma" since she noticed none of her Detroit friends called their mothers that.) "You sick?"

"Just tired, Alma May." Lizzie's worn face brightened as she gave Alma a welcome home smile. "Alma May, would you wash them dishes up before supper? Reckon them beans is just about done."

Alma cringed. Her own grammar had improved since coming up North. Why hadn't her family's? And why don't they remember to call her "Alma," not "Alma May." "Alma" sounded less hillbillyish. And beans again. The third time this week.

"Mom, you remember that dress I told you about last week? You know, the copper-colored silk one in Goldberg's window? Well, I tried it on and it fits perfectly. Do you think we could put a dollar down on it so I could get it out before Friday? I promise I'll earn the rest to pay it off." But I don't know how, Alma thought.

Her mother didn't answer, but instead said, "Reckon I've made up my mind. I'm goin' to vote, Alma May. Roosevelt's the one to get this country out a the mess it's in."

Alma made no reply, even though she knew her mother was waiting for one. She bit her lip and thought how many times lately her mother did not listen to her. Suddenly, Alma didn't feel like listening to her, either. And she was glad her mother was so tired. But she was proud that Lizzie had decided to vote. Most of her friends' mothers didn't think about it much.

Carrie Lou sat in her wooden high chair. When her mother wasn't looking, she grabbed a fistful of Pablum from her bowl on the tray and tossed it. She squealed with delight as she dropped her head to the side of her chair and watched the food plop on the floor. She pushed her fat little face forward for Alma's usual home-from-school kiss. But Alma was in no mood for Pablum kisses. She turned her back to Carrie Lou and began to wash the dishes. She picked up Carrie Lou's half-empty cup of milk from the counter.

"Put that in the icebox, Alma May. Carrie Lou can have that before she goes to bed. Every little bit we can save helps," Lizzie said. "Times is gettin' worse an' worse every day, Alma May. Whatever we do, we got to remember to either use things up, or--"

"--fix 'em up, or do without," Alma finished under her breath.

Out of the corner of her eye, Alma watched her mother. When she wasn't looking, Alma poured the milk down the sink. That made her feel a little better.

After supper the family moved the radio into the front room and listened to *Amos 'n' Andy.* Then Alma's mother carried Carrie Lou into the kitchen to bathe her in the galvanized steel tub, and Jimmie Lee spread his books out on the kitchen table to do his homework. Alma's father settled back into his worn mohair Morris chair, pulled out a small pouch of Bull Durham tobacco from his pocket, and began to roll a cigarette. Alma loved to watch her father's hands while he rolled cigarettes. He did it so effortlessly, and the cigarettes looked almost like store-bought ones. She'd watched her friends' fathers roll theirs. Theirs looked like lumpy, white string beans.

When he finished, he grabbed his guitar and began to sing a Kentucky coal miner's folk ballad. Alma sat by his feet and watched his hands move gracefully over the strings. She pretended to listen, while the sum of ten dollars and ninety-eight cents raced through her head.

> I'm sad and I'm weary, I got those
>   hungry, ragged blues.
> I'm sad and I'm weary, I got those
>   hungry, ragged blues.
> Not a penny in my pocket to buy one
>   thing I need to use. . . .

Then she told him all about the dress. He listened intently, patiently, as she talked. No one understands me like my father, Alma thought. We're Silks, and cut from the same bolt. She watched a painful expression flicker across his face. His eyes were just about the most beautiful blue eyes Alma had ever seen.

"Alma M--Alma, you know I'd buy you ten a them dresses if I could," he said with a sad shake of his head. "An' ten pairs a shoes to match. Ain't no use, baby, your hankerin' for somethin' you know from the start's goin' to be impossible to get. You been doin' that a lot lately. You know we ain't got that kind a money--"

"But, but--" Alma interrupted, clearing her throat and plunging ahead. "Do you think you could try again to find Mister McLaughlin? Maybe he'd loan me the money. It'd be just for a little while, and ..."

"Honey, you know I been lookin' all over this town for McLaughlin. It's like he's fell off the face a this earth. Besides, I'd never ask a friend to let me borrow money."

Alma frowned and stood up. He doesn't really care, either, Alma thought. All he cares about is going back to his old mountains and getting a dumb farm. And we don't even have a cent saved toward that.

She bid her family a curt good night and retreated to the bedroom she shared with Carrie Lou. Alma lay down on her bed under the posters of Clark Gable and Jean Harlow and made plans for the next day.

★   ★   ★

"Oh, A--a--a--l--m--a!" It was Gladys. Alma shuddered, hunched her shoulders up tightly, and tucked her head down. She hated her name. Why couldn't she be named something Silk-sounding like Felicia or Clarice? She tried to get lost in the crowd of students on their way to history class, but Gladys caught up with her. She linked her arm with Alma's and inquired from behind thick glasses in her intimate, isn't-it-great-we're-friends voice:

"Watcha going to wear to the dance, Alma?"

"Oh, I don't know. Haven't thought much about it. I have three or four choices. Depends on what mood strikes me on Friday night."

"I'm wearing my Sunday Church Dress," Gladys said.

Alma knew which one she meant. It was light brown, and had been ugly even when it was new two years ago.

"I dyed it navy blue and stitched lace on the sleeves and bottom hem to make it longer. Sewed some new buttons on it, too. No one will ever know it's the same dress," she said. She tossed her hair from her face as she headed toward her next class.

Cotton, Cotton, Cotton, thought Alma.

Albert Salvatore was slouched against the door to history class and talking with his buddies when Alma entered the room. She felt her knees tremble. He was the most beautiful creature she had ever seen (well, next to Clark Gable). Tall, but not too tall, dark curly hair with one adorable lock that kept falling over his forehead, and a smile like an Ipana toothpaste ad. He gave her a casual half-wave. If her father had the most beautiful blue eyes in the world, Albert Salvatore had the most beautiful brown ones. Two more days, Alma thought. She smiled shyly back at him.

Alma did not go straight home after again worshiping the dress that afternoon. Instead, she headed north toward Felicia Carlson's house on West Grand Boulevard. Mrs. Carlson had to be home: the Pierce-Arrow and Lincoln Town roadster were parked in the driveway. Mr. Carlson probably had the Packard. Alma felt guilty as she rang the doorbell. Her mother had forbidden her ever to come here again. Mr. and Mrs. Carlson made gin in their bathtub and sold it at a huge profit from the basement of their home. Alma didn't think this so wrong. She'd heard that a lot of people did that. Someone had told Alma that the Carlsons also sneaked whiskey into the country from Canada and sold it for double the price.

Alma had babysat after school and on Saturdays for Mrs. Carlson, making fifteen cents an hour, for a year and a half before her mother found out what the Carlsons did. Since her mother had made her quit, she had not had one offer to babysit. No one else she knew could afford it anymore.

"Why, Alma! Alma Combs. Long time no see. How have you been? Come on in. Susie is still napping." Mrs. Carlson wore a red velvet gown with a sequined flamingo across the bust. "I hope you'll excuse my casual lounging gown. I'm just about to dress for dinner," she said. She led her into the parlor.

Alma thought about the cheap housedress her mother wore for lounging, on the rare occasion she got to lounge at all. She also wore the same dress for dinner. And she wore it for scrubbing floors, for feeding the baby, and for shopping, too.

"Do sit down, Alma," Mrs. Carlson said, pointing to a new white plush overstuffed chair that just matched the thick white carpeting. She patted her tightly waved blond marcelled hair. "May I get you something? Lemon or cherry phosphate?"

"No, thank you, Ma'am. My mother will be expecting me soon." Alma sat down stiffly and thought of her father's Morris chair. Of the Combses' carpetless front room. The floor was covered with scrubbed but worn linoleum. It had once been blue flowered. Now it was mostly black from countless steps made on it, and impressions of the bare wood floor underneath showed.

"Well, then, Alma, what can I do for you?" Mrs. Carlson puffed on her mother-of-pearl cigarette holder.

Alma hesitated. Then she swallowed, shifted her eyes around the room, and said to the green and blue peacock feathers arranged in a mirrored pot in the corner:

"I, ah, I've been a little sick these past few weeks. That's why I haven't been around to babysit. But I feel a lot better now. And, ah, there's this beautiful dress in the window of Goldberg's and I tried it on and Mrs. Goldberg agrees it was made for me and the Autumn Fantasy Dance is Friday and I have to have a new dress because after all I'm the chairman of the Decoration Committee and if you'll advance me ten dollars and ninety-eight cents I'll work for half wages until it's paid off." There. She'd said it. Relieved, she continued to stare at the pot.

"Why, of course, Alma," Mrs. Carlson said. She walked over to the hall stand to get her purse. "Are you sure that's all you need? I could give you more to buy matching shoes."

"No, ten dollars and ninety-eight cents is fine," Alma said, rising to go.

"Well, I'll have to give you eleven. I don't have any change." She drew a ten-dollar and a one-dollar bill from her purse.

"Oh, thank you, thank you, Missus Carlson. I'll be around Saturday at the usual time," Alma said.

"Oh, you said once your mother does altering. I have a lot of new dresses that are a little too big in the waist. Do you think she could do them?"

"Ah, no, I'm sorry, Missus Carlson. Mom has so many back orders she can't possibly take any more for quite a while," Alma lied as she hurried down the walk, the money in her hand. "Bye, Missus Carlson. Thank you, thank you."

Alma didn't mind that she had to do a pile of messy dishes again that evening before supper. She was sorry her mother was still very tired, and told her so. She even gave Carrie Lou not one, not two, but three mashed potato kisses.

★　★　★

The next day, Thursday, she stayed after school for a few minutes to advise her committee of last-minute decoration plans. Then she half walked, half ran as fast as she could and still look like a lady, toward Goldberg's Fine Clothing Store. She ran up to the display window to admire the dress just one more time before buying it. She stopped short. The dress--it was gone! She blinked. It did not appear. Her face paled and she stood there in disbelief. They must have it on the rack inside, she thought, as she opened the door to the shop.

Mrs. Goldberg was standing behind a counter adding up a sales tally.

"Where's the dress?"

"What dress?"

"The copper-colored silk one with the little blue flowers that was in the window."

"Oh, that one. I sold it just a few minutes ago. To a young blonde girl. For her that dress was made. She was a little on the short side, and it made her look taller. Such a bargain. Smart she was to buy it."

"But, but, you said it was made for--"

"Ah, but we have another little number that was just marked down. For you it was made--"

But Alma was already out the door and running toward home.

Her mother was sitting in the messy kitchen again, feeding Carrie Lou. Alma did not greet them tonight. All she wanted to do was fall down onto her bed and get lost in the comfort and security of her old quilt.

She opened the door to her bedroom and stopped suddenly. Her books and pocketbook fell to the floor. There on the bed was the dress!

"How--?"

She ran toward it. How did it get there? She squinted her eyes and looked closer. It wasn't the same dress. She examined it carefully. Almost identical material, but this material was richer looking. And the details of the trim were more delicate, sewn better.

"How... ?" she asked her mother, who stood behind her now, holding Carrie Lou, and smiling.

"I been studyin' the dress from Goldberg's winder, too. An' Crowley's had a sale on silk. An' I figure them new side-draped pearls would look silly on someone like me anaways. Been sewin' on it for three days solid while you been in school."

Alma looked at her mother for a long while, as if seeing her for the first time. Finally, she spoke. "Mom, you're--you're Silk, too!"

Her mother gave Alma a bewildered look, but let her hug her tightly.

Chapter 12

Delicate papier-mache globes swayed gracefully below crisscrossed streamers of orange and green crepe paper. Leaves of brown and gold fluttered above and below them. The high school band under the spotlight struggled valiantly to play "Sunny Side of the Street" and almost succeeded.

Alma stood with Gladys Polaski next to the wall opposite the main entrance to the gymnasium, where she could not fail to be noticed. Her breasts under the beautiful copper-colored new dress swelled with self-pride and self-satisfaction. Miss Galbraith was right. Alma and her Autumn Fantasy Dance Decoration Committee had done a remarkable job. And with the gym dimly lit, no one could tell that the leaves were made from construction paper, that they dangled from wires wrapped around the ceiling's beams and girders, and that the leaves surrounding the scene were stuck to the walls with paste. They really looked like they were falling. She was truly in a scene of Autumn Enchantment. And in her new dress she was the Autumn Enchantress. Alma felt especially attractive in comparison to Gladys in her drab, navy blue made-over dress. Gladys was someone to stand with until Albert Salvatore arrived.

"You know," Gladys said as she scanned the room, "if the school wanted to save a lot of time and money, they could save these decorations and use them again next year. It seems a shame to just throw them away after using them once."

Spoken like a true Cotton, Alma thought.

Alma had wanted to lock the door of her bedroom and dress for the dance alone. She had wanted to look in the mirror and savor privately her beauty in the dress. But her mother entered carrying Carrie Lou and shyly asked if she could help button the tiny back buttons. Alma begrudgingly accepted her help, but balked when her mother awkwardly began to brush Alma's hair. Alma knew her mother had never heard of Botticelli. How could she know how to arrange Alma's hair like the women in his paintings?

While her mother smiled and Carrie Lou clapped her fat little hands together, Alma wound the last spit curl on her forehead and gave a final quick approving glance in the mirror. The unsuspecting Albert Salvatore didn't know that he would be hers tonight.

She had hurried from the room as Lizzie lumbered after her. Jimmie Lee, sitting on the davenport reading the funnies, looked up long enough to say, "Why you gotta get dressed up like that? You're only goin' to a dumb old dance." But Alma didn't miss the admiration and pride in his eyes.

Her father stood by the front closet and held Alma's coat open for her. "If you ain't a sight for sore eyes. Not only is my oldest young'n' an artist, but she's as pretty as the sunset on Big Black Mountain, too."

Uncle Darcas, who had hung around after supper, emerged from the kitchen. He held an almost-empty bottle of beer in his hand and was scratching his huge belly. "My, oh, my, if you ain't as fancy lookin' as a brick shit house!"

Alma recoiled. So now it's a brick shit house and not a privy. She couldn't protest her uncle's vulgar remark out loud, however. If he were not so generous with his Model T, her father wouldn't have a car to drive her to the dance tonight. Even her uncle was good for something. And nothing, not even Uncle Darcas's comments, could spoil her elation. This was the first time in her entire life she had felt pretty.

She allowed her mother's shy kiss on her cheek. Her father opened the door to escort Alma out. She looked at her brother, hoping for another approving glance from him, but be was still engrossed in the funnies. Uncle Darcas had taken Carrie Lou from Lizzie's arms and was teasing her with a bright red sucker, which he held up in front of her. "Give your ol' Uncle Darcas a big kiss, Carrie Lou, an' you can have a suck. You do nice things for your ol' Uncle Darcas and he'll give you what you want."

Alma had climbed up into the Model T and smoothed her dress out carefully before sitting down. The blood stains from her mother's near-miscarriage still remained on the seat, even though Alma had tried her best to remove them. Why should she care, though, when Uncle Darcas did not seem to. But she hoped that nothing would rub off onto her beautiful dress.

When they approached the high school, Chet had asked, "I'd like to see what my little girl has done to make the gym into an 'Autumn Fantasy,' as she calls it. Reckon I could peek in for a little bit?"

"There aren't any other fathers going inside, P--Dad," Alma had lied. In truth, she didn't want her schoolmates to see her father in his shabby clothes, or to hear his hillbilly drawl. Especially Martha Templeton. Alma had heard Martha, the most popular girl in her class, telling hillbilly jokes and ridiculing hillbillies in general.

Chet pulled up at the door of the gymnasium. Alma gave him a quick kiss on the cheek, partly to ease the guilt she felt for feeling ashamed of him. The smile returned to his eyes. "You run along now, Baby," he said softly, "an' have yourself a good time. What time should I pick you up?"

Alma's mind raced. The dance was over at ten-thirty. She should allow herself a few minutes to talk with Albert. But not too long. She didn't want to seem too eager. Maybe a half hour. "The dance is over at eleven," she said.

"Eleven it is. I'll be here waitin' at eleven. Bye, Honey."

Now the gymnasium was almost filled. Alma looked around. She wondered if she'd missed Martha Templeton and what she'd be wearing. Wait until she sees my dress, Alma thought. She'll ask me where I bought it. I'll say I've been to Hudson's. I won't be lying, because I won't actually be saying I bought it there. I'll just be saying I've been to Hudson's. Alma smiled a secret little smile.

She noticed a skinny, brown-haired classmate approaching. It was Joe Smith. He thought she was smiling at him. So now he'd come to ask her to dance. What should she do now? She didn't want to take the chance of not standing there for Albert to notice when he first came in.

Alma looked away and stared at the wall to her far right as the young man drew nearer.

"May I have this dance?" he said in a croaking voice.

Alma wished he'd disappear. She had nothing against him, but he was blocking Albert's view if he should enter the door now. Alma glanced at the entrance again to see if Albert was arriving. Not yet. She looked at Joe Smith. His Adam's apple bobbed up and down as he swallowed and smiled nervously. There were raw patches on his face. Most likely from shaving, Alma thought. She smelled the Brilliantine in his hair. He'd probably dumped about a gallon on it, but his cowlick still stood at attention.

"This--this dance has been promised," she said.

The smile faded from Joe Smith's face. Redness crept from his neck to his cheeks. He stood there, frozen.

Poor dumb cluck. She didn't want to hurt his feelings, but he might spoil her chances. Why didn't he leave?

To her relief, he asked Gladys to dance. She had just discovered another thing Gladys was good for. Alma was glad when they stumbled away to the beat of "When I Take My Sugar to Tea."

But it was scary standing alone now. Should she move over to the other end of the gym, near the punch bowl? Should she head for the girls room? No. She did not want to leave her vantage point.

Her face glowed when she overheard her name:

"Alma Combs did most of these decorations," the first voice said.

"She did a real good job," the second added. "She's really good in art. Have you seen the oil paintings she's done in Miss Galbraith's class?"

"Yeah, but she's no better'n Purlie Washington, even though I hate to admit it about a nigger," the third said. "In fact, sometimes I think Purlie is better."

"Well, I'm sure glad Miss Galbraith didn't pick her to head the decoration committee. I'd refuse to go to a dance decorated by a nigger, no matter how good she is," the second said.

"Me, too. I . . ." The first voice lowered to a whisper. "Oh, my god, there's Alma."

Alma's face lost its glow. It's not true, she thought. I'm much better than Purlie Washington. All Purlie knows how to paint are those gloomy old scenes of people suffering. Who wants to see those? My paintings are pretty. They make people feel good.

She was determined not to let the remark spoil the magic of the moment. She looked at the decorations again. Purlie could not possibly have thought up a scene like this. Too bad Purlie couldn't be there to see what a wonderful job Alma had done.

Gladys Polaski, the Cotton to End All Cottons, was dancing a second dance with Joe Smith. Good. Poor mousy Gladys with her greasy hair and dull dress should feel lucky to be dancing with anyone, even the painfully shy Joe Smith. Not that she, Alma, had turned down that many offers. The scene was not playing out exactly as Alma had thought it would. The boys were not all forming a line to dance with her. But it didn't really matter that they weren't, because Albert Salvatore hadn't arrived yet to see that they weren't. Alma frowned slightly. What if-- what if he didn't show up tonight at all? But that would not be possible. Alma had overheard him telling his friends that he'd see them here.

She looked over at the main entrance again. Her heart stopped beating and her hands grew clammy. For there--there she saw the tall figure of Albert Salvatore. Alma's stomach flip-flopped under the sash of her dress. She tried to appear casual.

Albert Salvatore scanned the gymnasium quickly. How confident he looked. How handsome in his dark brown suit. It will complement her copper-colored dress and hair perfectly.

There. He noticed her now.

Albert Salvatore's glance met Alma's and he waved casually in recognition. How sophisticated, how grown-up, she thought. Not like that Joe Smith and most of the other boys here.

The dance was ending. Alma hoped the band would play a slow number next. She felt awkward dancing the fast fox trots. For her first dance with Albert Salvatore, it had to be slow and dreamy.

As she watched Joe Smith escort Gladys back to her place, Alma reviewed the subjects she would talk about with Albert. Whether he liked his teachers and what he thought of the school, of course. She wondered if he knew anything about art, and if he realized she was responsible for the decorations. She could also talk with him about--

"How come you're not dancing?" Gladys asked. "I saw you turn down a couple of offers. And why didn't you dance with Joe Smith? What's wrong with Joe Sm--"

"Nothing," Alma said sharply. She was annoyed that Gladys had interrupted her thoughts. The music started again, and Albert Salvatore was approaching. The dance was a slow one. Good. She felt her knees get weak. Like when Pa was in that last mine explosion. Only this time it was different. It was deliciously different. And this time she knew she would not faint.

Albert Salvatore was closer now. His beautiful brown gaze held hers. One more minute and he would belong to her. She was acting out a scene whose ending was out of her control. He was destined to be hers. Alma wet her lips, pulled in her stomach, and smoothed her dress as Albert Salvatore continued walking toward her. His Ipana smile grew even wider.

The dancers stopped. Albert Salvatore stopped. All conversation stopped. All heads, including Albert Salvatore's, turned toward the main entrance. For there, standing under the bright light of the doorway, was the figure of a woman in a low cut, form-fitting red dress with a slit several inches up one side that revealed a shapely right thigh enclosed in a black silk stocking.

Alma's smile disappeared. Something was wrong. This was not supposed to be part of the Autumn Enchantment scene. *Who? Who was that?*

Alma looked at Albert again. He stood frozen, staring at the creature in red, his mouth open. Should she forget her manners and rush toward Albert to claim him for the dance? Should she continue standing there?

The woman in the red, red dress was now approaching the wall where Alma stood. The tops of her breasts above the neckline of the dress jiggled with every step. Her dark hair was fashioned in the latest marcel like Mrs. Carlson's.

Alma's mouth flew open. Behind the woman's heavy makeup she recognized that it was--*Martha Templeton!* She looked quickly back at Albert Salvatore. He had become unfrozen and was half walking, half running in the direction of the red dress. This was not at all the way the Autumn Enchantment scene should be played. Alma swallowed again. In spite of herself, she could not tear her eyes away from the Temptress in Red Silk and the helpless boy running toward her.

"M, Martha Templeton!" Gladys whispered. "She's cut her hair! Wow! She looks at least twenty-five! And that dress! You can actually see the top of her cleavage!" Gladys gulped.

"Holy smokestacks!" a raspy male voice said.

"How did she get past the chaperones?" an envy-tinged female voice asked.

"She probably wore her coat until she got past them," another said.

"Wait 'til they notice, though. They'll make her leave."

"Not Martha Templeton. She can get away with anything," someone else said.

"Leave it to Martha. She's a real trend setter," another said.

"Yeah," agreed several males in unison.

Alma continued to stare dumbly at Albert Salvatore and Martha Templeton as they whirled gracefully around the floor to "There's Danger in Your Eyes, Cherie."

The dance was almost finished. Next it would be Alma's turn. She hoped they would play another slow one. Alma reviewed again the places she would suggest to go on their first date. To the movies to see *Forty-second Street*? To the art institute where the admission was free? To the--

The music stopped. Alma cleared her throat and waited for Albert Salvatore to escort Martha back to her place and then ask her, Alma, to dance. But they made no motion to leave the floor. Albert stood there with a dumb look on his face, staring into Martha's eyes.

The band started playing "All of Me," as the Temptress in Red Silk and her partner resumed dancing. The floor became dense with dancers again. Most of them moved absently, their attention on Albert Salvatore and Martha Templeton.

Alma was one of the few remaining by the wall. Even Gladys had gotten another offer. Several young men had approached Alma, but she had shaken her head no. Surely Albert would ask her to dance next. After all, she was the Autumn Enchantress, wasn't she? And this was the Autumn Enchantment she'd created. She looked down at the neckline of her dress. She hadn't noticed before how high it was. She glanced at her flat patent leather Mary Jane shoes. The black ink she'd worked into them did not hide the cracks after all. She looked over at Martha's red silk high-heeled pumps as they twirled around the floor. They were as grown-up and stylish as all of Mrs. Carlson's. Martha's red, red nail polish glistened even in the semi-darkness and her graceful left hand rested possessively on Albert Salvatore's shoulder. Alma looked down at her own hands. They seemed suddenly much too big for her arms. What should she do with them? She hid them in back of her. No, that wouldn't do. That made the smallness of her bust even more noticeable. She decided to fold her arms in front of her and hide her hands in them.

The song ended and most of the dancers, including Gladys, returned to their places. Now, finally, it was Alma's turn. But the Temptress in Red Silk and her partner didn't seem to notice that the music had ended or that the spotlight was trained on them now. They continued to dance, oblivious to the stares and giggles of their audience.

Alma bolted for the nearest exit. She pushed her way through the crowds of male students who had their gaze fixed on Martha Templeton's neckline and female students who had theirs fixed on her dress and hairdo.

Gladys ran after Alma. "Hey, Alma! What's the matter? Where you going?" she called.

Alma's throat hurt from holding back the tears. She didn't answer, for fear she might lose control. Then Gladys would know what a fool she was. She hated Albert Salvatore. She hated Martha Templeton. She didn't know which one she hated the most.

"Alma! You're not going home already! It's only eight o'clock!" Gladys called. "Don't go! Don't go! Who will I stand with?"

Alma could not care less who Gladys would stand with! She ran as fast as she could through the halls and toward the side exit. "I'm Sitting on Top of the World" floated through the crisp night air as she ran across the athletic field on her way toward home.

★   ★   ★

Her family was sitting in the front room listening to the Detrola when Alma burst through the front door. Alma noted that, mercifully, Uncle Darcas had gone home.

"Why, Alma M--Alma, what you doin' home? I thought I was to pick you up at eleven!" her father said. "It ain't even eight-thirty yet."

"Oh, I had a headache. And it wasn't all that much fun. I was bored. The kids all acted like such babies." Alma shrugged her shoulders in exaggerated unconcern, and walked to her bedroom as casually as she could. She did not want her family to see her face.

Once inside, she turned the light on and shut the door tightly. Carrie Lou was asleep in her crib. Alma didn't bother to look at her, but went straight to the dresser. She looked in the mirror. Her long ringlets were tangled from running. She looked at the neckline of her dress. How had she ever thought this dress was the most beautiful thing she'd ever seen? She no longer felt she was out of a Botticelli painting. She was out of a Bo-Peep cartoon.

She reached into the top drawer of the dresser and grabbed her mother's sewing scissors. She cut swiftly, altering the neckline from high to plunging.

From another drawer, she grabbed two pairs of her stockings, which her mother had neatly balled. She stuffed a pair under each of her breasts. She stepped back to view her image. Hopeless. While Martha Templeton's looked like a Rubens, her own looked like a Vermeer.

Her eyes focused on the scissors again. She grabbed them once more. In less than one minute, the hair that had once cascaded halfway down her back now curled a little above her ear lobes. She stepped back again to view her image. She smiled with satisfaction. She looked at least fifteen years older.

She cleared the dresser top of telltale scraps of material and hair and hid them in a paper bag in the wastebasket. She tore off the ruined dress and threw it in the back of her closet. Feeling guilty, she retrieved it and placed it carefully on a hanger, but hung it way in the back of the closet where it would be out of sight and out of memory.

Noiselessly she opened the bedroom door. If she left it closed, she would arouse more suspicion. She turned off the lights and climbed into bed. She could be herself with the darkness.

Alma grimaced when she heard her mother's heavy, shuffling steps approaching. She hopes I'll talk about the dance and tell her what the kids thought about the dress, thought Alma. She pulled her old quilt up high around her face so that her newly shorn hair would be hidden as much as possible. She saw her mother's thick silhouette outlined in the bedroom doorway.

"Alma May," her mother began hesitantly.

Alma made no reply, pretending sleep. Besides, her mother had been instructed to call her Alma, just Alma. Would she never catch on?

"Alma May," her mother repeated. No answer. She turned and plodded back down the hall.

Alma yawned loudly. "The kids all loved my dress, Mom," she called. "They thought it was the prettiest one there."

She heard her mother's shuffle stop and the pleasure in her voice as she said, "Reckon you was the prettiest one there, too."

Her mother continued down the hall again. The hallway went dark when she switched off the light. "Alma May, you should a turned off the hall light before you went to your room tonight. You know every little bit a 'lectricity we save helps. Times is gettin' worse an' worse every day. We must all remember not to waste things. We must . . ."

She's back to Cotton, thought Alma, and buried her head under her old quilt. Now she could let go.

Chapter 13

A month later, Alma stood before a borrowed easel. It was Saturday, and since early that morning she had been on the ground level of the Detroit Institute of Arts copying the painting that hung on the wall before her. She'd lost all track of time, having gotten immersed in the Rococo world of Fragonard's *Park Scene*. Alma loved imitating the French master's fluid brush strokes. And his playful figures were so carefree and moved with a floating grace. And the colors, they were--how did Miss Galbraith describe them?--they were lush and sensuous. Alma had decided that since she was a dismal failure with men, she'd concentrate on the one thing in which she knew she could succeed: painting.

Through her many visits to the institute lately, she'd become acquainted with a kindly guard, who had gotten permission to let her use the wooden easel left by an art student who had never returned to claim it. And with the canvas, brushes, and oil paints generously offered by Miss Galbraith, Alma was well equipped to pursue her increasing interest in painting.

Alma stretched her legs and suddenly realized how tired they were, and how hungry she was. What time was it? she wondered. Still morning, or afternoon now?

After several more careful strokes on the canvas, she wiped the brushes with a rag. She put the brushes and paints and rag away in a paper sack. After removing the canvas carefully from the easel, she folded it up and carried it and the sack with one hand and the wet canvas with the other up the marble steps to the main floor.

Alma paused for a moment to glance into the huge Garden Court, then turned her head away. She did not like the subject of the frescoes by Diego Rivera in progress on the walls of the court. Since July, the famous Mexican artist had been painting scenes representing the production and manufacture of the automobile all the way from the raw steel at the blast furnaces to the final assembly. Alma thought it was dumb to go to all that trouble to glorify the boring world of the automobile worker. It was more fun to capture the delightful pleasure-seeking world of Fragonard's upper class. Besides, the huge frescoes reminded her of her father's job, and that any day it could be taken from him. She was tired of hearing about the forty-three percent unemployment in Detroit. She was tired of hearing about the ten million unemployed in America. She was tired of hearing about that Mahatma Gandhi and his self-imposed starvation and about that poor little Lindbergh baby and his cruel kidnapping and murder. She would rather insulate herself from all these scary thoughts by losing herself in the Fragonard painting. And after that, she would paint a carefree Watteau, and after that a happy Renoir, and after that a . . .

Alma headed toward the main door. She smiled as she handed her guard-friend the easel and canvas. He would put them safely away in one of the institute's storerooms, where they would await her next visit.

"Better hurry, little lady, or you'll miss the President," the middle-aged man said. He reminded Alma of the dour-faced man in Grant Wood's *American Gothic*, but with a bad complexion. When he smiled down at her, though, his brown eyes lit up, and his pockmarked cheeks grew round, becoming like two worn-out golf balls.

"The President?" Alma's eyebrows rose in surprise. "Oh, I forgot." President Hoover was coming to campaign today at Olympia Stadium. "But I've got plenty of time to get home and eat before seeing his ride to the stadium." Alma didn't want to admit that she wasn't planning on seeing President Hoover's motorcade. If she saw the President, she would be reminded again about the worsening Depression.

"Well, lots of luck. It's already past eight, and he's scheduled to speak at eight-thirty," the guard said.

"Eight o'clock!" Alma said. "It couldn't be that late!" She hurried out the big main doors of the institute. The guard was right; the darkness and the chill night air hit her as she bounced down the wide terraced steps and patted the feet of Rodin's sitting bronze nude sculpture, *The Thinker.*

Alma shifted the sack of art supplies to her other hand and buttoned her worn, out-of-style coat. She hated her coat. Her mother had bought it at a Salvation Army store the winter before. "This is a fine coat," Lizzie had said proudly, "an' for what I gave for it, I couldn't a made it as cheap, even if I used remnants."

She looked down at the frayed sleeves, which were too short for her this year. Mrs. Carlson's new coat from Russek's had luxurious leg-of-mutton sleeves. She might be sliding her arms into them at that very moment. Mrs. Carlson was in New York to attend the opening night performance of *Dinner at Eight.*

Alma's jaw set defiantly as she hurried in a northwesterly direction toward home, because she was thinking how she was challenging her mother by openly babysitting for Mrs. Carlson these days, except when Mrs. Carlson was out of town. Alma's resolute resistance was met with a disappointed and hurt look from her mother. "Them Carlsons ain't no good for you to be workin' for, Alma May, what with all their bootleggin' an' such," her mother would say. "They might have lots a fancy things, but you know how they got 'em. By lyin', an' cheatin' an' stealin'. Anybody that does that is just plain trash, an' I don't want you workin' for--"

"Ah, Mom, Mrs. Carlson is real nice," Alma would interrupt. "You'd love her if you ever met her. And you know there's no other way I can earn any money." Alma knew that her mother realized babysitting was really the only way Alma could earn money, and that she was powerless to stop her. Invariably, her mother would add: "But you wouldn't have to work for her at all if we all could learn to use less. We could give you the money we save, an' even start savin' for The Farm again. We ..."

Alma would cover her ears with her hands and run from the room.

She thought then of The Farm. The Farm was being mentioned less and less frequently now. Would they ever start saving for it again?

Alma turned her head away as she passed a new bread line on her left. Every week there were more of them. She noticed Purlie

Washington among the crowd. She smiled shyly at Alma, but Alma pretended not to see. She was glad that Purlie had missed several more days of school, including art classes. She'd heard it was because another family had moved in with the Washingtons and their friends. That made three families in one little flat.

She saw another familiar figure standing in line. Was it Joe Smith? She looked again at the tall and gangling young man. Yes, it was Joe Smith, all right. Were times getting so hard that Joe Smith had to beg for food, too? Alma's glance met his and she smiled. Her classmate turned his head away quickly. He was ashamed to be begging and still hurt because she wouldn't dance with him, Alma thought.

Alma noted that the heavy traffic of cars and pedestrians was all heading toward the stadium. She had read that the President's motorcade would be traveling down Third Avenue on its route. Alma had to cross that avenue on the way home.

She passed a hot dog stand on her right. The enticing aroma of cooking wieners and freshly chopped onions followed her far past the stand. She would probably get caught in the crunch of spectators already crowding along the curbs of Third Avenue, she thought, and it would take her forever to get home to eat. Alma poked her hand into her coat pocket and pulled out a nickel and six pennies and the monthly envelope to mail for Miss Di Inganno. She had just enough money for a hot dog and hot cocoa, with a penny to spare. She ran back to the stand, purchased the food and continued homeward, gobbling it down.

She thought of Miss Di Inganno when she mailed the envelope at the next corner. The old lady looked even more frail these days, and talked even more about her lover. It seemed as though lately whenever Alma knocked on her door, she was either playing with that dumb Valentino Shadow Cut-Out Book or reading old movie magazines. It was no fun going there anymore.

The crowd was looking south now toward where the approaching motorcade would pass. Alma looked around for her father. Jimmie Lee wouldn't be there. He was sick with the flu. And her mother wasn't interested in seeing Hoover. Her father had taken her mother to hear the Democratic presidential candidate, Roosevelt, and Mayor Murphy speak a few Sundays ago at the Naval Reserve Armory. Lizzie Combs had come home with a hopeful light in her eyes. "Alma May," she'd said with an uncharacteristic lilt in her voice, "I just know Mister Roosevelt is for us poor people. He really cares what happens to us."

The mood of the people around Alma was cheerful, expectant. Many held banners and signs reading, "Hold on to Hoover." Several fathers balanced small flag-waving sons or daughters on their shoulders. High above, young men were perched on telegraph poles. They floated literature down on the crowd below. The receptive mood of the crowd began to affect Alma, and suddenly she felt guilty for not wanting to see the President. How could she have wanted to miss the chance? To think that the President of the United States, the President of all these people around her--her President--was approaching! This was a moment she'd remember always. Someday, she'd tell her children about it. This was a lot different from what she imagined it would be. These people were not gloomy and sad-faced. They were almost merry, as if they had put their problems on the shelf for a little while and were determined to enjoy the moment.

A feeling of well being came over her. The hot dog had eased her hunger pains, and the cocoa had warmed her. And after all, her father was still working, wasn't he? And even if he did lose his job, he'd find another. He always took care of them, didn't he?

Alma looked around again for her father. Maybe Mr. Buckingham was there, too. Mr. Buckingham had become a friend of all the family. Often now he would bring her father home from work and stay for supper. He never failed to bring candy, or shiny red apples for dessert.

The first cars in the motorcade, the bannered limousines carrying the Republican officials, were passing now. And now, at last, the long black Lincoln limousine (Alma had read that Henry Ford would furnish it) carrying the President was almost before her. Alma's stomach fluttered in anticipation. She peered into the open front window of the creeping automobile. From newspaper clippings she recognized the smiling, round-faced man sitting by the window. It was Governor Brucker. The woman sitting next to the governor and wearing the cloche-style hat must be Mrs. Brucker. And now, finally, looking into the back seat of the approaching vehicle, she saw the familiar faces of President and Mrs. Hoover. She was wearing a cloche, too, Alma noted. Alma was surprised that the President's face was no longer round and healthy looking, as she remembered from newsreels and newspaper photographs and the painting hanging on the wall at school. It was drawn and tired, with circles around the eyes.

"My god," a woman behind Alma whispered, "how he's aged."

Alma heard a sudden shout from across the street several yards ahead. She and the spectators around her turned their heads toward it.

"All right, men!" the angry voice yelled, "Let's fly the Hoover flag!" A band of ragged men ran into the street in front of the limousine and pulled their pockets inside out. The crowd around Alma gasped. The ragged men thumbed their noses at the limousine.

"How dare they do that to the President!" a man next to Alma said.

Alma looked again at the President. His face was right alongside her now. She saw his smile fade and the pain in his eyes.

The band of men were jeering and hissing and booing the President. One man carried a sign reading, "Down with Do Nothing Hoover!" Another held up a sign, "We want jobs now!" Suddenly, one man, perhaps the youngest in the group, reached into a bag and, shouting obscenities, began throwing eggs at the limousine. One missed its target and splattered on Alma's coat. Another man ran up and spit at the open window, narrowly missing the President.

Where did these men come from, and how dare they do that to the President, no matter how they felt about him?

Just as suddenly as the angry men had appeared, another group of men in neat suits arrived. They circled the demonstrators and pulled them, handcuffed and kicking, from the view of the motorcade.

"That's the Secret Service," a man at Alma's left said to his companion. "They couldn't do anything about the signs, but the eggs and spitting and cuss words are going too far."

Alma fled from the crowd. She pushed her way through the crush of spectators. Some were still shaking their heads with disgust and disbelief.

After a few minutes, she found herself in a less crowded spot. She took a deep breath before bucking the onlookers again. Then, in the group of people ahead, she saw her father. "Pa! Pa!" she cried.

Chet grabbed her and hugged her tightly. "What's the matter, baby? You look upset. Where you been? I waited at home for you, thinkin' you'd want to come with me to see the President. You been at the art museum all this time? What's that on your coat?"

"Oh, Pa. Did you see all that? Those awful men? How could they do that?"

"Oh, you mean those demonstrators. Never thought I'd ever see somethin' like that. Hunger an' fear'll do awful things to some people." He patted Alma's head and added: "But don't you worry your pretty little head about nothin'. Your Pa'll always take care a you." He released her then, and said, "Alma, I'd like you to meet someone." He nodded toward a tall man standing next to him.

Alma looked up at the man. He was expensively dressed, like Mr. Carlson, and his dark, deeply waved hair was streaked with silver. She disliked him instantly. Maybe it was because the eyes staring back at her were deep set and beady and cruel, like the eyes in some of the paintings by Goya.

"Mister Standish, this is my oldest daughter, Alma," Chet said proudly.

Alma stared at the man. "Mister--Mister Standish? How do you do." Alma did not offer her hand. So this was Mr. Standish. No wonder she disliked him. But why was he was standing with her father? She thought her father's foreman never associated with his men.

"How do you do?" Mr. Standish said. His voice was not as cruel sounding as she'd expected it would be. And did she notice a flicker of admiration in those eyes?

"Pa. Let's go. I don't feel well," Alma said. It was true. Her stomach felt queasy.

Her father said goodbye to Mr. Standish and they hurried toward home.

A moment later they were out of the thick of the crowd. Alma felt better now: she had left the scene of the demonstrators, she had left that Mr. Standish, and she was with her father. After she got home and ate, she would curl up on the davenport and listen to *The Chesterfield Hour*. She liked to hear Ruth Etting sing, and to imagine her standing in front of the microphone dressed in a smart silk or satin gown.

"Dad, how come that Mister Standish was with you?" Alma asked.

"He wasn't until he saw you. He knew I was there, but he was standin' by himself. He seems to want to be alone all the time. He only came over an' stood by me when you got there. My pretty little girl must a impressed him," Chet said with a grin.

Alma dismissed Mr. Standish. "I wonder if Mister McLaughlin was there."

"Didn't see him. I'm still wonderin' whatever happened to Tom McLaughlin. I think about him a lot. Maybe he ain't even around these parts no more." Chet's eyes widened. "Say, look at that crowd a people in front a that big building over there. Wonder why they're here an' not at the stadium? Wonder why they're all lookin' up at the sky?"

Alma looked to where her father pointed. A large crowd of people were already gathered and others were joining it. Several of them were pointing excitedly at something way above them.

"What they looking at, Dad? I don't hear any airplane or anything."

"Don't know. Oh, I see now. They're all lookin' at something up on top a that building." He pointed to a speck near the top floor of the tall structure. "It's, it's … reckon if it ain't someone up on a ledge. But what in tarnation … ?"

They had reached the gathering crowd now. One middle-aged woman wearing a babushka that almost covered her tin hair curlers informed Alma and Chet, her voice excited, "He's been up there for five minutes. I was the first to notice him."

"But, but, what's he doing up there?" Alma asked.

"What d'ya think he's doing up there?" the woman replied. "He's going to jump, of course."

"But why?"

"Who knows? Maybe his wife left him. Maybe he's dying of TB. Maybe he lost everything in The Crash, maybe he …" The woman walked over to another group of people approaching. Alma heard her say again, "He's been up there for five minutes. I was the first to notice him."

"Has anybody called the police?" someone in back of Alma asked.

Another voice replied, "Someone said the police've been called, but they're not here yet. Either they're all guarding the President, or else they can't get through."

"Wonder who he is?" Chet asked.

"Maybe he's an investor. All kinds of investors have their offices in this building," a woman on Alma's right said.

Alma looked down at the big double brass doors of the building and the engraved bronze sign on the facade. She just realized that this was the Detroit Investors Building; she passed this building often on her way to and from Woodward Avenue. This was where Martha Templeton's father had his office. Martha Templeton. The popular Martha Templeton. But she didn't want to think about Martha Templeton and all her popularity with boys, and all her new clothes, and her wealthy father--

"He's been up there for over five minutes. I was the first to notice him," Alma heard the woman wearing the babushka say again to another group of newcomers. Alma looked over at her for the first time. The woman's face was animated, and the corners of her mouth were turned up in a smile. Her eyes shone.

"Why don't the police get here? Someone should go call them again," a white-haired man in front of them said.

"I'll go!" exclaimed a young man. He pushed his way out of the crowd.

Meanwhile, the man up on the ledge was moving slowly from side to side, his arms stretched out flat against the building.

"I'll bet he doesn't jump," an old man in back of Alma said.

"Most of the time they don't jump," a woman next to him agreed.

"Yeah. They just want attention."

"No, some of them are really serious about it. Remember those business men in New York who lost their shirt when the stock market crashed?"

"Hey, that reminds me of a joke," a young man on Chet's left said. "Did you hear the one about the two men who jumped hand in hand from the forty-seventh story of the Penobscot Building?" The young man paused for effect. "Yeah, they had a joint account."

The crowd around Alma and her father laughed as Alma looked about her. They're treating this almost like it's a show, she thought.

"Why don't the police get here?" the white-haired man asked again.

"Wonder who he is?"

Alma wondered, too. Who could be so unhappy that he'd want to end his life? Is it a young man? An old man? Where is his fami-- Alma's face paled and she swallowed hard. Could it--Could it be Martha's father? Oh, no, it couldn't be Martha's father. She'd seen him several times recently when he picked Martha up from school in his huge Packard. He seemed so happy, so sure of himself--like Martha.

"Bet he doesn't jump," someone said.

"Bet he does," the joke teller said. "Say, got an idea!" He raised his voice so all could hear. "I'll bet everyone here who thinks he won't jump, a quarter if he does." The young man looked around eagerly at the crowd.

"You're crazy!" the white-haired man said.

"You got my bet!" This from a middle-aged, cigar smoking man to Alma's right.

"Mine, too!" yelled a gum-chewing blond woman ahead, looking back at the young man.

"Mine, too! Mine, too!" other eager voices chimed in.

"Disgusting!" the white-haired man said.

Alma shook her head. "Dad, how can they be so cruel at a time like this?"

"Don't know, baby. Reckon people get carried away when they're in a crowd. They do an' say things they'd never do alone." He took her arm to leave. "Let's go home, baby," he said gently.

But Alma stood frozen. She had to find out if it was Martha's father.

"Hey, I got another good idea!" the joke teller said. "Any more bets?" he yelled as he looked around, his eyes shining. Several more added their bets. "OK. Betting's closed," he shouted. "Got a good idea. I know how I can collect on my bets. I'm going to make him jump!" He raised his face up toward the top of the building again, cupped his hands around his mouth and shouted: "Jump!"

Some of the spectators gasped. Some laughed nervously.

Chet tugged harder on Alma's arm and said, "Come on, Alma, we're goin' home. Don't want my little girl to be here anymore."

"No!" Alma said.

"Jump!" the young man shouted again.

Alma heard a siren in the distance.

"Finally!" the white-haired man said.

Alma looked at the faces around her. She saw the smiles disappear in disappointment as the sirens grew louder.

"Jump!" Jump!" the young man repeated.

The wbite-haired man shook his head slowly as several others joined in the shout: "Jump! Jump!"

Alma's stomach felt queasy again, and her heart began to pound faster. She looked up once more at the man on the ledge. The man leaned forward for a second, and then leaned back quickly against the wall again, his arms still outstretched. She squinted her eyes to see. Was it Mr. Templeton?

"Jump! Jump!" The chorus of voices grew larger and louder. The siren was even closer now. It must be only about a block away, thought Alma, covering her ears against the shrill noise.

The man above leaned forward again. "Jump! Jump! Jump!" More and more voices were joining in the shout.

Alma's father began to push her away from the crowd. "We're goin' home now!" he said in that high, scared voice like when her mother was so sick.

"No!" Alma said. She set her feet down firmly on the sidewalk as her father continued pushing her.

The chorus took up the chant again: "Jump! Jump! Jum--" Then suddenly there was silence as the man leaned forward and, after hesitating for an instant, pulled his arms from the side of the building and covered his face with his hands. Alma's throat grew dry. The crowd gasped as the man began to fall.

"Oh, no," the white-haired man whispered.

Alma stared at the falling figure. Was it really a person? It looked like a dummy. A doll. So limp ...

The crowd around her began to separate in all directions, so as not to be hit by the falling man.

Then she heard it. The thud. Heavy and loud. Sickeningly heavy and loud. Alma turned her head away from the sound as the crowd gasped. Her father began to push her again. "Alma May, let's go!" His voice was desperate now.

But Alma, horrified but fascinated, stood on her tiptoes and craned her neck over the shoulders of the people standing in front of her. She had to find out. Was it Martha's father? Martha deserved it if it was--she had no right being so popular. Alma hoped it ...

She wrested herself from her father's grip on her arm and began pushing through the line of people in front of her. She had the sensation of having gone through this before. It was like when her father was in that last mine explosion, and she was waiting to see if he was one of the victims.

The ambulance and the police had arrived now. The crowd around Alma began to speak again in halted, hushed tones.

"Do you recognize him?"

"No. Wonder who he was?"

"Poor devil."

"I was the first to see him ..."

"Whoever he was, he's well dressed. Look at that suit."

"Look at them fancy spats. Hey, he's only got one on. He musta lost one when he fell."

Alma was before the body. It was lying on its back with its face turned away from her. She could not see if it was Martha's father, but the man appeared to have the same build. Suddenly, for the first time she felt generous toward Martha and sorry for her. With her father gone, she wouldn't have the money anymore for all those clothes.

The police and the men with the stretcher were at the body now. "All right, everyone stand back," the officers said as they extended their arms out from their sides to stop the curious crowd from getting nearer the body. One of the officers squatted down beside it.

Alma held her breath as the officer gently turned the dead man's face toward her. Was it--was it ... ?

"Hey! I know who that is!" a voice behind her said. "That's that man who's been in all the papers. That broker guy who invested all his friends' money and lost it all in the crash. That's that James Man--James Manchester. That's who it is!"

"Hey, you're right! I recognize him from the newspaper pictures."

A fleeting pang of disappointment and a feeling of relief hit Alma. She turned around slowly and pushed through the crowd to her father.

"You shouldn't a seen that, honey," Chet said.

Alma said nothing, but began to walk in a westerly direction toward home. Her father walked beside her, one arm around her shoulder, the other holding the sack of art supplies.

"Amazin' to me how some people can be so cruel," Chet said in a low voice. He shook his head.

Cruel was right, Alma agreed. Those awful, awful, cruel people. How could they do that? She blinked her moistening eyes.

They were at last out of the thick of the crowd. She heard the ambulance siren grow fainter and the young man's voice shouting, "I'll collect those quarters now!"_

Suddenly, Alma stopped walking.

"What's the matter, baby?" Chet asked, tightening his arm around her.

Alma was silent. She--She herself was as cruel or crueler than those people. For a minute there, she had half-wished it was Martha's father. How could she have been so evil? She was worse than they were. A feeling of nausea overwhelmed her. Her stomach felt even queasier and like it was up near her chest.

The hot dog and cocoa erupted from Alma's mouth and splattered on the curb. She heard a woman say, as if from a great distance: "Look at that! Isn't that scandalous? That old man with that young girl! She's drunker'n a skunk!"

"Yeah," another woman said. "He's old enough to be her father. And look at that sack he's carrying. Probably full of that cheap bootleg hootch. Disgusting!"

Chapter 14

C het stood at the living room window and shook his head. He would never get used to Michigan's unpredictable climate. This Sunday afternoon in December was more like one in April. Its balmy breezes beckoned winter-weary residents, lured by a false sense of spring, out-of-doors. It was capricious, too: in early morning, there were sunshine and warm temperatures; in late morning a cold, still dampness; and now in early afternoon, balmy breezes and sunshine again. Chet preferred the steady, faithful climate of his home state.

His eyes grew wistful as he thought of his mountains and The Farm. After all these months in Detroit, and even with Lizzie's penny-pinching, they had managed to save only fifteen dollars and forty-three cents. Lizzie was right: "Things are so dear here. Why, I gave eleven cents a pound for bacon at the A & P today, an' …."

Chet pulled Lizzie's freshly laundered and starched curtains back from the window to afford a better view of his ten-year-old son in the yard below. Jimmie Lee had been outdoors in the Combses' shallow front yard for over half an hour attempting to make a snowman. Chet had advised him that it would be futile. "This snow ain't good packin' no more, Jimmie Lee. Not when it's been half thawed, an' then got hard again, an' now half thawed again." But Jimmie Lee, who was feeling better now after having been confined to the house for days with a cold, had begged a reluctant Chet and Lizzie to allow him to play outside.

Chet smiled and watched Jimmie Lee persevere. Making a snowman was a new experience for his son before last winter, the family's first in

Michigan. Back home, there were usually only two snowfalls of about an inch or so a year, and by afternoon, the snow would disappear.

Chet's smile waned when his thoughts turned to Standish. It had all started a few weeks ago, soon after the President's visit. The foreman had approached Chet as he was punching his time card before work that morning.

"I'd like a date with your daughter," Standish had said. It was more a demand than a request.

Chet's eyebrows had risen in surprise. Of course, his boss was not serious, he thought. He smiled at Standish. His little Alma May was getting so pretty. There were probably lots of fellows who'd want to date her. "Sure," he said, jokingly.

He'd forgotten the incident until lunchtime, when Standish had approached him again and repeated: "I'd like a date with your daughter."

Chet smiled and said, "You're funnin', a course. Why, my Alma May's only fifteen years old."

Standish did not smile back. His cold, dark eyes penetrated Chet's smiling, warm blue ones. "I'm going to date your daughter."

Chet's smile faded as the foreman walked away. He's serious, Chet thought. A cold uneasiness gripped his stomach.

The uneasiness lasted throughout the day. That afternoon Harry Buckingham looked over at Chet from the other side of the press and shouted above the noise, "Hey, Hillbilly, how come you're so silent? You've hardly said a word all day."

Chet confided in Buckingham, and watched his face grow angry.

"Why, that bastard!" Buckingham said. "What did I tell you? He's just been waiting to get you where it really hurts. He knows how much your family means to you. Leave it to that snake-in-the-grass to lie in waiting all this time until he thought of something."

"Way I figure is, my Alma May's old enough to start courtin' if she was back home," Chet said, "but she ain't even been out with a feller her own age yet, let alone one old enough to be her father, an'--" He had stopped talking when he noticed that Buckingham was not putting his end of the steel sheet in the correct place.

"Watch what you're doin', Harry!" Chet said. "Our fenders are comin' out wrong."

"What's the difference?" Buckingham said. "Standish never checks up. He's too busy thinking up devious things to do. He doesn't have time for his job."

Chet had shaken his head in disapproval, both at Standish and at Buckingham. In spite of his fondness for Buckingham, he did not agree with his work ethics. Chet had noticed Buckingham's carelessness before, and in each instance he was relieved that Standish hadn't checked their work at those times.

Late that afternoon when Chet punched his time card before leaving for the day, his foreman approached and said: "Soon."

Buckingham overheard and as Standish walked away whispered to Chet, "That slimy serpent. What you going to do, Hillbilly?"

Chet's face had grown white as he replied, "I don't know. But I sure ain't goin' to let him go out with my sweet an' innocent little baby. I figure I'd just as soon die first."

For three days, Standish approached Chet with increasing frequency and repeated: "Soon." Then he'd smile insidiously as he walked away. What should Chet do? Should he quit his job that he needed so desperately, or hang onto it in the hope that Standish would give up or find another worker to make miserable?

Then, suddenly, Standish stopped coming around. Chet began to relax again. He resumed his old cheerful demeanor. Standish had given up, Chet told Buckingham.

"I wouldn't trust that sneaky snake," Buckingham said. "He's just lying low on his belly, waiting to strike. I can tell by that glint in those cruel eyes."

Chet realized several days later his friend was right. On several occasions, when Chet had approached groups of laughing fellow workers engaged in conversation, they would abruptly stop talking as he drew near.

Buckingham tipped Chet off to what they were talking and laughing about. "That damn bastard Standish's been spreading it around that he's been dating Alma. If you're not arranging a date for him, he's pretending he's dating her anyway."

Chet's soft eyes grew hard. "So that's his game. You're right--he is a slimy bastard," Chet said, surprised at his own language. "But, no one for a minute would think that my little Alma May would even think a goin' out with him."

"They don't know Alma like you and I do, and they probably don't really believe it. But it's some new gossip to amuse them. Sometimes I think men are worse than women."

Chet was grateful that his thoughts were interrupted when Jimmie Lee entered from outside.

"That slush's no good for makin' a snow man. It just won't stick together," Jimmie Lee said. The corners of his mouth turned down and the rest of his face screwed up in a frown. "I think slush is snow with all the fun taken out." He yanked his stocking cap off to emphasize his disgust.

Chet smiled at his son. "I figure you couldn't a said it any better." He tousled Jimmie Lee's brown hair, which was already in disarray from having been under the cap. "Your ol' Pa was right about that snow."

Darcas entered from the kitchen holding Carrie Lou and a bottle of beer. He had stayed for an early dinner. Euella was at home, "sick" again, according to Darcas. He belched as he placed the beer on the lamp table and rubbed his belly. "Yummy. Like I always say, Lizzie's beans is even better second time around." He reached into his pocket and pulled out a sucker. He tore off the wrapper and let it fall to Lizzie's just-cleaned floor while be grinned and held the red candy up before Carrie Lou.

Carrie Lou squealed with delight and clapped her hands. "Canny, canny!" she cried, her bright blue eyes merry with anticipation.

Chet smiled proudly at his baby daughter. Carrie Lou was already saying a few words, like "canny," and "Da Da," and "pwitty," and "baby."

Darcas held the sucker up higher as Carrie Lou reached for it. "Give your ol' Uncle Darcas a big kiss, Carrie Lou, an' you can have a suck."

Alma, who was returning from Miss Di Inganno's with the *Sunday Free Press* in her hand, entered the room in time to see her baby sister reach for the sucker again.

"Come on now, Carrie Lou," Uncle Darcas said, "Give your ol' Uncle Darcas a big kiss an' he'll give you some 'canny'."

Carrie Lou planted her drooling pink lips on Uncle Darcas's slobbery mouth. Alma cringed.

"Dad, let's go house hunting this afternoon," Alma said.

Jimmie Lee's face brightened. "Yeah, Dad, let's go house huntin'! There ain't nothin' else to do, and it's so nice out!"

"What you mean there ain't nothin' to do?" Chet asked with a smile. "Why, you ain't even read *Dick Tracy* yet, or *Joe Palooka,* or--"

"Please, Dad, please?" Alma asked.

"Well ..." Chet said, weakening. Maybe it would be good to go for a ride and look at some houses. It would take his mind off Standish for a while. "If it's all right with your Uncle Darcas if we use his car."

"Reckon you can use the ol' Tin Lizzie anytime you want," Darcas said. He licked his lips after another sticky kiss from Carrie Lou and handed her the sucker. "But I don't know why you want to go house huntin'. You know you ain't got no money to buy no house. It's just a waste a time. Besides," he said, looking at Alma and grinning, "reckon Alma May'd rather go to that art museum an' look at them dirty pitchures again."

Alma glared at her uncle, but she did not blush this time. She was learning to hide the embarrassment she felt at his remarks.

"Darcas!" Chet said. "You ain't funny!"

"I was at the art institute all day yesterday," Alma said, "and I wasn't looking at any dirty pictures. I was copying a Renoir."

"My little girl's goin' to be a famous artist someday," Chet said as he smiled at his oldest daughter. "Say, honey, which one a them talkin' pictures did you see after leavin' the art museum last night?"

"I saw two of them, Dad--*Strange Interlude* and *Bill of Divorcement,*" Alma said. "All the movie places are starting double features now." She hesitated a moment before adding, "I met Gladys Polaski downtown." She was not lying. She did accidentally meet Gladys Polaski downtown. But she did not go to the movies with her as she hoped her father would assume she did.

★　★　★

Fifteen minutes later the Combses, including a reluctant Lizzie, were packed into Uncle Darcas's Model T on their way to a real estate office. Lizzie always protested the house hunting game. "Why, that's lyin' an' cbeatin' an' stealin'," she would say. "It's lyin' because we know we ain't really lookin' for a house, it's cheatin' because we're cheatin' the real estate man out a his time, an' it's stealin' because it's stealin' his gas when he drives us around--"

Chet would shake his head and interrupt. "Oh, Lizzie, you know this ain't hurtin' nothin'. Why, if nobody never went to the real estate feller's office, what would the poor feller do all day? Probably just sit with his feet up on his desk just a hopin' an' prayin' for someone to come in. Actually, we're doin' him a favor." He wished Lizzie could relax and learn to have a little fun. Worried and penny-pinching, that was Lizzie.

Alma sat in back with her sketchbook in her hand. She thought if they passed some nice homes, she might get out of the car and sketch one for a few minutes. "What real estate we going to, Dad?" she asked.

"Well, let's see now," Chet replied. The man at OK Realty was wise to them by now, and so was the man at Horkins & Cooney. "Where you think you might want to live, Alma M--Alma?" He said it seriously, as if the only concern was to select a neighborhood.

"Boston Boulevard," Alma said, thinking of the expensive homes that sprawled on big, well-maintained lots and smiled at each other across the wide, clean boulevard.

Jimmie lee's face screwed up in a frown for the second time that day. "Oh, no, Alma! Not Boston Boulevard. They're probly too ritzy to even have a playground. How'm I gonna learn to play baseball without some place to play? Let's find a house around here."

In the end, they compromised on an area in which they had not house hunted before--northwest Detroit.

★   ★   ★

Half an hour later, Chet sat in the year-old Essex automobile next to Mr. Baker, the broker. He looked out of his window at the neatly paved street with middle-class homes, some brick and some frame. Such fine, strong houses. When they got The Farm, they would have a fine, strong house like these.

Alma sat in the back next to the right window, her sketchbook still in her hand. This neighborhood was nicer than where they lived now. She wouldn't mind living here--for a little while. She leaned back into the comfortable seat. The real estate man's Essex was so much more--what was that word? "Streamlined," that was it. So much more streamlined and lower to the ground than Uncle Darcas's Model T. How could she ever have thought his high, box-like Tin Lizzie was nice? She rubbed her fingers over the still-new gray mohair upholstery. Mr. Carlson's new '33 custom Cadillac V-16 had velvet upholstery, but this was nice.

She glanced at her mother, who sat silently next to her, holding a sleeping Carrie Lou. The corners of Lizzie's mouth were turned down in disapproval. Alma's nose scrunched up. Her mother was no fun.

Alma looked over at her brother. His eyes were big with wonder. "This car's swell!" he said. "Don'cha feel just like we're almost ridin' on the ground?" Alma smiled and looked out the window again.

The Essex traveled north on Normandy Avenue, winding its way between the cars parked on either side of the street, as Alma's thoughts turned to Miss Di Inganno. She was growing a little concerned about the old woman. Alma had stood at her door for a full five minutes that afternoon, waiting for Miss Di Inganno's frail invitation to enter. It never came, so Alma had inched open the door. She was met by an odor that she'd noticed lately in Miss Di Inganno's place--a stale, slightly fishy odor.

Miss Di Inganno was sitting in her usual chair by the table. The only light in the room came from the kerosene lamp. The Valentino Shadow Cut-Out Book was open, but the old woman was not holding it up to the light. She was pouring over yellowed newspaper and magazine accounts of her lover's death.

Alma approached the table. Miss Di Inganno did not look up. She continued to move her withered finger across the printed lines, muttering the words out loud. It was almost as if she were a first grader just learning how to read, who had grown old and ludicrous in the process as she'd remained at her desk.

Alma noisily cleared her throat. "Miss--Miss Di Inganno," she said. There was no answer. "Miss Di Inganno--"

"Thousands of tearful mourners passed the gold casket draped with pink roses from the idol's latest love. ..." Miss Di Inganno continued to read, oblivious of Alma's presence.

"Miss Di In--" She stared down at Miss Di Inganno's fingernails. They were polished in a garish red color as usual, but the polish was chipped, and half gone. The tips of the nails curled down and under, like whiplash lines in an Art Nouveau illustration. Alma shuddered.

"Miss Di Inganno."

"Have you come to view my Rudy, too?" She looked up at Alma, noticing her for the first time. Her eyes were vacant and watery. She doesn't realize that she has her false eyelashes on upside down, thought Alma.

"Hurry along now, young lady," Miss Di Inganno advised. "Can't you see the others in line behind you? All come to see my Rudy. But he's not really gone, you know. ..."

Alma grabbed the unfolded *Free Press* and ran from the flat. She would not go back there again. Jimmie Lee would have to go from now on. Alma had meant to tell her father of her concern for Miss Di Inganno, but had forgotten about it in the excitement of going house hunting.

The old woman was forgotten again when Mr. Baker said, "Here we are."

He pulled up into the driveway next to a neat, two-story house of brick and stucco. A "Prestige Realty" sign was stuck in the snow on the front yard.

Mr. Baker, a tall, rangy man of middle age, was the first one out of the Essex. He reached into a pocket for a handkerchief and wiped his bulbous red nose, which protruded above a trim, graying mustache. "The house is vacant now."

Chet opened Alma's door. He played the game as he smiled at her and Lizzie as if to say, "Well, here we are, home again." He looked across the street and down the neatly snowplowed hill, thinking if this were The Farm, those houses would be standing where our pawpaw grove or a lespedeza field might be.

Chet followed a slow-moving Lizzie, who held Carrie Lou. Carrie Lou had just awakened. Mr. Baker led Lizzie up to the front porch. Alma followed behind, but Jimmie Lee ran to the back of the house. Chet smiled. Probably wants to see how big the back yard is.

The porch on The Farm would be bordered with clumps of tansy and catnip and maybe hoarhound, Chet thought. In summer, there would be honeysuckle climbing up the lattice on the side.

Mr. Baker selected a key from a giant ring of them and opened the front door. He motioned for Lizzie to enter.

Alma was annoyed that her mother was so hesitant. Why hadn't she stayed at home? Alma was anxious to inspect the foyer. That was what Mrs. Carlson called it--a foyer. The Combses didn't have one. Their outside door entered directly into the living room. Alma noted that the foyer was roomy and quite impressive with a curved stairway and wide banister leading to the upper level. This would be the first thing her future dates would see. Good. The closet was roomy, too. Plenty of space to hang her date's coat. Good. Alma had been thinking less and less lately about when they would return to Mountainview and buy The Farm.

She followed the broker and her parents into the large living room on the right. Mr. Baker was pointing out the features of the room. His voice echoed in the emptiness.

"Notice the marble mantle over the extra large fireplace opening. And the French doors opening to the sun porch on the east." Lizzie and Chet looked impressed, but Alma had seen French doors before. Mrs. Carlson's house had French doors opening from every room on the east side.

Lizzie sat Carrie Lou on the floor. Mr. Baker smiled and said, "She getting heavy for you, Mrs. Combs? You'll notice how spotless the owner left the floor."

All eyes looked down at it. Alma had never in her life seen such a shiny floor. It was almost like a mirror. She would be proud of this floor when her dates came to call.

"You'll notice that the floor is of oak hardwood," Mr. Baker said, "and not a scratch on it--"

Mr. Baker was interrupted by a delighted squeal from Carrie Lou, completely awake now. "Pwitty baby. Pwitty baby," she exclaimed as she leaned over and patted her own reflection.

Everyone laughed as Carrie Lou clapped her hands and repeated, "Pwitty baby. Pwitty baby."

"Lizzie!" Chet said, startled and proud. "That's the first time she's put two words together!"

Lizzie looked down at her baby daughter, and her eyes squinted together as she smiled for the first time that afternoon.

"Where are the bedrooms?" Alma asked Mr. Baker. The broker pointed upstairs. Alma ran toward the foyer. "I'm going upstairs," she said. "I want to see which bedroom would be good for me, where there's lots of north light for painting."

As Alma left the room, Chet thought it was about time to ask something intelligent of the broker. "Where do you put the stove?"

"Stove?" Mr. Baker asked.

"The stove," Chet repeated. "I figure you'd need a big stove to heat this room. I been seein' them big stoves that would heat up a whole room. They got icin' glass windows, an' a big pot belly, an'--"

"Oh, you mean a big base burner," Mr. Baker said, with a smile. "But those are becoming obsolete."

"Obsolete?"

"Everyone's switching to central heat now. That's why the trend is toward basements. The furnace is down in the basement, and the heat is forced up to the rooms through the registers." He pointed to grilled metal boxes protruding from the walls.

Chet had heard something about central heat from the workers at the plant, but he shook his head in wonder. "Reckon that furnace would have to be a right smart size. How would I carry in coal enough to feed it?"

"Oh, you wouldn't have to worry about that. Coal is delivered to the side of the house and dumped down a coal chute into a coal bin in the basement."

Chet shook his head again in amazement. Wonder if they knew about this back home? Maybe there could be a coal chute built into The Farm house!

Chet went in search of a door leading to the basement as Jimmie Lee came running toward him. "Dad! Dad! Can we buy this house? There's a huge back yard, plenty big enough for playin' catch, and there's a playground just down the street, and ..."

Mr. Baker smiled as he said to Lizzie, "Come, Missus Combs. I'll show you the kitchen."

On the way back to the real estate office, Mr. Baker confided in Chet. "The owner is very anxious to sell. I'll bet he'd reduce the price by three thousand."

"How, how much is the price now?"

"Eleven. It's a steal at that. But, as I say, I bet he'd go down."

Chet swallowed. That would make it eight thousand. It might as well be eight million.

"Dad," Jimmie Lee asked now from the back seat of the Essex. "Please. Can we buy that house? That back yard is swell for playin' catch in.'"

Chet looked back at his son and tried to sneak a warning glance without Baker noticing. Maybe the house hunting game was going a little too far. Maybe Jimmie Lee was too young to realize that they just wanted to get some ideas for when they bought The Farm house. He glanced at Lizzie, who was sitting next to Jimmie Lee and holding a cooing Carrie Lou. Lizzie's thin lips were turned down again in a disapproving scowl. What was happening to his wife lately? She was no fun to be around anymore. Couldn't she play the game? Chet looked at his daughter sitting next to the window, her sketchbook still in her hand. Alma was getting her head filled with big ideas. But she deserved better than the flat they were living in. She'll probably be dating soon-- He thought of Standish for the first time in an hour. That bastard! The anxiety hit Chet again.

"What do you think?" Baker asked. "Would you like me to make the owner an offer?"

Chet cleared his tbroat and said, "Well, Well, truth a the matter is ..." He paused a minute, thinking fast before continuing. "Truth a the matter is I think we need a bigger house. What with our baby girl growin' like a weed, an' all, she'll need her own bedroom soon, an'--"

"Ah, Dad!" Jimmie Lee cried. "That house's just perfect. Carrie Lou can sleep with Alma!"

Chet gave Jimmie Lee a warning glance, but his son was looking out of the window now, amused by a group of boys about his age who were attempting to slide on their sleds down a slush-covered driveway.

"Should I make the owner an offer?" the realtor repeated. "Or would you like to see something a little bigger?"

Chet was grateful for an out. "I, I think my family would like to see somethin' a little bigger, probably with four bedrooms, an', well..." Chet looked back at Lizzie's face, still set in a censuring scowl, before he continued defiantly, "Reckon we'd like to consider a little nicer neighborhood, too. But it's gettin' kind a late today. Maybe next Sunday."

★   ★   ★

Alma leaned back into the rear seat of the Model T as it chugged southeast on Linwood Avenue on its way home.

"Dad, can we get a car like Mr. Baker's?" Jimmie Lee asked, talking over the squeaks and thuds and jiggles of the Model T.

Chet didn't answer. He had grown silent.

Jimmie Lee repeated: "Dad, can we get a car like Mr. Baker's Essex?"

Finally, Chet replied. "No, son, we'll probably get a Dodge when we move back home an' get The Farm. Dodges are sturdier. Better for goin' around mountains an' back roads, an'--"

"Back home! We still goin' back home? But I wanta stay here'n learn how to play baseball. Nobody plays baseball back home. An' nobody plays marbles, neither." Jimmie Lee's face screwed up in a disgusted pout again.

Nobody does anything fun back home, Alma thought in agreement. Since coming to Detroit, she had gradually realized how small and dull her and her family's world had been back in Mountainview.

She still held the sketchbook in her hand. They hadn't passed a house fancy enough to sketch that day. Oh, the Normandy Street house would be all right to live in for a while, until she became rich and famous from her paintings. She had already sketched the Carlsons' house and the houses around it. Someday she would live in a house as nice as those.

"Someday we'll own a house as nice as the house we just saw," Chet said. "Maybe we can find a farm with a house almost like it, an' I'll have a coal chute put in on one a the outside walls, an'--"

"Oh, The Farm, The Farm, The Farm," Alma said, a little annoyed with her father for disturbing her thoughts. "I'm sick of hearing about The Farm. We're never going to get The Farm. And I don't ever want to live on a farm anymore, anyway. I'm going to live in a real big house in the city." She was immediately sorry for what she'd said when she looked in the rear view mirror and saw her father's face fall as his smile evaporated, and his eyes grew sad. But it was true, Alma thought. She did not want to live on a farm anymore. If she was stuck on a farm, who would see the nice clothes she would someday wear?

After Alma's outburst, the family grew silent, except for Lizzie. "Foolin' that nice Mr. Baker that way. That's a sin." She shook her head in disapproval. "An' you folks is just fillin' your heads with fancy dreams a things we'll never get. Why, what's wrong with where we live? It's a fine, clean place, an' if we'd all learn not to waste things, an'--what's that new word I been readin'--econ--econo--economize. That's it. Economize. We could learn to economize more an' save again for The Farm."

They all remained silent, then Lizzie continued, "I think it's about time we went an' saw that place I been readin' about. Then you'll all know how good we have it. You'll see what bein' poor really is. Why, we're all healthy, an' your Pa still has a nice job."

Alma saw her father's wince reflected in the mirror. What was he worried about?"

"An' if we hurry, we still can get home in plenty a time to listen to Father Coughlin," Lizzie continued. "Let's head toward the river, Chet. The paper said this place is by the river."

Alma's face twisted in a scowl. She did not want to go down by the river to see some poor people and she did not want to hear Father Coughlin. Why did her parents have to listen to Father Coughlin every Sunday afternoon? You'd think he was God or something, the way they sat glued to the radio, with her mother in the chair under the colored portrait of President-elect Roosevelt that Lizzie had clipped from the *Free Press* rotogravure section. She and Jimmie Lee could not utter a word when his program was on. Alma knew her mother liked the fiery priest from nearby Royal Oak because he was a supporter of Roosevelt. "Roosevelt or Ruin," "Roosevelt or Ruin." Alma sure got tired of hearing him say that all during the campaign.

Mr. Buckingham, who knew everything, did not like Father Coughlin. "You don't realize it, but that man's dangerous. Power hungry. He's a pompous demagogue and a propagandist and an anti-Semite. Just listen to him carefully. Either he's not saying anything but froth, or else he's twisting facts to suit his point." Alma suspected that Mr. Buckingham, being a former English teacher, also didn't like him because he mispronounced words. Like saying "the Treaty of Ver-sales" for the Treaty of Versailles. Alma didn't object to all this, but the sound of his voice, which started out low and soft and slow and ended up high and loud and--what was the word Mr. Buckingham used?--passionate, with ranting and raving, and screaming. THAT was scary! Alma sighed. Sundays with Father Coughlin.

They were near the Detroit River now. Lizzie pointed south. "There. It must be over there," she said. She gestured toward what appeared to be a junkyard.

As they drew nearer, they recognized it to be a fester of huts and shacks strewn together in rows.

"Lizzie!" Chet said, "We can't take our young'n's here."

"Just for a minute," Lizzie said. "Park the car here for a minute."

Chet parked the Model T next to a huge sewer pipe, and Lizzie, still holding Carrie Lou, opened her door and started toward the little colony of squatters. Why, she's really determined, thought Alma. I've never seen Ma lead the way anywhere. Not like Pa does.

They got out of the car and followed Lizzie as she walked under an entrance on which was painted a crude sign reading "Hoover Haven". Alma wanted to turn around and go back to the car to wait. She did not want to see any poor people, and she felt like she was invading their privacy. But her curiosity won out when she saw that the huts and shacks were constructed of packing boxes and fruit crates and strips of corrugated tin, all ingeniously wired or nailed together. Some of them even had strips of tarpaper. Alma thought if she pushed hard on one of them, the whole row would come crashing down.

Some of the gaunt and ragged inhabitants stared at her and her family when they passed, but others continued with whatever they were doing. One old man, squatting by an open fire, was cooking scraps of food stuck on a twig. Another was collecting cigarette butts in a rusted Campbell's soup can. The early afternoon sun had melted the snow enough to make a sticky combination of slush and mud underfoot. It squished under Alma's galoshes as she walked hesitantly behind Jimmie Lee.

Chet, following his wife and Carrie Lou, looked back at Jimmie Lee and Alma and whispered: "You young'n's all right? We'll just be here a minute to please your Ma. Don't know what got into her. Ain't like your Ma to do a thing like this."

Alma heard a small voice and felt a poke in her back. "You got a nickel, lady?" She turned around and saw a very young boy with outstretched palm. His hand and the rest of him shook involuntarily from head to toe. Alma had noticed some drunks shake like that.

"What's the matter with that kid?" Jimmie Lee whispered to his father.

"Probably got the rickets or somethin'," Chet said. "He ain't gettin' the right kind a food." Chet reached into his pocket for a nickel, but could come up with only three cents. "Here, little feller," he said, placing it in the boy's grimy palm.

The boy's thin face became all mouth when he smiled with appreciation and promptly placed the coins in the hand of an even smaller child, a disheveled little girl of about four or five.

"It's my sister's day to eat," explained the boy as he turned and walked away. Alma could tell even under his outlandishly big overalls that his legs were bowed.

"Dad!" Jimmie Lee whispered. "Look at them old cars! There's people livin' in 'em!"

Lizzie joined them as they walked toward a cluster of rusted automobile bodies. They passed a decaying Hudson, probably an early nineteen twenties model. Alma was startled when a head popped out from behind a window covered with curtains made from cardboard.

"Hey, girlie. What you readin'? I'm a reader, too," asked the head, which was surrounded by a shock of gray hair and a grizzled gray beard. After a moment, Alma realized that the old man with the gravelly voice was talking to her and that she still carried her sketchbook in her hand.

"Oh!" Alma said. "This isn't a book. It's a sketchbook." She hurried through the slush-mud after her father.

"Let me see your sketchbook!" the old man yelled.

"It wouldn't hurt to let him see your sketchbook," Chet whispered to Alma.

Alma and Chet walked back to the Hudson-house and Alma held the sketchbook in front of the man. "See?" she said, flipping the pages.

The man reached for the book, but Alma jumped back. She would not let this dirty old man touch her sketchbook. "Let's go home now, Dad. We've been here long enough," she whispered.

They hurried to catch up with Lizzie and Jimmie Lee. Alma stopped suddenly. She hesitated, then turned around and walked back to the man. She opened her sketchbook and tore out one of the pages. It was a scene of Big Black Mountain, which she had filled in with watercolors. She thought it was one of her best sketches.

"Here," she said softly, as she handed it to the man.

"You mean I can have this?" he asked. His watery eyes grew big with disbelief.

Alma nodded her head.

"Bless you, young lady."

Alma peeked into the car. Several books were stacked on the dashboard, which was being used as a bookstand.

"Would you like to have a book, young lady? How about this one? I'm almost done with this one." He reached down and picked up a book that had been lying open on the car seat next to him and handed it to her.

Alma read the title: *Dressing in Style for That Exotic Cruise—To the Bahamas and Other Exciting Places.* She shook her head no and ran to join her father, who was watching from several yards away.

"That was a nice thing for you to do, Alma--give him one a your pictures. An' one a your favorites, too," Chet said.

She was glad that she'd done something to please her father. She still felt a little sorry for her outburst about The Farm.

Alma looked over at Jimmie Lee and wondered why he was holding his nose. She soon found out when a sudden gust of wind blew a familiar stench her way, the same stench that she smelled back home when the school privy needed cleaning out. Here it came from a small lean-to fashioned from old boards and orange crates. A faded "Sunkist" was still readable. A small boy holding his crotch stood in front of the Sunkist privy. He wiggled and jumped first on one foot and then the other. "Hurry up in there! Hurry up in there! I gotta piss!" he screamed.

Alma and her family turned away. Chet shook his head. "It's a wonder the city would allow a privy here. It ain't healthy in such close quarters. But I reckon the poor devils ain't got no place else to make water."

They headed toward a tiny clearing where two ragged and muddy young boys were playing catch. One of the boys missed the ball and fell in the mud as the ball landed in the doorway of a hut made from corrugated cardboard. An old woman came out of the hut and screamed,

"What the hell you think you're doin'? If I told you once I told you a million times not to play ball here. You're ruining my front lawn. And if that ball lands just right, it could knock my whole house down!"

The boy sheepishly picked up the ball and stood up. Alma noticed that the muddy thing was really not a ball at all but a cloth bag. She wondered what it was filled with. Probably beans.

"See, Jimmie Lee?" Chet whispered with a grin. "If you really want to play catch, you don't need a fancy back yard to do it in."

"Let's go home now, Mom," Alma said. "We've seen enough."

"Reckon we have, Alma May," her mother said. "An' it's got chilly since the sun's gone down again, an' we don't want to miss hearin' Father Coughlin." She drew her coat tighter around herself.

They picked a different path on their way back to the car, but there was no way to avoid walking between more rows of huts. Alma noticed a shack fashioned from egg crates and corrugated cardboard. The strains of "Life Is Just a Bowl of Cherries" drifted out from the flimsy walls. Over the doorway was scrawled "Radio City". Alma's eyebrows raised in bewilderment. Radio City?

Next to the shack was another with the words, "Office of the Mayor", printed in more professional-looking letters above the doorway. The shack was perhaps the sturdiest one of all, Alma thought. It was made entirely of tin and wires and nails and even had a small window covered with isinglass. She peeked in the window. A gray-whiskered man seated on a car seat was eating from a fruit crate used as a table. A kerosene lamp's dim light illuminated his features. The man looked up from his plate and smiled at Alma. Embarrassed to be caught violating the man's privacy, Alma ran from the window and hurried to catch up with her family.

She trudged alongside her father in the slush-mud, which was becoming crustier now since the sun had gone down. Something began to prick her memory. Something from years back. There was something about that man back there eating in that shack. Something vaguely familiar about his smile. Something about how be moved his hands. Her steps became more halting as she strained her memory to recall. She stopped walking altogether. Could it be--? No. It was impossible. What would he be doing here?

"Alma, what's the matter?" called Chet, who had continued walking and was now several yards ahead of her. He hurried back.

"Pa! Pa!" Alma whispered as she yanked at his arm and pulled him back in the direction of the man's shack.

"What in tarnation--?" Chet said, while he motioned for Lizzie and Jimmie Lee to follow. "What's got into you, baby?"

Alma was already knocking on the shack's doorway.

"What you doin' that for, Alma May?" Chet asked. "Get away from there! You shouldn't be doin' that!"

The tin door opened and the owner of the shack stood there, a tall, bony man who, even with stooped shoulders, towered formidably above Chet and Alma.

"Yes?" the man asked. "Are you here to sign the petition?"

"Please excuse us," Chet said. "My daughter—I don't know what's got into her. She, She--" He stopped abruptly and his mouth flew open. He stood there for a minute and then the shock on his face turned to pleasure. "Well, if--if it ain't ol' McLaughlin!" he croaked. "McLaughlin! Tom McLaughlin!"

The man looked quizzically at Chet. He, too, stood and looked dumb for a moment. Then his face widened in a broad grin as he recognized his old friend. "Chet! Chet Combs!" he said. "Is it really you?" He stared hard at Chet. "Reckon it's you, all right! What in tarnation you doin' here?"

"What in tarnation <u>you</u> doin' here?" Chet asked. They both laughed and embraced each other.

"Look at the sign over your head," Tom McLaughlin said proudly, pointing to the top of the doorway. "I'm mayor of Hoover Haven." The mayor pulled at Chet's arm and continued, "But I'm forgettin' my manners. Come on in an' set yourself down."

Alma still stood staring in the doorway. Lizzie was behind her, holding Carrie Lou, and Jimmie Lee next to Lizzie. Both of their mouths were agape.

The mayor motioned for them to come in. "This beautiful young lady ain't little Alma May, is it? An' Lizzie, you got prettier'n ever. An' that young man ain't Jimmie Lee? He must a growed a foot. An' who is this pretty li'l thing?" He picked up Carrie Lou's pink little hand and shook it gently.

"That's Carrie Lou," Chet said proudly. "Born since we got here, an' already puttin' two words together. First time's today."

Alma and her mother crowded together on the car seat, while Chet sat on an oil barrel. Mr. McLaughlin and Jimmie Lee sat on the floor. Alma looked on the wall above the barrel. A colored portrait of Roosevelt, the same one as on the wall at home, smiled down on them.

The little shack was amazingly warm. A small stove fashioned from pieces of bricks rested on the floor made of scrap boards. A rusted pipe extended from the stove and was vented out the wall next to Mr. McLaughlin's "desk." The desk was a narrow, warped door, which had a few traces of white paint still clinging to it. It rested horizontally on stacks of bricks. On top of the desk were neat piles of correspondence and several stubs of pencils. Alma wondered what correspondence Mr. McLaughlin could have.

On the opposite wall was a pallet of rags over what appeared to be cardboard and old newspapers. Several ragged coats served as blankets. Next to the pallet was an upended orange crate on which a large, shallow tin can half filled with water sat. Next to the tin can was an almost-used-up bar of soap. A ragged towel was folded neatly next to it. Completing the furnishings was a cardboard box about one-quarter filled with food supplies--half a loaf of Bond bread, a can of sardines, a blackened banana, and an almost empty bag of A & P "Eight O'Clock" coffee.

"I'll just move this empty plate out a our way, an' fix us some coffee," Mr. McLaughlin said.

Chet shook his head no. "Thankee kindly, Tom, we just had some," he lied. He stared at McLaughlin and shook his head. "What's happened to you? I been lookin' for months an' months for you. Gave up hope a ever findin' you."

"Well," McLaughlin began. He scratched his whiskers in concentration. "Reckon I better start at the beginnin'."

McLaughlin told of having been transferred from the Ford Highland Park plant to its Rouge plant. Several months later, he lost his job altogether when Ford laid off more men. He hadn't saved a cent in all the months he'd worked, having blown it on clothes from Hudson's, and women, and cars, and such. "Oh, I was a real city slicker," he said, with a laugh. "An' the more money I made, the more it burned a hole in my pocket." He'd gotten a few odd jobs after being laid off, but they had lasted for only a few days. And then, suddenly, there was nothing. Nothing. "Things got from bad to worse," he said. He sold his car and pawned his fancy clothes. "Pretty soon, all I had was the clothes on my back. An' no place to go. Them fancy women an' all my friends gone, gone. Then I heard about this place. That must a been about six months ago. Been here ever since."

He looked around the little room. "Ain't a bad life here. Got a place all my own, a bed to flop on, little vittles once or twice a day. What more does a feller need? An' here I'm really liked for my own self. Respected. You know I been elected mayor a Hoover Haven three times in a row? Last time I even won over the feller livin' next to me. He's out there cookin' his scraps over that open fire." McLaughlin pointed out the window at the hunched-over figure of a skinny young man. "An' he's got himself graduated from college an' everythin'." He paused and poked his chest proudly. "Yep, when somethin' don't go right in Hoover Haven, they all come to see me for help." He pointed a long finger toward the right wall. "An' we even got us a radio next door in Radio City--that's why they call it that--the only radio in all a Hoover Haven. Soon we'll all be settin' around that ol' Atwater an' Kent radio hearin' Father Coughlin."

He smiled and said, "But reckon I been ramblin' on too much. My ol' mouth's been goin' up an' down as fast as the needle on a sewin' machine. Tell me what's been happenin' to you."

★　★　★

All that could be heard on the way home were the rattles and squeaks and groans of Darcas's Model T and the sounds of Sunday afternoon traffic. Chet sat with his hands loosely gripping the steering wheel. It was still hard to believe. Tom McLaughlin in a place like that. And to think that Chet had been too proud to look him up until he himself had found a job and was settled. Maybe if he had looked him up when he first came here over two years ago, he might have been able to help him. Maybe he and McLaughlin shouldn't have come here at all. If Chet hadn't come to Detroit City, Alma May wouldn't have got her head filled with all those hifalutin, fancy ideas. But Alma May couldn't have meant it about The Farm. And if they had never come here, he would never have met Standish, and--

"Pa, do you think Mister McLaughlin will come and visit us?" Jimmie Lee asked. "Why didn't he want to come and live with us? I told him he could use the couch. I can sleep on the floor. I like sleepin' on the floor. Why does he want to live in an old shack like that?"

Chet thought for a long moment. "Well, son, the way I figure it is, Mister McLaughlin, even though he ain't got much left a his very own, even though he once was makin' lots a money an' had lots a things, the way I figure it is he'd rather be independent an' not have much, than be dependent on someone else. Understand, son?"

It was Jimmie Lee's turn to think for a moment. "Sure, Pa. Guess I understand. But I wouldn't live there in a million years." He thought for another moment and then added: "Ma, you're right. We ain't so bad off."

Lizzie, who was holding sleeping Carrie Lou, turned around and gave Jimmie Lee and Alma her squinty smile.

Alma had been looking out of the window at the glittering marquee of the Paramount Theater, advertising *Grand Hotel* with John Barrymore and Greta Garbo, and at the smiling and smartly dressed patrons waiting in line. Alma did not smile back at her mother. Her mother had been reading too much lately. Alma liked her better before. She should go back to just cooking beans and scrubbing floors. If her mother thought that dumb trip to that Hooverville was going to make Alma content with beans and cold water flats and second-hand Goodwill clothes and a boring farm--well, she'd just better think again! Someday, when she became a famous artist, Alma was going to eat steak every day and live on Boston Boulevard and wear Chanel clothes like Mrs. Carlson and ...

Chapter 15

"Oh, shit! Here comes the son-of-a-bitchin' bastard now," Harry Buckingham said. He and Chet stood by the time clock early the following morning.

Chet's stomach began to knot again and his hands to grow clammy as the foreman approached. "Hey, Combs!" Standish said. "I want to talk with you." Buckingham gave Chet a sympathetic glance and walked toward his press.

"Have lunch with me today," Standish said. He squeezed his long, manicured fingers around Chet's arm. Again, it was more of a command than an invitation. Standish smiled and looked down at Chet. Chet's arm stiffened under his foreman's grip, and his face flinched in reaction to Standish's out-of-character attempt at sociability. His face paled and his eyes hardened while Standish walked away. Standish always ate alone. What was he up to today?

Chet told Buckingham about the lunch invitation. "Too bad," Buckingham said, "You couldn't have refused--you have to eat lunch with him." He shook his head in sympathy as he and Chet lifted a stamped fender form onto the conveyor.

All that morning they speculated on the foreman's motives. They agreed that Standish didn't need a whole lunch hour to fire Chet. He could do that in a minute, and make up any plausible excuse to write on the termination notice.

"Maybe he wants to swap jokes. Maybe he wants to compare the sandwiches he packs with Lizzie's," Buckingham said. A wry smile flickered across his lips.

Every few seconds, Chet glanced at the huge clock on the far wall. Never had the time dragged so slowly. Should he just quit now and get it over with? What would Lizzie and Alma May and Jimmie Lee think if he up and quit? No. He would stick it out until he got fired. Every minute he worked would mean another penny or so. And five pennies meant a loaf of bread. Eleven pennies meant a pound of bacon, and--

The lunch whistle blew. Chet's hands began to tremble. This was it. What was Standish up to?

The presses ground to a halt and the huge room was quiet except for the sound of the workers' voices and scurrying steps as they headed toward the cloakroom to get their lunch buckets. "Maybe Standish'll forget about it," Chet said to Buckingham, his voice unconvincing.

"Ah! The eternal optimist," Buckingham said. He gave his friend an empathetic pat on the back. "Here he comes now," he whispered.

The foreman caught up with them. "Ready, Chet?" he asked. This was the first time Standish had addressed Chet by his given name. He smiled and patted Chet on the back in an intimate, fond gesture. Several workers, upon seeing the unusual action, stopped walking and looked their way.

Standish selected a spot for lunch in clear view but out of earshot of Buckingham, Gajewski, Sobieski, Lombardi and the rest of Chet's lunchtime cronies. "Like a sandwich?" asked the suddenly friendly foreman after they settled down on an empty pallet used for stacking parts.

Chet felt awkward accepting, but was afraid not to. "Thank you," he said, his teeth clenched. Should he offer his boss one of Lizzie's? Hard telling what Lizzie had put in them today. Friday his penny-pinching wife had given him bread and oleo sandwiches. He decided against it, and offered Standish the jar of beans instead.

To Chet's surprise, Standish accepted enthusiastically. There was an awkward moment when neither one spoke. Finally, Standish began: "You know, Chet, ..."

There he goes again, thought Chet, using my first name.

Standish continued, "You're sure a lucky fellow." He paused and swallowed a mouthful of Lizzie's beans. "Ah, delicious," he said. He licked his thin lips. "Yes, you're sure a lucky fellow. You've got a wife to pack lunch for you, and waiting for you when you come home. And a couple of nice kids, ..."

Here it comes, thought Chet as his stomach knotted even tighter. He's going to demand a date with Alma May again. The slime!

"You know," continued Standish. "I've been thinking a lot about myself lately. Oh, I've got a good job, all right, but what else have I got? No kids, no wife, not even a girlfriend." He glanced at Chet, who began to squirm on the pallet and to almost gag on Standish's elaborate beef sandwich.

"Oh, don't worry, Chet," Standish continued as he patted him on his arm. Chet stiffened again under his touch and glanced over at his grinning friends. Walter Gajewski was nudging Lombardi with his elbow and pointing a fat finger at Chet and Standish. Meanwhile, Sobieski was winking at Chet. Buckingham was the only one of the crowd who was not amused. How Chet wished he was sitting with his friends.

"I'm not going to ask again for a date with your daughter."

Chet stopped eating and his eyebrows lifted. He looked at his foreman suspiciously. What kind of a twist was this?

"You were right. Your daughter's way too young for me. And, why in the world would she ever want to go out with an old bachelor like me? Someone as sweet-looking and pretty as she is probably has lots of young fellows after her." He hesitated and tapped his nails nervously on his lunch pail. "And, well, you can probably tell how difficult this is for me to say: You with that winning way about you, and the easy camaraderie you have with everyone, you could make more friends in one hour than I could in my whole lifetime. Truth is, I don't even have one friend to my name." He paused and swallowed hard. The corners of his mouth turned down.

Chet looked at Standish again. What kind of a dumb hillbilly fool does he take me for?

"Oh, I know, you probably don't believe a word of what I'm saying." He paused and worked his hands. "But that business with your daughter--of course I didn't really want a date with your little girl. I, I was just envious of you all these months and was scheming a way to get back at you." He looked at Chet. Chet saw a softness he had never seen before in his boss's eyes. Should he believe what he was saying? "What I'm trying to say, Hillbilly, is--may I call you Hillbilly like all your friends do? The fact is I'm a miserable, lonely man. And I need you for a friend--" He stopped speaking and looked shyly at Chet. "Oh, I can see you don't believe me."

Chet didn't know what to say. He'd sensed this about what drove Standish all along and wanted to believe that his words were sincere. But these past few weeks had been miserable.

"Let me prove that I mean what I say, Hillbilly," Standish said. "I've been watching your work closely these past few months, and you're probably the best worker we've got. You come to work early lots of times, you're never sick, you're conscientious about your work--I know it's Buckingham's fault that some of the fenders have to be scrapped-- you produce even more than your quota, you treat your superiors with respect. Fact is, you're a model worker. And I want to make up for all the misery I caused you. I'm going to recommend you to the super for a promotion. With your work attitude and your ability to get along with others, you'd be a model foreman."

Chet's eyes got bigger. Standish was going too far! But, oh, how he wanted to believe what he was saying!

The whistle blew. Chet glanced over at his buddies. They got to their feet, still grinning at him and Standish.

"This has been good for me, my little confession," Standish said. "And you'll see. Things are going to be different from now on. Do you, do you think we could have lunch together again sometime soon?" Standish stood up, dusted off the seat of his smartly tailored pants and looked down at Chet.

The eyes that had once been cold and cruel were now soft and pleading. Oh, how Chet wanted to believe him! Not knowing what else to do, Chet nodded his head yes as the foreman walked slowly away. The usually brisk-walking and proud figure was now shuffling and slumped.

Chet returned, dazed, to his press. He told Buckingham of Standish's confession and promise of a promotion recommendation.

Even Buckingham, seldom disconcerted, was surprised at the audacity of what he thought was Standish's latest trick. He shook his head and said, "Shit! Now I've heard everything! You got to hand it to that slimy bastard. He's sure got the imagination." He shook his head again and added, "I know you don't believe that snake."

"A course not," Chet said over the noise of the presses. But still, he *was* relieved. He was not fired yet. And every penny counted, especially with Christmas near.

He worked silently across from Buckingham, and thought of how wonderful it would be if Standish did have a desire to change. What if he did not lose his job. And what if Standish was sincere about that recommendation? Just what if it *were* all true? He began to relax a little, for the first time in weeks. He began to think about how wonderful it would be if he did make those few dollars extra each week as a foreman. Lizzie could really stretch those dollars and pretty soon they could start saving again for The Farm. Alma May didn't really mean what she said about The Farm. Wait until she got back home away from all these glittering stores and fancy houses and high muckamuck people. Like that Mrs. Carlson. Just wait until they got back to those mountains. Just wait until he and his little girl went back to their secret place and she started sketching their mountains again while he played his old guitar, and ...

"Hey, Hillbilly," Buckingham shouted, "what in hell you smiling about? I'm warning you, don't believe that bastard. He's just having some more fun with you."

Chet glanced angrily at Buckingham, annoyed with him for interrupting his thoughts. Buckingham was always so free with advice. "Don't you think a feller can change?" Chet shouted. "Don't you think every person deep down inside wants to be good? No matter what that person acts like on the outside?" Oh, how he wanted to believe Standish.

"Not that person," Buckingham said. "That person's not a person."

Late that afternoon while Chet and Buckingham were caught in the rush of workers heading to punch out, Standish approached Chet again. Once more, he gave Chet a friendly pat on his shoulder. He bent down and whispered warmly in Chet's ear, "Remember, now. Recommendation. Soon."

Buckingham frowned and the others grinned. Chet looked up at Standish's warm and smiling face. Standish's eyes, pleading and soft, had the same little boy look that Jimmie Lee's had when he'd done something wrong and wanted to be forgiven, like last week when Chet caught him taking a nickel from his pants pocket. Should he believe Standish?

For the first time in weeks, the worry lines were almost gone from Chet's face and there was a briskness to his gait when he stepped down from the crowded bus that evening and walked north toward home. His foreman's words kept returning: "Recommendation. Soon." Maybe Standish was sincere. Should he tell Lizzie and the children? No. He had better not. No use getting their hopes up if it were not true.

But late that evening, with Lizzie lying in his arms in the darkness, he felt such a closeness with her, such a need to share his hope. Hadn't he always shared everything with his Lizzie?

"Oh, Chet," Lizzie cried, shyly pressing her body into his. "Maybe it's true. Maybe he ain't goin' to be mean no more. Maybe we really can start savin' again for The Farm."

The next morning Chet stood at the press smiling across at his partner, ready to begin work. Buckingham grinned and said: "Hey, Hillbilly, you look twenty years younger today. Get a little last night?"

Chet didn't reply, but continued smiling. He did feel younger today. All morning, he couldn't stop the thoughts that kept recurring. Thoughts of the morning sun shining down on Big Black Mountain, and lespedeza fields, and morning glories growing up the side of his porch, and Sebright hens and Minorca roosters, and … Wasn't it his moral duty to help a fellow human being who was trying to be a better person?

Chet saw Standish approaching up the aisle. A graceful, erect, cruel-eyed Standish. Chet's smile withered. This--This was the familiar Standish again! What--?

The foreman walked directly to Chet, paused long enough to bend over and hiss into his ear, "Soon!" before parting his lips in the old smile so well-known to Chet, and continuing up the aisle.

The uneasy pang pierced Chet's stomach again. Soon? What did be mean by soon? Soon he would recommend Chet for promotion? Or--Or soon he wanted a date with Alma May? Chet's hands began to tremble as he looked across at Buckingham. His partner was shaking his head in sympathy and disgust.

Standish's meaning was apparent later that day when Chet stood in the noisy crowd waiting to punch out for lunch. In a voice loud and clear, the foreman yelled over the din of impatient, hungry men:

"Oh, by the way, Combs. Ask Alma May which one of those movies she saw with me last Saturday night she liked the best-- *Strange Interlude* or *Bill of Divorcement*."

Alma May? *Strange Interlude*? *Bill of Divorcement*? What--?

Chet's face hardened and he bolted after Standish as the crowd around him tittered. But the foreman had already disappeared.

Chet faced the grinning crowd. His fist trembled with rage. Surely they didn't believe that bastard!

"When's the wedding, Hillbilly?" Walter Gajewski asked. His fat cheeks got even rounder as he grinned, and his big eyes sparkled with amusement. The men laughed.

"You know it ain't true. My Alma May wouldn't--"

"Ah, we're just havin' fun with you, Hillbilly," Ed Sobieski said, still grinning.

"Lay off, you idiots!" Buckingham said. "Let's go eat," he said softly to Chet.

Chet followed Buckingham silently into the cloakroom, where they claimed their lunch buckets, and then to their customary lunchtime spot. He sat down slowly, and listlessly opened his lunch bucket. He did not feel like eating. He felt like kicking Standish in the balls. Buckingham was right. Chet had been a fool to even entertain the idea that Standish was sorry. Chet's hands paused while opening the wax paper from around his sandwich as he thought hard about where he had heard of *Strange Interlude* and *Bill of Divorcement* before. Suddenly, be remembered. Alma May had seen those movies last Saturday night with Gladys Polaski!

"Don't let it get you down, Hillbilly," Buckingham whispered. "Don't you see? That's what he wants. He's trying to get you where it'll hurt you the most. The guys know it's not true."

The good-natured chatter around them suddenly stilled. Chet looked up to see Standish approaching. His body stiffened as the foreman stopped walking and stood, tall and cool and superior, above him. What now?

Standish scanned the crowd. When all had paused in eating and every eye was focused on him, he looked directly at Chet, reached into the back pocket of his neat worsted pants, and pulled out a pink object.

Slowly, carefully, and with great flourish, he opened the object. It was a pair of women's bloomers, satin and lace-trimmed.

What--? Chet's pale brow wrinkled.

"Oh, Combs, I finally remembered to bring these in. Alma May must be missing them. She left them in the back seat of my car the other night." He smiled down at Chet and his eyes danced. The crowd around Chet gasped.

Chet sprang to his feet as Lizzie's beans splattered on the concrete floor. In one swift motion, Chet had his hands around Standish's neck and his knee kicking into his groin.

"You bastard! You lyin' bastard! Take that back!" Chet sputtered. "Take that back! You're a lyin', son-of-a-bitchin' bastard!" He felt the blood pounding in his temples and his ears ringing. He'd kill the snake! He'd kill the snake! Saying that about his little girl! Chet was aware of someone pulling at his arms and from a distance he could hear Buckingham's voice shouting, "Stop it! He's not worth it, Hillbilly! Stop it!"

Chet and Standish were on the floor now. Chet looked down at Standish's face. The foreman's eyes bulged and his face was turning blue. Good! He would kill the lying bastard!

Chet continued to feel a pulling at both of his arms as he pounded Standish's head against the oily concrete. Still sputtering, he whispered: "Take that back! Take that back! You know it ain't true!"

"Stop it! He's not worth it!" Buckingham's voice sounded closer now. Chet slowly loosened his grip from around his boss's neck, and with great effort, Buckingham and Sobieski pulled him off Standish.

Chet stood over Standish with his arms still pinned in the grips of Buckingham and Sobieski as the foreman gasped to catch his breath. The color slowly returned to Standish's face. No one in the silent crowd bent down to assist him to his feet. Standish lay there for a moment. When his breath came in a more normal rhythm, he stood up and dusted off the back of his pants and matching vest. With great dignity, he made his way through the parting crowd. He then turned around and his look met Chet's. Standish gave Chet a wide, friendly grin and walked erectly and gracefully away, some of Lizzie's beans still clinging to the seat of his pants.

★　　★　　★

Chet felt an odd sense of relief as he rode the half-filled DSR bus west toward home. It had finally happened. It was over. He was fired. No longer would he have to worry about when it would happen. It was over.

He had been called to the personnel office and shown the Termination of Employment form. Chet had read the neatly typed reason for termination of employment: "Quality of production output unsatisfactory. Fender forms defective. Warned three times previously." Chet had stood there dumbly and counted the words. Twelve. There were twelve words explaining why he was fired.

He was amazed that he was so calm now, after being in such a rage a short time ago. He looked absently out the bus window. A long line of shivering, ragged men and women and children wound around a building that housed one of the Salvation Army branches. Chet's face fell. Would he and his family be in a bread line like that soon? He quickly looked away. He would never permit it. Where could he find a job, and soon?

Chet decided to get off the bus at Woodward Avenue and walk the rest of the way home. He'd postpone telling Lizzie and the children as long as possible. And maybe during the long walk home he'd pass a place that was hiring.

He headed south. His stomach began to growl and he realized that he had not eaten lunch. He sat down on the next park bench and, with cold fingers, opened his lunch bucket. He unfolded the wax paper around the sandwiches. Just what he expected. Bread and oleo. Again. But, being ravenous, he gobbled them down and wished he had some coffee to warm him. He felt in his pocket for a nickel. He found one, along with a penny, and made his way down the crowded street to the nearest coffee shop.

When he opened the door to Shorty's Lunch, his ears were assaulted by jangling and rolling and clicking noises. The small place was empty except for the owner and two young boys about Jimmie Lee's age in the corner. They were playing one of those new contraptions that Chet had noticed seemed to be everywhere of late--a pinball machine. He wondered why the boys were here and not in school. Then be remembered that Alma May had said there was only a half day of school today. Chet hoped the pinball craze would die down before Jimmie Lee discovered it. Chet frowned. Where would Jimmie Lee ever get a nickel, now, to have a little fun?

Chet sat down at the neat steel-topped counter. As he took a sip of his steaming coffee, a familiar-looking young woman wearing bifocals walked in. She sat down next to Chet and loaded her books on the counter.

"A cup of hot water, please," she said to the diminutive man behind the counter.

"A cup of hot water? You kidding?" the man asked.

"Yeah. Just a cup of hot water, please. I brought my own tea ball." She reached into her coat pocket and came up with a small, perforated steel ball.

The owner shook his head and poured her a cup of hot water.

The young woman popped the ball into the water. Chet glanced at her face. It was plain except for the freckles. Where had he seen this young woman before? Then he looked at her hair and remembered. Alma May's friend, Gladys Polaski! No one else in the whole world had hair like that.

"Why, hello, Gladys. How are you?"

Gladys Polaski turned and looked at Chet. "Oh, hi, Mister Combs." She paused for a moment and her freckles wrinkled closer together as her face registered surprise. "How come you're not at work?" she asked, with more than a tinge of scolding in her voice.

Chet, a little taken aback by her brashness, thought fast. "Oh, I didn't feel very well, so I figured it was best to come home early."

Gladys's face showed a flicker of disgust. "My father never takes off work," she said. "He'd never miss a minute, even if he was almost dying."

Chet was silent, not knowing what to say to that.

"Don't forget, now," one of the boys at the pinball machine said. He dropped a coin in the slot. "If my Mom wonders why I didn't bring home a loaf of bread, what you gonna say?"

"That you lost the nickel she gave you," the other replied.

Chet asked Gladys, "Do you play them new pinball machines, too?" He nodded toward the boys.

"Oh, heavens, no!" Gladys replied. "That's a real waste! Why, for a nickel I can get a whole pack of typing paper. I'm going to get a job as a typist when I graduate, and I'm practicing as much as I can." She sipped her tea smugly.

How different from Alma May this young woman was, Chet thought. But they do have one thing in common. They both like going to movies together. "Alma says you an' her went to the show the other night," Chet said.

"Show? What show? I never went to a show in ages," Gladys said. She blew on her tea.

The familiar pang hit Chet's stomach again. "You--you remember. You an' Alma May went to see them two movies together last Saturday night. You remember. What were they called, now? Oh, I remember now. *Strange Interlude* an' *Bill a Divorcement*."

Gladys looked at Chet and her freckles bunched together again in bewilderment. "You crazy or something? Like I say, I never been to a movie in a long time. Why should I pay a quarter to see *Strange Interlude* when I can get the play from the library and read it for nothing?"

Chet's hands began to tremble so much that the coffee he was holding flooded the saucer and spilled over onto the counter. The owner picked up a cloth and rushed over to wipe it up, while Gladys leaned over to Chet and exclaimed: "Hey, what's the matter with you, Mr. Combs? You look like you seen a ghost. You're right. You must be really sick!"

Chet whirled slowly around on his stool and stepped down. He headed for the door.

"Mister Combs! Need some help going home?" Gladys called.

Chet shook his head no as he opened the door.

He stumbled in the direction of home. Gladys Polaski did not go to the movies with Alma May? thought Chet. But she must have, even though she says no. Gladys must be lying. He turned around and headed back in the direction of the cafe. He would tell Gladys that she was lying. He stopped. How stupid that would be. But why would Alma May pretend that she'd gone to the movies with Gladys? Unless, unless she'd gone to the movies with--with-- Oh, no, Alma May would never go anywhere with Standish. Chet felt his knees weaken. His Alma May would never--

Could he make it to that park bench over there? He staggered up the slope, almost falling into a pile of soot-crusted snow. He managed to make it to the icy bench, and plopped down.

Was Alma May lying? Had she just been pretending she was spending all that time at the art museum? Oh, no, not his little girl. Not his Alma May. Chet slowly shook his head. The thought of Alma May and Standish together--it couldn't be true. But maybe Alma May, because she was always hankering after fancy things, and Standish seemed to have lots of spending money ... He covered his face with his hands.

★   ★   ★

Alma absently fingered the monthly envelope Miss Di Inganno had just given her to mail, and said to Lizzie: "Mom, we just got to do something about Miss Di Inganno. She's getting weaker all the time."

"That old witch's got bats in her belfry," Jimmie lee said. "She doesn't even know me anymore."

"And that awful smell. Fishy and stale," Alma said. She wrinkled her face and pinched her nose.

Lizzie sighed and shook her head. "Reckon I don't know what we can do. If a body don't want to be seen by the doctor-man. An' if a body don't eat hardly nothin' like she probably don't, an' ..." Lizzie shook her head again and moved into the kitchen to mix cornbread for supper.

Jimmie Lee watched his mother as she reached into the cupboard and got down the sack of corn meal. He pulled Alma to one side and, standing on tiptoe, whispered in her ear: "Gimmee a nickel, Alma. Please. Me'n Eddie's goin' downtown."

Alma looked down at her brother and her lips curved in a smirk. "What you need a nickel for?"

Jimmie Lee studied the faded paper lampshade next to him and whispered: "I--I need a box of crayons for school."

"I'll bet. Then why are you whispering?"

Jimmie Lee continued to stare at the lampshade as Alma added, "Crayons, my foot! You just said that because you thought it'd please me if you were interested in art like I am. I know why you want that nickel. You want to waste it on that dumb pinball machine again."

Jimmie Lee looked up into Alma's eyes. "Please, Alma! Please?"

Alma hesitated and then reached into the pocket of her coat. She came up with a nickel. She placed it in her right palm, and held it under Jimmie Lee's nose. He reached eagerly for it, as she pulled her hand away and, giggling, put it behind her back.

"Aw, c'mon! Alma, please!" Jimmie Lee said.

Alma giggled again and handed the coin to Jimmie Lee.

His face broadened when he smiled and whispered, "Gee, thanks, Alma! You're swell!" He glanced into the kitchen at his mother, who was stirring the batter now, and whispered even softer, "Promise you won't tell Ma. She'd croak if she found out I spent a nickel on a pinball game. Y'know how she is."

Alma nodded her head emphatically.

Jimmie Lee scurried quietly to get his coat, and Alma looked down at Miss Di Inganno's envelope again. A concerned look crossed her face once more when she thought of her. But Alma did not want to dwell on sad things. She would think of something happy. Alma had a quarter saved for a movie ticket from the money Mrs. Carlson had just paid her.

The last time she'd gone to the Carlsons', Mrs. Carlson had greeted her with, "Come in my bedroom, Alma, and help me decide which of my new play suits to pack." She motioned with a silken-draped arm toward her bed, on which were laid so many new clothes that the pink silk spread underneath was barely visible.

"Playsuit? You going to wear a playsuit when you go skiing?"

"Oh, I won't be on the slopes all the time, silly," Mrs. Carlson said with a smile. "There'll be an indoor pool there, and when I don't feel like being in a bathing suit, I'll wear one of these." She pointed to several of the one-piece play suits and other strange new play garments-- wide-legged beach pajamas Alma had seen on mannequins at Hudson's, shorts and slacks she'd seen advertised from Russek's.

Alma gently fingered all of the four playsuits and then selected two in pastel shades of pink and blue. "With your blond hair and fair complexion, these will be most flattering," she said.

Mrs. Carlson smiled at Alma. "Thank you, dear. It's nice to know someone who's an artist, who knows about colors. Someday I'd like for you to paint my portrait."

Alma was flattered. She smiled shyly as Mrs. Carlson continued. "Oh, I'm getting so excited about our ski trip. Since the Olympics were held in Lake Placid, everybody, just everybody is going skiing."

Now Alma peeked into her parents' bedroom at the alarm clock on the dresser. Later than she thought! She called toward the kitchen to her mother: "Mom, I'm going now to mail Miss Di Inganno's letter."

She buttoned up her old coat in anticipation of the cold December afternoon. To her surprise, as she reached for the door, it slowly opened. It was her father!

"What--?" Alma asked. No need to ask more. Her father being home early meant only one thing. Alma stood there and stared at his wan face and slumped figure. Pa looked twenty years older this afternoon than when he had left for work that morning.

"Pa," she said gently. What would they do now? What would they do? "Pa--" Her father did not look at her, but headed toward his Morris chair.

Her mother called from the kitchen, "Alma May! Who's there?" Alma didn't have the heart to answer. She continued to stare at her suddenly old father as he fell into his chair.

"Pa. Why won't you look at me? Tell me, how did it happen?" She walked over and stood by him.

Lizzie came in from the kitchen, wiping her bands on her apron. "Who's there, Alma M--" She stopped, her apron still in her hands, when she saw Chet.

She came over and stood beside him, and gently patted his hand.

"Pa. Look at me. Why won't you look at me?" Alma repeated. Chet looked up at her, finally, and a wave of hurt crossed his face. He looked away.

"Was it Standish?" Lizzie asked, her voice barely above a whisper. Chet nodded his head.

"Oh, Pa," Alma whispered. Hearing Standish's name reminded her again of something she'd been feeling guilty about since last Saturday night. "That awful, awful Standish. He gives me the heebie-jeebies. I caught him standing and staring at me while I was buying a ticket to the movies last Saturday night. He didn't say a word. Just standing and staring at me with those awful eyes while I bought my ticket." Alma swallowed and hesitated before continuing. "And, Pa. I've been feeling bad about something." Alma bit her lip. "Remember you never wanted me to go to the show at night alone?" Alma paused again. "Well, I led you to believe that I went to the show with Gladys Polaski because I knew you'd get mad if you knew I went alone."

Her father stared up at her. "You--You went to the show alone?" Chet asked.

Alma nodded yes. Oh, why did she tell him? Didn't he have enough to worry about?

"My little girl," Chet whispered, his voice cracking. "I just knew my Alma May didn't do anything wrong."

Her father was actually smiling now. Alma looked down at him in bewilderment. Had her Pa gone loony? She'd just told him that she'd disobeyed him and he told her he knew she didn't do anything wrong. And why was he grinning as wide as a Cheshire cat when he'd just lost his job? Alma's pity turned to annoyance. Didn't he care what would become of them? Who would take care of them? Who would take care--

"Everythin's goin' to be all right, Alma May," Lizzie said. "Your Pa'll take care a us. Ain't your Pa always took care a us?"

Chapter 16

Alma stood in the doorway of the little upstairs flat. Her lower lip trembled as she took in its entire dimensions with one glance. So it had finally come to this, she thought. A place no bigger than the light housekeeping rooms they had first lived in when they arrived in Detroit. One small room that served as a kitchen, dining, living, and bedroom for her and Jimmie Lee, and a tiny bedroom for her parents and Carrie Lou. And not even a bathroom. The Combses would have to share one with the tenants on either side.

She shook her head when she caught her father's look. It was all his fault that they had had to move here. But she immediately felt sorry that her gesture caused a pained expression to cross his face. Alma knew jobs were scarce and he had tried, but couldn't he have found something in all these months?

At first Alma had believed him when he said he would find work soon. The morning after being fired by Standish, he'd gotten up earlier than usual, polished his worn shoes, and washed and dressed carefully. He'd set out before dawn, his lunch pail in his hand, his map of Detroit in his back pocket again, and a confident smile on his face. "I'm goin' to be the first in line. Ain't nobody goin' to be ahead a me. Today's our lucky day. Just you wait an' see. I'm goin' to find another job today."

He'd said the same thing for weeks. Then Alma began to notice that he no longer got up quite as early in the morning and he did not smile quite as much when he returned in the evening. For the first time, Alma suspected that he'd given up hope of finding a job.

One morning she came into the kitchen when he and her mother were arguing. Seemed as though they were arguing more and more lately, and usually about the same thing. Jimmie Lee was doing his morning chore, sifting ashes from burned coals. He held a small window screen over a tin bucket. The coals that remained on top after sifting, he put into another bucket for using again. Carrie Lou sat in her high chair, slurping a bowl of watery oatmeal. Lizzie had been extending the family's oatmeal lately with more and more water.

"But, Chet," Lizzie pleaded, "it would only be for a little while, till you found a job, an'--"

"No, Lizzie. I don't want to hear no more about it. My woman ain't goin' to work. A woman's place is in the home. It's a man's job to provide for his family."

"But, Chet, it ain't your fault there's no work, an' it'll only be for a spell till things pick up."

"No!" Chet said firmly as he traced the outline of his rubbers with a pencil on several thicknesses of newspapers. Chet had been going barefoot inside the flat every evening to save his shoes for job hunting. But eventually the holes in the soles had become so large from walking on pavement day after day that his shoes no longer held the newspaper or cardboard liners he stuffed into them each morning. So now he had to resort to wearing ordinary rubbers without the shoes. But the rubbers were beginning to get holes in the bottoms, too. "I don't want to hear no more about it, Lizzie," he said, as he cut around the outline with a pair of scissors. "You ain't goin' out an' clean houses for no other people." He stuffed the liners into the rubbers and emphatically stuffed his feet into them, too.

The Combses had been able to stay in their flat for several months after Chet lost his job. They had paid the landlord a month's rent in advance when they had moved in and, with their tiny savings and Lizzie's increased frugality, they had managed to stave off moving to the smaller flat for several months.

Alma watched her mother now as Lizzie positioned the photographic portrait of the new president above the radio on the little table. Lizzie dusted it carefully, as Alma's mouth twisted in a slight sneer. You'd think that picture was a portrait by Rembrandt, the way her mother babied it. It was only a cheap reproduction from the *Sunday Free Press*. Her mother didn't pay half as much attention to the pictures Alma painted.

It hadn't taken the Combses very long to move. They had sold much of their furniture for a few dollars. They didn't have room for it in the new flat, and desperately needed the money it would bring. But they did not part with the radio.

"I'd better go call the doctor for Miss Di Inganno," Alma shouted now, "and mail her letter for the last time." She had to raise her voice to be heard over the sound of the baby in the flat next door. The baby had begun to cry again, a lusty, steady cry--a cry of hunger that Alma remembered from Carrie Lou's infancy. These walls must be made of tissue, Alma thought, holding her hands to her ears.

She was glad for a reason to leave, and she would take a long time doing the errands. She was even gladder to leave when she heard a man's voice shouting above the baby's cry, "Feed that goddam brat, will ya? I can't stand the noise!"

"You know my milk's dried up, and there's no money to buy any!" a woman's voice shouted in reply.

Alma slammed the door and ran downstairs. She buttoned her coat against the March wind. After making the call and mailing the letter, she would head for the quiet orderliness of the art institute. It had become her second home lately--a sanctuary, an escape from quarrels about whether or not her mother would work, the increasing hang dog look on her father's face, and Jimmie Lee's whining for bigger portions at mealtime.

Alma hung up the pay phone receiver after talking with Dr. White, the kindly doctor who had tended her mother during her near-miscarriage. He assured her that he'd call on Miss Di Inganno that afternoon. Her thoughts turned to her visit to the old lady's flat that morning.

Alma had knocked on the door, but did not wait for Miss Di Inganno's invitation to enter because she knew it would not be forthcoming. She opened the door to the familiar scene, which to Alma was like a painting grown old and faded and yellow. It should be entitled *The Yellow Room*. For there, as usual, were the yellowed newspaper clippings and photographs on the walls, the yellowed Miss Di Inganno wearing the yellowed lace outfit and sitting at the table staring vacantly at the yellowed movie magazines. When Alma had approached the old woman to say goodbye and to plead once more to allow the doctor to come, she had thought how unbelievable it was that she had once looked forward to her visits there. Now she was repulsed by the sight of her.

The stale, fishy smell, expected now, became more pronounced as Alma drew nearer. And in spite of herself, Alma checked again the condition of Miss Di Inganno's fingernails. No, she still hadn't trimmed them. The once manicured nails were completely devoid of polish now. The Art Nouveau curve was even more pronounced, and for the first time, Alma noticed that the nails were thick and yellow, too, and had deep lines in them.

Alma's glance moved down to the table. The movie magazines were placed exactly as they had been yesterday. Even the one in front of Miss Di Inganno was open at the same page. Alma shuddered when she noticed the shriveled remains of a dead centipede on it. Upon closer inspection, she noticed that it was not a centipede, but one of Miss Di Inganno's false eyelashes that had fallen from her eye and had become curled into a ball.

Alma looked down at the top of the old woman's mantilla. The tendrils of hair escaping the mantilla, once a fascinating sumac color, had now grown as white as dead dandelion fluff.

"Miss Di Inganno," Alma said in a loud voice, "I've come to tell you goodbye." Alma knew there would be no answer on the first try, so she waited for a moment and repeated in an even louder voice, "Miss Di Inganno, I've come to tell you goodbye."

The old woman slowly turned her face up toward Alma and gazed through her as if Alma were not there at all. Then for a brief moment her gaze became lucid when it fixed on Alma's face. The deep furrows in her cheeks under the makeup came together as she twisted her face in a frown. "You've cut your hair!" she scolded in a clear voice. "That was your best feature! You'll never be a big movie star without it!"

"I cut my hair months and months ago," Alma said, a little hurt. Didn't she have any other good features? And who wanted to be a movie star, anyway? Oh, at one time when she was young she had been torn between wanting to be a movie star or an artist. But now, there was no question: one day she would be a famous artist.

Alma seized upon Miss Di Inganno's moment of clarity. "Please Miss Di Inganno. Let me get a doctor for you."

"No! No! No doctor!" Miss Di Inganno cried. "Those doctors let my Rudy die!"

"But it would be a different doctor," pleaded Alma. "Please."

"A different doctor," she whispered. Her eyes became vacant again and she turned her face back down toward the table.

"A different doctor, a different doctor." Alma pleaded again.

"Y…es. A different doctor. A different doc..t..o..r." A faint smile lit the old woman's face. "No. Get Dr. Meeker. The same doctor Rudy had. Rudy's doctor." Miss Di Inganno's smile got a little wider. "Y…e…s. The same hands that touched my Rudy's body will touch mine. The same hands that touched my Rudy's body will touch mine. The same h…a…nds …"

Alma had picked up the envelope addressed in Miss Di Inganno's faltering scrawl that waited for her on the table next to the plaster of Paris bust of Valentino. Alma would ask the landlord again to mail any future envelopes for Miss Di Inganno. She took the unopened Detroit *Sunday Free Press* and paused at the door for one final look at the old woman.

Miss Di Inganno was staring straight ahead again and still muttering, "The same ha..nds …"

Alma closed the door softly behind her.

She continued to hurry east now toward the art institute after depositing Miss Di Inganno's envelope in a mailbox. She thought again that, even though she was glad of it, how strange it was that Uncle Darcas did not offer to have Alma and her family live with him and Aunt Euella and share expenses. Although nothing was said by her mother or father, she knew they wondered why, too. But as usual, Uncle Darcas was generous with his old Model T, and helped them move the embarrassingly small amount of remaining furniture.

Mr. Buckingham would've offered to help them move, and maybe even offered to have them live with him if he'd known about what had happened. She missed Mr. Buckingham's cheerful visits and wondered how he was. Would they ever see him again? He had dropped by the same evening after her father lost his job and tried to inject a bit of gaiety with candy treats, as usual. That night it had been Cracker Jacks and Tootsie Rolls and a big bag of fresh fruit. Buckingham had also told several long and detailed jokes, which under normal circumstances would've left the family holding their bellies from laughter, but on that night brought only polite smiles.

Poor Mr. Buckingham, Alma had thought. He was trying so hard.

"Say, I've got a bright idea," Buckingham had said. "Let's all go out to dinner. The treat's on me."

Jimmie Lee's face began to crinkle in a smile at the prospect of going out to a restaurant, a rare treat, but his smile left when Chet quickly squelched the idea. "Lizzie already has supper ready, Harry. Reckon there's plenty. Why don't you stay? It's your favorite, cornbread an' beans. An' then we could listen to *Amos 'n' Andy* like we always do."

Alma knew Buckingham sensed that they would rather not have a visitor that evening, even a friend as close as he was.

"No, thank you kindly, Chet. On second thought, I really should be getting home," Buckingham said. There was an awkward pause. Buckingham seemed embarrassed, unusual for him, as he headed for the door. He placed his hand on the knob to open it, turned and said softly to Chet, "Oh, damn it, Hillbilly, you know if I could I'd trade places with you. You need the job more than I do. I wish it had been me fired instead of you."

Her father smiled up at him. Moisture glistened in Mr. Buckingham's eyes as he blinked them rapidly.

"I know, I know, Harry," Chet said gently. "I know how you feel. An' thanks for sayin' it."

There was another awkward pause. Buckingham reached into his wallet and pulled out two twenty dollar bills. "Please, Hillbilly. You'd make me feel better if you'd take this."

"Oh, no, Harry. I couldn't," Chet said, embarrassed.

"But it's not like I was giving it to you. Consider it a loan."

Chet shook his head. "Thanks anyway."

Buckingham reluctantly put the bills back into his wallet. He stroked Chet's back, looked around the room at everyone, and said in a low voice, "See you soon."

He closed the door behind him. They would not really see him soon, Alma thought. His feelings of guilt for still having a job while her father did not would keep him away.

Alma looked up now as she walked, and saw that another family was being evicted from their home. Alma had lost track of the number of evictions she'd witnessed in the past few days. She'd heard that in Detroit alone they were numbering in the hundreds every week.

A small crowd was gathered around a pile of furniture on the lawn in front of a deteriorated three-story brown clapboard flat. She saw an old woman fingering a shiny black ceramic table lamp with a base made to look like a reclining panther. A younger woman had a tape measure and was measuring the width of a kitchen table, while a middle-aged woman was attempting to fit her huge buttocks into a dilapidated rocking chair. *The vultures!* Alma knew they were aiming to cart off that poor family's furniture if the furniture company didn't get there fast enough to reclaim it.

The door to the flat opened. A woman shouted from the doorway: "You give me back my radio, you bastard! You dumped everything else out. The least you could do is leave me my radio. You can take everything else, but not my radio!"

The crowd turned to see the excitement as the obese young woman, shaking with rage, struggled for an object that a heavyset man, whom Alma took to be the landlord, was attempting to carry down the steps of the porch.

"Dump everything else out, you bastard, but not my radio!" The woman was screeching as loud as she could now. Two frightened, dirty little girls stood a little behind her. One girl was crying and sucking her thumb while she tried to hold onto the hem of the woman's dress. The other girl was also crying and sucking her thumb, too. She held a paper bag.

"You ain't paid me no rent for six months and your furniture's being repossessed and all you can think about is your goddam radio!" the man shouted.

"Give me back my radio!"

"No! Everything goes out!"

The man and woman continued to argue over the radio as the crowd, which had grown larger now, began to shout: "Give her back her radio! Give her back her radio!"

The more the woman shouted and the more the crowd chanted, the redder the man's face grew and the more determined he was to wrest the radio from the woman's grip. After several more minutes of pulling and shouting and chanting, the superior strength of the man won out. When the woman finally let go, the man lost his balance in the struggle and tumbled down the steps, the radio still in his arms.

The crowd began to laugh and cheer and clap. The man, humiliated, rose awkwardly and brushed his clothes off. He still clutched the object of the battle.

A black city police car pulled up to the curb beside Alma. Two officers jumped out and rushed toward the porch.

"This is it," one said. "Three oh four four West Penrod."

The officer closest to the porch was about to address the glaring woman when the woman turned to the girl who held the paper bag and said something. The girl did nothing but continue to cry and suck her thumb and hold the bag.

"Now!" shouted the woman. "Give me the bag now!"

The frightened girl handed her mother the bag. In one swift motion the woman threw the black contents of the bag onto the approaching men. "You ain't gonna evict me without a fight!" she screamed.

The crowd around Alma gasped again and grew more delighted when the men staggered back and covered their eyes with their hands. "My eyes! My eyes!" the officers shouted.

The woman yelled for the children to step back inside, and slammed the door as she and the children disappeared behind it.

"What was that black stuff?" a child to Alma's right asked.

"Pepper," the big-buttocked woman answered. She had succeeded in fitting her derriere into the seat of the rocker, and was now struggling to get it out.

"Oh, my god," a man's voice said. "Pepper! Maybe she blinded 'em!"

"Good!" a woman said.

"Yeah. Serves 'em right. They ain't got no business evicting that poor woman and her kids!" agreed the woman with the tape measure as she began to take the dimensions of a bookcase.

"Yeah! Good!" Alma heard a woman's voice behind her shout.

"Good! Good! Good!" Shouts were coming from all around Alma now.

She had the urge to run to the steps and help the men, but she had a stronger desire to run from the scene. She threw a final guilty glance at the officers on the porch as she hurried from the yard.

The crowd continued to chant, while the landlord stood in the yard with the radio still clutched under his arm, and the woman with the tape began to measure a chest-of-drawers.

Those cruel people, Alma thought, as she turned the corner onto Woodward Avenue. Just like when that man jumped from that building. But she did not want to think about that. She wanted to think about how quiet and peaceful it would be at the art institute.

She passed a group of people forming a bread line and turned her head away. If there were someone in the line that she knew, she did not want to see that person. Was Purlie Washington there with her family and relatives? Alma had seen them often lately, waiting for a handout of what was probably watery soup and stale bread. She, Alma Combs, would never, never, wait in line for a handout, even if she were starving.

Alma continued south on Woodward and crossed the avenue to admire the latest Graham-Paige automobile models in the windows of an auto display room. She stood with her nose pressed to the glass as a sudden ray of sunlight warmed her back and shone on one of the automobiles. Alma gasped in admiration, for the light blue paint job, shimmering and sparkling in the ray of sunlight, seemed to be several different colors at once. This remarkable paint must be that "Pearlessence of Blue" she'd heard about. Made with powdered fish scales, of all things!

She would have a more luxurious car than a Graham-Paige one day, Alma thought. Her glance fell upon an attractive poster in red, white and blue in the window. "Get Behind the President," it read. It was good to see something optimistic.

She thought, then, of the new President, Mr. Roosevelt. And of her mother and father, who had sat spellbound in front of the little radio last week, staring at the round orange glow of the dial as if the dial itself was their friend, the President. It was as if he were right in the same room, speaking to them personally. His voice, even though firm, was natural and warm and friendly. So full of life. Not ranting and raving like that Father Coughlin.

"Things is goin' to be better now that Mister Roosevelt's the President, just you wait an' see," her mother had said that night after the new President's first "fireside chat." Lizzie had picked up the broom and begun to sweep the kitchen's old linoleum floor with new and unusual vigor and determination. "Why, just look how he's takin' charge a things already." Alma had been surprised at the confident smile on her mother's face. "We must all remember what our President said: 'Confidence an' courage are the essentials in our plan,' 'Confidence an' courage are the essentials in our plan,' 'Confi ...'"

Alma shook her head and smiled. Her mother had a brand new phrase to say over and over.

She noted with dismay now a note signed by the Governor. It was glued to the door of the bank she passed. She'd seen many of these notes lately announcing that another bank had been closed. Not that it mattered to her family; what little savings they had, her father kept in a Mason jar in back of the bottom drawer of the chest in her parents' bedroom. But the whole bank thing was scary and depressing.

But Alma felt a stir of excitement as she anticipated continuing her work on copying a happy little Renoir-like oil by Glackens at the art institute. She loved the luminous, radiant reds and yellows and greens of the painting of a young woman about her age riding on a horse. Oh, to be, just for a moment, the subject of that carefree scene!

She stopped suddenly as she neared the wide marble steps leading up to the building. What are all those people doing here? They couldn't all be here to see the special exhibit of old Italian masterpieces, even though it was said to be the best since the Rembrant show. For whatever reason they were here, Alma wanted to quickly push through the crowd and escape to the security of the quiet corner where the little Glackens painting hung.

"Pardon me, please. Excuse me," she said, threading through the maze of people to the quadruple doors. She encountered disgusted and annoyed looks along the way.

"Better watch out, little lady," said Alma's friend, the guard, when she finally reached the lobby, "or you'll get crushed."

She looked up at his smiling and concerned face. "What's going on today?" she asked.

"They're all curious. Just curious," he said. "They been hearing about the Rivera frescoes and they want to see for themselves what all the stink being raised is about. I never seen anything like it. There's never been this many people here at one time since I've been here."

"Oh, the Rivera frescoes. I forgot all about them," Alma said. "But how am I going to get to my easel and paints in the storeroom?"

The guard shook his head in sympathy. "Don't know, little lady. I'd get 'em for you, but I'm not allowed to leave my station, not with all these people coming through." He smiled down at her again. "And even if I could get 'em for you, you'd never be able to copy that little Glackens in peace today. Now that you're here, though, you might as well see what all the fuss's about."

Alma shook her head. "I couldn't care less about those frescoes. I'll come back tomorrow."

But Alma found herself suddenly pushed forward by the rush of the crowd, and up the stairs through the Great Room. She tried to turn around, hoping to buck the flow of traffic headed for the Garden Court.

"Alma! Alma Combs!" Alma heard a familiar voice call. She craned her neck over the heads of the people in the Garden Court ahead. Alma searched the crowd until she saw the owner of the voice. It was Miss Galbraith, her art teacher. Of course, Miss Galbraith would be there! Alma was very fond of her, but she didn't want to be delayed by talking with anyone.

"Try to move over here, Alma," Miss Galbraith shouted over the din. "Purlie's here, too!"

Oh, no. Not Purlie. Not poor, shy, no-talent Purlie. She thought she'd be in that bread line she'd just passed.

In spite of her efforts to turn and run from the scene, Alma found herself being shoved to where Miss Galbraith and Purlie Washington stood.

"I'm so glad you're here, Alma," Miss Galbraith said. "Now two of my best students are here." She smiled happily up at Alma and gave her an affectionate pat on the arm. Miss Galbraith was a short, round woman of about forty, whose fingernails were never entirely clean of oil paints or India ink, and whose cherubic face was constantly rounded in a smile. Alma wondered whether Miss Galbraith smiled in her sleep, too.

Miss Galbraith nodded her head toward Purlie and said over the noise, "Purlie brought her parents to see the murals, too. Isn't that nice?"

Alma looked next to Purlie where a Negro man and woman stood. They both smiled timidly at Alma and then proudly at Purlie.

"Alma, this is my momma and daddy," Purlie said. "Mamma and Daddy, this is Alma Combs. You remember--I told you what wonderful paintings Alma does? Well, this is <u>Alma</u>." She said her name as if Alma were special. Purlie looked at Alma and smiled that shy smile of hers.

Why is she always smiling at me and trying to be friendly when I don't want to be friends with her? Alma wondered with irritation.

The man shyly extended a hand to Alma. She took it hesitantly, never having shaken a colored person's hand before. It was dry and callused. Mr. Washington, a skinny, wizened man, looked too old to be Purlie's father. His kinky white hair, contrasted with his black face, reminded Alma of a swirled scoop of vanilla ice cream on top of devil's-food cake.

Alma rarely had seen a colored person in the institute, and thought Purlie and her family looked out of place. She felt sorry for them.

"Oh, Alma, ain't these murals wonderful?" Purlie asked. "If I could paint one-tenth as good as he does."

"Now, now, Purlie. You always underestimate yourself," Miss Galbraith said. "Both you and Alma keep on learning and working the way you have been, and maybe someday people will come to see both of your work."

Miss Galbraith's voice was drowned out by a man's voice in back of her: "There they are! Right up there on both those walls. All those Communist fists. What'd I tell you? The gall of that Rivera guy!" The man pointed to the uppermost murals above the center of the two main murals on the north and south walls of the huge room.

Miss Galbraith shook her head in amusement. "Don't believe him," she said to Alma and the Washingtons. "Those aren't Communist fists. They must be a symbol of some kind. Probably mining. They must each be grasping metals used in making steel. All those fists must be grasping to capture the riches of the earth. Besides, I read that Rivera has become disenchanted with Communism, and no longer belongs to the Party."

Miss Galbraith looked over at the huge main mural on the south wall. She pointed to the section in the right corner, where several men were depicted working at a giant press. "You must be very proud, Alma," Miss Galbraith said, "that your father is part of such a huge industry that makes life easier for all of us."

"Proud?" Alma asked. Proud that her father worked in an automobile factory? It had never occurred to her to be proud that her father stood at a press all day and did dumb work. Why, anybody could do that. "Yes," lied Alma.

"You did tell me once that he works at a press, didn't you?" Miss Galbraith asked.

"Yes," Alma replied, "but not anymore. He's between jobs now, and looking for something more challenging."

Alma was glad when Miss Galbraith changed the subject. She did not want to think about her father and the fact that it was his fault that they had had to move to that ugly flat.

"If you study this mural for a while," Miss Galbraith said, continuing her art lesson as she pointed to the main mural on the opposite wall, "you'll see how imaginative Rivera is. Even though all these activities depicted in the mural may occur in different areas of a factory, Rivera combined them into one picture by using those snake-like conveyor belts to unify his composition. And see those two huge machines?" Miss Galbraith pointed her chubby finger at two awesome-looking machines in the middle of the mural. "His wonderful sense of design uses them as vertical accents in the overall composition--"

"Oh, Miss Galbraith," to Alma's surprise, the bashful Purlie interrupted, "this is just about the greatest work I've ever seen in person." Purlie stood on tiptoes trying to look around over the heads of the crowd at the four walls filled with Rivera's work. The whites of her eyes looked whiter than ever against her black skin as they grew big with admiration.

Alma stifled a look of pity. Of course Purlie would think the murals were great. Purlie herself is always painting those dumb pictures, too, about common subjects doing common things.

"I ain't noticed that vaccination picture yet," Mrs. Washington said, giving her daughter another proud and loving glance. She continued to scan the four walls. "The one that all the fuss is about." Mrs. Washington was a stooped and withered version of Purlie with the same dumb, shy smile.

Alma felt a tinge of envy. Her own mother never took an interest in art. She never would have come here.

"There it is. There's the vaccination panel," Miss Galbraith said. She pointed to a smaller panel in the upper right corner of the same wall. A doctor In the mural was vaccinating a blond-haired baby held by a nurse. In the foreground were animals, and in the background were what appeared to be scientists.

"A lot of people think it looks just like a nativity scene, what with the blond hair on the baby looking like a halo, and all," Miss Galbraith explained. "But the way I look at it is, Rivera just happened to choose the baby to be blonde. It's a medical laboratory. And the animals, they're there because that's where the serum for the vaccination comes from—animals' blood. And the men in the background--the scientists--they're transforming the serum into vaccine."

Miss Galbraith looked around the room and nodded her head in admiration. "Oh, yes, Rivera is quite an artist. Remember, girls, when we were studying last month about Michelangelo and the other Italian Renaissance painters? Well, Rivera has revived the fresco technique of painting with watercolors on wet plaster, but he's improved on it with his own scientific flair, and ..."

Alma wasn't listening. She was bored with Miss Galbraith's lecture. Who wanted to hear about these murals, the subject of which was dull, dull, dull? She, Alma, wanted to see something with beauty. And these had no beauty. As soon as there was a break in the crowd, she'd sneak away before Miss Galbraith discovered that she was gone. She didn't want Miss Galbraith to know that she wasn't the least bit interested in these murals.

She tuned out Miss Galbraith and listened instead to the excited voices around her:

"There it is. The vaccination panel!"

"That ain't really no vaccination panel. That's the Holy Family. Degrading. Halo around the baby's head. Blasphemous!"

"Look at that fat, ugly baby. Sacrilegious!"

"Look at them naked women on the east wall."

"Yeah. If that ain't pornographic, I don't know what is."

"And I hear that Commie artist got twenty thousand from old man Ford's son to do these. After all those men he laid off, too. Twenty thousand dollars would put a lot of men to work."

"All the people laid off in this city, some of the banks still closed, and they give twenty thousand dollars to some foreign Commie for art."

"And this ain't really art. Art ought to be beautiful. This ain't beautiful."

"This doesn't do the city of Detroit justice. It's a travesty. These walls should be painted over and they should get another artist to paint some murals with dignity befitting the city of Detroit."

"I agree. Maybe a graceful young woman draped in classic robes, holding a little automobile in one hand and a torch in the other."

"And look what they've done to this lovely Garden Court. They've mutilated it. I used to like to come here and sit and look at that fountain in the middle of the room, and just relax and take in the beauty. Now look at it."

It was stifling in the room filled with so many warm, excited people. Alma brushed back a lock from her perspiring brow.

Miss Galbraith's face was still happily animated as she continued her art lecture. Apparently, Purlie's father had asked her a question, because she was looking at him as she talked. He kept turning his battered slouch hat nervously in his hands and nodding in agreement with everything Miss Galbraith said.

"What style is it? I think Rivera incorporated art of the ancient Aztecs and Mayans with Cubism." Miss Galbraith looked around the room and her eyes got round again. "Oh, yes. I think it's truly an accurate portrayal of Detroit. But it doesn't matter what I or anyone else thinks. It's Rivera's interpretation. And long after you and I and everyone else in this room are dead and gone, people will still be coming here to see the murals. I think he's really captured our indomitable industrialism, which has made Detroit famous all over the world. It will take a lot of visits here to take it all in. And …"

And these murals are boring, thought Alma. And I was dumb to come here today. She looked around for an opening in the crowd. Should she pretend that she's sick and has to leave? No, she will wait until Miss Galbraith isn't looking at her, and sneak quickly away without explanation. Alma tuned out her teacher's voice again and listened to the crowd around her once more:

"Look how big he made those nude men in those pictures way up on both walls."

"Yeah. Much bigger'n the factory workers. Why you think he did that?"

"Maybe he didn't think the factory workers were very important."

"Yeah. Maybe. And look how sickly and bored some of the workers look. But I guess I'd look sickly and bored if I worked in a factory all day. After all, it doesn't take much brains to work in a factory, especially on a press."

Alma bit her lip. It doesn't take much brains to work in a factory, especially on a press. Why couldn't her father be smart like Mr. Carlson, and be in business for himself? She hated this room and all these murals.

A hush fell over the crowd. A man in a business suit walked to the edge of the large, stepped fountain in the center of the room. It was Dr. Valentiner, the director of the institute. Alma had seen him several times in the past as he walked purposefully from floor to floor, carrying important-looking papers.

Now. Now's a good time to sneak away. Miss Galbraith and the Washingtons were intent on looking at Dr. Valentiner, who had begun to speak to the crowd.

She turned and pushed her way through the throng, as it grudgingly made way for her. A few minutes later, she was at the front lobby again.

"'Night," she said with relief to her friend-guard.

"Don't you want to stay and hear about the murals, little lady?" Surprise registered on the guard's face as he opened one of the four big metal doors for her.

"I've heard enough about those murals," Alma said, hurrying out the door.

It was wonderfully cool outside. She breathed deeply of the fresh air.

It doesn't take much brains to work in a factory, especially on a press. It doesn't take much brains to work in a factory, especially on a press ...

She was ashamed of herself for being ashamed of her father for being only a factory worker. And only a coal miner before that. And she was ashamed of him for being fired from his dumb job, and for not being able to find another one, and for forcing them to move to that dump that was even worse than the last dump, and for being too proud to let her mother go out to work.

Where could she find some beauty today? She had to have some beauty every day, or she would wilt. What an ugly day this was! First there was seeing Miss Di Inganno grown so ugly, then moving into that wretchedly ugly flat and hearing those ugly shouts of the neighbors, then seeing that ugly eviction, and now that little-talent Purlie and her family and Miss Galbraith thinking those murals were so great, when really they were so ugly. She, Alma, knew what beauty was, even if they did not. Beauty was happy people, dressed in happy clothes, doing happy things. Where could she go today to sketch some beautiful thing? Must she resort to looking in the window at the new Graham-Paiges again?

Her lips turned up in a smile when she thought of the answer. She knew where she would go!

Alma patted the toes of Rodin's sculpture as usual, rushed down the wide steps of the institute, and hurried south. She buttoned her Salvation Army coat, grown even shabbier these past few months, with one hand and clutched her pocketbook containing her sketch pad and pencils with her other.

Fifteen minutes later she had reached her destination. Never before had she seen such luxurious and lovely gowns in one store window. Her eyes gleamed as she reached into her pocketbook and took out the pad and a pencil.

Alma worked quickly, oblivious to the curious and amused glances of the pedestrians who passed her while she stood engrossed in front of the huge J. L. Hudson Co. window. Here, at last, she had found some beauty. And here, at last, she was with her old friend. Her artistic talent was her old friend, one who would not fail her. As her father had.

Chapter 17

"Please, Ma, please!" Jimmie Lee wailed. "Let me have a little more milk. I'm starvin'!"

Alma saw her mother bite her trembling lip as she took the almost-empty bottle from the table and put it in the brown oak icebox. "Jimmie Lee, wish you could have all the milk you could drink. But you know this here's all there is. Carrie Lou ain't hardly had none, neither."

And I haven't had any for weeks, Alma thought. She looked at her brother's thin face across the table. Jimmie Lee was going through a growing spurt. He reminded her of the Life Everlasting weed back in Mountainview that suddenly shot up in the springtime. She'd been studying about nutrition lately in Miss Nelson's class. At Jimmie Lee's age, he needed lots of milk and good food.

"Reckon I can stir up a mess a bulldog gravy for you directly," Lizzie said. She walked toward the coal stove.

"Bulldog gravy. Bulldog gravy. That ain't nothin' but flour an' water an' a speck a grease. I'm sick a bulldog gravy! I want some milk!" Jimmie Lee looked at his father sitting next to him. Chet had suddenly picked up the latest United Farm Agency catalog from the table. He opened it at a random page and began to read.

Why did her father always have his nose in that dumb catalog, Alma wondered. If we don't have enough money for milk, we certainly don't have enough for a farm. Alma felt a tinge of guilt. She herself had three cents left from the money she earned babysitting for Mrs. Carlson. But she was going to buy a Saturday *Detroit Free Press* with that. Alma had become an avid reader of the "Chatterbox" society column.

It seemed every day she read about a member of one of the clubs Mrs. Carlson belonged to. It might be the beautiful Mrs. Farrington, reported planning a cruise to Nassau, or maybe the fashionable Mrs. Van Delore, glimpsed stepping into her new LaSalle while wearing an afternoon jacket dress by Schiaparelli with elbow-length pleated sleeves and a huge satin bow.

Mrs. Carlson. Alma's mouth twisted slightly. She was secretly irritated with Mrs. Carlson for being on another vacation. This time it was a visit to Kentucky for the Derby. Mrs. Carlson should be staying home more so Alma could earn some money.

"Jimmie Lee," Lizzie said. She bit her lip again and glanced at Chet before continuing. "Maybe--Maybe you should go wait in that line down there in the street."

A distressed look crossed Chet's face. "No, Lizzie. No. Ain't none a us goin' to wait in no bread line," he said. He got up from the table and began to sweep the floor.

Jimmie Lee glared at his father. "Why you always sweepin' the floor an' makin' beds an' doin' dishes around here? That's Ma's work. A pa's work should be out a the house. Only Ma an' Alma May's supposed to do housework!"

"Jimmie Lee! You apologize to your Pa! Right now!" Lizzie said.

Chet stopped sweeping and rested the broom against the sink counter. "It's all right, Lizzie," he said, his voice low and barely audible. He returned slowly to the table, picked up the farm catalog, and walked with bent head and stooped shoulders into the bedroom. He closed the door behind him.

"Pa sick. Jimmie Lee bad boy. Pa sick. Jimmie Lee bad boy," Carrie Lou said. She picked up her bowl and licked the last of the oatmeal, slid down from her chair and ran toward the bedroom. "Carrie Lou kiss Pa. Carrie Lou kiss Pa."

Alma frowned. Carrie Lou's always kissing. Kissing, kissing, kissing. If she's not kissing one of us, she's kissing Uncle Darcas.

There was a knock on the door that led to the hallway outside. The knock sounded again before Alma could reach the door to answer it.

The caller, a young woman carrying a baby, had her fist raised to knock once more when Alma opened the door. "Please," she whispered, "my husband'll be back in a few minutes. He don't want me to be borryin'. But my baby, she's so hungry. She's just cravin' some milk, and I'm all dried up, and no money to buy none. Do you think you could let me have a little, just until ..."

Alma didn't know what to do. The woman glanced around the hallway and then stepped into the room and closed the door behind her.

"We live in the flat next door," she said in a rush. "My husband, he's so proud. Been lookin' for work for months, but there's just nothin'. Too proud to let me wait in a bread line, too. Please, just a little milk," she pleaded, her deep-circled eyes fixed first on Alma, then on Lizzie and Jimmie Lee.

Alma glanced at her mother's worried face, then at Jimmie Lee, who sat staring at the baby. In between whimpers, the baby chewed on its fist or the flowered bodice of its mother's cotton housedress.

Lizzie looked at Jimmie Lee, but he avoided his mother's pleading eyes and turned his gaze to his empty cereal bowl.

Lizzie's strained face turned first toward the icebox, then to Jimmie Lee and Alma, then to the baby, who had deep circles around its eyes, too, and then back again to the icebox. "I, I reckon you can have a little."

Jimmie Lee stared angrily at his mother. He blinked his eyes and his chin began to tremble. He jumped up from the table and ran toward the door.

"Jimmie Lee! Jimmie Lee! Come back!" Lizzie cried. But Jimmie Lee was halfway down the stairs leading to the street below.

Why isn't there school on Saturdays, so I could be away from here, Alma thought, as she grabbed her worn cardigan from the closet. Away from her father, who seldom went outside of the flat anymore and was no fun to be around. Away from her mother, who was yacking more and more these days and interrupting Alma's thoughts by quoting President Roosevelt from the Detroit *Free Press*, when they were lucky enough to find a used one. Away from Carrie Lou, who--

"Don't forget, Alma May," Lizzie said, in spite of her distress over the unexpected caller, "fetch a poke an' pick some a them dandelion greens--the young, tender'n's."

Alma did not heed her mother. She was not going to pick dandelion greens for supper. She hurried down the stairs and slammed the door of the flat behind her. She hoped none of her classmates had seen her exiting. She didn't want them to know she'd moved into one of the low-rent flats around here. And she'd die if they saw her picking dandelion greens.

If only Miss Galbraith hadn't been sick and away from school this past week! Miss Galbraith would've given her some art supplies to use at the art institute. That substitute teacher, Miss Leslie--she watched the students like a hawk, and every piece of canvas, every jar of tempera, every brush was accounted for. Alma jingled the three pennies in the pocket of her shabby skirt. Three pennies would not buy art supplies to start another oil painting, but it would buy a society page. She smiled in anticipation.

Alma picked up a copy of the newspaper at the next corner. Where could she go to savor it alone, in peace? She glanced up at the dark clouds above the J. L. Hudson building; they were moving in her direction. Could she make it to Hudson's quiet and comfortable women's lounge on the thirteenth floor before a downpour? She decided not, and noticed a park bench in a clearing. Maybe she could sneak a look at the "Chatterbox" column before returning to the gloom of the flat.

But as soon as she'd settled on the bench and opened the paper, a young boy of about six or seven approached and shoved a filthy hand under her nose.

"Got a coupla pennies for some milk, lady? I ain't had nothin' to drink but water for days." The boy's voice sounded surprisingly childish, for his face looked old and wise.

Alma frowned in annoyance at the wispy figure. She felt flattered at being addressed as a lady, but guilty because she was reminded of Jimmie Lee's begging for milk.

Alma shook her head no. "Why don't you wait in one of the bread lines? There're plenty of them around."

"Takes hours to get to the front of the line and they don't got no milk left in any of 'em. I waited in all of 'em."

"Sorry," Alma said. She looked down at the paper again and turned toward the society pages. *It was her three cents, and she had a right to spend it on a paper if she pleased, didn't she?* But she raised her eyes and watched the boy while he walked away, a dejected figure in baggy overalls. He

looked vaguely familiar. Alma strained to remember. Was he the same
boy who had begged money from them at that Hooverville her mother
had dragged them to that Sunday? But Alma didn't want to think of
babies and boys wanting milk. She wanted to read about the wedding
at St. Hugo's chapel in Birmingham that morning and the cabaret party
at the Colony Club that night.

She scanned the pages, and noted that "free-form flower patterns
rival dots, stripes, and broken checks in new fabric designs," that--

"I'll bet you don't have a Bible as nice as this at home," a voice
above her said.

Alma, startled, looked up from the paper and saw an old woman
standing in front of her. She was dressed all in black, including a scarf
that almost covered the coarse white hair protruding from under it. In
one hand she held a Bible, which she pushed forward for Alma to see.
In the other, a peeling leatherette bag filled with something.

The woman sat down beside Alma. "See?" she said. "The cover
is genuine leather. And the pages, they're edged in gold." She shoved
the Bible under Alma's nose and flipped the pages. "And look at these
full-color illustrations."

Alma moved farther away from the woman, and held the paper to
the side to block her view of her. She pursed her lips and began again
to skim the page. Hudson's offered complete luncheons for fifty cents.
Afternoon frock in the new non-crushable linen--

"What you reading, young lady?"

Alma set her lips even tighter and continued to read.

"What you reading?"

Alma stared at her paper, but did not know what she was reading now--

"You reading the religion page?"

"No."

"Well, what you reading?"

"The society page," Alma said, her voice flat.

The woman made a clucking sound with her tongue against the
roof of her mouth. "The society page. The society page. Now, why
you want to read about all those selfish people's comings and goings
and spending all that money on silly things at a time like this, with all
these people hungry and out of work? Those selfish people should--"

Alma slammed her paper down on her lap, and rose from the bench. The woman reached up and grabbed her by the arm.

Alma looked down at the woman's face. It was as wrinkled as a dried apple. It reminded her of how Miss Di Inganno probably looked without makeup. "Leave me alone! I've got a right to read what I want!"

"You should be reading this fine Bible." The woman shoved the Bible up toward Alma again.

Alma shook loose from the woman's grasp and sloppily folded the newspaper as she began to walk away.

"Look at you," the woman yelled after her. "Dressed in those old worn clothes and worrying about what high society is doing! 'Pride goeth before destruction, and a haughty spirit before a fall!'"

Alma hurried toward home. Half a block later, she heard the woman's shout: "'Pride goeth before destruction, and a haughty spirit before a fall!'"

Alma didn't know what the old hag meant by that and didn't care. She looked down at her clothes. Her lower lip began to tremble like Jimmie Lee's had. If even that old woman had observed how worn her clothes were, then everyone else must, too. Oh, she was sick to death of her old clothes, and--

Alma saw the small, familiar figure of a young boy in the line ahead. No. It couldn't be. When she drew closer, she saw that it really was whom she feared. Jimmie Lee, how could you? Wait in line for a handout.

Alma slowed to a casual walk to avoid drawing attention to herself. As she approached her brother, his glance met hers. He turned his face away.

She passed him and whispered, barely moving her lips, "Get out of this line. Don't you have any pride?" She continued walking casually, even though the clouds still threatened rain. She glanced at the faces of the others to see if anyone there might recognize them. No. Thank heaven for that.

Alma turned around to see whether Jimmie Lee was still in line. Yes. Looking down at his feet. His glance met hers again, and he gave her the same pathetic look he'd given her mother before.

Jimmie Lee sprang from the line and ran in the direction opposite of home. Alma was relieved, but wondered where he was going.

She felt a sprinkle of rain on her forehead and hurried again, glad that soon there would be fewer bread lines to pass. Last week Lizzie had read aloud from the *Free Press* to anyone who would listen that the President had appointed a Mr. Hopkins to head a federal emergency food relief agency. Soon most of these people would be getting food from a commodity office. Her mother said they would apply for it, too. Well, she, Alma, would never go to a government office for free food! And she knew her father would not, either. Lizzie and Jimmie Lee could go if they wanted. "But it's all right to get a little food from the government, Alma May," her mother had said, "just until the country gets back on its feet. Whatever President Roosevelt thinks is all right, must be all right. Why, President Roosevelt is treatin' us folks with respect, an' ..."

Roosevelt, Roosevelt, Roosevelt. Her mother was always talking about Roosevelt these days. As if he were God, or something.

When Alma drew nearer home, she was surprised to see an ambulance parked in front of her flat. Her heartbeat quickened along with her steps. An ambulance! What was the matter? Who was sick? Or ...

A crowd was forming around the long white vehicle with a flashing light on top. Oh, God, don't let it be Pa! Alma started to run.

Pa, Pa, I'm sorry for the way I've been treating you lately, thought Alma. If you're spared again this time, I'll do anything. I'll even pretend about The Farm.

Alma pushed her way through the crowd. She felt a nervous sensation in her stomach, like during that other awful time.

A police officer was approaching a squad car. He had his arm around a young woman. The same woman who had begged the milk from them earlier!

The woman was murmuring with lips almost as white as her face: "My baby. My baby. He's beat my baby to death. He's beat my poor baby to death. It's not true. It's not true. He loved the baby. He loved the baby. ..."

It's not Pa! It's not Pa!

The officer helped the woman into the car as another officer pushed a man in, also. The man had handcuffs on, and, even though his head was bent low, Alma could see a glazed expression in his eyes.

"That must be her husband," someone in the crowd said.

"How could anyone beat his own baby to death?" someone else asked.

Alma ran toward the door to the flat. She must see Pa and know that he was really all right. And Ma, and Carrie Lou, too. She almost collided with two white-uniformed men carrying a stretcher. Alma looked down at the sheet, which rose slightly in the middle from a small lump under it. She was struck with the fleeting thought that how ridiculous it was for two men to carry such a light load.

She ran up the stairs and pushed open the door to the flat. Lizzie was sitting in her father's chair, rocking Carrie Lou.

"Where's Pa?" asked Alma.

Lizzie nodded toward the bedroom.

Alma ran into the room. Her father lay on the bed with the open farm catalog by his side. He was staring, expressionless, at the chipped plaster in the ceiling.

"Pa," Alma said. Her voice was softer as she repeated again, "Pa."

Her father continued to stare at the ceiling.

"Oh, Pa. You're okay." Her father's face didn't change as Alma waited for him to speak. "Oh, Pa, say something." Alma reached down and shook his hand. "Talk to me. Talk to me!"

He turned his eyes slowly toward her.

"Pa," Alma whispered. "You're all right. You're all right. I was so afraid. . . ."

"A course I'm all right. Why did you think I wasn't, baby?"

"Because of the ambulance."

"Ambulance?"

"The ambulance. Down in the street."

"Ambulance in the str...e...e t?"

Alma hurried from the bedroom and stood over her mother, who was still rocking Carrie Lou. "What's wrong with Pa?" she asked.

"Don't know. He's been layin' there all mornin', not sayin' a word. Not even when that poor woman pounded on the door screamin' for help. Not even when I went to call the policeman--"

"She was here again?"

"Yes, but it was already too late. The poor little thing was already dead."

"Why? Why did that man kill his own baby?" Alma felt her eyes moisten.

"I, I'm still wonderin' how he could. Reckon he just couldn't stand no more cryin'."

"I thought when I left that you were going to give her the last of the milk for the baby."

"I did. But the poor little thing was still hungry for more. An' pretty soon I could hear it cryin' an' cryin' an' cryin'. An' pretty soon I could hear him yellin', an' the woman cryin', an'--"

"Oh, Ma. Stop. I don't want to hear any more," Alma said. She collapsed into a chair by the table. She suddenly felt very tired. Alma folded her arms on the table and rested her head on them.

"Did you see Jimmie Lee?" asked Lizzie.

"Uh, no," Alma said, shutting from her mind the picture of him running from the line. She casually picked up the newspaper, which had fallen to the floor in a messy pile as she hurried into the room. At last she could look at the society page in peace. Even though she was no longer in the mood, maybe reading the newspaper would help to blot out the memory of her brother's face, and that poor baby, and her father lying listless on the bed, and that old woman on the park bench, and …

She heard a crack of lightning, followed by a rumble of thunder. She'd gotten home just in time.

"Where could he be?" Lizzie asked.

Alma lifted her head. The room had grown dark, even though it was only late morning. She lit the kerosene lamp on the table. Her mother had the electricity shut off to save money.

Carrie Lou pulled her thumb out of her mouth to comment. "Jimmie Lee not here." She stuck it back in.

Alma laid the paper flat on the table. She was about to turn to the society section when a familiar name on the front page caught her eye.

Her eyes widened and her mouth parted. No. It couldn't be true! Alma read the short item again:

> "An elderly man dressed in woman's clothes was found dead in his flat in the 6100 block of 15th street yesterday afternoon. Coroner's examination revealed death was caused by starvation.
>
> No food was found in the flat's cupboards, but empty cans of cat food were discovered in the bedroom. Police surmise he had been existing on the cat food, since no trace of an animal was found.

Memorabilia of the late movie idol Rudolph Valentino were pinned on the flat's walls along with that of other movie stars. On the table were other Valentino mementoes, including a small bust of the actor dressed as The Sheik, from the movie of the same name, and an empty cigar box with his picture on it. Beside a tin box, which also had his picture on it, was an envelope containing a ten dollar bill and addressed to the caretaker at Hollywood Memorial Park Cemetery in Hollywood, Calif.

"The man's landlord, who found the body, said the man was known as Miss Di Inganno, who came from Hollywood. He said he was shocked to learn that the tenant was a man.

Police are searching for the man's relatives."

Alma rose from her chair and walked into the bedroom, still holding the paper. "Pa," she whispered, barely getting the word out. "I, I can't believe it's true. Miss Di Inganno is a …"

Her father was still lying in the same position and looking at the ceiling. Alma, beginning to get a little impatient with him, left the room. She silently gave the paper to her mother to read and pointed to the item. She lay down on the day bed. It was not true. Miss Di Inganno was not a man. It was not true.

"Poor creature," said Lizzie, after quickly reading the item. "Poor, tormented creature."

Carrie Lou pulled her thumb from her mouth again and mimicked her mother. "Poor kweecher. Poor, tormennen kweecher." She stuck her thumb back into her mouth once more and, after a minute pulled it out again. "Pa sick. Baby dead. Jimmie Lee not here."

Oh, be still, Carrie Lou, Alma thought. I want to fall asleep. Maybe if I fall asleep and wake up I'll find this day never happened.

She suddenly remembered the fishy smell of Miss Di Inganno's flat. So, that was it. That was it. It was cat food.

Alma closed her eyes. The thunder and lightning had stopped and she was able to doze off in spite of the sound of the heavy rain on the roof. Fragments of scenes drifted into dreams. There was her father, lying on his bed, staring at empty cat food cans, which were nailed to the ceiling. There was Jimmie Lee, running after five men in white uniforms who were carrying a stretcher with a sheet protruding slightly in the middle. There was the old woman standing by a bench selling cat food labeled "Bible." The woman's scarf flew off in the thunderstorm and Alma saw that she was not the woman by the bench but really Miss Di Inganno. But Miss Di Inganno wasn't really Miss Di Inganno, but--

Lizzie's voice awakened Alma. "Alma May. Alma May."

Her mother was tapping her on the shoulder. "Alma May, you take care a Carrie Lou while I go an' look for Jimmie Lee. He should a come home long ago before it started rainin' so hard. It's almost supper time."

Alma, thankful that her dream was interrupted, rubbed her eyes and sat up.

"Want me to go, Mom?" she asked. "I know better where to look."

"No," Lizzie replied. "Reckon I have to look for him myself. I can't bear waitin' no longer." She closed the door behind her.

Alma was grateful that Carrie Lou was asleep. She didn't want to put up with her slobbery kisses and having to reward her for them with pinches of sugar.

She peeked into the bedroom. Her father still lay in the same position, but his eyes were closed now. Carrie Lou slept beside him.

Alma felt hungry. She avoided looking in the icebox, because of the memory of Jimmie Lee and the milk. Nothing in the cupboard but a box of oatmeal a third full, a sack of cornmeal almost empty, and a bowl containing about half a cup of sugar. The bean pot was on the stove. One-third full of watery beans. Her mother had extended them for several days. Alma frowned, but filled a bowl. After finishing it, she was still hungry, but dared not take more. She filled her stomach with four glasses of warm water from the teakettle and pretended it was good, hot soup.

Several hours dragged by. Alma tried to concentrate on the paper, but couldn't. What was taking her mother so long? Had she found Jimmie Lee?

She heard the door open finally. Lizzie walked in, her clothes sopping wet. Alma had never seen her mother so tired-looking, her face so drawn from worry.

"Been all over. Ain't nobody seen'm."

Lizzie took off her soaked oxfords at the door and laid them on a newspaper to drain. She walked with great effort into the bedroom to change her clothes.

Back in the living room, she flopped down in a chair at the table. "Where could he be?" she cried.

"Oh, he'll probably be home any minute now," Alma said.

"Where could he be? Where could he be? He ain't never been gone so long before." Lizzie leaned her elbows on the table and rested her head in her hands. "An' the way he left, so hurt an' cryin' for milk." She slowly rose and shuffled into the bedroom again.

From the day bed, Alma heard her mother pleading, "Chet. Chet. Wake up. Jimmie Lee. He ain't home yet." After a moment, she continued. "Wake up, Chet. It's dark out an' still rainin' an' Jimmie Lee still ain't home."

"Jimmie Lee…ain't…home…yet?" Alma's father finally asked, his voice weak and barely audible. "He been…gone?"

Lizzie came back to where Alma sat. "You pick them dandelion greens, Alma May? Figure I just a soon be cleanin'em as settin' here not doin' nothin', just a waitin' an' waitin'."

"Forgot, Mom," Alma lied. How could her mother remember the dandelion greens at a time like this?

Her father entered the room, dragged to the sink, and filled a glass with water from the faucet.

How messy he looks, thought Alma, with his wrinkled shirt hanging out of his baggy pants, his hair falling down over his eyes. About as limp and listless as something a cat would drag in.

"How long's Jimmie Lee been gone?" her father asked, fully awake now.

"Since early this mornin'," replied Lizzie. "He was cryin' for milk when he ran out a here. I been all over lookin' for him. If he don't come home soon, we'll have to call a policeman to find him."

Seeing her parents' concern, Alma frowned in concern, too. Where could Jimmie Lee be all this time? He didn't have any money for the pinball machine. He didn't have the price of a child's ticket to see Clyde Beatty in *The Big Cage* at the Fox. And even a double feature would've been over long ago.

She thought again of her little brother in that line and the look on his face when he ran from it. She thought, too, of the three cents she'd spent on the *Free Press*. She gathered up the newspaper and threw it into the wastebasket.

"What you doin' that for, Alma May?" her mother asked. "You know you shouldn't waste paper like that. Why, we can use that for lots a things. Like linin' our shoes, an'--"

Lizzie was interrupted by a knock on the door. She rushed to answer it, moving with unusual speed for her.

An unsmiling police officer stood in the hallway with an arm around a frightened Jimmie Lee.

"You this boy's mother?" the officer asked, as he took his hat from his head. His voice was stern.

Lizzie slowly nodded her head.

"Your son was picked up early this afternoon. Stole a bottle of milk from the Risdon Dairy. He's been at the station for hours, afraid to tell his name, finally did."

Lizzie found her voice at last. "Oh, Jimmie Lee. Jimmie Lee."

Jimmie Lee rushed to his mother and buried his face in her belly.

"We'll let him go this time, m'am. I think he's learned his lesson," the officer said. "But if it happens again, it will be on his record."

Jimmie Lee ran to his father and covered his face with his hands. He pushed his head into Chet's thin chest.

Alma, who stood by the doorway now, heard the officer whisper to her mother in a gentler tone: "Don't be too harsh on him, Mrs. Combs. People'll do anything for food sometimes." He smiled sympathetically as he put on his hat and left.

Lizzie slowly closed the door and turned around. Her face was colorless.

She looked Chet straight in the eye, and said in a voice firmer than Alma had ever before heard her use: "I'm goin' out an' lookin' for a job tomorrow mornin'."

Chapter 18

T he early evening light filtering through the fluttering leaves
above made dancing shadows on the brown paper sack that
Alma was using as drawing paper. She sat leaning against a
large oak in the woods that had been home for the Combses these
past few weeks. The woods were located at a busy intersection on the
outskirts of the city of Dearborn, adjacent to Detroit's west side. She
sketched from a library art book. Carrie Lou, at Alma's side, crooned to
the doll Lizzie had fashioned from rags too small for any other purpose.

Alma found it hard to concentrate on the frolicking rococo scene
by Fragonard: The rumbling noise in her empty stomach would not be
stilled. It competed with the same noise from Carrie Lou's. The rumbles
were getting so frequent now, it was difficult to tell from whose stomach
they came. She wished her mother would get home with her pay so that
Jimmie Lee could run to the store to buy something for supper.

Alma thought about how proud her mother had been when she
returned home from her first day of work and showed them the two
dollar bills she'd earned. To think of it! Her mother had actually gone
to a pay phone and answered an ad for an "honest, reliable, experienced,
mature woman" to clean once a week for a "generous wage." She had
gotten on a Department of Street Railways bus all by herself, and
transferred to two more buses before getting to her first cleaning job
in Grosse Pointe, a city bordering Detroit's east side. Mrs. Gottleib had
been so pleased with Lizzie's scrubbing and polishing and waxing the
fifteen-room Tudor, that she had told her friends at the Colony Club.
Before long, Lizzie was taking the ninety-minute trip each way Monday

through Saturday. She was paid two dollars a day at each of the houses, but carfare was eating up one-third of that. Every night that she was fortunate enough to have a newspaper given to her, Lizzie would scan the classified ads to find jobs closer to home.

The rumbling noise sounded from Alma's stomach again. She'd just die if she didn't eat soon!

"Carrie Lou hungry, Alma May," Carrie Lou cried, rubbing her own stomach. "Ma home soon?" She nodded her head and looked up through pleading blue eyes at Alma.

Alma didn't answer, but looked around the woods. Her eyes grew sad when she saw her father in the distance, still sitting in the dilapidated wooden kitchen chair near the entrance to the Combses' home, a makeshift tent. He had been sitting in the same position for hours, staring down--at what she did not know. If he wasn't sitting in the chair, thought Alma, he was lying on the cot pretending to be asleep. What did he think about all day long, and why wouldn't he say hardly a word to anyone? Alma had made every effort to draw him out, but to no avail. Where was Mr. Buckingham when her father needed him most?

She thought how disgraceful it was to have had to move here among all these people, some so dirty looking and dirty talking. This was almost as bad as that Hooverville where Mr. McLaughlin lived. She and her family had come here when they could no longer pay the rent on the flat, and the landlord had suggested this place. They sold even more of their belongings to scrape together enough money to pay the dollar to the property owner for one week's rent and to buy a big piece of used tarpaulin, which Lizzie had patched with scraps of canvas. They had piled their remaining possessions into Uncle Darcas's Model T and had come here to set up a place to live under the tarpaulin, between a family from Ohio and a man from Dearborn.

"Carrie Lou hungry, Alma May," Carrie Lou whined again.

Alma looked down at her baby sister. She was filthy from playing in the woods! Alma would have to clean her up before her mother got home. "Ain't no excuse for us to be dirty, Alma May, even if we're poor," her mother would say, "but be careful, an' don't waste no soap."

"Mom will be here soon, Carrie Lou," Alma said.

If only there were even some prunes or salt pork left from the family allotment her mother got from the new government Surplus Commodity Department. But they were used up days ago, along with the flour and lard.

She glanced over at her father again. Poor Pa. Still in the same position. They even had to sell his favorite old Morris chair. Her gaze shifted to the trailer next to the Combses' area. There was that man from Dearborn, the one who loved to talk so much. He was raking around his trailer, pretending he had a real yard or something. She tried to avoid him, The Philosopher, as the woods people called him, whenever she could. Alma did not want to get trapped into talking about Technocracy, whatever that was, or Socialism, or--

"You do portraits, honey?"

Alma looked up, startled. It was that vulgar woman from two trailers away standing over her; the one that the other renters called a floozie. She did not like this middle-aged woman with her bleached hair, black at the scalp (Missus Carlson's, though bleached, was soft and natural looking), or her overpowering Evening in Paris perfume. Most of all, she did not like this woman because of the way she'd been flaunting herself in front of Alma's father.

"Pay you if you draw a pitchure a me. Ain't had my pitchure done in a long time." The woman smiled down at Alma, showing dark, neglected teeth.

"I don't do portraits," Alma said, her tone curt.

"Ah, please, honey. It'll only take a few minutes."

"I don't have the right kind of paper for doing portraits," Alma said in a flat voice. She did not like being addressed as "honey" by strangers, particularly this woman. Alma looked down at the Fragonard painting and resumed copying it with her penny pencil.

"Just use some a that paper bag. There's a whole nickel waitin' for you here in my pocket for just one little old pitchure." The woman patted the pocket of her dirty, too-tight dress. She sat down next to Carrie Lou, who was staring at the woman's red lipsticked mouth.

"Wed! Wed!" Carrie Lou said as she reached up and touched the woman's lips, her eyes big with fascination.

"Ain't she the cutest little thing?" the woman said. She patted Carrie Lou's head.

Carrie Lou puckered up her mouth and leaned over and kissed the woman on the lips.

"Well, ain't that cute, now," the woman said. She bent down and returned the kiss on Carrie Lou's cheek.

"Carrie Lou want nickel now," Carrie Lou said, holding out her palm.

"Well, don't that take the cake," the woman said. "Gives me a kiss and then wants a nickel for it." She shook her head. "Ain't got no more nickels, honey. Just one for your sister."

A nickel. A whole nickel! If Alma had a nickel she could walk to the store and buy a whole loaf of bread. Her stomach began to growl again. "Well," she said to the woman, "maybe I could try a portrait."

The woman lost no time in sitting erect and striking a pose. "Which side do you prefer? My right or left profile?" she asked, turning her head from side to side.

"Oh, the left would be good." She would get this over quickly. She took a large piece of brown sack paper and began. Visions of fresh, sliced Bond bread bounced in her brain. She did not care to draw the woman as she truly looked. She disregarded her sagging jowls and gave her a smooth, firm chin line. She ignored the puffy eyelids and lines around the eyes. The worldly hardness in the eyes was replaced by a soft innocence. Alma finished the sketch by framing the face in a cloud of pale hair as soft as an angel's.

"There," Alma said. She handed the picture to the woman. Now she wanted the nickel.

"Oh, you flatter me," she cried. "I ain't looked that good in years. Wait till my man sees this!"

Which man? Alma wondered. She'd heard that the woman had many. Did she mean her husband, who was gone half the time and drunk the other half?

The woman rose and reached into the pocket of her dress. Her brow puckered in surprise. "Well, if that don't take the cake! My nickel! Where'd my nickel go to?" She poked the toe of her peeling patent leather pump into the grass where she'd been sitting, and stooped down. "It was in my pocket just a minute ago," she said, patting the grass with both hands.

The image of the Bond bread disappeared from Alma's head.

"Forget it," Alma said, trying to hide her disappointment. In her pocket, my eye, she thought. She never intended to give me a nickel. She never had a nickel any more than I do.

The woman walked away with the sketch in her hand. She turned her head back and called, "You draw real pretty-like! I'll bring you a nickel tomorrow when my man comes home. Honest."

Alma leaned back against the oak. What a dummy she'd been, wasting her talent on someone like that. She'd never fall for such a trick again.

If only their share of the thrift garden planted by the Combses and the other woods people was ripe. The sprouts were just now pushing up and it would be weeks before anything could be eaten.

"Alma May! Alma May!"

Oh, Lord, it was Uncle Darcas coming her way now. From the direction opposite the one the woman had taken. Here just in time again for Ma to get home with the money for supper. Maybe there'd be enough to go around if Uncle Darcas didn't hog half of it. And look at that belly protruding from his unbuttoned shirt. Jiggling like Jell-O with every step. What does he want this time? He must know after all these years that I can't stand the sight of him. And I'm getting more and more annoyed with him lately, if that were possible. The way he seems to be gloating over our misfortunes, our having to move here and all. And never once offering to let us stay with him and Aunt Euella. Like before when he never offered when we moved from that other flat. And the way he seems to be getting happier and happier the worse Pa gets.

"Unka Darcas coming," Carrie Lou said, pointing to her uncle.

He was standing over them now. "Alma May, they's havin' a party!"

A party. Who was he trying to kid? Who in this place could afford a party? Alma's lips curled up in a sneer.

"'pon my honor, if they ain't. An' they's plenty for all, they says. They's roastin' a piece a meat big as this." Her uncle spread his arms apart as wide as he could. Dark hairs curled around his navel. She winced and turned her head away.

"Sure as a skunk stinks, they are, Alma May! Reckon we better hurry before everybody here smells that tantalizin' aroma with all the juices drippin', an' the outside gettin' all crusty brown-like, an'--"

Uncle Darcas stuck out his tongue and circled his huge lips with it. "Reckon if it ain't about the best meat I ever tasted. They already give me a bite."

"Carrie Lou hungry, Alma May," Carrie Lou cried. "Carrie Lou go with Unka Darcas." She jumped up and grabbed her uncle's hand as her doll fell from her lap.

Uncle Darcas began to walk away with Carrie Lou as Alma stood up. "Carrie Lou! You stay here! I'm supposed to be watching you!"

She ran after them. "Uncle Darcas! Leave her here! Ma wouldn't want her to go! And she'll be home any minute!"

Alma caught up with them. She'd pretend to go along, and as soon as Uncle Darcas let go of Carrie Lou's hand, she'd grab her and run home.

"Where is this party?" Alma asked, carrying on with the pretense.

"Down at the end a the woods. Where that family what's got all them young'n's is," her uncle said. He licked his lips again in anticipation as he began to walk faster. Carrie Lou was having difficulty keeping up with him, so he bent down and scooped her up into his arms.

They were in view of the family's ramshackle hut now. It was true! There was a huge chunk of meat being roasted. The mother and father and what appeared to be all of their fifteen barefoot children stood around a pit sloppily fashioned from cement blocks. The meat sizzled on what looked to be an automobile radiator grille. The aroma wafted toward Alma. How delicious it smelled!

"See? What I tell you, Alma May? You thought your ol' Uncle Darcas was funnin' you, didn't you?" Uncle Darcas said accusingly. He lowered Carrie Lou to the ground.

Alma's stomach growled again. She hadn't had meat since that salt pork days and days ago. She wondered what kind of meat it was--pork? beef? And where this family could have gotten it. She figured them to be worse off than her own family.

Alma scanned their unkempt faces. They were all silently chewing. No one was speaking. If this were a party, why weren't they smiling and having fun?

The smoke from the sizzling meat floated toward her. Oh, how good it smelled! Meanwhile, Jimmie Lee and other children from all around the woods were gathering near the fire, their eyes big.

"Can this young lady have some a your meat?" Uncle Darcas asked.

The family glanced at one another. Then they all looked at whom Alma took to be the head of the family, as if for approval. The man stopped chewing and after a moment he spoke. "Help yourselves."

An old man who Alma hadn't noticed before was sitting on the ground, resting against a tree. He pulled a jug from his mouth long enough to shake his head and say, "What's this country comin' to? What's this country comin' to?"

Uncle Darcas bent down and picked up a knife that lay on top of one of the cement blocks. He sliced a big chunk of meat and placed it on an empty tin plate. He shoved it toward Alma.

Alma looked down at the meat. The savory aroma teased her nostrils again. How delicious it looked! Uncle Darcas was right. It was cooked to perfection, with the outside all browned and the inside all juicy. But she hated to take food from this family. And they all looked so dirty. Still--even if her mother was getting off the bus right at this very moment with her money, it would be like an eternity before they could eat.

"Carrie Lou want some!" Carrie Lou cried, reaching for Alma's meat.

Alma grabbed the meat from the plate before Carrie Lou could, and bit into it as Uncle Darcas watched. It was tougher than she thought it would be, and tasted like no meat she had ever tasted, but she was so hungry.

"Can we have some, too? Please! Please!" cried Jimmie Lee and the other children around Alma.

"Reckon it's dog eat dog around here!" Uncle Darcas said, in a voice loud enough to be heard over the begging children. He snorted his noisy pig-like laugh and slapped his thigh.

Alma quickly swallowed her share and smiled shyly at the head of the family.

"Here, Alma May. Have some more," Uncle Darcas said as he snatched the knife before anyone else could. He cut off another big chunk and put it on her plate.

Alma ate it slowly this time, letting the juices trickle on her tongue before swallowing. All the while, Uncle Darcas watched her, a grin spreading across his face.

The old man sitting next to the tree pulled the jug from his mouth again and looked up at Alma. "Girl, don't you know what you're eatin'? You're eatin' dog."

Alma stopped chewing. Her eyes widened. "D, Dog?" She shook her head slowly and looked all around at the family. A silence fell on the group again. Some of them stopped chewing and looked down at the ground. "Not true. Not dog," she whispered. She looked at the head of the family. His glance met hers, and he nodded yes.

Alma dropped her plate and bent her head low and spat on the ground, but she'd already swallowed the last bite.

She spun around and ran toward home, forgetting about Carrie Lou and Jimmie Lee and Uncle Darcas, forgetting about everything but getting away from there. *Dog! Dog meat! I've eaten dog meat!*

She heard Uncle Darcas's raucous belly laugh behind her. "The high muckymuck Alma May Combs eats dog meat. The Famous Arteest Alma May Combs dines on dog meat!" he shouted after her. She felt the vomit rushing to her throat as another of his laughs followed her, but she did not stop running. *Oh, Uncle Darcas is cruel, cruel! I hate him! I hate him!*

The vomit gushed from her mouth and splattered on the front of her dress and on the bushes that tore at her face and arms as she ran. "Pa! Pa!" she cried.

Chapter 19

Maybe if he sat there a while longer and concentrated real hard, he could gather enough strength to get up from the chair and stir the pot of beans. That was his job for the day. Stirring the pot of beans. Before leaving for the bus stop that morning, Lizzie had insisted they be cooked all day long so that they wouldn't spoil from the summer's heat. Alma May and Jimmie Lee did not like to see him doing woman's work, so he tried to do it when they were away. The icebox had been sold for a quarter. But even if they still had it, they couldn't spare the dime for the chunk of ice needed every day in this hot weather.

Chet strained his memory to recall where Alma May had said she and Carrie Lou were going. Where Jimmie Lee was, he didn't know and didn't have the strength to go and find out.

Chet's head was bent and his eyes were focused on an ant crawling on the ground below him. He envied its strength and determination as it wove its way around the stones and twigs and bits of paper. The ant was carrying a crumb of bread on its back three times its own size. Probably taking it home for his family. It was a provider. Chet was not.

Oh, how he'd failed! He'd failed miserably at everything. He could not be depended on for anything anymore. He hoped he wouldn't fail with the beans.

At first, long ago, he'd tried so hard to find another job after Standish fired him. How he had tried! How optimistic he'd been those first few weeks. Foolishly optimistic, looking back at it now. He'd actually thought that someone would want his services and pay him for them. How long ago was that? The exertion of trying to remember was too much. ...

Chet looked down at his body. His clothes hung on his frame like rags on a scarecrow. He knew he should eat more. His appetite was gone. Gone along with everything else. Gone with his dream of The Farm. ...

Should've stayed back in the mountains. Should've never left his mountains. Should've never brought his family here. He'd had a job there. Now Lizzie had a job and he did not. Lizzie was getting stronger and he was getting weaker. Every day she was growing farther and farther away from him. Every day she was reading more and more and using more and more words. Like today--was it today or yesterday or last week--she'd said, "We must all endure, Chet. Endure. If we can endure this, we can endure anything. ..."

But he did not want to think of Lizzie. He didn't want to think of how he was hurting her, and how--and how he was failing her at night, too. At night, in bed. ... She didn't understand. How could she understand? "Chet, honey," she'd said, finally, with her face growing flushed--even in the darkness then he could see her dear face--after what must have been weeks but he couldn't remember how long of no lovemaking. "How, how come you ain't been wantin' to be near me no more, Chet? Is it, is it...I, I've tried my best to keep myself clean and sweet smellin' for you. Chet, honey, please tell me. Please. If I'm doin' somethin' wrong, I'll change."

"Oh, Lizzie, Lizzie," he'd cried. "How could you think that? Ain't that at all." He had tried making love with her that night, after Alma May and Jimmie Lee and Carrie Lou were finally asleep. But it was no good. He'd failed at that, too. She didn't understand. He had no desire, no need. "Ain't nothin' wrong with you, Lizzie. It's me," he'd said, turning his face away.

He had tried again a few nights later, to prove to himself and to her that he was still a man. But his failure again had only reaffirmed his worthlessness. ...

Lizzie, oh, Lizzie, I'm not good enough, not nearly good enough for you.

He must be worthless in everyone's eyes. The children had given up on him. How could he blame them? He was no longer a father to them. Could no longer provide for them. It was almost as if he no longer was a part of the human race. ...

Even the birds were against him. The whippoorwill kept him awake in early morning. The yellow-billed cuckoo laughed at him. The tufted titmouse scolded him. Even the bobwhite no longer called its name from the nearby field. Its message was "Go to work! Go to work!" But Chet was in empathy with the mourning dove, for it was almost as if he, himself, were calling out in its melancholy, cello-like song.

Chet looked over at the cot. The cot was his friend. He could escape for hours at a time on the cot.

"What you thinkin' about all this time? I been noticin' you, day after day, just settin' there and starin'. You must be solvin' the problems of the world."

Chet lifted his head with great effort. A woman stood over him. What was she doing there?

"I can see you don't recognize me. Name's Loretta, but my friends call me Blondie. I'm your neighbor. Two trailers down." The woman gestured toward a silver trailer, its roof glistening in the dappled sunlight. It was perhaps fifteen or twenty yards away, parked beyond the trailer next to the area where the Combses lived.

The woman plopped down on the grass beside Chet.

Chet glanced at her. He hadn't noticed her before in the woods. He'd hardly noticed anyone. He shifted his focus back to the ground before him. Maybe if he didn't pay any attention to her, she'd go away.

"Don't you get lonesome settin' here all day?"

Chet didn't reply. Oh, how he wanted to lie down on the cot.

"Your daughter draws real pretty-like. She done a pitchure a me. Got it hangin' in the trailer. My man ain't been home to see it yet."

Chet glanced at the woman again. She was smiling up at him. "Of course, I know I'm not half as pretty as the pitchure," she said as she ran her fingers through her yellow hair. "But she's got real talent. You must be real proud a her."

Chet felt obligated to say something. "Alma May's got real talent," he said. He looked over at the cot.

"Say! Why don't you come and see how the pitchure looks hangin' on the wall?"

Chet slowly shook his head.

"Oh, c'mon. It'll only take a minute. You'd be real proud to see it."

Chet shook his head once more. "No, thank you. I've got work to do here." He thought of the beans again.

"You mean you can't spare even a minute to see your own daughter's pitchure?" The woman reached up and tugged at his rolled-up shirtsleeve. "Ah, c'mon. It'll only take a minute, and then you can come right back and do all your work."

If he went with her, that would get rid of her. Then he could come back and stir the beans and lay down on the cot. Chet looked over at her trailer. It looked so far away. Too far for him to walk.

The woman sprang up and stood before him. He hadn't noticed before how dirty her dress was.

"C'mon," she repeated, smiling at him.

Chet slowly lifted himself from the chair and stood up. His legs were unsteady from sitting in one position for so long. He began to wobble after her.

The woman linked her arm with his. It was smooth and soft. "You been settin' too long," she said. "Me, I could never set that long." She looked over at the trailer next to the Combses' tent. "Ain't seen The Philosopher all day. Wonder where he could've gone to? He's usually doin' his run around the woods, or doin' sit-ups or somethin'."

The Philosopher. Philosopher. Fellow next door is The Philosopher. Chet had forgotten all about him. He hadn't been over lately pestering Chet with his endless talking.

They were finally at the woman's trailer. The outside of the vehicle was plastered with faded and peeling advertisements. One showed a man swallowing a sword and another a scantily dressed bearded woman. "My man and me used to follow the carnies," the woman said. "He worked the games and I did the hot dog stands."

She climbed the three steps leading into the trailer. Her lisle stockings had runs and the seams were crooked. Smooth, white flesh bulged slightly over the garter tops under the short dress.

Chet leaned against the side of the trailer and rested for a moment before attempting the climb.

The woman looked down from inside the trailer. "C'mon. Don't be shy. I ain't gonna bite ya."

Once inside, he looked around the walls for Alma May's sketch. "Where is it?" he asked.

"Where's what?" the woman asked. "Oh, the pitchure," she said, as if she'd forgotten all about it. She pointed to the wall in back of Chet. Alma May's sketch was thumbtacked next to a colored poster of a midget sitting on a throne. "See? Ain't it good?" she asked.

Chet leaned against the wall opposite the sketch and looked at it for a moment. Yes, Alma May had done real good work. Alma May always did real good work. And the woman was right: Alma May had really flattered her.

"Thank you, Ma'am," Chet said. "It's a very nice picture. Reckon I better go now." He walked toward the door.

"Ah, now. Ain't no need to hurry. Set down for a minute."

Chet shook his head. "Reckon my work ain't goin' to get done if I ain't there."

"It'll wait a few minutes on ya," the woman said. "C'mon. Set down, set down. I'll warm us up some coffee."

Coffee, thought Chet. I haven't had coffee for days. Coffee would taste real good, even on a hot day like this. "Well ..."

Chet sat down slowly at the tiny oilcloth-covered table cluttered with dirty dishes. The woman felt around the little counter, also strewn with dirty dishes, until she found a box of matches. She lit the propane burner, placed a smoke-smudged enameled coffee pot on it, and sat down opposite Chet.

"Feelin' low, ain't ya?" she said.

Chet's eyes widened slightly at her candidness. He nodded his head.

"Me, too," the woman said, her tone confidential. "My man, he ain't home half the time. A girl can get pretty lonesome with nothin' to do all day. Nothin' to do but remember the good times. The good times before the bottle got to him."

The woman rambled on but Chet wasn't listening. He was glad when she rose and rinsed out two dirty cups with water from a saucepan. He would pretend to listen, gulp the coffee, and leave.

"Hey, you sure don't talk much," she said. She placed the cup of coffee before him.

Chet managed a faint smile.

"That's okay," she said. "No need to talk. Just set there'n enjoy your coffee."

Chet took a sip of the hot liquid. It was strong and stale tasting, but good. He began to relax. For the first time in months, he was with someone with whom he didn't feel guilty.

"I like men who don't talk very much, anyways," she said with a little smile.

He hadn't noticed before that her teeth had black spots. But, still, her smile was appealing, innocently friendly.

"I like men who're a little mysterious. You're mysterious."

How comfortable to be with someone who doesn't care that I don't feel like talking, Chet thought. He began to relax a little more and took a big swallow of coffee.

"More?" the woman asked.

Chet smiled and raised his cup. "Yes, thankee kindly, Ma'am. I could use another cup."

"Say, now, if that ain't the most you've said so far," she said. She filled his cup again, then filled her own and sat down once more. "Bet you been lookin' all over for work for months and months and can't find a thing, huh? And finally figured what's the use and gave up. And now you feel kinda like, like a failure or somethin'."

Chet nodded his head. He was with someone who understood. Not like Lizzie and Alma May, who were always trying to cheer him up and who only made him feel guiltier.

The woman had her hand on his in a gesture of understanding. How smooth and white and small it was.

"More coffee?" she asked.

Chet smiled. "Thank you." What was the harm in being with this friendly woman who only wanted to show a little kindness? He'd have another cup and then leave. Alma May might be home soon with Carrie Lou.

The woman poured more coffee and continued to talk on and on about her carnival days. "A different week, a different town. Toledo, Peoria, and every little burg this side a the Mississippi. Them was the days. When people had quarters to spend, and dollars. ...

"That was before Tony--that's my man--hit the bottle and couldn't hold onto a job no longer, even for a coupla days at a time. Oh, he used to be a good provider. He was a good husband. Good at everything, if you know what I mean." The woman winked at Chet. "Say, if you ain't got just about the prettiest blue eyes."

It had been a long time since anyone had told him that. A long time since anyone had complimented him on anything. Chet finished his coffee and slowly rose to go.

"Please," the woman said, grabbing his hand. "Don't go just yet. I, I get so lonesome sometimes. So lonesome. No one to talk to all day. No one to understand me. I, I think you understand me. Even if you don't say hardly nothin', I get the feelin' you understand me."

The woman was standing closer to him now. She put her other hand on his arm. "Please," she said softly. He could smell her perfume. "You make me feel good just bein' with you. Important, like. It's been so long since anyone made me feel important. Know what I mean?"

Know what she meant? Oh, my god, how he knew what she meant. Chet turned and hurried to the door. He was surprised to find that it was now closed. "I'll be goin' now, Ma'am."

The woman still had one hand in his and the other on his arm, and was leaning forward a little awkwardly in an effort to hang on to him. He hadn't noticed before how tightly the dress fit across her breasts.

"Please. Stay for a little while. I need someone like you," the woman said, looking at him with pleading brown eyes, almost like a child's.

Needs him. How long had it been since someone needed him? The woman had both of her hands on his shoulders and was standing in front of him, blocking the door. In the light filtering in through the dingy little windows, her face looked softer, more like in Alma May's sketch. It was pretty and appealing. Oh, how he wanted to feel needed.

She had her arms around him now and was kissing his cheek. He had to get out of there before—before …

"My man won't be home for hours and hours," she whispered in his ear, her voice strangely husky now. "And no one will miss you for a few minutes more. Just--"

"I, I--" Chet began, before her mouth on his silenced him. Oh, my god, Chet thought. How dumb he'd been to let her talk him into staying.

"I need you. I need you," the woman whispered as she moved her lips from his mouth to his cheeks and ears and back again to his mouth.

Here is someone who needs me, Chet thought as he felt himself being pushed backward and onto a narrow bed. Her lips were on his again, warm and demanding.

"Fuck me, fuck me," she whispered.

He felt a stirring in his privates. A feeling he hadn't had in months and months. I must get out of here, thought Chet, as the woman climbed on top of him and began to unbutton his shirt. Oh, what a fool he'd been to come here. This woman is nothing but a ...

She was unbuttoning his beltless pants now. "Knew when I first laid eyes on you that you'd be a good lay," she said, panting. "I like the silent, mysterious type. Never know what they're thinkin'. Never know how they're goin' to be in bed." She had his pants and B.V.D.'s completely off now. "So, this's the game you like to play, eh? Lettin' me undress you like you was a baby, eh? Whatever you want, Blondie'll give you. I'm a hundred and sixty pounds of untamed woman." She jumped off of Chet and with fumbling, impatient fingers began to unbutton her dress.

As it slid to the floor, he saw that she was without a brassiere or other underwear, even bloomers. Her breasts, no longer confined by the dress, were like two giant ripe gourds. The stretch marks on her white belly mingled with the purple network of veins traveling to the blackness between her dimpled thighs.

Chet lay there, unable to move as the blood began to surge and pound through his privates. Maybe, maybe, if he did not fail with this woman, he would not fail again with Lizzie. He would be a man with this woman and then he would be a man again with Lizzie.

The woman rolled down her stockings and garters and tossed them on the floor, kicked off her shoes and climbed on Chet. "Oh, we're goin' to have a good time," she said, straddling him, her breasts flopping against his ribs. "Say, what's your name, honey?"

He could smell her then. He could smell her unwashed crotch.

"How you want it?" she asked. She scooted down toward his feet and began blowing on his navel with her mouth.

He could smell her dirtiness.

She looked up at him and smiled. Her hair fell over her ears and forehead. "Oh, I git ya! You're a mystery, and I'm supposed to guess what's goin' on in your head."

Chet felt all desire leave him. He lay there, motionless. The air was stifling. A feeling of fatigue overwhelmed him. He closed his eyes but could not shut out the smell of this woman. He must leave, but did not have the strength to move.

The woman was kneeling on the floor now with her face in his crotch. He had to get out of there!

"Hey, what happened to it?" she cried. She moved her mouth down. "Ol' Blondie'll fix it."

With great effort Chet lifted himself onto one elbow.

The woman paused long enough at her job to mutter, "Baby be better in a minute. Blondie fix it."

Chet pushed her away and swung his legs to the floor. He reached down and picked up his underwear.

The woman stared up at him from behind sweat-dampened hair.

Chet pulled on his B.V.D.'s and put one leg into his pants.

"Where, where you goin'?" the woman cried, jumping up.

"Sorry. I never should've …" He did not look at her as he reached for his shirt.

"Where the hell you think you're goin'?" she repeated.

Chet put on his shirt and began buttoning it.

The woman wrapped her arms around him and rolled her body against his. She stepped back and began to unbutton his pants again. "Blondie'll fix it up fast--"

"I have to go," Chet mumbled, buttoning his pants once more.

The woman stood there with color mounting in her face. The yellow hair against her red face was like a caution light turning red. "What kind of a fuck are you?" she sputtered. "The mystery man! The mystery man! If this is your big mystery-- Boy! What a cheat! A swell fuck you are!"

Chet shoved his feet into his broken-down shoes. He winced when he caught a glimpse of Alma May's sketch as he walked to the door.

"Come back here!" yelled the woman. "You ain't goin' home 'til you at least pay me for my trouble! Think I would a wasted my time on a hillbilly bag a bones like you if I'd a knew what a dud you are? Shit! I've had better fucks with a gearshift. At least a gearshift stays up!"

"Sorry," Chet said in a low, cracking voice. "Ain't got no money."

He opened the door. The air outside was blessedly fresh smelling and cool.

"Mean to tell me you ain't even got a nickel so's I can get me a cold beer?" the woman shouted.

Chet slowly shook his head.

"Dead dork! Dead hillbilly dork!"

Chet closed the door behind him. With bent head he dragged his feet toward home, his unlaced shoestrings flopping in the dirt. He stole a glance to see if The Philosopher was at home, and was relieved to see that he wasn't.

The tarpaulin ahead looked miles and miles away. Could he make it? Chet leaned against a tree for a moment. Suddenly, the enormity of what had happened overwhelmed him. He slid slowly down against the trunk of the tree and fell to the ground, whispering, "Oh, Lizzie! Lizzie! What have I done? What have I done?"

Chet hid his face in the coolness of the grass. "Oh, Lizzie, I love you so much, so much! How could I have done that to you? You, who are so good. So good. Too good for me. I don't even deserve that woman back there. ..."

He lay there for a moment longer, then rose slowly. Somehow he managed to drag himself home. His arms outstretched, Chet fell on the cot and buried his face in the clean white pillow, shutting out the sound of the rustling leaves and the smell of the burning beans.

Chapter 20

"**C**an you believe it, Combs? They've eaten everything! That Pollard family with the fifteen kids has eaten everything out of our thrift garden. Nothing's even ripe yet, and they've already eaten the leaves from the tomato plants and the tops from the squash."

Chet lifted his head from studying the Nehi bottle caps on the ground before him and saw his neighbor, The Philosopher, beside him. The Philosopher had apparently been doing his twice- daily run around the woods, and was now running in place. His tennis shoes moved up and down in perfect rhythm, like pistons in a well-cared-for engine.

"After all the work we did in it all these weeks. ..."

The garden. Chet shut out his neighbor's voice, and tried hard not to think about the garden.

Mayor Murphy had provided seeds and tools for the people of Detroit to plant gardens in vacant lots throughout the city this year. The Combses and the other woods people shared a city-owned plot next to the little camp. Jimmie Lee had hauled water every day from the comfort station across the highway, run by the city. Every day he poured six buckets on an allotted portion of the garden. At first Chet felt guilty because he didn't have the strength to carry some of the loads of water himself. But as the weeks went by--or was it months?--he'd tried hard to forget the garden.

"Maybe if I had fifteen kids, I'd allow them to steal everyone else's share just to survive, too, you know," The Philosopher mused in a bumpy, up-and-down voice, as he began to run in a small circle in front of Chet. "Yes, survival is the name of the game these days, you know," he asserted again. He reached into the pocket of his faded khaki shorts, pulled out a handkerchief and, without missing a step, wiped the sweat from his narrow brow. "Yes, poverty is our common denominator, you know. Especially here. And some people are survivors and some people aren't, you know. Take for instance that one there." Downs pointed in the direction behind Chet.

Chet slowly turned his gaze around to where The Philosopher pointed. A woman was walking up the path toward the comfort station on the arm of a young man carrying a bucket. Chet flinched and quickly turned his head back. He began to stare at the bottle caps again.

"That one's a tough broad, you know. She'll survive. But watch out for her. Blondie's tried to seduce every man here for a loaf of bread or a cold beer. She'll no doubt reward the young man later for carrying water for her." Downs grinned. "But keep alert and don't fall for her wiles. I didn't. I keep on my toes, you know."

Chet covered his face with his hands, remembering. He wished his neighbor would resume his run around the woods and leave him alone. He looked longingly over at the cot. He had almost gathered enough energy to rise from the chair and plop on the cot again when Downs had come by.

The Philosopher stopped running and lowered his long, wiry body to the ground in front of Chet and began to do pushups. Beads of sweat trickled down from his silver-gray hair, matted from perspiration, and dripped to the grass under him. "Seven," he counted, between grunts. "Eight …"

Chet ignored his visitor and looked over at the Detrola next to the cot. They had put off selling it as long as they could, but it would have to be the next thing to go. What could they get for it? A quarter, fifty cents?

"Twelve," counted Downs. "Yes, Combs. Have to keep your mind alert, no matter what happens, you know. Know what keeps your mind alert? Exercise. Exercise. Fourteen. Don't let yourself be immobilized. Fifteen. If a man feels good in body, he feels good in spirit, you know. Sixteen. Combs, you're punishing yourself for a failure you're not responsible for. Seventeen. To feel guilt when no sin is present is neurotic, you know. Eighteen …"

What would they do when fall came? When it was too cold to live out in the open?

"Twenty-two …"

Oh, how weak he felt. Chet closed his eyes to shut out the sight of his neighbor. Watching him go through all those motions only made him feel more tired.

"Twenty-four. … Our dreams have ways of falling by the wayside, you know. Put my three sons through college. One graduated summa cum laude from the U in Ann Arbor. Twenty-six. Degree in architecture, you know. What's he doing now? Collecting garbage. Happy to have a job. Twenty-nine …"

When Chet opened his eyes, his neighbor was standing on his head before him. How strange his red face looked, with the mouth above the eyes and sounds coming from it.

Downs continued his steady stream of advice. "I'm not going to allow myself to submit in quiet desperation, you know. …"

Chet closed his eyes again. When he opened them, Downs was sitting on the grass beside him, his tanned legs crossed tailor-fashion.

"Look at all those cars," The Philosopher said, pointing toward Telegraph Road and shaking his head. "All those people traveling to and fro, looking for work that doesn't exist. One wonders where they get the fourteen cents for the gallon of gas. They're all lined up, waiting for their gallon of Joy gas. *Joy gas.* Perfect brand name for the times we're in, you know." His thin lips curled up in a grim half-smile as he pulled his handkerchief from his shorts pocket again and wiped his long, lean face. "Yes. Look at all those cars, and each one different. Know why Technocracy never had a chance of catching on? Because we Americans would never go for having one kind of car available, you know. This country could never be run by engineers and technicians, you know. Most of them don't understand people's emotional needs, you know. Americans would never go for one kind of car, one kind of everything else, and being rationed by some sort of 'central committee' with a punch-card system.

"Yes, Combs, what you should do is run six miles a day like I do. …"

Chet winced and closed his eyes again.

"To feel worthwhile, a man has to feel productive, you know. And since I no longer have a job to be productive in, I'm being productive in maintaining a good body. Yes, Combs, exercising facilitates an attitude of accomplishment. You have to be a survivor, you know. …"

Chet crossed his hands in his lap and made his mind a peaceful blank. He had discovered his own way of survival. Sleeping and making his mind a peaceful, white blank. Only a few of The Philosopher's words seeped through to disturb that calmness:

"And, no, the new National Recovery Act will never work, either. ... And socialism will never catch on in this country. In America, the measure of a man's success is the amount of money he's accumulated, you know. So, Roosevelt's not really going to solve our economic woes. ... Yes, that's why what this country needs is a good war."

Chet was startled out of his tranquility by his neighbor's last words. He opened his eyes and spoke for the first time. "Reckon I didn't hear you right."

"What this country needs is a good war."

"You're funnin', a course. How could any war be good?"

"That's the only thing that's going to unite this country and provide jobs to get most of us back to work. Oh, the Civilian Conservation Corps is already helping a few of the young men, you know--too bad your boy is too young--and Roosevelt will probably invent some schemes to get some of us working. But what we need, of course, is something big enough happen to provide employment on a massive scale. ..."

Chet did not want to hear about war, and was glad when his neighbor finally stood up and began jumping up and down.

"But, I'm afraid this country is going to be on its back for a long, long time. It's like we're at the bottom of a pit, and no way to climb up. Well, when the time comes for me to climb, I'm keeping myself in shape to do it." With that, he was suddenly off, resuming his run.

Chet closed his eyes again and folded his hands. He would will his mind a white blank once more, and then get up and make his way to the cot. But he could not clear his head. A phrase spoken by Downs kept returning to intrude on that white tranquility: "At the bottom of a pit." "At the bottom of a pit." Chet sat there, letting the late morning breeze fan his face as his eyelids grew heavy. "At the bottom of a pit, at the bottom of a pit." He could not will the words from his tired head.

Then, suddenly, he opened his eyes and sat erect in the chair. Of course! That was it! At the bottom of a pit. It was clear what he must do. As clear as the summer sky around Big Black Mountain. At the bottom of a pit. For the first time in months, a faint glint of hope flickered in his eyes.

Chet rose from his chair and walked toward the path that circled the inner perimeter of the woods, a new determination in his stride. He stood by the edge of the path and waited for The Philosopher to go by on another lap of his run. When Downs found out what a good idea he had, Chet was sure he'd help him. He'd be a fool not to, when he understood how much money he'd make. For what seemed like an hour, but in truth was only a few minutes, Chet stood, a slight, stooped figure in sagging clothes, and waited for Downs to appear.

"Oh, Lizzie. Oh, my wonderful Lizzie," he whispered, as a new hope fluttered across his pale face and turned his lips up in a little smile. "We'll be rich. Rich. I've found a way to make us rich. We'll be leavin' here soon. Things'll be all right for us an' the young'n's again. You'll see. You can quit your jobs. I'm goin' to start takin' care a you an' the young'n's again."

Chapter 21

"**Q**uick! Quick, Alma May! Hide this!" Jimmie Lee cried. He ran toward Alma with something in his hands.

Alma dropped the folded newspaper she was using to fan Carrie Lou and grabbed a half-rotten onion and the wilted remains of a head of cabbage from her brother's hands.

"One of them Pollard girls is chasin' me. Tryin' to steal it from me. But it's ours. I grabbed it first!" Jimmie Lee's face was flushed from running and his hair wet with perspiration and falling in his eyes. He hesitated just long enough to inhale a deep breath. "I'm goin' to see Pa!" he called over his shoulder as he ran toward the highway.

"Hey, wait a minute!" Alma shouted. She stuffed the cabbage and onion under the cot on which Carrie Lou lay. "Come back here! It's my turn to be by Pa!" But Jimmie Lee was already out of earshot. Alma frowned. She picked up the newspaper and resumed fanning Carrie Lou. Of all times for Carrie Lou to go and get sick! At a time like this, when she, Alma, was so worried about Pa. She looked down at her sister's flushed face and straightened the rag filled with fast-melting ice chips on her forehead.

"Aw right, where is it?" Alma heard a coarse approaching voice yell.

Alma looked up to see one of the Pollard girls running toward her. She did not answer, but continued fanning.

"Where's the cabbage and onion? It's mine! I picked it off the garbage truck first!"

Alma gave a sidelong glance at the intruder. It was that girl with oozing pimples and body odor.

"I don't know what you're talking about. Go away!" Alma said, her tone icy. She hoped the girl couldn't smell the onion under the cot.

"Yer brother hid 'em here, di'n't he?"

"No! Go away! My sister's sick and you're disturbing her!" How repugnant the girl looked, with her uncombed hair falling in her eyes, and her baggy boy's shirt failing to conceal her budding breasts. And those grimy bare feet.

Carrie Lou began to whimper. All she needed was for Carrie Lou to wake up again.

"I'll go away if you give me a nickel," the girl said, her voice suddenly wheedling.

"Don't have a nickel."

"Aw, c'mon. You must have a nickel. Yer ma works every day."

Alma was not lying. The money that her mother brought home last night had to go for aspirin and ice and cough medicine for Carrie Lou.

"I'll make it worth your while." The girl lowered her voice in a throaty imitation of a mixture of Jean Harlow and Mae West, and raised her skirt up above her skinny knees. "For a nickel I'll let you play with my privates for ten minutes. And if you're nice, I'll even let you--"

"Get out of here!" Alma felt a hot redness creeping from her neck to her face.

Carrie Lou began whimpering again. "Get out of here!" Alma repeated, this time in a whisper.

The girl stepped back. "You think yer something special 'cause yer an artist, don'tcha?" she said over her shoulder as she walked away. "You ain't no artist! All you draw is pretty pitchures! You don't draw things the way they really are, ugly-like an' everything!"

"What do you know about drawing? You're just a cheap little, little--"

"At least I ain't no hillbilly an' my pa ain't no loony like yers!" yelled the girl, running now. "An' I'm gonna find yer brother an' beat his ass in!"

Her father was not a loony. And what did that trashy girl know about art? She was *glad* that one of the girl's brothers had become violently ill yesterday from mistaking toadstools in the woods for mushrooms and eating them. Alma immediately bit her lip when she realized what a cruel thought that was.

If only they could leave this place! It was supposed to have been only a few days that they would have to live here. "Mister Roosevelt's doin' wonderful things, Alma May," her mother had said the day they arrived. "Pretty soon your Pa'll find another job. We just all have to endure for a while longer." Well, the few days of endurance had strung into weeks and weeks. And what would they do when fall came? Where would she and Jimmie Lee go to school?

Oh, who was she to put on airs when she lived in a dump like this? she thought dejectedly. Who was she to think she'd be a famous artist someday?

Alma's glance fell upon the little radio. If they ever sold the Detrola Alma would die. That was her only link with the important world. With Walter Winchell and the new daytime story, "The Romance of Helen Trent."

Alma looked up with relief when Jimmie Lee returned. "I just had to see Pa again for myself," he said. He took the newspaper from Alma's hand and began fanning Carrie Lou.

Alma picked up a small bouquet of wild chicory flowers from a glass of water on the table. She'd gathered them earlier from the meadow next to the woods, and was surprised and glad that they hadn't died yet. She loved them for their bright blue petals, which were so perfectly formed and showy. Alma hurried up the path toward the highway.

"Oh, Pa. Stubborn, stubborn Pa. Where did you ever get the idea to do this?" Alma whispered. She skirted quickly around the heavy traffic on Telegraph Road toward the Joy gasoline station.

She saw the crudely written letters on the corrugated cardboard sign nailed to a telegraph pole in the vacant lot next to the station:

"See Man Berried Alive! Only 25¢"

The "25¢" had been crossed out and "15¢" scrawled above it. *Oh, Pa, down in that box in that pit.*i

Alma's hurried walk changed to a run as she approached the mound of freshly dug dirt near the pole. *What if, what if he's--?* But she must not think of that.

She fell to her knees and, dropping the flowers, peered down into the hole next to the mound. There lay her father six feet under the surface of the earth. His arms were folded across his chest and his eyelids closed. The sides and bottom of the box in which he lay were constructed of wood and the top of glass. The box was partly covered with dirt so that her father was visible only from the waist up. *Oh, Pa. Desperate Pa.*

Alma placed her mouth to a pipe that rose from inside the box to several inches above the ground. "Pa! You all right, Pa?" she called.

She waited for a moment but there was no answer. Her hands began to grow clammy and her throat dry. Alma swallowed hard and yelled again: "P, Pa! You all right, Pa?" Still no answer.

Oh, God. Make him answer. Make him answer!

Alma put her ear to the pipe and strained to hear. She placed her mouth to the pipe again and shouted: "Answer me! Answer me, Pa!"

Finally, from what seemed like miles away, Alma heard her father's faint voice. "That you, Alma May? Reckon I must a drifted off for a minute. ..."

Alma let her breath out in little puffs of relief. *Oh, Pa! Thank heavens.* She pushed her hair off her brow with a shaking hand. "Please, Pa. Please. I'm begging you again to let us dig you out of there!" she shouted down the pipe, knowing how useless her pleading was.

"We're goin' to be rich, Alma May," was her father's weak reply.

Alma slowly shook her head. Rich. Rich. "Pa. I brought you a bouquet of chicory flowers. I'm holding it up high for a few minutes so you can see something else pretty besides the sky."

"They're real pretty, Alma May. Thoughtful a my baby to bring 'em." After a moment's pause while Alma grew worried again and her heart skipped several beats, Chet continued. "I don't mind lookin' at the sky, baby. Been playin' our game. Remember, Alma May? Our game about The Farm, an' pretendin' the clouds are tractors an' hens, an' things?"

We never played that game with the clouds, Alma thought. Poor Pa. Maybe that Pollard girl is right. Maybe Pa *is* getting loony--

Alma remembered then. The game. The game with the clouds she and her father used to play while lying on their backs near the edge of the mountain ridge back home. They'd spent countless lazy Sunday afternoons going over and over in exact detail how The Farm would be run and how wonderful it would be. It seemed so long ago now.

"Of course, Pa. I remember." After a moment, she continued. "You been eating, Pa? How's the food lasting?"

"There's a heap a food left, Alma May."

Alma hoped her father was not conserving the bread and water. The beans they sent down with him had to be eaten the first day, before they spoiled.

"Alma May," came her father's voice again. "I'm tired now, an' feel like sleepin' for a spell again."

"All right, Pa," Alma replied, shouting down the pipe again. "I'll be right here if you need me. I'm staying here until Ma gets home." She got up and sat down on a pile of concrete blocks close enough to the pipe so that she could hear her father's voice if he should call.

Alma looked around. She sat twenty or thirty feet from the busy highway in front of her. Several vacant, dilapidated buildings to her left. The Joy gasoline station to her right. Weeds growing around uneven stacks of tires and overfilled, uncovered ash cans that lined the station wall nearest her. They would make a good subject for a work from the Ash Can School of painting, whose artists painted realistic scenes of ordinary subjects, Alma mused.

This is insane, Alma thought. Once her father had gotten the idea that he'd make lots of money quickly, there was no stopping him, no matter how hard they had all pleaded. Even Mr. Downs had shaken his head and advised that he see a doctor. But in the end, her father had persuaded The Philosopher to dig the hole, saying that Mr. Downs would reap half of the profits from all the curious passersby who paid to see him.

Jimmie Lee had refused even to find the materials to make the box. "No, Pa! I ain't helpin' you get buried!" he'd cried as he shook his head and blinked back tears.

So it was left for the still-protesting Mr. Downs to do the digging of the hole and the begging of the wood, nails, glass and pipe from a nearby hardware. He did most of the building of the box, too, because her father ran out of strength after a few swings with the hammer. Alma had stood by, with her hands to her shaking head, begging her father to change his mind.

She was startled now by a shiny black limousine that pulled up and parked a few feet away. A man in a smart brown chauffeur's uniform got out on the driver's side and opened the back door nearest to Alma. He took the arm of a woman in white as she stepped onto the running board, and then to the ground. She was followed by a little boy of about six or seven wearing a suit with short pants, also white. The boy ran to the hole and looked down.

"Mommy, Mommy!" he cried. "It's true! That sign was right! There really is a man down there! Look, look, Mommy!"

The woman, dressed in a linen afternoon suit, spectator pumps and a cloche, frowned daintily. "Charles! Be careful you don't get your hands dirty! And if your suit gets soiled, you know you can't go to Richard's party."

"Look, Mommy!" Charles repeated. He began to jump up and down in excitement. His thin, straight legs reminded Alma of a puppet's.

The woman frowned again and said to the man, "I suppose we'll never get him out of here if I don't have a look, too. I should have never let him talk me into stopping."

The chauffeur nodded his dignified, expressionless face, replying in a French accent, "One moment, Madam. I'll get a blanket for you to kneel on." He hurried to the limousine trunk and returned with a neatly folded plaid blanket, which he shook open and laid on top of the mound.

"Thank you, Marcel," the woman said. She kneeled gracefully on it, gave a quick look, and rose. "Yes, sweetheart," she said to the boy, "a man buried alive. Mommy saw him blink his eyes." The diamonds on her fingers flashed when she reached her soft, white hand out to catch the arm of the boy. "We'll have to go now," she said.

The boy ducked under her arm and jumped on the mound again. "Mommy," he cried, looking into the hole once more, "where does he go to the bathroom?"

The woman looked at Alma for the first time and her face grew pink. "Marcel," she said, walking toward the limousine, "get Charles into the car." She opened the back door of the vehicle herself and climbed in.

"Come along, Master Charles," the chauffeur said, "you'll be late for the party. And you're getting your white shoes soiled." He took the boy firmly by the arm and pulled him toward the limousine.

"I don't want to go to the party!" the boy yelled. He twisted his body toward the hole and tried to run back to it. "I'd rather stay here and look at the man!"

The chauffeur scooped him up as the boy's arms and puppet legs thrashed about, and lifted him onto the back seat of the car next to his mother. "I want to see the man go to the bathroom!" he screamed, all the while.

"Shh," the woman said, putting her finger to her puckered lips. The chauffeur slammed the door shut, and through the open window between her son's screams, Alma heard the woman say, "You don't want to see that lazy old man again. Anyone who would do that for money must be lazy. There must be some kind of a job he could get."

Alma ran after the car as it sped away. "My father's not lazy! My father's not lazy!" she yelled after it. Not until she returned to the cement blocks and sat down again did she remember that they had not paid their thirty cents.

How could she persuade her father that he should be brought up from that hole? Should she lie and tell him they had already taken in lots of money, so he didn't need to stay any longer? Or should she tell him the truth, that there had been many cars that had slowed while the gawkers read the sign, but few had actually stopped? Would that make him want to stay even longer down there, reasoning that he was making no money at all above the earth, but at least he was making a few cents below it?

Reasoning. What reasoning? Her father was beyond reasoning. If her mother only knew that he was in that pit all day long! Lizzie had a fit two evenings ago when she came home from work later than usual and found Chet there. She had fallen down on her knees to the soft mound and cried, "Oh, Chet! Chet, honey! Don't do this! We can survive as long as we stick together. I'll ask for a little raise tomorrow an' I'll even find a house to clean on Sundays!"

But when Lizzie had realized she couldn't reason with him, either, and that he did not plan to surface even after dark--"Why, that would be cheatin' to climb out at night, Lizzie," Chet had said, "An' you always say we shouldn't cheat"--she'd made Alma and Jimmie Lee promise that he'd be brought up at least for several minutes each day while she was at work. Her mother didn't know he'd refused that, too. Maybe it was a good thing her mother *was* gone all day.

If only Mr. Buckingham would get here. If her father would listen to anyone, it would be Mr. Buckingham. Alma had saved two nickels for phone calls from her mother's earnings two days ago. In desperation, she'd called the personnel office at Dodge Main twice and left word for him where they were living now. Would they relay such a personal message? she wondered.

Alma was chilled now by a sudden fear. Was her father still all right? She jumped up from the blocks and peeked down the hole again. Her father's eyes were closed, his arms still folded across his waist, a faint, peaceful smile on his pale lips. Just like, just like—

Her trembling lips could barely form the words: "Pa! You, you all right?" Her voice was high and hoarse, and didn't sound like her own. "Pa! Pa! Answer me!"

Finally, her father opened his eyes. "I'm all right, baby." A smile lit his pale face. "This is a new beginning. This…is a…new…begin…ning."

"Oh, Pa," Alma whispered. She turned her head from the pipe and stood up. She walked with unsteady legs to the pole on which the sign was nailed. Alma reached into the pocket of her dress and pulled out a black crayon. She crossed out the "15¢" and wrote "10¢" above it.

Alma dragged herself to the pile of blocks and sat down again. If only she could earn some money. Mrs. Carlson was away for the summer and she didn't know of another soul to work for. And no money for carfare if she did.

She couldn't even get her mind off her father by sketching, because all her pencils had been used up and all the paper bags had been used for drawing paper. The store owners had gotten tired of Jimmie Lee begging sacks from them. All she had left was the black crayon.

No stamp to send a letter to Mr. McAllister, either. And if she did, what was there good to tell him?

No use expecting Uncle Darcas to help them. The more depressed her father became, the happier Uncle Darcas seemed to be. He'd come by that first night--at suppertime, of course--and acted like it was a big joke that her father was down there. He shoved his way through the crowd of curious onlookers from the woods gathered around the mound--not one of them had the quarter to pay, naturally--and peeked down the hole.

"Reckon if you ain't sunk to a new low, big brother!" he called. Then he stood up, slapped his thigh in amusement, took a swill from his bottle of beer, and looked around the crowd, "Yup, reckon my brother's sunk to a new low!"

Realizing that Lizzie wouldn't be home from work for quite a while, so there was no food ready, he took another swig of beer and climbed back behind the wheel of his Model T. "Reckon bein' as I'm kin, I don't have to pay no quarter!" He wiped the streams of beer running down his chin with his shirtsleeve as he grinned and drove off.

Now, not even the woods people came to see the passersby pay for a peek. The novelty had worn off. Not that that many had actually paid. Three the first day, two the second, and none so far today. Oh, Pa, Alma thought. Her lip began to tremble again. So far you've earned only a grand total of a dollar and a quarter.

"How's your father doing, young lady?"

Alma gave a start. Because of the heavy traffic, she hadn't heard the running footsteps of the approaching Philosopher.

"He's sleeping now."

"You ought to take a run around the woods, you know. It would take your mind off him for a while," The Philosopher said, his up-and-down voice sounding like an un-tuned radio as he continued to run in place before her.

Run around the woods? Run around the woods? How could she leave her father and go run around the woods? "No," she said. She hoped her brusque tone would encourage him to leave.

"Ah, yes, your father's desperation and pride are making him do this, you know."

Alma did not need The Philosopher's explanation. And how could he be so small as to take half of her father's earnings, even if that was the agreement?

The whistle of a train sounded in the distance. Mr. Downs cocked his ear in its direction. "Another train with its passengers escaping to and from the pains of life."

She was glad when Mr. Downs finally turned to go. "Yes, survival is the name of the game these days, you know," he shouted over his shoulder as he resumed his run.

The crickets began to warm up for their nightly concert. The cars traveling on Telegraph Road were almost colorless now in the twilight. Alma was relieved that the temperature had fallen a little. But it was getting dark now. That meant another night of her father being down there. Why hadn't she thought to ask Mr. Downs to have Jimmie Lee come? She did not want to leave her father for a minute. She remembered then that Jimmie Lee was with Carrie Lou and couldn't leave her. She hadn't thought about Carrie Lou for hours.

The sound of a car driving up in front of Alma and braking to a sudden stop jolted her from her thoughts. She waved the cloud of dust away from her face and hoped none of it would seep down through the pipe to her father. Two young men jumped from the rumble seat and two more opened the doors and piled out. Alma's pulse quickened and a vague uneasiness enveloped her: One of the young men looked familiar.

"Lookit, yous guys, if it ain't Little Miss Muffet sittin' on her tuffet, whatever that is," said one of them. The white skull and crossbones against the background of his black short-sleeved cotton undershirt stretched across his muscular chest and stood out in the near-darkness. "What in hell is a tuffet, anyway, Scatelli?"

"Dunno, Pisoni. I allus wondered what a tuffet is, myself," a familiar voice said. "But whatever it is, I betcha hers ain't tough." His companions laughed. "Betcha hers is real smooth." The tall, stooped young man grinned and stared at Alma.

Alma's eyes widened. She turned her face away. It was, it was that foul Scatelli kid who'd teased her whenever he could since that very first day in grade school. But she thought he was still away in that reformatory in Ionia.

"Holy shit!" Scatelli said. "If it ain't Little Alma May Combs, the little hillbilly artist who wears shoes but no stockings and no bloomers!"

"No bloomers!" one of them cried. "This I gotta see!" He made a move toward her. The others laughed.

Alma jumped up and stared at all four. They were all wearing the same skull and crossbones design on their black undershirts, and wore no outer shirts. She swallowed and felt her throat tighten.

"Hey, look! The sign was right! There's a man buried down there!" one of the young men cried.

Scatelli grabbed Alma by the wrists as the other two stepped to the hole.

Alma stared up at her old classmate's face, which was distorted in a lopsided grin. The pimples of grade school had now become pockmarks and his breath smelled of beer and un-brushed teeth.

"Well, now, if you ain't got even prettier than I remember you." he said, pulling her toward the car, his grin wider. "At long last we're gonna have some fun together."

Alma struggled to wrest herself free as her mouth opened to form a scream. She could not make a sound come out. She looked over at the gas station. It was closed for the evening. She glanced at the highway.

"Hardly no cars going by now. And it's getting too dark for anyone to notice us," Scatelli said, reading her thoughts. He pulled her to the side of the car not visible from the highway.

"Ma! Ma! Come home," Alma whispered. "Please, please come home!"

Alma kicked her toe as hard as she could, aiming for his shin, but he jumped out of the way just in time.

"Hey, Scatelli!" one of his friends shouted. "You gotta see this! Come and see this nut down in this hole!"

"Hold this little bitch for me!" Scatelli yelled. "But watch out for her! She's got a temper. Then we'll all take her somewheres and have some fun with her." He grinned down at Alma. "But I'll have my turn with her first!"

The shortest of the gang grabbed Alma's wrist and Scatelli stepped to the hole.

"Now, ain't that real purty-like," Scatelli said. "They even got flowers on the grave. But they're all wilted." He looked over at Alma and grinned again. "Just like Alma May's gonna be when I'm through with her." His companions laughed. Scatelli looked down into the hole. "Well, if that don't look real, his hands folded and all." Scatelli placed his lips to the pipe and began to sing the lyrics of "Indian Love Call" in a loud voice:

> "When I'm calling you
> "Will you answer, too?"

He put his ear to the pipe and wrinkled his face in exaggeration, as if he were listening intently. "He don't answer!" he cried in mock concern.

Alma's heart began to pound even harder.

Scatelli placed his lips to the pipe again and repeated:

"When I'm calling you
"Will you answer, too?"

Once more he put his ear to the pipe and listened. "He *still* don't answer!"

One of the young men who was standing next to the hole giggled, a high, girlish giggle.

"Oh, Scatelli!" the short one cried, tightening his grip on Alma's wrists. "Where'd you learn to sing so <u>boot</u>-ee-ful?"

"Told ya I got couth," Scatelli answered. "Us artists'n singers, we got couth. We're above the likes of yous." He looked over at Alma and smirked. "And our shit don't stink like the rest of yous. Kee-rect, Alma May?" He looked down in the hole again. "Hey! Just thought of something! How's this guy do his shittin'?"

"They prob'ly got a miniature outhouse stuck in his pants!" cried the one holding Alma's wrists. Scatelli and his friends laughed.

"Let's see if you're right," Scatelli said. He placed his nose to the pipe. "Don't smell nothin'," he said in simulated disappointment. "Hey, you down there!" he shouted into the pipe. "You got an outhouse in your pants?" He put his ear to the pipe and listened again, then lifted his head and looked around at the group. "He don't answer!" he cried as his eyes widened. "I'll make him answer," he said with determination. He reached down and picked up a small stone.

Alma, who had been exhausted from pulling, began to struggle again with sudden renewed strength. "Leave my Pa alone! Leave my Pa alone!"

Her captor removed one of his hands from her wrist and placed it over her mouth. A gust of wind blew the odor from his armpits her way.

Scatelli dropped the stone down the hole. Alma flinched when she heard it land and hoped it hadn't broken the glass, as the other two youths laughed and searched for more stones. She looked over her captor's shoulders to the highway. Even fewer cars than before and it was dark now and nobody could see the sign. *Jimmie Lee! Jimmie Lee!* she thought when she saw the woods. *Read my thoughts and run for help!*

The young men took turns dropping stones down the hole while Alma yelled muffled shouts and continued kicking and struggling. One of her kicks landed on her captor's shin, causing him to jump up and down and twist her arm backwards in retaliation.

Scatelli and the others were no longer taking turns now, but were having a free-for-all, seeing who could drop the most stones and who could drop them the fastest.

"Careful we don't get none down the pipe," one said.

"Yeah. We don't wanna get none down the pipe," Scatelli said. "They might get stuck halfway down, and-- Hey! His lips are moving!" Scatelli put his finger to his mouth. "Shh! Be quiet! I wanna hear what Mister Combs is saying!"

The other two paused and watched while Scatelli put his ear to the pipe. After a moment he lifted his head and grinned. "'It's all r..i..g..h..t Alma M..a..y,'" Scatelli said, imitating Chet's feeble voice. "'They can't h..e..l..p the w..a..y th..e..y a..c..t. ...'" Hear that everybody? We don't know what we're doing!" He and his companions broke into delighted laughter and giggles.

Pa! Pa! They know what they're doing. *Oh, please, somebody--anybody--please come--!*

"Hey!" Scatelli said. "Got an idea! And we won't even know we're doing anything wrong!" He reached down and grabbed a fistful of loose dirt from the mound. "Just think how easy it would be to snuff out this old coot's breath!" He slowly released his grip on the dirt and let it pour down the pipe as he looked over at Alma and grinned. "We don't even know what we're doing!"

The one next to him gave another girlish giggle. He, too, bent down and picked up a fistful of dirt. He poured it down the pipe and continued to giggle. The third one and Scatelli picked up a handful and waited impatiently for their turn.

A passing bus drowned out Alma's muffled, "Pa! Pa!"

"Hey! Somebody come over and hold this bitch while I have a turn. Yous guys're having all the fun--"

Alma felt the pressure on her wrists increase when the arms of the young man holding her suddenly stiffened involuntarily. Then, to her amazement, he just as abruptly freed her.

"Holy shit!" he shouted to his companions. "Let's beat it! Here comes a car!" He jumped into the rumble seat.

Scatelli and the other two looked in the direction of the approaching headlights. Then, like scared animals, they bolted to their car, jerked open the doors and piled in.

Alma stood stunned. She watched their rusty jalopy speed erratically away with Scatelli at the wheel. She blinked her eyes and looked again to make sure what had happened so fast was really true. *Yes, they were driving away. They were really gone!*

She looked over at the parked vehicle whose headlights made long rays of light in the darkness. Never before had she been so happy to see a car!

Alma stumbled toward the white roadster, her hand before her eyes shielding them from the glare. She blinked, and through the white spots floating before her face she saw a familiar figure approaching.

"Alma, Alma," Harry Buckingham said as she fell into his outstretched arms. "You all right?" He patted her head. "Yes, yes, Alma, it's really me."

Alma lifted her head from the shoulder of his white linen jacket and looked up at his face, wrinkled in a happy grin. "You found us! You found us!" she whispered, her voice choking.

"Just got back in town today. Ed Mansfield in personnel gave me your message. He's a good guy. I found Jimmie Lee and he said you and your father would be here. He's been with Carrie Lou for hours, afraid to leave her to give you a rest. He told me about the hole. I--"

Pa! Pa! Alma broke from Buckingham's embrace and ran to the hole. "Pa! Pa!" she cried down the pipe. "They're gone! They're gone! Did they hurt you?"

In spite of the light stretching across the ground from the car's headlights, it was impossible to see her father now. "Answer me, Pa! Answer me!"

Finally, Chet's voice, even weaker now, came up slowly through the pipe. "I'm all right, baby. ..."

Alma, relieved, placed her mouth to the pipe once more. "Pa! Pa! Mr. Buckingham's here. Mr. Buckingham's here!" She jumped up and motioned for Buckingham to take her place.

Buckingham's brow creased. "What did you mean? Did they try to hurt your father?" he asked anxiously, and kneeled down.

"Oh, Mister Buckingham! They dropped stones down the hole. And then they started pouring dirt down the pipe. You came along just in time."

"Oh, my god!" Buckingham put his mouth to the pipe. "Hey, Hillbilly! This is Harry! You okay?" He put his ear to the pipe for a long moment. Then he looked up at Alma and smiled. "He can't believe it's really me," he said. He placed his mouth on the pipe again. "It's really me, Hillbilly! It's Harry. I thought you said you'd never work under ground again. Well, you can come up now. I've finagled a job for you at Consolidated, but you have to apply tomorrow." Once more he listened for Chet's reply. "It's really true, Chet! I've gotten acquainted with the girl who works in personnel there."

In the light from the car's headlights, Alma saw a smile cross Buckingham's face. "This was a dumb idea you had going down there, Hillbilly!" he called. "Besides that, your sign is misspelled." He looked up at Alma and grinned, then called to her father, "Want to go to Chicago with me next weekend? I hear the Century of Progress exhibition is swell!"

PART TWO

Chapter 22

Alma paused before the door and read again the classified advertisement she had clipped from the clerical help wanted section of the *Detroit Times*. Yes, this was it. Three-oh-two Ambassador Building. She straightened the seams of her rayon stockings, pulled her shoulders back and cleared her throat before opening the door.

The middle-aged receptionist with sleek, short hair at the desk looked up from what she was typing only long enough to hand Alma an application form, a card on which was written the number fifteen, and then motion for her to take the last remaining seat against the wall. Alma, aware of the other young women looking at her, walked a little self-consciously across the black and white asphalt tile and sat down. The receptionist hadn't even asked her what she was there for.

Alma looked around. A young woman wearing a dark dress and dark hat was typing nonstop at a typewriter stand against the wall across from Alma. On a wall opposite the entrance a sign read, "Laury & Greyson, Designers." It was of bright chrome, and parallel lines whisking through the forward-sloping letters gave it the appearance of moving at great speed. The design of the furnishings suggested motion, too, and--what was that word that was being used so often lately? "Dynamism," that was it. The desk at which the receptionist sat was clean-lined, made of brushed metal and Bakelite, and trimmed in chrome strips.

Alma looked at her own chair. The arms were of the recently developed tubular aluminum. The sculptured design suggested a forward look, too. She reached down to the chrome and glass table before her, picked up a Laury & Greyson brochure, and scanned it quickly. *"A uniquely American look.. .... A new age, in which mass consumption of well-designed machine-made products will help restore social harmony. ... If a product is made desirable enough, reluctant buyers will respond. Streamlining a product strips it for action, throws off impediment to progress. Laury & Greyson designs flow, have resistance-minimizing streamlined contours. ..."*

Streamlined, she thought. *Streamlined*. Yes, everything here is streamlined.

Alma hadn't known to what company she would be applying. The ad had said only, "General office. Efficient young woman. Excellent salary." She began filling out the application form. It was brief. And streamlined.

Alma peeked at the other young women sitting in the room. She hadn't thought there would be so many applicants for a general office job. The economy was a little better now, so jobs should be more plentiful, shouldn't they? She counted fourteen other women, all almost uniformly dressed--dark tailored dress, white gloves, small dark hat over short, trim hair. Alma looked down at her own dress and peeling patent leather pocketbook. How impractical her pink flowered voile with its ruffled collar looked! And suddenly she was aware of how casual her shoulder-length curls must appear with no hat. She was the only one carrying a sack, too. She had to bring her low shoes and the overalls for changing into before painting the mural later.

Only one line remained to be filled out: "Typing speed: ..."

Typing speed? How naive she'd been not to realize she'd be given a typing test. But she would get by. She'd learned to type a little during her senior year of high school five years ago. Had Gladys Polaski read the ad?

Alma finished the form and settled back into her chair. The aluminum arms felt agreeably cool against her own bare ones. The temperature outside was pleasant for an early September afternoon, but it felt hotter in here.

"She could at least give us a few minutes to practice," whispered the girl on Alma's right, a plain thing with eyeglasses as thick as Mason jar bottoms and the scent of Packer's Tar Soap about her.

"Practice?"

The girl nodded toward the girl typing across from them. "The receptionist is giving each of us applicants a three-minute typing test without even a chance to warm up first. Then she corrects it on the spot and if you pass, you get to go into that room"--she motioned toward a door near the far left corner--"probably for more tests. And if you don't, she sends you packing. Three minutes! Three minutes isn't enough for a fair test. It's a good thing my typing speed is really high. Seventy-one the last time I tested. What's yours?"

"Oh, um, I don't know, but it's pretty high, too. I haven't been tested lately." She couldn't remember. Who besides Gladys Polaski cared about typing? Painting was the only important thing in life then and it still was now, even with no sales yet. Alma thought about the mural she was helping paint at the Clifford Street branch post office. It was demeaning to paint a scene that was designed and directed by some other artist. But with the small wages she got from the Work Projects Administration for assisting on it, she could buy paints and brushes for her own paintings.

"It's my turn now," the girl whispered when the receptionist beckoned her with a fresh sheet of paper.

Alma counted the applicants again. Still fifteen including herself. Two had been tested and were lucky enough to enter the next room, and two new applicants had arrived. She glanced anxiously at the clock. She hadn't thought the interview would take this long. She had to be at the post office in forty-five minutes. If she ran there after her interview she could still make it. She had better not be late again. Mr. Angelo saw that her wages were docked for every minute she was tardy. "You are not treating this like a real job, Miss Combs," he'd said when she was late a few minutes several times before. "If Edward Bruce should come by and inspect all the murals in the Detroit area and see you come running in late, I'd have to dismiss you right on the spot." Alma would begin painting furiously and say to herself, Edward Bruce, my foot! The big Federal Art Project director doesn't have time to inspect every mural being painted in federal buildings and libraries all over the country.

The Mason glass girl had finished her test, apparently with flying colors. The receptionist did not make a single mark on it and motioned her into the next room. She gestured for the girl on Alma's left to begin hers. Alma looked at the clock again. She began to wiggle her foot. She would be late for sure in getting to the post office! Should she excuse herself and leave now? No, she had better see this through. She really needed this job. If she was making more money, she could start paying her family for board (not that they had ever hinted that she should, of course), and buy some decent clothes and art supplies. Things were a little better for her family, now that the UAW was in at Consolidated and her father was working full time. Even Jimmie Lee was more independent than she was and paying board, now that he was working full time stocking at an A & P store.

The last girl had done well, too, and had entered the next room. Alma began to be anxious about her own typing as a new girl confidently took her place at the typewriter. If she didn't need the job so much, she'd walk out the door now. Would she remember where all the keys were? She made a mental picture of the keyboard and moved her fingers in her lap in pretense of typing. What was that sentence she used to type over and over when she first learned the keyboard? Oh, yes--she remembered: "Now is the time for all good men to come to the aid of their country." Alma's lips turned up in a slight smile as she changed it to, "Now is the time for all good men to come to the aid of Alma Combs. Now is the time--"

She stopped suddenly: The girl in the chair to her left was looking at her curiously. I must be acting like an idiot, Alma thought. She turned her face away and felt a blush coming on.

The next applicant did well, too. The room must be filled with efficient young women. Alma never thought she'd be applying for an office job. She thought by this time she'd have her own painting studio like in that big oil painting by William Merritt Chase--*Tenth Street Studio*, that was it--where wealthy art patrons dressed in stylish clothes admired her paintings on the walls, and were surrounded by upholstered couches and chairs that were luxurious, comfortable. ...

The receptionist beckoned for Alma to take her test now. Alma stood up slowly, feeling relieved, but anxious.

Her legs began to tremble a little as she walked across the room. She felt awkward carrying the sack with her, but was afraid she might forget it if she left it on the chair.

The woman took her card with the number on it as Alma sat down in front of the sleek L. C. Smith. She was a little surprised to find that the woman had bad-smelling breath when she leaned over and pointed to the copy that Alma was to type. Somehow, bad breath didn't seem efficient. Alma brushed a curl from her forehead. Her hands grew clammy. The woman looked at her watch and walked briskly back to her desk. Alma sat up tall in the chair. Were all the other girls in the room staring at her? Her arms felt like lead. She exercised her fingers in preparation and then placed them on the keys, trying to remember where the correct position was for "home plate," as Miss Cummings, the typing teacher, had called it.

Alma skimmed over the first few sentences of the copy:

> "We at Laury & Greyson believe that efficiency is next to godliness. In order for an office to be efficient, it must be streamlined in every way. Our employees do not waste precious time engaged in unnecessary conversation.

Alma took a deep breath and began typing. She typed a few lines-
-*Oh, why were the keys so hard to push down?*--and peeked up to see how well she was doing:

> "Er sy Lsuty & Htrymsn nrlirbr yhsy rggivirnvy id nrcy yo hoflinrdd—"

Alma winced. No, her fingers were not on home plate. She moved her left hand over one key to the left as her face grew hot and she began perspiring. *It must be 100 degrees in here.* She took another deep breath and began again. After a few words, she peeked up at her paper once more:

> "We at Laity ★ Greyman beliebe—"

Oh, lord, what was she doing here? She was not like these other applicants. They were all efficient and--

She wiped her brow, rolled her paper up a few lines, and began again:
"We at Laury--
Her fingers were wet with perspiration and sliding from the keys--
"Stop!"
Alma glanced up and saw the receptionist by her side, looking at her watch again. Could her three minutes be up already?

The woman pulled Alma's paper from the typewriter carriage in one swift motion. She pruned her face up into a frown as she read it and shook her head. "You've wasted our time and yours. Worst typing I've ever seen." Her breath assaulted Alma again when she motioned for her to leave by the front door and beckoned for the next girl.

Alma fought back hot tears. "I--I'm sorry. I didn't know you'd be testing. Please give me another chance."

The woman looked impatiently at Alma.

"I, I'm an artist. That's what I'm really best at."

The woman gave her an annoyed look. Alma cleared her throat and swallowed. "Do, do you need any more designers?"

The woman tapped her foot and looked at her watch. "No. And they're all men."

Alma glanced around and saw that all eyes were focused on her. She could feel her face redden as she gathered up her pocketbook and sack from the floor. She wanted to crawl under the typewriter stand and die! She hurried awkwardly out the door, not bothering to close it behind her. She ran for the stairway--it would be faster than waiting for the elevator. *Oh, how humiliating!.. And for a common office job!* And to think that she'd actually almost begged. Why had she ever gone there?

Outside, the bright sunlight hurt her eyes, but the breeze cooled her cheeks as she half-ran, half-walked north on Clifford Street. How she hated that woman! Alma wished now she had grabbed her test, torn it into bits, and thrown it in her cold, efficient face and screamed in front of everyone, "You've got bad breath! Bad breath!" Why was it she could always think of what she should have done after it was too late?

What time was it? She hurried even more, weaving in and out of the crowd of pedestrians. She could not afford to rile Mr. Angelo again. The WPA money was even more precious now that she didn't get that job. How woefully unprepared she'd been! Oh, she felt so inefficient and so--so--unstreamlined.

Another insult hit her ego when she thought again that in all the years that she'd been painting, she had not sold one painting. Not one. Oh, Mr. Buckingham had bought a little sketch, but she knew he'd only bought it to boost her self-esteem.

She skirted the mail trucks by the ramps at the rear of the post office and the men who were exiting the door with bags loaded for their afternoon deliveries. In the restroom she hurried into her low shoes and overalls, dumped her dress and pocketbook into the sack, and placed it on a shelf. She walked toward the front of the building, where work on the mural was underway on a side wall. Alma glanced at the big clock on the right wall. Nine minutes late! If she were lucky, she could pretend she'd gotten here on time but, not feeling well, had been in the restroom all this time.

Mr. Angelo was standing on the scaffolding. He glared down at her. He was a greasy, potbellied pork chop of a man, with body odor and hair on his arms like on a coconut. "What's your excuse this time, Miss Combs?"

"I, I was here in plenty of time, but I didn't feel well, so I went to the restr--"

"Oh? Here in plenty of time, eh?" Mr. Angelo raised one corner of his thick upper lip in a sneer. "How come I didn't see you, then? I was here twenty minutes early today."

Alma glanced around. She was glad the customers waiting in line and the clerks behind their windows were not paying attention. "I, I--"

"Get up there and start working. You know we're behind schedule as it is." Mr. Angelo turned his fat face toward the mural again and resumed painting. "I'm docking you double this time."

Docking her double! Now that she and the other helpers were on half days, there would hardly be anything left. She scrambled up the scaffolding, careful not to bump into the open jars of tempera. The last thing she needed to do was knock over some paint.

She positioned herself alongside the other young woman, Mary Scarfino, where they had left off painting the afternoon before. The room was hotter today. The ceiling fan was not working. She and Mary were painting the section of the mural that represented salt mine workers on the job. Alma squatted down, opened a jar of black tempera, and stirred it well. She poured a little of it on her palette, stood up again, and stirred the paint with the tip of her brush. Alma took a deep breath and began to fill in the shadow behind the right arm of a man loading a flat car.

"Don't mind old Mr. B.O.," Mary whispered out of the side of her mouth. "He's just envious of you. He knows you've got more talent in your little finger than he's got in his whole greasy body. I don't know how he ever got to be director of this job."

Alma looked anxiously at Angelo, who was working on the automobile assembly scene on a higher part of the scaffolding to their left. She was glad to see that he wasn't looking, so hadn't seen Mary's lips move. Mary, a tall, thin, mousy haired girl, was the eldest of ten children, and grateful for the chance to be painting anything. "Just think, Alma," she'd said several times, "we're getting paid a living wage by the government to paint an American scene that will be enjoyed by thousands and thousands of ordinary people for years to come. If I didn't need the money so much, I'd paint it for nothing. And for the first time, we're bridging the gap between the artist and the general public."

Alma stole a glance at the entire mural. Yes, it certainly was about the common people and about the environment and time in which it was being painted: The tempera-on-gesso mural was tentatively called *Detroit Muscle,* and included in the montage were the automobile assembly scene Angelo was working on, the building construction scene Bobby Johnson was painting, and the salt mine scene. Alma had been surprised when she saw the sketch for the salt mines. She hadn't realized that there were any under the city of Detroit. She had gone home that evening and jokingly announced to her startled family, "I'll be working in the salt mines for the next few weeks!" And there was the boxing scene, too, showing Joe Louis defeating Max Schmeling last year. Purlie Washington will be happy when she sees this, Alma thought. Colored people didn't get a chance to be in the limelight very often.

She thought of Purlie now with a fleeting tinge of envy. Purlie was really enjoying her Federal Art Project job, teaching art classes to underprivileged children. "Oh, Alma," she'd said the other day when Alma had seen her waiting for a DSR bus on Woodward, "the WPA is a wonderful thing." Purlie still had the habit of opening her eyes wide when she spoke, making the bulging whites contrast even more against her black skin. "If it wasn't for the WPA, most of those little kids would never hold a palette or paintbrush in their hands. And you should see their little faces light up when they see what they can do."

Not that Alma really wanted to teach art classes. But where was the "espirit de corps" here on this mural project? Where was the spirit of devotion and enthusiasm that she had been hearing the other Project artists had for one another and the work they were doing? Where was--

Angelo was scowling down at them. But mostly at Alma. Oh, why didn't he like her? Could it be, as Mary had said, that he was envious? "Shhh!" Alma hushed just loud enough for Mary, who had started to whisper again, to hear. She was relieved when her partner stopped.

Angelo had resumed painting, but now Bobby Johnson was staring down at her from the same level on which Angelo stood. One of his big blue eyes closed in a compassionate wink.

He continued to look at her, now with more than sympathy. Alma feared he'd get her in trouble with Angelo. She gave him a pleading look. He turned his face toward the mural and began painting again.

Bobby had been begging Alma to date him since they met that first day of the mural project, but she had declined. Not that he was ugly or anything like that--actually, his wide bright smile was sort of appealing and his manner was pleasant, but--why should she waste time going on dates he suggested to places she herself could afford? Alma knew Bobby didn't own a car and couldn't afford to take her to places she longed to go, such as the Detroit Yacht Club, or that expensive restaurant called the London Chop House, or to the Bowery supper club, or ...

Bobby was looking at her again. Alma gave him another pleading look and glanced over at Angelo, his face twisted in another scowl. He laid his palette and brush down on the scaffolding and descended the steps. Bobby had really ruined it for her now!

Alma began to paint faster, pretending complete concentration on the shadow she was filling in. She did not look up until Angelo was beside her. He smelled even sweeter in the heat of the room--

"I will not tolerate spending government money to carry on a flirtation."

"But--but I wasn't--"

"Hell you weren't! I saw you looking up at him with those moony eyes--"

"But I wasn't flirting--"

"Excuses. Excuses. You're full of 'em." His voice was cold.

"I was just--"

"Mr. Angelo, Alma wasn't flirting. It was me." Bobby had climbed down and was standing beside her. "Please--"

"Back to work, Bobby." His voice was not as cold toward Bobby. What did Angelo have against her?

But Bobby remained standing there, looking at Alma with sympathy. Mary looked up from her painting long enough to glance at Alma in the same way.

Angelo studied the spot on the mural that Alma had just completed. "This is terrible." He shook his head. "Who told you you could paint? This supposed to be a shadow?"

Alma felt the anger swell in her. First she couldn't type, and now this greasy jerk is telling her she can't paint!

Angelo grabbed the brush out of Alma's hand. Alma got a whiff of his underarm as he reached up and began painting over her strokes.

"This is the way we paint in the big city," Angelo said. "Maybe back in them thar hills where you came from, they taught you different."

Alma felt the anger mounting even more and the room getting even hotter. Mary was looking at them openly now. Her lips silently formed the word, "envious."

"If you don't improve soon, I'm going to have to write a report on you to Holger Cahill."

Holger Cahill. Holger Cahill! The big, big Federal Art Project boss?

She could take no more of Angelo. "I've got you figured out now. You're afraid everyone will find out you don't have any talent yourself, so you keep drawing attention to other things. Like every time I'm late, even for a minute, and--"

"How dare you talk to me like that!" Angelo's voice got louder and higher. An ugly red crept up under his oily cheeks.

"Talk about WPA boondoggling!" Alma's voice got louder, too. She glanced around the room. The customers were all listening in amusement. "My uncle was better at his WPA job digging ditches than you are at directing this mural! Any fool knows you can't get the best work out of an artist by treating him like you do. An artist has to work in a relaxed atmosphere and do work at his own speed--I've heard Holger Cahill is very understanding about this--and not have to work under a no-talent little dictator who keeps a time card on us. I just know you're the only mural director in the whole country who's obsessed with petty little rules, and I know why, too--"

"You're fired!" Angelo sputtered. The red had reached his forehead.

"Fired? Fired! Who ever heard of getting fired from a WPA job? You're not firing me. I'm quitting! But not before I finish telling you I know why you like keeping us nervous and afraid of you. So that we can't do our best work. You're afraid our painting will turn out better than yours--"

"Get out!"

Alma turned abruptly to leave, accidentally knocking over the open jar of paint with her foot. The black tempera splattered against the bottom of the mural, making a dripping Rorschach-like design on the feet of one of the salt miners.

Angelo covered his eyes, then shook his fist.

"Gee, I'm sorry, Mr. Angelo! Now the mural will never be finished on schedule. YOUR schedule." Alma was standing on the floor now. She looked up long enough to see the smiles in the eyes of Mary and Bobby and the hesitant grins on their lips.

"Oh, and another thing, Mr. Angelo!" Alma shouted as she looked up at him. Mr. Angelo seemed to have shrunk a foot shorter. "You have b.o.! B.o.!" Alma caught the shocked expressions on the faces of Mary and Bobby and the other spectators before she turned and walked toward the restroom.

Outside, the breeze was blessedly balmy again. She hurried away from the post office, her fingers clutching the bag containing her pocketbook, dress and shoes. Had she really said all those awful things? Where had she gotten the nerve? Now what was she to do? She had failed at everything.

But what she'd said was the truth. And think of what he'd said to her! For the second time that day, she fought back hot tears stinging her eyes. What if--What if Angelo was right? What if she had no talent for painting at all?

Alma slowed her walk. She realized that she was not headed toward home, but was moving in an easterly direction. Alma had promised her mother before leaving that morning she would hurry home and arrange the supper table colorfully for Mr. Buckingham's special birthday dinner. But it was still early, and Alma needed a little time to get over the scene with Angelo. Besides, she was avoiding her mother lately. She was tired of her constantly questioning why Alma did not accept a date with so-and-so or so-and-so. Alma could just imagine her mother now, looking up from mixing cornbread or scrubbing the linoleum floor, with her face squinting in that concerned expression. "But, Alma May, you don't have to be sweet on a feller to be keepin' company. An' even if he don't have no money now, that don't mean he might not someday be makin' a decent livin'. I just don't know what's goin' to become a you. Since we came to this city when you was a little girl, you got your heart set on the moon. Best you learn to be happy with things the way they are."

Alma would change the subject and talk about topics she knew interestd her mother. Such as "Ma Perkins", or the latest popular radio program, "Information Please", with Clifton Fadiman ("A body can learn lots a things listenin' to that program, Alma May.") Alma was glad her mother didn't listen to Father Coughlin's radio program anymore. Her mother did not like the "Shepherd of the Air" since he'd changed his slogan from "Roosevelt or Ruin" to "Roosevelt and Ruin", and had called the President a Communist, a great betrayer, and a liar.

Her father didn't seem quite as concerned as her mother about Alma's lack of marriage prospects. "Alma May, I'm glad you're fussy," he would say, looking up from his farm catalog. "My baby's got a right to be fussy. But it's true what your Ma says. You have to be happy with things within your reach, an' not hanker for things that'll never be."

Most of the girls Alma knew were married or about to be. Even Gladys Polaski was engaged. Alma had run across Gladys one day last year in the fabric department at Crowley's. "Oh, Alma! Guess what?" Gladys hadn't waited for Alma to guess, but had continued breathlessly, "I met this simply wonderful boy--his name's Frankie Czarmiewski and he drives a delivery truck for Robinson Furniture--and we're getting married in two years. By that time we'll have enough money saved for the down payment on a little bungalow. We would get married sooner, of course, but why waste money on rent? Oh, you'll be invited to the wedding, of course, but we both think it's silly to have a reception, when that money could go toward linens, or a stove or ..."

Once a Cotton, always a Cotton, Alma had thought.

Oh, Alma was a failure, all right. A failure at finding a boy she liked, a failure at selling her paintings, a failure at getting an office position, and a failure at keeping even a WPA job. In her own way, she was just as much a failure as the National Recovery Act, whose faded emblem was still displayed on the window of the building to her right.

Alma suddenly realized how tired she was, and that she was approaching the Ambassador Building again. She kept her head averted until she was sure she had passed it.

"Alma! Oh, Alma!"

Alma turned around. It was Gladys Polaski, in person. Dressed in a dark brown dress, dark shoes, and a hat over her short bob.

"Oh, Alma, Alma! Something wonderful just happened! Guess what? I just got a new job! It's with Laury & Greyson. They're designers in that building"--she pointed back to the Ambassador Building--"and guess how much I'll be making? Thirty-five dollars a week! Can you imagine? That means Frankie and I can be married sooner. You should've seen all the girls up there trying out for it. But the typing test was easy. I got the highest score. Eighty-one words a minute without one error. Oh, I have to run over to Robinson's and tell Frankie!" Gladys turned and joined the crowd of pedestrians heading south.

Alma stood speechless staring after her, as Gladys glanced back at Alma and shouted, "Alma, why don't you apply for a typing job? You could make lots of money!"

Alma walked even slower now. *That's real good news, Gladys. Real good news. Now maybe you can afford some shampoo.*

A few minutes later, she found herself walking south on Woodward. Across the street and a little south, banners decked the huge J. L. Hudson building, proclaiming its fifty-eighth anniversary sale. Alma joined the throng heading for the store. She looked down at her casual outfit. Everyone dressed up to go to Hudson's. She hoped no one she knew would see her.

Once inside, the anticipated scents of expensive perfumes and toiletries wafting her way delighted her. She inhaled deeply. Alma glanced around the huge, high-ceilinged, marble-walled first floor.

Should she browse at the jewelry counter to her right, where diamond and precious stone creations beckoned behind sparkling glass display cases? Or should she finger the fine silk scarves and linen handkerchiefs to which an entire counter was devoted? Alma marveled at the number of customers milling in every direction, carrying dark green paper packages and shopping bags with "Hudson's" printed on them.

She crossed the white and gray marble floor to the counter selling Chanel perfume. She loved the scent: at once elegant and sophisticated. A scent a woman of style would wear, thought Alma. She found an open spot at the crowded counter next to a smartly dressed blond woman. The woman was softly humming the melody to a popular ditty, "A-Tisket, a-Tasket." Alma reached down and picked up a tester bottle. She sprayed a little Chanel No. 5 on her wrist. The woman suddenly stopped humming and cried, "Alma! Alma Combs! Is that really you?"

Alma turned and found familiar pale blue eyes staring at her. She stared back at the pretty woman with the flawless complexion. It was-- Mrs. Carlson! And she hardly looked a day older than when Alma had last seen her.

"Alma Combs! Long time no see! Where have you been hiding? I tried to find your name in the phone book, but I couldn't."

Alma thought fast while she found her tongue, and glanced down again at her own casual clothes. "Ah, um, we had our phone taken out. We were getting too many calls." In truth, the Combses had never had a telephone. Even if they had the money for one, her mother thought it a luxury.

Mrs. Carlson pouted prettily. "Well, I wish you had called me. Or at least dropped over." She peeled off one white glove, reached into her blue silk clutch purse, and pulled out a pad of paper and a gold Parker pen. "I'll give you my number. We moved to the Pointe several years ago."

Alma knew that the Carlsons had moved to Grosse Pointe. She'd kept up with Mrs. Carlson's social life through the "Chatterbox" column. Mrs. Carlson almost rivaled New York City debutante Brenda Frazier for publicity. Alma remembered in particular seeing a photo of her and Mr. Carlson doing the Big Apple at a Grosse Pointe Yacht Club dance. Mrs. Carlson had looked very smart and nicely faddish in her dress with several big apples appliqued on it.

Alma stole a look at her as she wrote. She wore a blue silk print dress. Her smooth, shoulder-length hair, done in the latest page boy style, was set off smartly by a felt pillbox hat, with the new bustle in the back made of the same silk print as her dress.

Mrs. Carlson handed Alma the paper with her address and phone number on it. "I'm so glad I'm doing the errands myself today. Otherwise, I never would've seen you. Robert--you remember Robert, our dear old chauffeur--Robert has the flu and I just don't trust the other help with any of our cars." She puckered her smooth brow in a slight frown. "Oh, I do hope I remember to buy everything. Let's see, now, there's that Benny Goodman record with Ziggy Elman on trumpet. What's it called, now? Oh, yes--'And the Angels Sing.' I just adore Benny Goodman, don't you? I suppose you're going to see him tonight at the fairgrounds. Oh, I'll bet all you young ladies and fellows will be out there jitterbugging the night away." Mrs. Carlson paused long enough for breath, and waited for Alma's answer.

"Uh, I have other plans for this evening." Her father had been asking her to go to the state fair with the family sometime before it closed. Alma suspected he wanted to drag her to see the livestock displays. She felt a little guilty letting him spend money on her at the fair, when she knew he was beginning to save for The Farm again.

"Of course. A pretty young lady like you must have lots of dates." Mrs. Carlson stuffed the bag containing the perfume she had just bought into her purse and pulled her glove on. "But I hope you're not too busy to paint a portrait of Susie for me. Our little girl is growing up so fast. Why, it won't be too many years before she'll be old enough for her debut!"

Alma stood there, speechless, while Mrs. Carlson chattered on. A portrait? Mrs. Carlson wanted her to do a portrait of her daughter?

"I've been thinking of having you do one for years. Remember, I've always said I adore the way you paint, and all my friends have been raving about that little pastel sketch you did of Susie once when you were babysitting her? But, as I say, I couldn't get hold of you. Do you think you'd have time? Oh, I'll pay you the going rate, of course. And if I'm pleased with it--oh, I'm sure I will be--maybe you wouldn't mind painting mine. What do you think is a fair price?"

Alma's knees felt weak. She leaned against the counter, almost knocking over a display of shiny white and black Chanel perfume boxes.

"I--l don't know."

"Shall we start at one hundred for the first portrait?"

Alma cleared her throat. "Y-Yes. That would be fine."

"Good. Does that mean you'll do it, then?"

Alma nodded her head yes.

"Call me after the flower show, then." Mrs. Carlson grabbed her purse from the counter and gave Alma's arm an affectionate squeeze. "Don't lose my number," she said, before disappearing in the aisle congested with shoppers.

Alma walked outside in a daze and hurried north on Woodward. She hadn't noticed before what a beautiful day it was. Mrs. Carlson "adored" her painting. *Oh, wonderful, wonderful Mrs. Carlson. And one hundred dollars to start!* She reached into her pocketbook and pulled out the piece of paper Mrs. Carlson had given her and read it again. She was glad now that she'd had that terrible scene with Mr. Angelo. Otherwise, she never would have run into Mrs. Carlson. Just wait until she told her family the good news!

The smile faded from her lips: She recalled what her mother had said years ago about Mrs. Carlson. "I'm glad you don't babysit for that Mrs. Carlson no more, Alma May." Her mother had paused long enough to squint at a needle she was threading before continuing to darn her father's stockings. "I saw that Mrs. Gottleib--you remember how I used to clean for Mrs. Gottleib--well, I saw Mrs. Gottleib waitin' in her limousine today for her driver-man to come out a the store. An' you remember how Mrs. Gottleib likes to talk about all a them Grosse Pointe ladies? Well, she says Mrs. Carlson an' her man owns stock in all a them factries that's makin'--what you call 'em?--munitions for them German Nazis. Reckon if that ain't wrong, I don't know what is. I figure any fool knows that Hitler man is aimin' to take over all them countries an' is goin' to have to do lots a killin' to do it."

Alma dismissed her mother's dislike of Mrs. Carlson from her mind. She *would not* let anything spoil her elation. *One hundred dollars to start!*

She paused for a moment to admire the diamond necklace in the window of Wright-Kay's jewelry store. Ninety-five dollars. Should she blow her first check on that? No, she decided, walking faster again. She would spend her first money on oils and brushes and canvas and board money for her family and some much-needed clothes for herself and ...

Alma gradually became aware of the rush of pedestrians passing her, hurrying in the direction of Grand Circus Park where she was headed, and of a newsboy's shout:

"Extra! Extra! Read all about it! Hitler invades Poland! Extra! Extra! Read all about it! German warplanes bomb Poland."

Alma, too, rushed toward the crowd gathering at the newsstand. She peeked over the heads and shoulders of men and women scrambling to buy copies of the *Free Press*. One man kept his copy steady long enough for her to read the huge headlines:

WAR!
GERMAN WARPLANES BOMB POLAND'S CAPITOL:
NAZIS ANNEX DANZIG, HEAVY BORDER FIGHTING

Alma strained to read more as she heard anxious voices around her:

"England and France will be in it for sure, now."

"Those poor British! Listen to what it says here: 'London Evacuates Children; Parliament Is Summoned.'"

"I'll bet it won't be long before we're in it, too, now--"

"No, we won't. Not if we continue our policy of non-intervention."

"That's right. I'm all for supplying them with weapons, but let them fight their own wars."

Alma agreed. We should remain neutral. And she was very glad she was living in this country, and not over there. When she turned to leave the crowd and continue toward home, she glimpsed a stack of the latest *Time* magazine, out that day. Under Winston Churchill's cover picture was the caption, "Hitler Is on the Run."

Once away from the crowd, the memory of the headlines began to fade. The war in Europe was far away. The long Labor Day weekend stretched before her. Yes, it might be sort of fun to go to the state fair. She would pay her father back what he spent on her.

The mid afternoon sunlight glistened on the upper windows of the buildings lining Woodward, making them sparkle like jewels. Alma began to plan how she would decorate the supper table for Mr. Buckingham's special meal. And maybe she would give him a birthday gift of one of her favorite mountain sketches. She avoided walking into a small boy, in his innocence drawing a Nazi swastika in chalk on the sidewalk. Alma began to sing, "A-tisket, a-taskit, a green and yellow basket. …"

Chapter 23

The steering wheel of the used, late-model white Oldsmobile coupe felt smooth and cool in her hands in autumn of the following year, as Alma joined the mid-afternoon traffic going south on Linwood toward home. She removed a hand from the wheel and ran her fingers down the calf of one leg. Her legs felt smooth and cool, too, hugged by stockings made of the new nylon material.

She was glad that Mr. Buckingham had helped her pick out this make and model, which she'd bought on credit. It had a completely automatic shift. Each time she stopped for a light, Alma glanced smugly at the other drivers who had to go through the mechanics of shifting gears. She had asked her father and Jimmie Lee to help in the selection, too, of course, but they hadn't wanted to aggravate her mother. Alma could picture her mother now, her face twisted in a disapproving frown as she looked down at the green beans she was snapping. "No, Alma May. Long as you insist on takin' that blood money for paintin' them pictures for that Carlson woman an' her man, leastaways none of us in this family is goin' to help you spend it."

"But Mom," Alma had protested. "I hear Mister and Missus Carlson have stock now in American companies building armaments to help our allies."

"They's probably still got stock in them Nazi companies, too. Playin' one side against the other. Oppor--Opportunists, reckon that's what they are."

Alma said nothing. Mrs. Carlson never mentioned her business dealings.

Alma turned the radio on now and tuned it to station WJR. "President Roosevelt signed the Burke-Wadsworth Selective Service Act into law this afternoon," the cool, crisp newscaster's voice announced, "and fixed October 16 as registration day for sixteen million, five hundred thousand young Americans between the ages of twenty-one and thirty-five now subject to compulsory military training. This is the first peacetime military draft bill in the nation's history. The President said that the United States is marshalling its strength to avert what he called the terrible fate of nations whose weakness invited attack--"

Alma frowned and flicked the dial a little to the right to CKLW. She was glad her father was too old and Jimmie Lee too young for the draft. Too bad Uncle Darcas was too old, too.

"England's Royal Air Force claimed its biggest victory of London's siege, with one hundred and seventy-five Nazi planes knocked out of the skies yesterday--"

War, war, war! That was all Alma heard these days. Defense and war. She moved the dial a little to the right again. From WXYZ came the pleasant, bouncy sounds of the Kay Kayser orchestra's "Playmate." Good. That was more like it.

She began to think of happy things again. Like the new dress she'd just picked up from Sak's. She would wear the black silk crepe with velvet collar and cuffs and jewel-like buttons tonight to the Cass Theater with Felicia Carlson. Felicia (Alma was flattered that Mrs. Carlson had today insisted it was about time Alma called her by her first name) had two tickets to see Clifton Webb in "The Man Who Came to Dinner," and had asked Alma to go with her since Mr. Carlson was out of town. This was the first time Alma had been invited to go somewhere socially with her, and Alma wanted to look her best. The dress was worth the twenty-five dollars. Oh, Felicia and the past year had been good to Alma! If only her mother wouldn't spoil Alma's happiness with her constant disapproval.

Alma looked down at the sales pamphlets on the seat next to the dress. Her mother would not even accept board money from Alma, since she didn't approve of the source from which it came, but surely she'd be thrilled at the prospect of owning one of the new Maytag white porcelain enamel washing machines with a wringer. Just wait until she saw the brochure. She couldn't refuse.

The other pamphlet was for her father. "Plymouth--the 'One' for '41," the cover said. Alma would point out the sporty little coupe on page two. Her father certainly deserved a Plymouth, after working on them all those years, and she was excited about telling him she wanted to put money down on one for him, and pay the balance in installments.

Alma was almost to the Combses' flat now. She hoped that Carrie Lou wouldn't notice when she pulled up. Carrie Lou always pestered Alma to take her for a spin in her car, and Alma did not have time this afternoon. She decided to park half a block from the flat and walk the rest of the way.

Alma smoothed the hem of her new pinafore and hurried up the sidewalk. She noticed three young girls of about Carrie Lou's age standing by the Combses' yard. When she drew nearer the flat, she was able to make out the words of their singsong chant:

> "Carrie Lou's a friend of mine.
> She will do it any time,
> For a nickel or a dime,
> Fifteen cents for overtime."

Alma stood there, not conscious of the meaning at first, until the girls repeated he chant.

The children became aware of Alma's presence and covered their mouths with their hands. They giggled nervously and scrambled away as Alma yelled after them, "Don't you ever come back here again! Hear me? I don't ever want to see you here again!" Alma stood there, her eyes blazing, while she watched them run from sight.

Carrie Lou appeared from behind the flat and ran toward her. Alma was surprised at how tall her little sister looked for her nine years.

"Carrie Lou! Did you bear those girls? What did they mean?"

Carrie Lou hung her head and smoothed down the grass with her toe.

"Wh, What girls, Alma May?"

"Don't lie to me, Carrie Lou. You heard what they were singing." Alma looked down at the top of Carrie Lou's head, which surprisingly reached almost to Alma's shoulder now. "Carrie Lou, have you been doing something you shouldn't?"

Carrie Lou looked up, her big blue eyes growing larger behind thick black lashes. "Oh, no, Alma May. What do you mean?" She hung her head again.

"Have you been doing something you shouldn't with--with boys?"

Carrie Lou looked up once more. Her little-girl eyes focused on Alma's. "With boys? Don't know what you mean, Alma May. I ain't been doin' nothin' wrong." Carrie Lou smiled her wide smile, intended to be disarming. "Take me for a ride, Alma May. Please, please!" Her thick black hair bounced on her shoulders as she jumped up and down.

Alma was glad to change the topic. "I don't have time tonight. I have to get dressed and drive way out to Missus Carl--Felicia's. I'm going to the theater tonight."

Carrie Lou's dainty mouth turned down in a frown. "How's come you're always goin' somewheres an' I ain't? Take me with you. Take me with you!"

Alma could just imagine how it would be with Carrie Lou along. She'd be begging for candy after every act, and then would be rewarding Alma with kisses and hugs. Carrie Lou was getting too big for that kind of stuff. Alma's mother should be talking with her about that. But knowing her mother ...

Her mother was sitting in the chair under the latest rotogravure portrait of President Roosevelt. She was smiling and reading Eleanor Roosevelt's *My Day* column. An open dictionary on the table beside her rested on a starched white doily. Lizzie had found the dictionary in the Salvation Army store for a nickel. Her mother would be lost without her dictionary, just as her father would be lost without his farm catalog.

Alma was glad Carrie Lou was still outside, and her father and Mr. Buckingham, who was coming for supper, were not home from work yet. And that Jimmie Lee wasn't, either. She didn't want them to hear. "Mom. Do you keep track of what Carrie Lou does all day?"

Lizzie looked up from the *Free Press*. Her brow wrinkled as she gave Alma a puzzled look. "What you mean, Alma May? When she ain't in school or helpin' me, I figure she's just playin' with her little friends."

"Did you hear those girls outside?"

"What girls?"

"Those girls. They were singing--"

Carrie Lou walked in. Alma made a mental note to talk with her mother later.

"Alma May, Alma May, buy me a pinafore just like yours," Carrie Lou begged. "Will ya, will ya? All the girls in school are gettin' them. Will ya, will ya?

Alma sighed. "We'll see."

Carrie Lou smiled her disarming smile again. "'We'll see' means 'yes,' I know it does." She ran to Alma and hugged her tightly. "Oh, you're the best sister in the whole wide world!"

Lizzie lowered her paper and gave them both a censuring look. "Never you mind askin' Alma May for no pinafore, Carrie Lou. I can make you one myself."

★   ★   ★

Alma, dressed in her new theater outfit, headed for the living room. Now, after supper when her mother was usually feeling her mellowest, would be a good time to show her and her father the brochures.

Jimmie Lee approached her in the hall. He was on his way out, as usual, for an evening with his friends. He stopped abruptly in mock helplessness. "Wow!" he said, and gave a long, low, appreciative whistle. "If you don't look swell! You look just like one of them society dames! If you weren't my sister, I could go for you. Of course, you *are* a little old for me."

Alma puffed on an imaginary cigarette holder and blinked her eyes in simulated seduction. "Silly," she said, in an exaggerated, sophisticated tone.

Jimmie Lee smiled, and Alma reached into her rhinestone-studded silver evening bag. She pulled out a twenty-dollar bill. "Jimmie Lee, I'd like--"

"Oh, Alma, you don't have to do that. I'm making enough to get by now."

Alma looked up at her brother. He had grown so tall these past several months that he towered above her. He was all legs and arms now, but his freckles remained as prominent as ever.

There seemed to be an unspoken conspiracy between Jimmie Lee and Alma against their mother, Alma thought. No, it wasn't exactly a conspiracy, but it was as though Jimmie Lee was the one family member who was the happiest for her and her new prosperity. "I happen to know that you just had to pay a huge repair bill on that old Terraplane of yours. Let me help you with that," she said.

Jimmie Lee shook his head. "I'll manage."

Alma protruded her lower lip, mimicking Carrie Lou's little-girl pout. "Well, at least let me give you enough to go to Eastwood Gardens to hear Harry James."

Jimmie Lee shook his head again.

"I hear the Tigers are playing the Senators tonight at Briggs Stadium. Let me give you enough for you and your buddies to go."

Jimmie Lee's eyes brightened at mention of the Tigers. "Well, maybe--"

Alma stuffed a bill in the pocket of his checkered cotton slacks and, standing on tiptoe, kissed him on the cheek.

Jimmie Lee returned the kiss on her forehead. "You're swell."

When Alma entered the living room, her mother and Mr. Buckingham were engaged in a friendly argument. Her father sat in the Morris chair her mother had found for him at a rummage sale several years after they were forced to sell the first one. He pretended to pay attention, but Alma knew he'd prefer to read the farm catalog he was leafing through. Strange how her father had grown more silent these past few years, while her mother had grown more talkative.

She was glad Uncle Darcas hadn't dropped by. Alma didn't want to put up with some stupid remark when he saw her in her new dress. Or his boring bragging about how Briggs was producing so many aircraft sub-assemblies for defense. To hear Uncle Darcas tell it, he was the most important employee there. But most of all, she was glad she didn't have to listen to his inane insinuations of why she didn't have a serious boyfriend. "Back home," he'd said the last time be was there as he took another swill of Stroh's beer, "if a woman ain't married by the time she's Alma May's age, folks'd be sayin' they's somethin' wrong with her." He had raised his shaggy eyebrows, rolled his little eyes, and left in a hurry, before her mother and father had time to bawl him out. Alma didn't know how poor Aunt Euella could put up with him. Of course, Aunt Euella was in a drunken stupor most of the time, anyway.

"But that Wendell Willkie ain't right, Harry," Alma's mother was saying now, making her point by jamming her darning needle deeper into Jimmie Lee's stocking she was mending. "Mister Roosevelt ain't goin' to become a dictator if he's elected for a third term. Way I figure, it ain't smart to change horses in the middle a the stream. What with the war in Europe, an' Mister Roosevelt knowin' all there is to know about foreign policy, an'--"

"He knows all there is to know about foreign policy, for sure, Lizzie," Mr. Buckingham replied. "Willkie's right on one thing, at least. Can't you see that Roosevelt's scheming to involve us in the war? He's been methodically trying to steer us, even though most of us don't want--" Mr. Buckingham stopped to admire Alma when he noticed her in the doorway. "You look very lovely this evening, Miss Combs," he remarked in exaggerated gracious formality.

Alma curtsied and smiled at him. Mr. Buckingham always made her feel special. Not like her mother, who was looking down at her mending, her lips pursed in a straight line as she began to darn faster. Her father said nothing, but smiled proudly at his daughter.

Mr. Buckingham tapped his Lucky Strike on the rim of his ashtray. "Hey, what's this I read about you in the *Free Press* yesterday?"

"*Free Press?*" Alma's tone was casual. "Oh, that. It was nothing. Just a little item in the *Chatterbox* column." In truth, Alma had memorized every word: "Who is this young new-on-the-scene Alma Combs? The young Detroit artist has painted several portraits of the Smart Set, including Felicia and Alfred Carlson."

Lizzie looked up briefly and gave Alma another one of her disapproving looks before resuming her darning.

Alma glanced down at her wristwatch. Not much time left. She was glad when Mr. Buckingham asked her what she had in her hand.

"Ah--just some brochures I was going to show Mom and Dad." She handed Chet the Plymouth pamphlet. "Dad," she said hesitantly as she stole a glance at her mother, "You know how all those years you worked on all those Plymouths and we never could afford one? Well, now I'm starting to earn a little money and there's no reason why I couldn't buy one for you on credit."

Chet looked up at his daughter, surprised. "Alma May, baby, I couldn't let you buy me a car."

"Oh, Dad, if anyone deserves a car, it's you--"

"But, honey, I don't need a car. The only places your Ma and me go, we can take the DSR. An' if we ever really need a car, Jimmie Lee'll loan us his Terraplane--"

"Please, Dad. Let me do this one thing for you."

"No, baby, don't want to hurt your little feelin's, but I can't let you buy me a big thing like that. Besides, soon as I get a little more money saved, we'll be goin' back home an' buy The Farm--"

"That's another thing I was going to mention, Dad. I'd like to start giving you some money toward The Farm--"

"Blood money," Lizzie said.

"Please, Dad. If you and Mom won't let me pay board money, at least let me buy something."

Lizzie dropped the darning to her lap and looked up, her eyes angry. "No, Alma May. None of us is takin' no gifts from you, long as you're associatin' with that mer--mer--mercenary Carlson woman."

"Lizzie, don't be so rough on Alma May," Chet said.

Alma blinked back the tears that started to mist her eyes. She could not have her freshly mascara-ed eyes ruined. "Mom, you've never even met Felicia. She's a real nice lady. I want to be just like her. She and Mister Carlson are always giving big sums of money to charities, and--"

"Blood money!"

Alma faced her mother squarely. "Why can't you be happy for me? Finally, I'm getting a little recognition for my paintings, and getting paid very well for them, and starting to meet some important people, and--"

"There ain't nothin' wrong in your wantin' to be successful in paintin' and makin' lots a money, long as you go about it right." Her mother's voice was getting louder. "An' as far as you 'startin' to meet some important people'--them people ain't our kind a people, Alma May. We're hillbilly people. Since we came to Detroit City you've been gettin' a big head. Ain't I always told you there ain't nothin' wrong in bein' hillbillies, long as we don't lie or cheat or steal? An' I can't forget how that Carlson woman got her money in the first place, by bootleggin', that's how. An' if that ain't lyin' an' cheatin' an' stealin', I don't know what is. Way I figure it, I'd rather be a poor, honest hillbilly any day, than a rich, unhonest--"

"Well, maybe you want to remain a hillbilly all your life, but I'm not going to."

"Once a hillbilly, always a hillbilly, no matter where you go or how much money you got. Sooner you learn that, the better off you'll be. You shouldn't be ashamed a bein' a hillbilly. You should be proud."

The mascara ran down Alma's hot cheeks. She fumbled for a handkerchief in her purse as Mr. Buckingham handed her his.

Alma's father stood helplessly between Alma and her mother. "Lizzie, Lizzie. Alma May, Alma May. Don't quarrel like this."

Alma dabbed at her cheeks. "At long last, I might have this wonderful chance to be someone really important, and I'm not giving it up for anything! Not for anything!" Her voice was louder, too, and choking.

"Well, reckon you better not bring none a them 'important' people to this house--"

"Don't worry! Don't worry! Think I'd bring anyone here? Knowing the way you'd treat them? They'd die laughing if they saw this place, anyway."

The Maytag brochure fell from Alma's hand as she dabbed at her cheeks again and blew her nose. Her father and Mr. Buckingham moved to pick up the brochure. Alma gave it a kick with her new black silk pump. "And to think! I was going to show you the new washing machines, hoping I could pay down on one for you so you wouldn't have to work so hard."

"Reckon my washboard works just fine, thank you--"

Alma turned from her mother and ran to the bedroom she shared with Carrie Lou. She reached into the closet and grabbed her suitcase, yanked open the drawers of the chiffonier and began stuffing the contents, blurred by her tears, into the suitcase.

"Whatcha doin'?" Carrie Lou stood in the doorway, drinking milk from a blue glass mug with a likeness of Shirley Temple on it.

"You sure do ask dumb questions! What does it look like I'm doing? I'm leaving!"

Carrie Lou lowered the mug from her bright red lips and her eyes got big. "Leavin'? Why, Alma May, why?"

"Oh, you wouldn't understand!" Alma threw a tortoise shell brush into the suitcase and tried to close it. She stuffed the straps of a silk slip that protruded from the side and struggled with the locks. "I know one thing you'll understand, though. You won't be able to sneak into my lipsticks anymore and make your lips up like a clown's."

Carrie Lou covered her mouth with her free hand. "Lipstick? I don't know what you mean, Alma May."

Alma's mouth wrinkled in disgust both at Carrie Lou and at the stubborn suitcase lock as her father entered the room.

"Alma May! Alma May! What you doin', baby?"

"I should've left a long time ago, Pa. I'm way too old to be still living with my parents. And Ma won't even let me pay board."

"Oh, Alma May, Alma May! Don't go! I'll talk with your Ma, an'--"

"No, Pa. You heard what she said. You could talk till Big Black Mountain was an ant hill, and she'd still be the same."

"Oh, we should never've left our mountains. I should never've brought you here. You never would've met all them high muckymuck people."

Alma glanced up at her father, whose eyes looked even bluer now as they began to mist. "I'm glad I met those 'high muckymuck' people, as you call them. Those high muckamuck people are the beginning of a wonderful life for me. I have hopes of making more money than I ever dreamed possible. If you both weren't so stubborn, I could share it with you. I could buy all of you everything you ever wanted."

"You know the only thing I ever wanted was The Farm, an' for all of us to be happy livin' there."

"And you won't even let me help you with that."

Her father's voice was low and firm. "No."

Alma at last succeeded in locking the bulging suitcase. She reached over and hugged her father tightly. How small and frail he was. "I'll ask Jimmie Lee to bring over the rest of my stuff tomorrow."

"But, but where'll you go, baby?"

"Oh, don't worry, Dad. I'll find a nice place to live." Alma gave her father a little smile. He looked older to her. "Don't worry. I'll be okay." She picked up the suitcase and her purse from the bed.

"Please don't go, honey."

"You know I have to, Dad."

Alma walked through the doorway of the bedroom. She did not look back.

"Alma May, you still takin' me to see 'Pinocchio?' Are ya, are ya, huh?" asked Carrie Lou.

Her mother was darning a different stocking when Alma entered the living room. The silence was as thick as the saw briars on the mountain slope back home. Lizzie looked up, her face red and blotched. "Where you think you're goin'."

Alma did not look at her mother. Her lips began to tremble. She gave Mr. Buckingham a feeble smile. "Bye, Mr. Buckingham."

Alma opened the door as Lizzie jumped up from her chair and ran toward her. "Alma May! Alma May! Come back! You don't have to go. If you promise to give up that bunch you been runnin' 'round with--"

"Can't do that, Mom. I finally have hopes of living the way I should. I won't give it up for anything--"

"Alma May! Alma May!"

Alma walked down the steps and glanced back. Her mother's thick figure was framed in the doorway.

My name's not Alma May, thought Alma. My name's Alma. Just Alma.

Alma turned the key in the ignition, the suitcase by her side on the seat, as Mr. Buckingham closed her car door. "Don't shut her out, Alma," he said gently. "Keep in touch. She loves you very much." He reached his hand through the open window and patted hers. "Take care of yourself."

Alma glanced back at her mother. In the light of dusk, she could barely make out her mother's features, but what she could see of them were contorted in a painful expression. She rolled up her window. Alma could not hear her mother now, but she could see her lips moving, calling her daughter's name.

"I will, Mr. Buckingham," she whispered.

The streetlights were turning on as Alma drove north on Linwood. The steering wheel felt cool and smooth in her hands.

Chapter 24

"Why you so nervous?" Tommie asked one early December evening. He and Alma turned off Lakeshore Drive with its towering elms onto the private road leading to the Van Delore mansion.

"Nervous? I'm not nervous," Alma said. She looked over at her escort behind the wheel of his Lincoln Victoria cabriolet. Actually, she was anxious about whether she would remember what she had recently crammed into her head from several etiquette books. Alma had learned that, as guest of honor this evening, she would be sitting at Mr. Van Delore's right at the dinner table. She should stand behind her chair until--

"They'll adore it." Tommie grinned at her. Tommie Tender (an unlikely name, but Felicia assured her it was real) was a young dress designer whom Felicia had befriended and taken under her wing. She had arranged for Tommie to escort Alma this evening. Tommie, tall and thin as an artist's paintbrush, had dark straight hair and penetrating brown eyes that missed nothing. "Tommie's always good for a laugh," Felicia had said. "You never know what he's going to say next." She was including him and Alma in more and more of her social engagements lately. Felicia had promised to wear a gown tonight that he had designed, a lovely white beaded crepe cut low in the back. She'd assured him that the ladies would be so impressed with it. They would want him to design one for them.

"Adore what?" Alma asked.

"The portrait, of course." Tommie's full, sensuous lips turned up in another grin. "I'll bet before the evening's over, you'll have at least ten more commissions."

265

Tommie pulled the Lincoln up the circular drive in front of the stone baronial dwelling, and parked. The mansion looked very grand at night with all the windows glowing and the floodlights making giant emerald and crystal jewels of the snow-topped shrubs. A uniformed attendant helped Alma and Tommie out of the car. Charles, the dour-faced butler, escorted them into the parlor. "He's probably gone to every Arthur Treacher movie a dozen times to see how a butler should act," Tommie whispered.

Most of the guests had already arrived, but the Carlsons were nowhere in sight yet. Clara Van Delore put her glass down and approached Alma and Tommie from across the room as they entered. Her size eighteen body was squeezed into a size fourteen black silk Schiaparelli that Alma had seen at Sak's. Alma smoothed the waist of her own blue crepe.

"Can you believe that face?" Tommie whispered. "She's got as many wrinkles as a marble egg that's been dropped."

"Oh, Tommie! You're terrible!" Alma kept her voice low.

"Alma, my dear. How lovely you look!" Mrs. Van Delore was holding a cigarette in a gold holder. She squeezed Alma's hand in a familiar, welcoming gesture. "And, Tommie, how nice that you could make it."

Mrs. Van Delore lowered her voice in mock conspiracy. "Everyone's just dying to see it. But the suspense will be even greater if we have the unveiling after dinner."

Alma smiled and accepted a glass of champagne from a pretty young servant girl. She took a sip, being careful to hold the glass by the stem, as she'd learned from the books. Tommie selected a glass from the tray as Mrs. Van Delore rambled on and Alma scanned the guests, trying to guess which one might be retired Col. Ezra McIntosh. Felicia had been elated upon finding out that Colonel and Mrs. McIntosh were to be guests at the party tonight. "If Colonel McIntosh is impressed with Clara Van Delore's portrait, your future is assured, Alma. He's looking for an artist to paint a portrait of each of his four sons and five daughters. And he's let it be known that if he's pleased with those portraits, he might consider having some done of his grandchildren, too." Felicia's eyes had grown bright with excitement. "And who knows where that could lead? Old Colonel McIntosh pulls a lot of weight in this town. Did you know that he ordered the Lutheran church to stop ringing its bells on Sunday morning? It was disturbing his sleep. And the church stopped it! The old colonel's got a lot of friends who follow his lead. Before you know it, you'll have enough commissions to last you for the next ten years."

How like Felicia Carlson to wish for such big success for Alma. Hadn't she been the one to launch Alma's career in the first place, what with the portraits of each of the Carlsons, and a few of her friends this past year, including the one just completed of Mrs. Van Delore? Felicia was wonderful.

"But how thoughtless of me to keep you all to myself," Mrs. Van Delore was saying. "Let me introduce you two young things to the other guests."

★ ★ ★

The tinkle of sparkling Waterford crystal mingled with the clink of gleaming Gorham silverware around her as Alma sipped her shrimp bisque. She was glad that she remembered to dip her spoon correctly into the bowl, from front to back. She glanced casually around the dining room. How beautiful it looked. Rich teak paneled walls shone in the candlelight both from the table's silver centerpiece and two candles set in crystal holders on the Regency buffet to her left. To her right, past Mrs. Van Delore, who was sitting at the end of the table opposite her husband, Alma saw the moonlight shining on Lake St. Clair through the huge bay window. Felicia sat near Mrs. Van Delore. Was it really true? Was she, Alma May Combs, actually sitting here, guest of honor no less, in the home of one of the city's leading society couples, whose names she had been reading for years in the "Chatterbox" column?

"We feel honored, Miss Combs, that you were free to be here tonight."

Alma smiled at her host. Percy Van Delore, an obese, wheezing man, had a flat nose and jowls that jiggled when he talked. He was likeable enough, Alma thought. "Oh, I'm the one who should feel honored. I'm having a lovely time. And what a beautiful home you have! I've been here quite a few times, of course, but only during the day for Mrs. Van Delore's portrait sittings. Your home is equally beautiful during the day, but at night it takes on a whole different atmosphere." Alma looked out at the lake again.

Mr. Van Delore wheezed in appreciation. "Yes, the lake is beautiful, isn't it?" He looked out the window beyond his wife and smiled. "You know, it's getting more and more fashionable to have a psychiatrist. But me, I don't think I'll ever need one. Not when I can sit in my comfortable leather chair and gaze out the window at Lake St. Clair. I feel at peace. Every day, it's different. In the summer you see the freighters and the boaters. You can feel the warmth. And in the winter--in the winter the ice formations are always changing."

Alma thought fleetingly of her father sitting in his shabby Morris chair looking at his United Farm Agency catalog every day in both the summer and the winter.

"Why isn't a pretty young lady like you at the Bundles for Britain Ball tonight at the Statler?" Colonel McIntosh's voice was loud and gravelly. He sat at Alma's right (Felicia had asked Mrs. Van Delore to arrange for this) and ate his bisque as he waited for Alma's answer. The Colonel had several chins, partly hidden by a polka dotted bow tie and a handlebar mustache that moved up and down as he ate. His white hair was combed forward from the back of his head in an attempt to hide his baldness. It did not work, because the hair kept separating and falling down over both ears, which made him look like an unkempt, mustached Humpty Dumpty.

How should Alma answer the Colonel's thoughtless question? Should she say she couldn't be at the ball because she was the guest of honor here? Or should she say that she hadn't paid much attention to it, and had forgotten about the ball intended to raise money for Britain, and appear unfeeling about the plight of England? She decided to say neither, and just smiled. Too much was at stake to answer Colonel McIntosh in the wrong way.

She was glad when her host began babbling on, and was grateful that what he was saying did not require an answer. It gave her a chance to pretend to be listening and to smile at Colonel McIntosh and devote one ear to the conversation around her:

"I hear that Chrysler is doing away with most of the bright work on its '42 models. You know--the chrome. Except for the bumpers. They're replacing it with materials not needed in the defense program."

"You know, of course, that Olds is now in mass production of automatic cannon for airplanes and shells for field artillery..."

"Work's coming along fine on that huge new bomber factory of Ford's. You know, the one in--what's that strange name? Ypsilanti, that's it. I can never remember that name. I'm glad they're going to call it the Willow Run plant..."

"Well, it's 'business as usual' for me. I'm not going to risk my fortune on anything as transient as the defense boom. Not when the public is finally demanding more and more consumer goods again. Let Uncle Sam worry about defense, at least for a while longer. ..."

"I can't pronounce their names, but I'm talking about those two Japanese envoys that Hardhat's sent to Washington. They've been talking all week with Roosevelt and Cordell Hull, trying to persuade the United States to stop helping China and Russia. And trying to patch things up with us. They seem like pretty decent fellows. Did you see that great picture of them in *Life* last week? Grinning like crazy. ..."

Alma stiffened at the talk of defense and possible war. It reminded her that Jimmie Lee was over eighteen now and could enlist any time he wanted to, something he'd been hinting at doing more and more lately as he devoted increasing attention to the newscasts and bulletins from Europe.

Alma stole a glance at the label on the bottle of wine that the servant brought for Mr. Van Delore's approval. Chateau Beychevelle, 1922. Mr. Van Delore took a sip, inhaled, rolled the liquid slowly around his tongue, and paused for a moment before swallowing. He nodded approval. While the servant filled Alma's glass, she smiled across at Mrs. McIntosh, but was met with a cool, uninterested response. Mrs. McIntosh had a flat, floury-white face like an uncooked pancake. Her veiny left hand kept fiddling with her long Chanel pearls, which were coming dangerously close to falling into her Hollandaise sauce.

Alma felt snubbed and looked quickly down to the opposite end of the table, where Tommie sat next to Felicia. Tommie caught her glance, and gave her a wink in empathy. While Mr. Van Delore chattered on and Colonel McIntosh answered a question from the woman on his right, Alma strained to hear the conversation around Tommie:

"I can't believe you haven't been invited to Rose Terrace. I'm seeing Anna tomorrow, and I'll be sure to drop the suggestion. ..."

Felicia had told Alma about Rose Terrace, Anna Thompson Dodge's mansion down the road from the Van Delore estate. Some say it has seventy-five rooms, and others say ninety. It was an imitation of the Palace at Versailles (Alma wondered if Father Coughlin had ever learned how to pronounce "Versailles."). Alma had often seen peacocks roaming the grounds when she drove by last summer. Felicia said she heard Mrs. Dodge employed two men full time just to polish her silverware and gold treasures.

"Felicia Carlson! Did I hear you right? This gorgeous creation was designed by this young man?"

"Honest. I have quite a few of Tommie's designs. After a while, those Paris designs can be boring."

It was Alma's turn to wink at Tommie. He was making a good impression tonight on the Grosse Pointe set.

"Do you know many other portrait artists in town, Miss Combs? For instance, Beresford Moore? I read that his portraits of Detroiters will be on exhibit starting Thursday at the Hanna galleries." John La Follette, who was sitting across from Alma at Mrs. McIntosh's left, was speaking. La Follette, a big, pleasant man and a baron of automobile producing machinery, reminded Alma of the kindly movie actor, Herbert Marshall. Felicia had told her that La Follette lived across the river in Canada to avoid paying huge United States income taxes.

"I don't know Beresford Moore personally, but I've seen his work. It's very good." Alma smiled back at Mr. La Follette.

"Good? His work is abominal! Abominal!" Colonel McIntosh interrupted, his voice booming. The other guests grew silent and listened. "You should have seen what he tried to pass off as a portrait of me last month. No resemblance at all!"

Alma was worried. Beresford Moore was well respected as a portrait artist with a lot more experience than Alma had. If Beresford Moore had not pleased Colonel McIntosh, how did Alma have the gall to even entertain the idea that she might? She may as well dismiss that chinchilla coat and matching hat and muff and the new '42 Packard Clipper from her thoughts right now. "What--What didn't you like about it, Colonel McIntosh?"

"Everything! Bags under my eyes down to here." Colonel McIntosh raised a gnarled finger to his cheek. "No hair on my head, exaggerated my chin. It just didn't resemble me at all!"

Tommie rolled his eyes and winked at Alma as the others smiled indulgently at the colonel.

"You should have commissioned Alma," Mrs. Van Delore said. "Just wait until you see her work."

Felicia smiled proudly at Alma while the others asked in unison when they were going to get the chance.

Mrs. Van Delore's lips turned up in a smug little smile. "Very soon. Here comes Mary with our dessert now."

So this is baked Alaska, Alma thought, as she dipped her spoon into the brown and white meringue. *That old curmudgeon McIntosh. There would be no pleasing him.*

"I hear you're from Kentucky, Miss Combs. What part?" Mr. La Follette asked.

Alma thought fast. If she told the truth, then she would have to explain that Mountainview was near Harlan, and right away they would think of coal mines and poor people and that awful "Bloody Harlan" strike of '34, and Appalachian hillbillies, and--

"Near Louisville?" Mr. Van Delore asked.

Alma nodded her head and crossed two fingers under the tablecloth. She hadn't actually come right out and said yes. What harm was there in letting them think it? Her mother's disapproving face flashed in her mind.

Mrs. McIntosh looked directly at Alma for the first time. "Oh? How interesting. Are you from the family that owns the famous Combs stables?"

Colonel McIntosh chuckled, his anger with Beresford Moore apparently forgotten for the moment. "My wife's ears always perk up when Louisville is mentioned. She's crazy about race horses."

Mrs. McIntosh looked at her husband in pretended annoyance. "Now, Ezra. Let someone else speak. Miss Combs was about to tell us about the Combs stables." She looked back at Alma and repeated, "Are you related to the Buford Combs family?"

Alma crossed her fingers tighter and smiled modestly. "Distantly."

"But you are from Louisville?" Mrs. McIntosh insisted.

Alma swallowed and nodded yes. She glanced at the other guests. Was that a skeptical look in Tommie's eyes? She looked back quickly at Mrs. McIntosh.

Mrs. McIntosh gave her a radiant smile. "Oh, you'll have to tell us how it is living in Louisville. It must be wonderful being a part of the racing scene--"

"Why, Alma Combs!" Felicia scolded gently. "If I had known you were from Louisville, I would've taken you there last spring for the Derby. It would've been a lot more fun with someone who's familiar with the area."

"Well, now. We should all plan to go together next May and have Miss Combs as our escort!" Mr. Van Delore's motion was seconded enthusiastically by everyone at the table. Except Tommie. He just grinned.

To Alma's relief, her hostess placed her napkin on the table and stood up. "Wonderful idea! But now, if everyone is finished, coffee and cordials are served in the east parlor. And then"--her eyes, as small and dark as shoe buttons, flashed in anticipation--"there is something I would like you all to see!"

★   ★   ★

Alma stood with the other guests before the silk-draped portrait, balancing her third cup of coffee on a Limoges saucer. Her hostess had dragged out the time for the unveiling as long as she could. Alma noticed several of the men looking discreetly at their watches. Colonel McIntosh had looked at his, too, but not discreetly.

Alma picked a spot to stand where she could see the colonel's face when Mrs. Van Delore removed the drape. Would he like it? Oh, please, make him like it. Even if he didn't care for it well enough to order a commission from Alma, don't let him say anything derogatory about it. Alma was sure if the Colonel didn't like it, he wouldn't pretend he did, contrary to what etiquette dictated. One negative remark from him, and no one else would risk having their portrait painted by her. Word would soon get around that she could not really paint well, after all.

Mrs. McIntosh was standing indifferently by her husband's side. Tommie bent down and whispered in Alma's ear. "Can you believe that? She's got a face that'd stop a ten-day clock!"

Mrs. Van Delore walked to the side of the easel and looked around at the faces of the guests.

"Trumpets, please! Toot-ta-toot-ta-toot!" Tommie whispered.

"And, now! Ladies and gentlemen. I give you the work of Detroit's newest artist--Alma Combs!"

"More trumpets," Tommie whispered. "Toot-ta-toot-ta-toot!"

Mrs. Van Delore flung the drape back with a flourish. Alma glanced at the colonel's face. It was expressionless. That meant he did not like it. Why did Mrs. Van Delore have to invite him? The vain old geezer.

Tommie whispered in Alma's ear again. "No wonder old cracked-egg face likes it so much. It makes her look twenty years younger. You did a heroic job!"

Felicia and Alfred Carlson, a tall, undistinguished looking man, walked over to Alma. "Oh, Alma, I knew it would be good!" Felicia cried. Then, lowering her voice and turning her head so the Van Delores could not hear, she whispered: "You did such a great job--you made her look good!"

"Thank you," said Alma, her eyes still on the colonel's face. "But I don't think Colonel McIntosh--"

The colonel was walking toward her now. His face was still inscrutable. Would he humiliate her in front of all these important people?

The colonel reached into his breast pocket and pulled out a small engraved card. "Miss Combs, you paint with great sensitivity. I don't know when I've seen a portrait I've liked better. You will do portraits of my children." He placed the card in Alma's perspiring palm. "We'd better start soon, though. I'd like to live to see them all finished."

★   ★   ★

Sunlight filtering in through half-closed Venetian blinds cut narrow shadow tracks across the silk bedspread and awakened Alma. She turned slowly over onto her back and rubbed her eyes. Alma stretched her pajama-clad legs and wiggled her toes between the silk sheets. How luxurious it felt! She yawned, spread her arms, and looked around.

She was glad that her new apartment's spacious rooms allowed her to indulge in creative decorating. Before the blank wall directly in front of her, she would place faithful reproductions by Beacon Hill that she hoped to splurge on from Hudson's: a nineteenth-century cherry French armoire (She thought briefly of her family's scarred pine chiffonier) and an eighteenth-century Regency secretary. Soon Alma hoped to ingeniously place a modern, plump-pillowed white velvet couch and a chrome and glass coffee table between the two formal pieces, which would lend an unexpected and daring air of casualness to the room.

"How clever of you to mix furniture periods," Felicia will say as she pats her hair, done in the new upswept style, and looks around the rooms after Alma finishes the apartment's final touches. "Oh, you artists can get away with anything and make it look smart!"

Alma smiled and wiggled her toes again, as she recalled the previous evening at the Van Delore party. As far as she knew, she had not committed one social blunder. Felicia had been proud of her. And besides all those commissions from Colonel McIntosh, three other guests had said they would be calling her soon to set up a schedule for portrait sessions. Alma ran her hand over the bedspread. Life was getting more and more wonderful! And she owed a lot of her new success to dear Felicia.

And so did Tommie his. All he could talk about on the way home last night were the three orders he'd just secured, and the one hinted at. "With a little imagination, I can design something to make Missus Van Delore and Missus La Follette and Missus Clark look good. But that old biddy married to the colonel--that will take a little doing." His smooth white brow wrinkled in exaggerated concentration. "I know. I've got it! I'll design something with a hood on it, and sew the hood on wrong with the opening in the back!" Alma had giggled in appreciation.

"I'm so glad Felicia has befriended us," Alma said. "I know why she likes you. You're very talented and amusing. But--But I wonder what she sees in me?"

Tommie thought for a moment. "You're talented, too. And, I don't know. Probably because you're young, and being around you keeps her young. But probably mostly it's because of the way you act when you're around her."

"What do you mean, how I act around her?"

"It's obvious you admire her a lot. And Felicia basks in admiration. She craves admiration and acceptance."

Alma lifted her head up from the pillow now and glanced at the Lucite clock on the nightstand. Her father and Jimmie Lee would be here soon! Her mother had forbidden Carrie Lou to come here.

("Carrie Lou's already got big ideas for her age. Why fill her li'l head with thinkin' she's got the right to fancy things, too, 'cause her sister's got 'em?") She jumped out of bed. Alma smiled as she padded to the door in her rabbit fur mules to get the *Sunday Free Press*. She'd scan it quickly. In a few months, maybe she could afford a maid who'd bring breakfast and the morning paper to her.

Alma scooted back into bed, two pillows at her back against the headboard, the paper resting on her raised knees. She turned immediately to the society pages. Yes--there was an item in the "Chatterbox" column about the dinner party last night:

> Alma Combs, who may someday rival Beresford Moore in the number of portrait commissions of leading Detroiters, was honored last evening at a dinner given by Mr. and Mrs. Percy Van Delore of Lake Shore Road. Afterwards, guests were treated to the unveiling of a portrait of the hostess painted by Miss Combs. Among the guests "oohing and ahing" were Col. and Mrs. Ezra McIntosh of Lake Shore Road, Mr. and Mrs. Alfred Carlson, also of Lake Shore Road, Mr. and ...

Alma smiled and reached into the nightstand drawer for the scissors. Her scrapbook would someday bulge.

She scanned the rest of the paper, noting from the headlines that "F.D.R. Sends Personal Appeal to Hirohito as Jap Troops Move"; that Edgar A. Guest, Jr. had written a story on civilian defense, saying that Detroiters should be prepared; that Sonja Henie was still at the Olympia Stadium with her Hollywood Ice Review (Carrie Lou had been pestering for weeks for Alma to take her); that Hudson's was using its slogan again this year: "It's Christmas Time at Hudson's."

Alma thought what a wonderful Christmas it would be. For the first time, she'd have enough money to splurge on gifts for everyone--

Oh, her mother was so stubborn and narrow-minded about Felicia Carlson! Alma slapped the newspaper together and jumped out of bed.

She took a hurried bath, dressed, and whisked a comb through her shoulder-length curls. She glanced in the dresser mirror and frowned at her image. Her hair was just too curly to stay in a page boy style.

The buzzer sounded. She smiled in anticipation as she returned the buzz.

Jimmie Lee leaped from room to room, his eyes wide with wonder. "Wow! To think that my sister lives in a place like this!" Jimmie Lee was still a gangling young man. Alma wondered whether the rest of him would ever catch up with his arms and legs.

Chet quietly surveyed the rooms. Alma could see the pride in his eyes. "Reckon you must be real happy here, Alma May."

"Of course, Dad. Anybody'd be a fool not to be." Alma hesitated a moment before asking, "How--How is she?"

"Your Ma's fine, baby. She was readin' one a her library books when I left. Think it was another one a them Bess Streeter Aldrich novels."

Alma noticed the changes in her father: his hair thinner and more gray now, his shoulders stooped and bony under the baggy overcoat. "Dad. That job's getting to be too much for you. I wish you and Mom weren't so stubborn. If you'd let me--"

Chet held up his hand in a gentle silencing gesture. "Got somethin' to tell you, baby." He walked slowly over to one of the overstuffed white chairs by the huge rectangular window that overlooked the Detroit River. "Reckon if that ain't just about the prettiest view ever," he said as he looked out the window at the sun trying to shine on the ice-capped water and on the sailboats sleeping on the shore. "Except for the mountains back home, a course." He looked at Alma. His eyes twinkled for an instant.

Alma smiled. Pa and his mountains. "Of course," she said. She helped him out of his coat. He pulled his farm catalog from one pocket, and sat down. "What is it you have to tell me, Dad?" She suspected he wanted to talk about The Farm again.

A concerned look crossed her father's face. "Alma May, I figure first I ought to tell you somethin'. Somethin' your Ma an' me's worried about." Chet paused for a moment and began to work his hands.

Alma felt her heart beat faster. "Pa! Tell me! Are you sick? Is that what you're worried about--?"

Chet smiled up at her. "Oh, no, baby. It ain't that. It's, it's Carrie Lou. Your Ma an' me--we're worried because she stays out so late. An', an' hard tellin' what she's doin'. Though she's probably not doin' nothin' wrong, bein' she's only ten years old, not quite eleven.

Pa was not sick. Pa was all right. Alma sat down slowly in the matching chair across from her father. "Oh. Carrie Lou. I thought ..."

"Your Ma an' me can't do anythin' with her. Don't know what's got into your little sister lately." He began to fold and unfold his hands. "Carrie Lou's gettin' so wild. You an' Jimmie Lee was never like that at her age." Pain clouded the blue of his eyes. "Alma May, could you talk to Carrie Lou? A course, your Ma don't know I'm askin' you."

Alma reached over and patted her father's hand. "Sure, Dad. I'll try talking with her. I don't know what good it will do, but I'll try." She could just picture her mother, attempting to give advice to Carrie Lou on being careful around the boys, all the while blushing and stammering, and not even looking directly at Carrie Lou, and then changing the subject abruptly.

Chet's face brightened a little. He sat back into the chair and began to relax. "Thank you, baby."

Alma leaned forward in her chair. "Now, what else were you going to tell me, Dad?"

Chet smiled and opened the farm catalog to where a slip of paper protruded. "Alma May, reckon I found our Farm. An' darn if it ain't near Mountainview, too!" His voice was excited and the words tumbled over each other as he began to read:

> "On graded county road. Forty acres. All tillable, sixteen cultivated, ten bottom, nine lespedeza hay meadow, balance spring-watered lespedeza pasture. Four-room frame house, composition siding, thirty-foot front porch, spring water, good twenty-four by thirty frame barn, fair one hundred an' twenty-five hen poultry house, dandy two hundred an' fifty chick brooder house. Taxes only six dollars an' forty-five cents--

Alma smiled while she watched her father read. She hadn't seen him this animated in a long time--

> "outstanding buy at only one thousand, five hundred an' fifty cash!"

One thousand, five hundred and fifty cash. If things went really well, Alma could give them that in no time.

"I figure in another month," Chet said, his eyes shining, "I'll have enough saved to go right down there an' buy that sweet little farm before it's gone, an'--"

"You mean you've got that much saved?" Alma's mouth parted in surprise.

"Like I always say, Alma May, your Ma can stretch a nickel so far the buffalo on it begins to moan."

Oh, Pa, Alma thought, if you had put that money in the bank instead of in that Mason jar, you would've had enough money way before this. But Alma knew there was no use mentioning it again. "Goin' through that Depression changed your Pa in lots a ways, Alma May," her mother had said, "An' one a them is he don't trust no banks. Since all them banks failed onct, he ain't never goin' to put his hard-earned money in none a them--"

"Alma May." Her father's voice was hesitant but pleading. "Did you ever think that maybe someday, someday--I--I know you think you're gettin' too old to be livin' with your Ma an' Pa, an'--well, wouldn't it be nice if you had your own little farm next to us, so you could be close to your Ma an' Pa an' Jimmie Lee an' Carrie Lou, an'--"

"Oh, Pa. You're always goin' on about that Farm," Jimmie Lee said, walking in from Alma's bedroom. He smiled over at his father. "Alma'd be crazy to give all this up to go back to them mountains. Bet they don't even have electricity yet. She couldn't even hear the radio."

Chet's smile disappeared.

Alma was relieved that Jimmie Lee had been the one to answer her father. She didn't want to hurt her father about The Farm again. Jimmie Lee was right. Why in the world would she want to leave Detroit, especially now that she finally had prospects of making it big as a painter, and--

"Hey, that reminds me!" Jimmie Lee walked over to the shiny new Stromberg-Carlson. "Mind if I turn on the radio? I think the game's on now. The Bears'll probably win the championship."

Alma jumped up to help Jimmie Lee with the floor model combination radio-phonograph. There were so many dials, Alma was not used to them herself yet.

She flipped on the dial and the familiar, mellow music of Glenn Miller playing "Chattanooga Choo Choo" filled the room. Alma fiddled with the tuning dial until she heard the sound of an excited crowd in the background, and an announcer describing the mayhem: "... first and ten. Ball on the thirty-four--"

Then silence. Jimmie Lee looked at Alma in bewilderment. "What happened? Is the connection loose?" He reached behind the radio.

"We take you to Washington for a special bulletin." The announcer's voice was crisp. A few seconds passed as they all exchanged glances. Then the announcer continued, tentative now, as if not certain that he was reading correctly: "President Roosevelt has just announced that the Japanese have attacked Pearl Harbor--"

"Pearl Harbor? What's Pearl Harbor?" Alma asked.

Jimmie Lee put his finger to his mouth to shush Alma, while the announcer continued: "American battleships Arizona and Oklahoma are on fire--"

"What? What does it mean?" Alma cried.

"... waves of Japanese warplanes attacking the United States naval base--"

"Them dirty Japs!" Jimmie Lee's eyes blazed. "Having the nerve to attack us! How dare they do that?"

Alma looked over at her father. Chet collapsed back into his chair. "Reckon we're really in it now." His voice was low and tired.

★　★　★

Jimmie Lee was at the Federal Building the next morning when the Army Recruiting Office doors opened at seven o'clock. By midafternoon, he was on his way to Fort Custer in Battle Creek.

Chapter 25

Alma smiled at Isabelle Charles and masked the revulsion she felt when she looked at her. The poor woman's face was demonic and twisted, like something out of Goya's *The Witches' Sabbath*. "Turn your head a little more to the right, please, Mrs. Charles. That's good. Hold it right there, please. Good. That's great!" Alma took a deep breath and continued. By scheduling the wealthy matron's portrait sittings in late afternoon when the light was less harsh, and by having her turn her head so that only her profile showed, she could muster all the painting techniques she had learned to make the subject's face appear softer. Alma *would* get through these sessions!

Alma was barely listening to Felicia and Tommie as they sat on her new brown plush couch in the corner and stuffed their mouths with Sander's chocolates from the coffee table in front of them. Although they were her dearest friends, she was a little annoyed with them for dropping by her new studio so often lately. It did not seem to matter to them that her days were filled with important portrait sittings and their presence intruded on the privacy she needed with her subjects.

Then she immediately felt guilty for being irritated with Felicia. Felicia had done so much for her. Just last week she had demonstrated faith in Alma's artistic ability again: She'd asked Alma to help her think of a theme for the tea, fashion show, and bridge event at the Downtown Women's Club for which Felicia was chairwoman. In just a few minutes, Alma had come up with an idea in keeping with the war effort. She had suggested the club's huge banquet room be decorated with red tulips, white lilacs, and blue bachelor buttons. There would be blue lights shaped to form the letter "V" for victory on either end of the room, with American flags displayed next to each. For bridge prizes, Alma suggested envelopes with a blue "V" printed on them and a book of war savings stamps inside. Felicia had been delighted. Alma hadn't cared that the club members assumed it was mostly Felicia's idea. It was the least she could do for her best friend.

That was enough of Mrs. Charles's face for today. Alma would concentrate on her subject's gown now. Maybe if she made the gown appear more elaborate, it would draw the viewer's eyes away from the woman's face.

After a few minutes on the gown, Alma glanced at the porcelain clock on the marble mantle. She stifled a sigh of relief. "That's all for today, Mrs. Charles," She said, forcing another smile. "It was a good session today. See you again the same time tomorrow?"

Mrs. Charles nodded yes and said goodbye to Alma and her visitors.

After Alma had closed the door behind her, Tommie said, "That woman really lights up a room--by leaving it."

"Oh, Tommie Tender! That's really cruel." Felicia grinned in spite of her admonition.

Tommie hung his head in mock shame. "I know. That was terrible. The poor woman can't help it that her face looks like a baked apple."

Alma hoped they would take Mrs. Charles' lead and leave, too. She wanted to get downtown to a little costume specialty shop and pick up a veil to wear with the harem costume Tommie had helped her design for the party at John and Betty La Follette's tonight. But Felicia and Tommie popped more chocolates into their mouths and settled back on the couch. So Alma picked up her brush again and continued painting the gown, only half listening to their chitchat.

She glanced around her studio. Yes, it was finally on its way to looking like the one pictured in William Merritt Chase's paintings. Expensive rugs over fine hardwood floors; thickly upholstered, comfortable couches; lush green plants protruding from tall, shiny urns; ornately carved antique furniture, oil portraits and other paintings hung on fabric-covered walls ... She was proud to have all of her newly acquired friends here. She would write Mr. McAllister about the studio soon.

There was only one thing missing to make the setting complete. Alma longed for someone to share all this with her. Someone to hold her at night, to cover her face and body with tender ... Whenever this longing arose, she submerged herself deeper into her painting.

While she continued now on the gown, she thought again about something that Tommie had done last week that had shocked her. It was during Detroit's first blackout. The three million residents of Detroit and Windsor, the Canadian city across the Detroit River, were to cooperate in an air raid practice. All motorists were instructed to park and turn out all lights. Every home, advertising sign, office building, apartment, and hotel were to go into total darkness. Felicia thought it would be fun to have a "blackout party" at her home that Sunday evening. She invited a small group, including Alma and Tommie and a new friend of his, a young blond dress designer named Carl.

As the siren sounded for three minutes and the servants flicked off all the lights, there was much giggling and joking and laughing and tinkling of cocktail glasses as the guests walked around the parlor, probing for the furniture and each other. Fifteen minutes later when the all- clear blew and the lights were turned back on, Alma blinked her eyes for a few seconds, partly to adjust them to the sudden light, but mostly out of surprise at what she had witnessed. Tommie was standing next to Carl, moving one of his hands up and down Carl's buttocks in a familiar, possessive manner. When Tommie jerked his hand away, Alma was hit by a sudden realization. So that was why, even though Tommie had casually mentioned his many girlfriends, she had never known him to have a date, other than when Felicia had arranged one for him. And that was why, although Tommie had had ample opportunity to make a pass at Alma, he had never once even tried to steal a kiss.

Something Tommie was saying now caught Alma's full attention. "I hear Martha Templeton Revere's donating the wrought iron fence from the front of her estate to the scrap drive for the war effort."

Felicia gasped. "You're kidding!"

"Yep. That beautiful iron fence."

Alma stopped in the middle of a brush stroke. At the mention of Martha Templeton's name, a long ago half-forgotten hurt began returning. "Martha--Martha Templeton?"

Tommie pushed the box of candy to the end of the table. "Yep. Martha Templeton Revere. You know, the young trendsetter from

Chicago. She and her husband--you know, the up-and-coming heart surgeon--she and her husband have moved back to Detroit. They bought the Parkinson estate on Lake Shore Road. Things'll really start popping in this town now."

"Do you know Mrs. Revere, Alma?" Felicia asked. "You and she are probably about the same age. Maybe you could introduce us."

"Not--not really, Felicia. I vaguely remember her from school. But she wouldn't remember me. Sorry." How had she, Alma, missed hearing that Martha had moved back to Detroit?

Felicia hastily gathered her purse and gloves. "I must be going, dear. I just remembered an errand. See you both at John and Betty's tonight." She smiled absently and waved one hand in a halting gesture. "Don't bother, Alma. I'll see myself out."

After she had gone, Tommie grinned "There she goes. Mrs. Sycophant."

"Tommie! How could you say such a thing! Of all people, Felicia is certainly not a sycophant. I wish I could be just like her. She has everything in the world she needs--"

"Except talent. She has no creative talent of her own, so she surrounds herself with people who do, like you and me. By being a hanger-on, she gets attention, too."

"I can't believe my ears, Tommie." Alma's voice grew angrier. "How can you say anything against Felicia, after all she's done for us?"

"We would've made it on our own, Alma. It just would have taken longer. Just look at you now. Sure, Felicia got you started by having you paint portraits of her family and friends, but now you get your own clients by word-of-mouth. People she doesn't even know."

Tommie finally stood up, to Alma's relief, and walked toward the door. He turned and chuckled. "What you want to bet Felicia's on her way to Mrs. Anderson's now? You know--that gossipy old witch with the reporter friend. Felicia will no doubt casually mention that she, too, is donating her entire fence to the scrap drive, and also that she'd like to meet Martha Templeton Revere. We'll read about Felicia and her fence in the "Chatterbox" column in a couple of days. And in a few weeks, we'll see her pictured with Mrs. Revere."

★   ★   ★

The late afternoon traffic was tangled, as usual since the war, when Alma drove her Packard east on Bagley. Detroit was suffering from acute congestion, Alma thought, with too many war workers driving to too many new jobs or getting on or off too few busses and streetcars. And her father was one of them. He could have used Jimmie Lee's Terraplane, but insisted "ridin' the bus is good enough for me. Save the tires for the war effort." She was glad that, even though the sale of new tires was banned, she would not have to worry about getting a new set when hers wore out. Felicia had assured her that a top executive friend at the Goodrich tire company in Akron could get her tires anytime. Except for minor inconveniences, to Alma the war was a distant echo. Since Jimmie Lee was still in Michigan in training at Battle Creek, and hitchhiked home on most weekends, she only half listened to the recent news of fighting: The Americans had defeated the Japanese in the Battle of the Coral Sea somewhere in the Pacific, Corregidor had fallen, sixty British Spitfires had landed several days ago from the carriers *Wasp* and *Eagle* on the island of Malta; and for the first time in months, the pendulum began to swing against the Axis. Alma put out of her mind that someday soon Jimmie Lee would have to be shipped overseas.

She turned left onto Clifford, noted that Ronald Reagan, the handsome young movie actor, was featured in *King's Row* at the United Artists Theater. She was about to turn right into the parking lot next to the costume shop, when her glance fell upon a group of four or five sailors gathered around a young woman wearing bright-colored clothes. One of the sailors had his arm around the woman, and was helping her into a car parked next to the curb.

Alma slammed on her brakes, almost causing a collision. *That young woman couldn't be--no it couldn't be*! She craned her neck out the window and looked closer. Yes, it was Carrie Lou! Alma pulled into the entrance of the parking lot, not caring about the snarl of traffic and honking of horns she caused. She jumped out of the car and ran over to Carrie Lou. *My god!* Carrie Lou looked like an overdone flamingo, with her red skirt and shiny pink blouse, and long, skinny legs.

"Carrie Lou! Get out of this car this minute!"

Carrie Lou, who had just sat down in the back seat, looked up and saw Alma. Her eyes bugged. "W--What you doin' here, Alma May?"

Alma shoved one of the sailors who was about to climb into the car out of the way. She pulled at Carrie Lou's arm. "Get out of this car immediately!"

The sailor yanked at Alma's arm. "Now, wait just a goddamn minute. Who the hell d'ya think you are? This is our friend--"

"And this is my sister! My baby sister. My eleven-year-old sister!"

The sailor's mouth dropped open. "Eleven. Eleven. She's only eleven?" He released his grip on Alma's arm.

"Jail bait! She's jail bait," one of the other sailers cried.

"But, Alma May, I ain't doin' nothin' wrong. Just goin' for a little ride, that's all." Carrie Lou's innocent eyes pleaded with Alma.

"Out! Out! I'm taking you home." Alma pulled harder on Carrie Lou's arm and succeeded in getting her out of the car, because the sailor no longer resisted her.

"We're sorry, ma'am. We never dreamed ..."

Alma pulled Carrie Lou over to the Packard, shoved her in, and locked the door. "Carrie Lou! Don't you have any sense in that little bird brain of yours? You're going to get yourself in a peck of trouble someday! It's a good thing I came along when I did!" Alma drove out the exit of the parking lot, the veil forgotten.

"But, Alma May, I wasn't doin' nothin' wrong."

Alma looked over at her sister and shook her head in disgust. "And look at those hideous, garish clothes!"

Carrie Lou looked down at herself. "But these are beautiful, Alma May. This is my newest outfit."

Alma sighed. "Where'd you get the money for it, anyway? You couldn't still have any left from what I sneaked to you behind Mom's back."

Carrie Lou didn't reply, but blew a huge pink bubble from the gum she was smacking.

"And speaking of money--Dad tells me he caught you selling Mom's sugar on the corner last week. How stupid! Don't you know you could get ten years in prison and a ten thousand dollar fine for selling sugar without getting ration stamps for it? And you could get whoever bought it from you in trouble, too? Only store owners can sell sugar." Alma doubted that an eleven-year-old would be prosecuted, but Carrie Lou should have some sense drilled into her little head. "Oh, Carrie Lou, what in the world's getting into you? And how much money did you get selling sugar?"

Carrie Lou shook her hair, which she had attempted to style in a page boy in the back and a pompadour in the front, but the hairdo had fallen loose from the bobby pins securing it. She smiled at Alma. "Wasn't sellin' sugar. Honest, Alma May. I was just carryin' it around." She gave Alma another big smile and, as if the subject were over, looked out her window and started to sing in a high, childish voice: "I got spurs that jingle, jangle, jingle, as I go ridin' merrily along. I got spurs--"

Alma flicked on the radio, turned up the volume, and tuned it to WJR: "And Keep 'em Flying. The more bonds you buy, the more planes will fly! The sooner you buy U.S. Defense Bonds, the quicker we will win the war. And remember, you get a twenty-five dollar bond for every eighteen seventy-five you invest--"

"Ma's savin' to buy a defense bond. Did you know that, Alma May? An' every week she saves the change from the groceries an' buys some war savings stamps. She's got almost a whole book filled already. 'course, Pa doesn't know."

Of course, he wouldn't know. Her mother would be afraid to tell him. Her father still didn't trust the banks or trust his money with the government, so he continued to keep his savings in that Mason jar. "What are you waiting for, Dad?" Alma had asked the last time she saw him. "You must have enough money, and then some, for The Farm now. What's keeping you from going back and buying it?"

A look of longing had clouded his eyes. "I know, baby. We've got enough for The Farm an' them Sebring hens an' Minorca roosters an' the down payment on a 9N tractor, too. But you know I can't leave yet. My place is workin' right here in Detroit for the duration in the job I'm doin'. You know my job's frozen. An' you know I got to do what I can to help the war effort."

Alma pulled up in front of the Combses' flat now. Her mother was in the yard, picking dandelion greens. The flat looked even seedier than the last time she saw it, with its sinking porch and wavy roof. The landlord was probably using the fact that the government had just put restrictions on building materials as an excuse for not repairing it. Well, at least the OPA had ordered a rent limit in the area because of the large number of war workers living there.

Her mother had hung a banner, sewn with a single blue star, in the window of the living room, in honor of Jimmie Lee being in service.

Carrie Lou opened her door and stepped out. "You comin' in, Alma May?"

"No. I have to hurry home. I'm going to a party tonight."

"You're always goin' to a party or somethin' fun!"

Lizzie stood on the porch. Her mouth twisted in a sneer. "Carrie Lou, Mrs. Gottleib told me that Carlson woman is buildin' a huge addition onto her house." Her voice was extra loud. "Wonder where she's gettin' the buildin' materials?"

Alma stepped on the accelerator and made a U-turn. She sped smoothly away as she heard her mother's voice: "Carrie Lou, you finish pickin' these greens while I go in an' start the cornbread. Pick the young, tender'n's. Them'll be good for supper. ..."

★   ★   ★

Alma smiled at Max, the ruddy faced uniformed security guard. He tipped his cap and closed the ornate double doors of the big iron gate behind her. Her mind was still on Carrie Lou. She'd have to tell her father about seeing her with the sailors.

It was serene living here. Who would think that only a few yards away, on the other side of that gate, were the noise and overcrowding and chaos of a wartime city?

She parked her car in her reserved space and hurried up the brick walk shaded by an umbrella of oaks and pines. She had only a few minutes remaining to bathe and dress before leaving for the party. Without a veil, the harem costume was out. She would have to think of something else.

Inside her apartment, she tossed her mail on the Venetian marble coffee table before the living room fireplace. She would open it late that night after she returned from the party.

But the return address on one of the envelopes caught her attention. She bent over the table and slowly picked up the letter. The neat, engraved gold letters on the quality ivory bond paper read: Martha Templeton Revere, Lake Shore Road, Grosse Pointe 30, Michigan.

Alma's hand trembled slightly as she held the envelope and read the address again. Was it some kind of a joke? A letter from Martha Templeton? Why would the popular Mrs. Revere be writing her? She carefully opened the envelope and pulled out the message. She scanned it once, then read it again slowly. Martha Templeton Revere would like to commission Alma Combs to do a portrait of her. She had seen her work and had been impressed. Would Alma call her at her earliest convenience?

There was no indication that Mrs. Revere had remembered her from school. Of course not--who would have remembered Alma May Combs, the hillbilly girl from Mountainview near Harlan?

Well, Martha Templeton Revere, she thought as she smiled and carefully slipped the message back into the envelope and placed it on the fireplace mantle, Alma Combs would savor the message and take her own sweet time answering it.

Chapter 26

Alma smiled as she sipped her glass of champagne: Everyone seemed to be enjoying the "aspiring artists" party she was hosting at her studio that February evening. The guests had gotten into the spirit of it, and some had even come dressed in artist's smock and beret. They all had taken turns at her easel and drawn caricatures of other guests of their choice. Amid much laughter and clapping of hands, especially by Percy Van Delore, she had just awarded the prize for the best drawing to Tommie. He had done a comic representation of Van Delore, exaggerating even more his flat nose and fat jowls.

She had been wise to instruct Sarah, the maid, to have several tables of hors d'oeuvres and finger foods placed around the room. Detroit was experiencing a meat famine. If Alma had planned to set a buffet, the lack of meat would have been even more apparent. Yes, everything was going well. She listened to the voices of the guests around her:

"Sneaky of the OPA, I'd say--not telling us in advance they're going to ration shoes. ..."

"Oh, we all knew Errol Flynn would be acquitted. Rape, my eye. I'd bet my last ration stamp those two young gals threw themselves at him. ..."

"Did you read what that Satterlee gal said after the trial, all the time dabbing at her eyes, acting the sweet little innocent? She said, 'I knew these women on the jury would acquit him. They sat there and just looked at him adoringly, just like he was their son, or something. Here I am, just two days from seventeen, and I feel like a broken old woman. ...'"

"Well, if the truth be known, I'd say it was mutual consent. 'In like Flynn,' you know. ..."

That brought hearty laughter. Alma thought she'd scream if she heard "In like Flynn" one more time.

"We'll have to use stamp seventeen from the sugar and coffee ration book. Good for only one pair of shoes until June 15, then a new stamp will be designated. Only three pairs of shoes a year--"

"I think the OPA is expecting too much. I buy at least three pairs a month! And they've even put a ban on making evening shoes, and no heels over two and tbree-eighths inches high, and no two-tones, and no men's patent leathers, or hardly any sports shoes, and--"

"But no ban on rubbers or storm wear--"

"Oh, goody! I'll go to the Downtown Women's Club's Valentine dance in my arctics!"

More laughter.

"... and who could resist those Hansen and Satterlee girls? Hubba-hubba!"

Alma winced. Another overused, tired "word."

Alma suddenly realized she, herself, was a little tired, too. She wouldn't have planned the party on a Monday evening when she had a portrait sitting early the next morning, but Felicia's social calendar had been filled all weekend.

"I was reading that the people who once bootlegged liquor now have moved into the meat market," one of the guests was saying. "Now steaks are selling for as much as five dollars each!"

Tommie stood in the group next to Alma. He looked at her and then at Felicia and then at Alma again before winking. Was Felicia selling meat on the black market?

"And all those hillbillies flooding Detroit are bringing TB and diphtheria and meningitis up here," someone said. "Glad they can't afford to move into our neighborhood."

"Me, too. Even though they're making more money than they ever dreamed possible up here in the factories, deep down they're still ignorant hillbillies. Feel kind of sorry for them, though. They think as whites they're members of a superior race. Their feeling of superiority to the colored race is one of the few compensations they have."

Alma stiffened. She wished she had the courage to say something. Of course, none of her new friends thought of her as a hillbilly. They thought of her as a genteel, young southern woman.

Tommie winked at her again. He seemed to be tuned into her thoughts often. Did he suspect her real background?

Tommie had brought a new acquaintance, who stood next to him. Ashley Whiteford, tall and anemic looking, was the son of a Canadian distiller. He slouched self-consciously as he picked at his food and dabbed his thin lips with his napkin.

Felicia was by her side now. "Alma, dear, your party is a huge success. What fun!" She lowered her voice to a whisper. "And I don't think anyone noticed there was no meat." She made her voice even softer. "If I'd known, I could have gotten you all you need."

"Oh, it worked out fine, Felicia."

"Well, anytime." Then, changing the subject, Felicia said, "Martha tells me she's sent you numerous notes and left phone messages with Sarah maybe ten times this past year about doing a portrait of her. But you never answer. She wonders if you're getting her messages."

"Ah--Sarah did say something about it, Felicia. But you know how busy I've been. I can't possibly think of taking on more commissions right now--"

"But Alma, dear." Felicia scolded gently, "Martha Revere? How can you refuse someone as important as that? Half the ladies in this town would give their right arm to be in her company."

"I--I'll see what I can do to juggle my schedule." In truth, Alma was relishing her power over Martha. For the first time in her life, Alma had something Martha wanted. She had instructed Sarah to say she was not at home when Martha phoned, even though she might be. Alma savored the growing stack of messages from Martha that she kept in her desk drawer.

"Promise?" asked Felicia.

"Promise."

Tommie had been right. Felicia had lost no time in getting acquainted with Martha. Soon they were pictured together at opening nights at the Shubert Theater. And at the Red Cross giving blood for American servicemen during a drive spearheaded by Mrs. Revere. And wearing slacks while walking arm in arm down Woodward (Mrs. Revere had been the first young Detroit matron to wear slacks in public.)

"Miss Combs, there's a phone call for you." Alma turned to see Sarah standing behind her, brown-haired and handsome and efficient in her black rayon uniform and white frilly apron. "It sounds like your father."

Her father. Why would he be calling so late? Alma glanced at the clock on the fireplace mantel. One o'clock in the morning!

"Excuse me, Felicia?" Alma asked.

Clara Van Delore smiled as Alma passed on her way to the study. "Alma, dear, how in the world do you keep a maid these days? And Sarah's so pleasant and neat. I've had two quit this past month to go work at the Willow Run bomber plant."

Alma smiled back at Clara. "Because I'm paying her twice as much as she'd earn in a factory."

Stephanie Wallington turned from the group with whom she was standing and tapped Alma on the shoulder as Alma passed. She was tall and angular and long-toothed. When she parted her lips in a smile, she reminded Alma of one of Mrs. McIntosh's whinnying prize thoroughbreds. Stephanie was on her fifth marriage. "Alma, great party!" She inhaled on her cigarette in its sequin-studded holder, which looked incongruous in her large, bony hand, but went well with her sequined smock and beret. "You'll have to advise me on the George Washington's birthday party I'm planning."

Alma was flattered. "Love to," she called back from the hall.

Her father's voice was high and croaking, like it was that terrible night her mother almost miscarried Carrie Lou. "Oh, Alma May! Alma May! Can you come by the house an' help me look for Carrie Lou? I'm callin' from a pay phone. Can't get Jimmie Lee's old car started, an' I walked to everywhere I could think of she might be, an' your Uncle Darcas can't help, he's workin' midnights this week. Called Harry, an' he's out lookin' for her, too, an', oh, Alma May, she's never been out this late before--"

"Dad. Dad. Calm down now. Hear me? It'll be okay. We'll find her." Alma picked up an ivory-handled letter opener and absently tapped it on the glass-topped teak desk. She would have to excuse herself for a while and ask Felicia to host in her absence. "I'll be over just as soon as I can. Don't worry, we'll find her."

Oh, that Carrie Lou! What kind of boys has she let pick her up this time?

★   ★   ★

Her father must have been waiting on the porch. When Alma drove her Cadillac up in front of the flat, his approaching steps made loud crunching sounds on the snow in the still darkness. Her mother was framed in the window of their upstairs flat, peeking out beside the banner with the blue star. Oh, her mother! If she hadn't been so penny-pinching, they would have a telephone now and it would have saved a lot of this anxiety. They could have called around town and helped track down Carrie Lou. And now, when her mother and father could surely afford one, there were no new residential installations allowed for the duration.

Chet opened the door to the car, jumped in, and quickly slammed it closed. His face was drawn, and as pale as the leather upholstery around him.

Alma patted his bare, rough hand with her own leather-gloved one. "She's probably on her way home now, Dad. But we'll go look, anyway."

Her father managed a feeble smile. "Thank you, baby."

Alma headed southeast toward the heart of downtown. "You probably checked at her friends' houses," Alma said. Then she thought a moment. "You know, it just occurred to me that I don't even know the names of any of her friends."

"Ashamed to say I don't, either. Never did see any of them around the house. She always left the house alone, promisin' to be back soon. But she never came back right away--always stayin' out late. But never late as this. Oh, Alma May. Your Ma an' me should a locked her in her room every night after supper. We did a couple a times, but then we gave in to her. Alma May, I should a takin' to whippin' her little behind, or--"

"Oh, Dad. You could never have spanked any of us kids, no matter what we did." Alma looked down at her father's callused hands, clenched tightly in hs lap. She could not conceive of those hands doing anything but work or gentle, tender things for his family.

"You're right, baby."

Alma looked out her window. "I'll keep looking on this side and you do the same on yours, Dad."

Even though the hour was late, the streets were still noisy with traffic and the sidewalks still filled with pedestrians. Alma slowed the car as she drove by an all-night movie theater. Maybe Carrie Lou might be in the crowd exiting from one of the sets of double doors. Alma looked carefully. No, she was not. She was not in the line waiting to buy tickets, either. Those were no doubt mostly factory workers, taking in a movie after the afternoon shift. She scrutinized the interiors of the brightly lit bars while she continued to creep by, hoping and not hoping to catch a glimpse of Carrie Lou. Two soldiers, who were leaving one of the bars, their arms around each other's shoulders and their caps askew, blew kisses at Alma and called when she passed: "Hubba-hubba!"

"Oh, Alma May," Chet said, "I shouldn't a asked you to come down here this time a night."

"It's okay, Dad, it's okay."

Where could she be? Alma remembered, then, the time she had seen Carrie Lou getting into the car in the parking lot near the United Artists Theater. She stepped on the gas pedal and headed in that direction, all the while looking as best she could at the passersby.

"We got to look in the cars, too, Alma May," her father said, "Carrie Lou might not know any better'n accept a ride home."

The marquee of the United Artists Theater was lit, but the theater was dark. Several groups were standing in front or walking by. Carrie Lou was nowhere in sight.

Alma pulled up near the attendant's booth in the almost-empty parking lot. She rolled down her window and reached into her coin purse.

The Negro attendant shook his head and waved her on. "We're closin' now," he called through the opening in his glass window, his breath making white puffs in the cold air. "Park free, but at your own risk."

Alma started to drive forward as Chet said, "Wait a minute, Alma May." He reached into his worn overcoat pocket and pulled out his wallet. He took out a snapshot of Carrie Lou and handed it to Alma. "It's a couple a years old, but see if he remembers possibly seein' Carrie Lou around here."

The attendant looked at the picture closely. "No. Ain't seen nobody look like this." He handed the picture back and turned some of the lights off in the lot and in his booth.

"I figure we better park the car an' look around, anyway. Wouldn't do no harm," Chet said.

Alma pulled up beside a green DeSoto. She left the headlights on to help illuminate the darkened lot.

"Got a flashlight, Alma May? You stay here'n lock the doors while I look around."

Alma reached into the glove compartment and handed Chet a shiny Eveready. "I'm going with you, Dad. I feel creepy this time of morning alone, even with the doors locked. Don't know what you expect to find but empty cars, though."

Chet grasped Alma's arm and shined the light into each car as they searched up and down the rows. After they had just about completed the task, Chet said, "You're right, Alma May. Ain't nobody here. I figure we better go." He steered her back toward her Cadillac. "Hey, I just noticed that car parked way over there by itself."

They hurried across the lot toward it. It was useless, Alma thought. And her feet were getting colder, even in the fur-lined motor boots. But as they approached the car, and Chet shined the light inside, Alma saw what appeared to be two feet resting on the top of the front seat. One was on the driver's side and one on the passenger's side. She walked slowly closer, and saw that the feet were attached to a pair of nylon-clad woman's legs. The legs were spread apart. They were long and skinny, like--like--

"Get back, Alma May!" Her father's tone was shrill and frightened. He sucked in his breath sharply.

Oh, god. Was it Carrie Lou? Don't let it be Carrie L--

"Get back!"

But Alma had to know. Was it Carrie Lou and was she d ... ? She looked with dread into the back seat as her father shined the light into it.

The bare buttocks and startled face of the young man on top of the woman looked white in the harsh, sudden light. Alma stepped back and turned her head away. This was the first time she had ever seen something like this.

Her father rapped on the window. "Open that window!" He stood there a moment, and repeated, "Open that window!"

Her head still turned away, Alma heard the window being rolled down, the sound grating the cold air.

"If my baby girl's in there, I'll kill you," Chet said in that high, croaking voice.

He stood there a moment longer. Then Alma felt his arm around her shoulders. "It ain't Carrie Lou." Alma could almost reach out and touch the relief in his voice. "Sorry you had to see that, baby."

Alma drove aimlessly around Grand Circus Park, looking into the lobbies of the Statler and Tuller hotels, looking under the marquees of the Madison and Adams theaters, looking at the young women as they crossed the streets. "Where to now, Dad?"

"I wish I knew." Her father's voice was faint and tired.

The streets were no longer crowded. Here and there were groups of men leaving a movie theater, or servicemen leaving a pool hall, or …

Seeing the servicemen gave Alma an idea. She turned the car abruptly onto Washington Boulevard and headed south.

"Where you goin', Alma May?"

"The Downtown USO."

"The USO? Carrie Lou wouldn't be there. She's way too young for that."

Alma parked the car on Lafayette Boulevard near the building. Most of the lights were out, but a few groups of servicemen and their girlfriends were standing in front. Some were waiting for taxis, some were attempting to hitch rides.

"Carrie Lou wouldn't be here, Alma May."

"Carrie Lou might be anywhere, Dad. Get that picture out of your wallet and we'll ask around. Maybe someone remembers seeing her."

They looked up and down the street as they approached the first group. No Carrie Lou. Chet handed her picture to a freckle-faced young sailor as the rest of the young men and women smiled at them. "This here's a picture a my little girl. You probably never seen her around here."

The sailor looked at the picture. "No, sir. Sorry." He started to hand it back to Chet and then paused. "Hey, wait a minute." He looked at it again. "Maybe I do remember seeing someone looked like this. But a lot older looking. Not lately, though. Maybe a coupla weeks ago." Alma saw the worried lines on her father's face, exaggerated by the harsh overhead streetlight. The sailor passed the photograph around the group, but no one else remembered seeing Carrie Lou.

One member of the second group, a young brunette who looked cold but stylish with a pink snood covering her pageboy hairdo, said between shivers while she clung to her Marine friend, "Oh, yeah, I remember seeing her. Just a little bit of a thing. She was here tonight, but left real early--"

Chet sucked in his breath again. "A--Alone?"

"I saw her putting on her coat, but I can't remember if she was with someone--"

"What color was her coat?" Alma asked.

"Ah, um--red. Bright red."

Alma looked at her father. Chet nodded his head yes.

"What time was that?" Chet asked, his voice excited.

"Let's see now. Maybe about eight or so."

Chet thanked the girl and gave a wan smile to the others. He put the picture back in his wallet, and guided Alma back to her car.

"Dad. I'm sure you must have called the--the police." Alma watched her father's face as she said it.

"Oh, I called them long before I called you. They won't start lookin' for her until she's missin' longer'n this."

Alma started the engine. "Dad. We've done all we can. Let's go home and wait. For all we know, maybe she's home in bed by now."

★   ★   ★

Lizzie met them at the door. Her look was anxious and questioning.

"Carrie Lou was seen at the USO early tonight." Chet sank wearily into his chair. "But the girl who said she saw her didn't know if she left alone, or--"

"USO? That ain't true! Carrie Lou's way too young for the USO."

Alma, exhausted, tossed her coat and hat on the lumpy overstuffed couch and flopped down next to them. "Carrie Lou's way too young for a lot of things she's been doing."

"What'll we do now?" Lizzie asked Chet.

Chet closed his eyes and rubbed his temples. "Way I figure is, there ain't nothin' we can do now but wait. We've been all over town."

The door opened and Harry Buckingham came in. He looked at all three of them and shook his head. "Nothing." He took his hat off and sat down next to Alma, not bothering to remove his coat.

"Harry." Chet's voice was tired and small. "'bout time you went home an' got some sleep. It's almost time for you to get up for work."

"Think I could sleep?" Buckingham turned his hat around and around in his hands. "I'm not leaving until she's home."

Lizzie started toward the kitchen. "There's a fresh pot a coffee an' I could warm up the cornbread if anybody wants it."

"No, thank you, Lizzie." Buckingham sat back in the couch. "I'm about coffeed out." Alma and Chet shook their heads no.

Lizzie lumbered over to the rocker she had proudly acquired from the Salvation Army a few weeks before, and sat down. An open library copy of *See Here, Private Hargrove* lay on the table beside it. The humorous book about the war probably brought Jimmie Lee closer to home for her mother, Alma thought. Next to the book was a letter addressed to him and stamped with the new purple "Win the War" postage stamp.

Buckingham glanced at the letter. Alma knew he wanted to get her mother's mind off Carrie Lou when he asked, "What do you hear from Jimmie Lee?"

"Nothin' much." Lizzie picked up the darning needles from the sack next to the rocker and began mending one of Carrie Lou's red bobby socks. "'ceptin' he's in a trench somewheres--must be somewheres in North Africa, bein's he's got a New York APO address. Every time he writes any details, they go and censor it. But we figure from the war news he must be in Tunisia. He must be where that red thumbtack is." She pointed to a map of the North African invasion tacked on the wall. Alma recognized it from the *Sunday Free Press* graphic section. Her mother followed the newscasts and moved the dozens of thumbtacks as each battle progressed.

That subject exhausted, Buckingham went on to another, while Alma traced and retraced her finger around the design in the stiffly starched doily that covered a hole in the arm of the faded couch. Chet rose and paced the floor from his chair to the kitchen and back again.

"I see you've got a lot of seed catalogs on the table, Lizzie," Buckingham said. "You must be going to plant a victory garden come spring."

"The government wants all of us to put up at least eighty-five quarts a fruits an' vegetables this year," her mother replied. "Reckon I can do that quicker'n a jack rabbit jumps. I always put up more'n that, anyways. I ain't worried about no food shortage. If the OPA chief's wife can feed her own big family on rationing, I figure I can feed this little'n. Far's the meat shortage goes, we can use cheese instead. Bet them rich people"--she looked at Alma, although supposedly talking with Buckingham--"bet them rich people don't worry about no meat famine. Bet they get it on the black market, or just go an' get it in a restaurant."

Alma got up from the couch and started to put on her hat and coat.

"Lizzie, Lizzie," Chet said. "Can't you talk about nothin' without you bring up them rich people? Turn the radio on for a minute." He sat down in his chair again.

Lizzie fiddled with the dial of the Detrola. The announcer's voice was pleasant and well-modulated: "In a surprise flanking maneuver, American forces have moved in from the rear on the dwindling Japanese troops on Guadalcanal, and now have the enemy pocketed in the northwestern tip of the island, the United States navy reported today--"

There was the sound of the front door opening. Lizzie turned off the radio and she and the others rushed to the door.

It was Carrie Lou. Her face was flushed and her lips were parted in a strange new little smile.

"Oh, Carrie Lou! Carrie Lou!" her mother cried. Carrie Lou almost disappeared from Alma's and Buckingham's view as Chet and Lizzie threw their arms around her.

"Where in the world you been?" Chet cried, his voice cracking with relief.

"Oh, Carrie Lou. We was all so worried." Lizzie stepped back and felt Carrie Lou's hair. "Carrie Lou! You're all wet. How come you're all wet?"

Carrie Lou's hair looked like it had been drenched in the rain--but there had been no rain--and was now partly dry.

Alma's lips quivered in relief, but at the same time she shook her head in disgust. "Look at her. She's drunk!"

Mr. Buckingham stared at Carrie Lou's face. "No, she's not drunk. It's something else."

Alma embraced her little sister. Her sweater felt damp under the open red coat. There was a look in Carrie Lou's eyes that Alma had never seen before. Sort of a happy, secret look almost as if it was coming from deep inside her. Almost a look of--of joy.

"Who brought you home?" Lizzie asked.

Carrie Lou smiled that new little smile again. "Sister brought me home."

"Sister?" Lizzie exclaimed. "Your sister's been here for an hour or more. Before that she was out lookin' for you."

"Sister brought me home. Sister Hester." Carrie Lou looked at each of them and then cried, "Somethin' wonderful's happened to me! I'm saved! I've been saved!"

Lizzie and Chet exchanged glances. "Saved?"

Carrie Lou raised her arms and said quietly, "But God commendeth His love toward us, in that, while we were yet sinners, Christ died for us."

"What ...?" Chet and Lizzie exchanged glances again.

Alma shook her head. "I can't believe this--"

"Jesus saith unto him, I am the way, the truth, and the life: no man cometh unto the Father, but by me."

"Carrie Lou! Carrie Lou!" Chet put his hands on Carrie Lou's shoulders and began to shake her gently. "Where you been? Where you been?"

"Oh, Pa! I been to a wonderful place. I been to Everyone's Tabernacle. They got singers, an' trumpets, an' they show the latest war newsreels, an', an' lots of people goes there, an' lots of people got saved tonight just like me, an' Sister Hester thinks I'm wonderful--"

"Sister Hester who? What's her last name?"

"I don't know. But it don't matter, Pa."

Lizzie began taking Carrie Lou's coat off. "How'd you get to the tabernacle?"

"I met some sailors at the USO. They were bored an' they heard about the tabernacle an' wanted to go there for a few laughs." Carrie Lou looked at all of them and smiled her new inner peace smile. "But I'm all through goin' to the USO or downtown. I promise. I've given my life to the Lord. I've been baptised in His Holy water."

"Oh, Carrie Lou, Carrie Lou." Lizzie walked to the closet and hung up Carrie Lou's coat. "You go to your room an' take those wet things off. You'll catch your death a cold. Reckon what you need is a cup a Life Everlastin' tea to ward off a cold 'fore it happens, an' a good night's sleep." She walked into the kitchen and began filling the teakettle.

Carrie Lou walked slowly toward her bedroom and began singing, "I was loaded down with sin, but my Savior took me in. ..." She closed the door.

Chet sat down in his chair. "She's all right. Our Carrie Lou's all right." He closed his eyes. "But I wonder what kind a place this tabernacle is. I hope it ain't like that Aimee Semple McPherson's church."

Mr. Buckingham picked up his hat from the couch and adjusted the brim before putting it on. "Oh, it wouldn't be quite like Aimee Semple McPherson's tabernacle, Chet. At least today's followers wouldn't be as gullible. I've been reading about all the salvation shops that're springing up in Detroit since Pearl Harbor. Detroit's got nearly a hundred. This city's become the Greater Armageddon."

"But why?" Alma asked, as she put her hat and coat on again.

"Because throngs of people have come to Detroit to work in the factories. And with throngs of people comes sin. And after sin comes salvation. All these preachers from the Bible Belt of the South and other places are jumping on the bandwagon. All they need is a vacant store, a--oh, I'm not saying they're all like that. And war brings big wages. Big wages means big donations. You figure it out."

"Well, I for one can't figure it out. I'm too tired." Alma bent down and kissed her father goodbye.

"Why don't you just stay here the rest a the night, baby." Chet rubbed his forehead. "You must be too exhausted to drive."

Alma looked into the kitchen where her mother was pouring boiling water into a cup. "No, thanks, Dad. I'll be fine."

★   ★   ★

The bulldog edition of the *Free Press* was hitting the newsstands and the Twin Pines milk delivery trucks were out as Alma traveled south on Woodward. Carrie Lou was safe and sound. She would be all right. The novelty of the tabernacle would soon wear off, Alma was sure of that.

Chapter 27

While Alma waited for Max to open the iron gate, she was still smarting over a parting remark Gladys Polaski Czarmiewski had made. As Alma was about to enter Hudson's, she saw Gladys waiting for a bus. Gladys had just been to Kresge's dime store, where she'd stocked up on bargain diapers for the baby she was expecting. "I'm making receiving blankets, and night shirts and night gowns out of the old ones," she explained. Gladys and Frankie and their two toddlers, two-year-old Johnny and fifteen-month-old Betty, were now living in a new four-room, two-bedroom frame "defense home." It was one of four hundred of identical design in the housing project at Seven Mile near Morang, built to accommodate war workers. Frankie worked at Chrysler now. Somehow, the subject of the man shortage came up. As they parted, Gladys patted Alma on the arm and said, "Me and Frankie--we'll keep our eyes peeled. There must be some nice fellow out there, in spite of the man shortage, just looking for a nice girl like you."

"I'm going home now to get ready for a date," Alma had replied, making her tone bright and dismissive.

The only reason Alma had gone to Hudson's was because Felicia broke a luncheon date with her at the last minute. "I didn't think you'd mind, Alma dear. This is the only time Martha has available to plan the Colony Club's white elephant sale with me. You know how busy she is, heading the war bond drive." Alma had suppressed a pang of jealousy. It seemed as though Felicia was spending more and more time with Martha Templeton Revere lately.

It was true. Alma did have a date. Huntington Westlake III was the son of Huntington Westlake II, the New York financier. "Hunt," as he was called by Felicia and his other friends, had been visiting the Carlsons for several weeks. Alma had a feeling, and she hoped, that his intentions were getting serious. "He's a prize, Alma." Felicia's eyes had reflected the excitement she felt when she had arranged his introduction to Alma. "Comes from the best of families, his mother--Rose Bradford Westlake, you know--grew up friends with the Vanderbilts. And he's being groomed to take over his father's financial empire. Fortunately, an old polo injury has kept him out of the service. Lucky is the girl who snares him! Especially since he's the only heir when his mother and father pass on. Not that they're expected to for years and years, of course."

Besides all that, Alma thought, as she inserted the key into her apartment door lock, Hunt was fun to go out with. He seemed to know instinctively the best places to take her.

The phone was ringing. It was Sarah's day off, so Alma threw her purse and light spring coat on the couch and ran to the study to answer it. She glanced at the clock on the mantle. Hunt would be here soon.

She hoped it was not Carrie Lou again. Since that night when her sister had joined that church, she had been calling and begging Alma for donations toward the building of a permanent tabernacle, and the calls were getting more frequent. And if that weren't bad enough, she would read verses from the Bible to Alma. Carrie Lou's fascination with the church and with Sister Hester Phillips had grown until now it was an obsession. A truant officer from school had even been to the flat the other day, her father told her, saying that Carrie Lou was skipping school.

"Alma May, whatcha doin'?" Carrie Lou's high, childish voice had taken on a new intensity since her salvation. Probably trying to mimic Sister Hester.

Alma took a deep breath. "I have a date with Hunt. Remember I told you about that real nice fellow Felicia introduced me to? And I only have a few minutes before be gets here."

"Alma May, do you think you could spare a few dollars?"

"For what?"

There was a pause. "Oh, for somethin'."

"If it's for a new dress or even a pair of jodhpurs--all the little girls your age are wearing them now--okay, I'll buy them myself for you. But I'm not giving you any money for that tabernacle."

"Alma May, I don't care about clothes no more." Carrie Lou's voice was getting that familiar whine in it now. "Sister Hester needs more money for the Lord. It's for the glory of the Lord, Alma May."

Alma tapped her fingers impatiently on the new gold-plated phone. "Oh, Carrie Lou, Carrie Lou. I wish you'd stay away from that tabernacle and that Sister Hester. Mom and Dad are so worried about you. It's taken over your whole life."

"Stay away from the tabernacle? Oh, no, Alma May! I could never leave Sister. She told me just yesterday she thinks I'm wonderful. Oh, Alma May, I want to grow up to be just like Sister Hester--"

"I really have to hang up now, Carrie Lou."

Another pause. "You're not givin' me no money for the glory of the Lord?"

"Sorry, Carrie Lou."

"I'm worried about your soul, Alma May." The words sounded incongruous spoken in Carrie Lou's little-girl voice. "Spendin' all that money on yourself an' not givin' any for the glory of God. 'For what shall it profit a man, if he shall gain the whole world, and lose his own soul?'"

Alma sucked in her breath. "I'm going to hang up now, Carrie Lou--"

"Love not the world, neither the things that are in the world. If any man loves the world, the love of the Father is not in him. For all that is in the world, the lust of the flesh, and the lust of the eyes, and the pride of life--"

"'Bye, Carrie Lou." Alma slammed the receiver down. *Carrie Lou, Carrie Lou.* What were they going to do with her?

Alma ran to the bathroom and began filling the tub. Her father said Carrie Lou was trying to get money out of them, too. She was even playing on their worry about Jimmie Lee. Her father said she was probably mimicking Sister Hester by saying, "Got troubles, have you? Heartaches? Afraid for those loved ones out yonder? Afraid for that boy in Africa? Give your dollars to the Lord, sisters and brothers. The Lord will bring that boy back safe. Hallelujah! Hallelujah! Glory to God!"

Alma splashed in the bubbles. Carrie Lou was getting overly modest, too. She even ripped out the short sleeves on all her blouses and dresses and insisted that Lizzie replace them with long ones so that her bare arms didn't show.

A few minutes later, Alma, dressed, stood at the mirror and carefully brushed on mascara. Her father said that Carrie Lou no longer went around the house singing popular songs such as "Mairzy Doats" and "Pistol Packin' Mama" as she did before. Now she was singing "Bringing in the Sheaves" and "Jesus Loves Me, This I Know." And her father had called one time and said, "Your Ma an' me was scared to death last night. Carrie Lou was in the bathroom with the door closed, an' Harry was visitin', an' all of a sudden if we didn't bear her screamin' some gibberish that sounded like 'cory a bally oh dah dah dah dah! cory a bally oh dah dah dah dah! shub ba ba! shub ba ba!' We all ran to the bathroom an' pounded on the door, an' then your Ma suddenly figured that Carrie Lou probably was talkin' in tongues. Remember we used to walk by that Faith Healing Holiness Church back home an' hear that funny soundin' screamin'?"

In spite of Alma's concern over Carrie Lou, the thought of all of them running to the bathroom door and pounding on it made her smile now as she ran the comb through her curls. Tomorrow she would call the police department again and request that the tabernacle be investigated. Her father and Mr. Buckingham had been there several times, checking up on it. They said they couldn't really be sure, but it might be just a fly-by-night operation with temporary quarters out of that storefront.

The buzzer sounded. Alma's heart fluttered in anticipation as she gave one last look in the mirror.

★   ★   ★

The wind blowing her hair over her face and into her eyes partly hid Alma's view of Huntington Westlake III, who sat beside her behind the wheel of his open cream-colored Cord 812 convertible. They were returning to Alma's apartment after a candlelight dinner at Chastane's in the Penobscot Building, Detroit's tallest structure. Throughout dinner, Alma had felt Hunt's gaze on her as they listened to the tuxedoed piano player at the baby grand, and as she glanced out the window at the lights turning on in the city below. The sun had gone down now and Alma was cold. She wished he would ask her if she wanted the top up.

Hunt looked over at her. His lips parted in a smile, baring white, beautifully shaped teeth. "That's one of the many things I like about you, Alma. You're carefree and fun-loving. Any other girl I know would have begged me to crank the top up a long time ago."

Alma did not feel carefree. She felt cold and disheveled. But to hold his interest, she must appear to be enjoying herself. She was glad they were almost home. She would fix them a pot of hot coffee. Alma brushed the curls out of her eyes and peeked at Hunt. Someday she would like to paint that profile--the fine aquiline nose, the firm, full lips, the high forehead brushed with thick blond waves. It reminded her of Michelangelo's *David*.

Back in the warmth of her apartment, Hunt casually threw his coat on the white plush couch by the living room window, and plopped his long frame beside it. Alma ran a hand through her tangled curls and walked toward the kitchen. She felt his eyes traveling from the top of her head, over her new spring blue print silk dress, and down to her blue silk pumps. He whistled appreciatively and stretched his arms out toward her. "Come here," he said, his voice low.

Alma smiled and shook her head. "After I put the coffee pot on."

While in the kitchen, it occurred to her that, since Sarah wasn't here, this was the first time she was alone in her apartment with Hunt. What would her mother think of that?

A few minutes later, she returned with the coffee pot and empty cups. She poured them both a cup, and then stood up. "Would you like to see my latest portrait, Hunt?"

"Why are you avoiding me? Don't you like me?"

"Yes. Yes, of course I do."

Hunt stood up and followed her to her studio, which adjoined the living room. "Then why won't you let me get close to you? Every time I try to kiss you, you move away or change the subject."

She must answer carefully, so as not to discourage him too much. "It's because--don't you think things are happening too fast, Hunt? You've taken me out every day for three weeks, and I've gotten behind in my work, and--"

"Oh, damn your work! What's important is how I feel about you!" He took the cup and saucer from her hand and placed both of their coffees on the table in front of the couch. Hunt turned her toward him.

"But my work is important--to me." Alma looked up at his face. His blue eyes, usually playful, were now serious.

"Oh, Alma, you must know how I feel. Come back to New York with me."

Alma gasped. She knew he was beginning to care for her, but the suddenness of it all--

"You don't have to work. Forget all this painting nonsense. Let me take care of you--"

He had not said a word about marriage. Unless she had missed something. "But, but I can't forget about my painting--"

His lips, firm and demanding and tender on hers, muffled her words. His shoulders felt hard under the tweed jacket as she encircled them with her arms. "Hunt," she cried.

He released her and held her at arm's length. "Look at me. You care for me, I know you do. I know you do! Oh, Alma, Alma!" He pulled her toward the couch and gently sat her down. "Say you'll come with me. Say it!" He ran his fingers through her hair, his eyes daring hers to look away. In the strong light from the fixture above, Alma could count almost each yellow speck in his eyes.

"Our lives will be one long holiday," he cried. "We'll go to the Caribbean, we'll go to South America, we'll tour Europe--when the war's over, of course. We'll go to--"

"You know I couldn't do that without being, without being"--oh, she felt foolish finishing--"without being married."

Hunt's eyes opened wider. "Married? I, I ..."

Flustered, Alma changed the subject. "But what about your work?"

"Oh, who cares about my work? You know I don't have to work. Dad gives me a huge allowance. I don't want to waste my time in boardrooms.."

"But what about some other kind of work, then--?"

"Oh, let's not talk about something as distasteful as work. Let's talk about us." His smile was confident as he pulled her toward him.

Alma's head was spinning. Did he think her answer was yes?

The phone rang. For once, she was grateful for the interruption.

"Don't answer. Don't answer. Whoever it is will give up."

Alma gently pushed his arms away and stood up. "It might be important." She hurried to the study.

Alma picked up the receiver. "Hello."

There was no answer.

"Hello," she repeated, annoyance in her voice.

"Alma May--" The voice sounded small and weak. There was a pause.

"Dad. Is that you?"

There was another pause and then, finally: "Oh, Alma May. It's gone. All gone."

"What's gone, Pa?"

More silence before her father sobbed, "The money. All the money we been savin' for The Farm. Gone. Gone. Every last penny."

Alma swallowed hard. "Are--are you sure, Pa? I can't believe it."

"I called the police, but there ain't no way we can prove we had all that money in that jar. Oh, Alma May--"

"I'll be right there, Pa."

★   ★   ★

A short while later, after telling a reluctant Hunt goodbye against his protestations that he wanted to accompany her to her parents' house, she found her father sitting in his chair, his elbows bent and resting on his knees, his head cradled in his hands. *Oh, Pa. The money--it just couldn't be gone.* She ran to him and threw her arms around his neck. "We'll get it back, Pa!"

Chet looked up at her, his face ashen.

Her mother came and stood by the chair. She patted Chet's arm.

"Where's Carrie Lou?" Alma asked her father.

"We locked her in her room again, but she's gone. Must a climbed out the window." Her father covered his face with his hands again.

"When did she leave?" Alma's voice was worried.

"We don't know." Chet looked up at Lizzie. "Maybe an hour ago?"

Lizzie nodded yes.

"And when did you discover the money was gone?"

"Maybe a half hour or forty-five minutes ago. I went to count it again--I hadn't looked at it for a couple a days--an' then I discovered it was--gone."

"Do you think ..." Alma's heart pounded harder. She took a deep breath. "Do you think Carrie Lou took it for the tabernacle?"

Her father's eyes grew round. "Oh, no, Alma May. Carrie Lou wouldn't do a thing like that."

"Carrie Lou wouldn't take that Farm money," Lizzie said. "She knows how much The Farm means to your Pa."

Alma sighed. "All the same, I think we should go to the tabernacle. Get your coat, Pa."

Alma's throat felt parched and tight. She walked to the kitchen to get a drink. She turned the faucet on and absently read the signs her mother had probably clipped from the newspaper. Glued to the cabinet were the instructions:

> Use more of the plentiful non-rationed foods. Use 8 and 5 point stamps when you can. Save 1 and 2 point stamps to make the count come out even. Your grocer cannot give you change in blue stamps.

And below it another clipping:

> Fat is scarce--use it wisely--save every drop.

Alma filled a glass and swallowed the water eagerly. She poured another and drank that, too.

Her father had his coat on now. "Do you think you could drop your Ma off after at the Telenews Theater, Alma May? I was goin' to take her on the bus, but ..."

Alma remembered, then, that the Telenews was showing *At the Front in North Africa*, an on-the-spot newsreel of all the United States branches of service there.

"Oh, I ain't in no mood to see no newsreel, now, Chet. I thought maybe I'd catch a glimpse a Jimmie Lee in it, but--" Her mother stopped, as if suddenly remembering something. She turned and pointed to the living room wall. "Look at this picture, Alma May. Be darn if that ain't Jimmie Lee on the right. I think he's fightin' under that ol' 'Blood an' Guts' Patton man."

Alma looked at the newspaper photograph her mother had thumbtacked under the invasion map and next to the photograph of President Roosevelt. Two unidentified American infantrymen were pictured at Kasserine Pass, checking out a captured Italian tank for booby traps after the Tunisian counterattack. The faces were so shadowy and distant from the camera that the features were not discernible. But the shape of the head did look slightly like Jimmie Lee's. Alma looked at her mother's hopeful face. "Sure, it might very well be Jimmie Lee." Alma made a mental note to write to Jimmie Lee when she got home that evening. She hadn't written in over a week.

There was a sound of approaching footsteps. They all turned toward the door as it opened.

It was Carrie Lou. Her face was expressionless and her eyes blank. Forgetting to close the door, she walked slowly to her bedroom.

Lizzie's voice was scared-sounding. "Carrie Lou! What's the matter? What--What happened?"

Carrie Lou did not answer, but continued walking.

"You been to the tabernacle?"

Carrie Lou slowly nodded her head yes.

"Carrie Lou." Alma's voice was sharp. "Did you, did you take the savings for The Farm?"

Carrie Lou didn't answer.

Alma grabbed her by the shoulders and turned Carrie Lou's face to hers. "Answer me! Did you take the money from the Mason jar?"

Carrie Lou's face was still expressionless. "M-Money? Oh, the money. Yeah, I took the money.

Alma shook Carrie Lou by her shoulders until her head lolled. "Where is it?"

"I gave it to Sister Hester yesterday for the tabernacle building fund. For the glory of the Lord."

Alma breathed in sharply. "Well, you're going with me and Pa to the tabernacle, young lady, and get that money back."

Carrie Lou slowly shook her head. "Can't."

"Can't? What do you mean, can't!"

"Sister Hester left town. They all left town."

Chapter 28

"Hunt, it all sounds wonderful, it really does, but--I have so many appointments scheduled in the next few weeks, and--don't you know there's a war on? I'd feel guilty about riding the train when we're supposed to be saving seats for the servicemen. And my four gallons of gas a week will go only so far--"

"Alma, please say you'll come," Hunt said on the phone from New York. "We wouldn't have to worry about the train. It'd be more fun driving. I can get plenty of gas."

"I--"

"If you can't come for a month, how about for a few days? Your painting can wait. Mom and Dad would like to meet you, and I want to show you off to all my friends. And I'll take you everywhere--the Waldorf for lunch, the Stork Club for dinner, and--and I'll even get box seats for *Oklahoma*, and ..."

Out of the corner of her eye, Alma saw Felicia emphatically nodding her head yes. Alma talked for a few minutes more before Hunt allowed her to hang up, and then only after promising that she would seriously consider his invitation.

"Alma Combs, I don't know what is the matter with you," Felicia said. She held up two long formal gowns Tommie had designed for her. "Anyone else would jump at the chance to be a guest of the Westlakes."

Alma hesitated. "He hasn't said a word about marrying me, Felicia. He's only said he'd like to take care of me."

Felicia ran her hand over the waist of one of the dresses. "Oh, Alma, you're so old fashioned. Do all you can to please him no matter what it takes. Play your cards right, and he'll ask you."

"What--What does he see in me?"

"He told me it's because you're unspoiled. Not like the other girls he knows. You're not--what did he say?--you're not jaded. You're more fun. I'll never speak to you again if you don't visit the Westlakes. They're the creme de la creme. And that Hunt Westlake--you'd be a fool to let him slip away."

"Oh, I know, Felicia. I told him I'll think about going."

"Well, good. Good." Felicia held one dress up under her chin. "Now, Alma, dear, tell me which one I should wear to the dance tomorrow night at the Book-Cadillac Hotel. I kind of like this pink better than the black. Remember a long time ago you told me I look best in pastels? But Martha is wearing pink and I don't want to compete with her. But, then, how could any woman compete with Martha Revere? Anyway, which one looks best on me?" Felicia laid the pink dress down on Alma's couch and held up the black.

Alma cupped her hand under her chin and looked at Felicia and the two dresses for a long moment, as if giving the matter serious consideration, while Felicia switched from one dress to the other. "The pink, definitely," she said at last. "And you wouldn't be competing with Martha Revere at all--she's very brunette and you're very blonde."

Felicia's face brightened. "Why, I never thought of it that way."

"And I have just the thing to set off this dress. I bought a pink fan several years ago before--before I left home. I think it's still packed away in my parents' attic. I'll go there this afternoon and then drop it off for you."

"Oh, Alma Combs, you're wonderful! What would I do without you?" Felicia hugged her. Alma loved the scent of Felicia's Chanel No. 5 perfume.

"I wish you were going, too," Felicia said. She picked up the dresses and her purse and headed for the door. "You and Hunt would have had a great time at the dance if you hadn't shooed him back to New York."

Alma smiled. "He's got to work once in a while. And I couldn't get any painting done with him here."

"And I could have introduced you to Martha."

"Oh, that reminds me," Alma said casually. "This was delivered last week." She handed Felicia an engraved ivory-colored card.

"An invitation to Martba's pre-dance cocktail hour!" Felicia said. "Now, see--if you and Hunt were going to the dance, you could have gone to this with us."

Alma grinned. "I think she probably wants to make sure she sees me in person so she can pin me down about doing a portrait."

"Once you've seen her, you couldn't resist doing her portrait."

"Oh, I'll call her--soon. Promise." Alma waved goodbye as Felicia closed the door behind her.

She could have asked Tommie to escort her to the dance, of course, but Alma was in no mood lately for dances. Thoughts of her father filled her days. *Poor Pa. How could Carrie Lou have done that, knowing how many years he'd been dreaming of and saving for The Farm?* In the weeks since Carrie Lou had taken the money, her father seemed to have aged terribly. His walk was that of a man twice his age, with shoulders sagging and destination uncertain. *Carrie Lou, Carrie Lou!* Sometimes the anger over what Carrie Lou had done swelled up within Alma so much, she felt she would explode from it.

Chet had been dropping by and telephoning Alma more frequently. Alma's anger with her sister was matched by her father's concern for Carrie Lou. "Alma May," he had said again just last week, while sipping coffee at Alma's new chrome and black lacquer kitchen table, "Carrie Lou ain't actin' like the little sister you once knew. Remember how lively and smily she used to be? Now she just sits on the davenport with her little face all sad lookin', or lays for hours on her bed, face down, but she ain't really sleepin'. An' Ma said a truant officer from school has been by three times. An' lost her appetite, too. Your Uncle Darcas tried to cheer her up by offerin' her candy--remember he was always givin' her candy?--but she don't even want that no more. She don't even want to go to the movies, either. Your Ma an' me think the guilt over what she's done is eatin' at her--"

"Guilt!" Alma said. "I should think she should feel guilty! Has she ever really apologized?"

"Oh, yes, Alma May. Lots a times. Every day. An' she keeps sayin' 'Everyone would be better off without me, everyone would be better off without me.'"

"She called me yesterday and said that, too, and wanted to give me that old blue Shirley Temple mug. I was still so mad at her I hung up."

"Oh, Alma May. You shouldn't a done that." Chet rested his elbow on the table and put his hand up to his forehead. *How old and worn his hand looked, like the surface of a gnarled hickory.* Alma took it in her smooth white one. "How like you to be worrying about Carrie Lou when you should be furious with her."

"Lots a times, 'specially these past few years, I been thinkin' we never should a left Mountainview, Alma May. If Carrie Lou had never come to this big city, she never would a got so boy crazy."

"Carrie Lou was bound to be boy crazy, no matter where she lived."

Chet sighed. "Maybe you're right, Alma May." He rubbed his forehead with his other hand. "But you never were."

"I've always had my painting. I've filled most of my time with it." Somehow, the time didn't seem right yet to tell him about Hunt.

Chet patted Alma's hand. "Yes, an' I'm real proud a you, baby."

"Dad, please, please let me give you money for--" Alma stopped. It was futile to offer again. If only he had put that money in a bank.

Chet slowly shook his head no. "Your Ma an' me's already started savin' again." He rose from his chair and gave Alma a weak smile. "Someday, someday we'll get The Farm. Besides, we couldn't leave 'til after the war. You know my job's still frozen."

Alma pulled her car up in front of her parents' flat now in midafternoon, and thought again how exciting it would be to visit New York. It seemed incredible, with all the money she was making now, that she'd never taken time off from her painting for trips. Maybe she just would this time. Could she pull it off? Would Hunt's family and friends think she really was a genteel modern-day Southern woman, as he did?

The weather was cold and windy for April, and a combination of light rain and snow fell on her as she got out of her car. When she approached the flat, she noticed the ubiquitous popular words some child had scrawled in chalk on the sidewalk: "Kilroy Was Here." This brought a smile to her lips.

Her smile turned to a frown as she glanced at the flat. Besides the familiar sinking porch and wavy roof, the paint was peeling badly now. She remembered how well her father used to maintain their Fifteenth Avenue flat. Maybe he didn't even notice how in need of repair this one was.

In the days before Carrie Lou had discovered Sister Hester, she would have run down the stairs to greet her and beg for a ride. Alma almost wished for those days again. Then, at least, her father had been in better spirits.

Her mother was sitting in the front room. As usual for this time of day, Lizzie had been reading. The *Free Press* was folded at the page containing Ernie Pyle's roving reporter column. It lay on the table by her chair. The popular American war correspondent's writing of at-the-front experiences brought the war and Jimmie Lee closer to her mother and father. Lizzie held in her hand a library copy of a *Reader's Digest* magazine. She was shaking her head in horror at what she was reading. "I can't believe this's true, Alma May. Even a cruel madman like that Hitler man--by the way, today's his birthday, he's fifty-four--even a cruel madman couldn't a been responsible for two million Jews massacred. An' this writer says before the war's over at least two million more'll be killed."

"I know, Mom, I heard that, too. But it couldn't be true."

Lizzie put the magazine down at last. "Got another letter from Jimmie Lee." She reached into the pocket of her freshly ironed housedress. "Course they censored a lot out, but he says he's real homesick, poor boy. An' he misses my beans 'n' cornbread an' he'd give anythin' for a mess of 'em." She smiled smugly. "Imagine that."

Alma took the letter eagerly from her mother's outstretched hand. Jimmie Lee did not write often. He never had been good at writing. And maybe he really was in the thick of battle, as her mother thought, and didn't have the opportunity. Alma read the short message twice, and smiled over one part:

> "Alma will be proud of my work of art I made from the base of a German 88 milameeter shell. I made a real pretty ashtray. Our mashine gun bulluts are still sticking out of it. I cant keep lugging it with me anymore so Im going to see if I can get it sent home to you. ..."

"I figure now that the Allies is chasin that Rommel man into the sea now," Lizzie said, "that battle in North Africa will be over soon, an' maybe Jimmie Lee'll be comin' home on furlough." Hope brightened her mother's eyes. "Look at the map, Alma May. You'll see." Her mother pointed to the invasion map still tacked to the wall near her chair. Lizzie had stuck thumbtacks on the names that Alma remembered from recent newscasts: Tunis, Bizerta, Enfidaville, the Mareth Line. Alma didn't keep up with the war news like her mother did, so she didn't understand what it all meant. "I see, Mom," she lied, "Maybe Jimmie Lee really will be getting a leave soon."

Then, changing the subject, she asked, "Where's Carrie Lou?"

Lizzie's face clouded. "She finally got up from her bed--been layin' there for hours. Wouldn't eat nothin', as usual. But she must be feelin' a little better now, because she says she wants to find her old doll an' give it to me. Ain't that strange? She's been up in the attic for a spell, probably lookin' for it--"

"Oh, no! Not in the attic," Alma said. "Carrie Lou better not lay her hands on my fan."

Alma ran toward the hall that led to the attic. Her feet made loud clumping sounds as she bounded up the bare wooden steps. Of course, Alma could always buy a fan for Felicia, but her old one was perfect for Felicia's dress.

She opened the door to the attic and yelled, "Carrie Lou! Carrie Lou!" There was no answer. "Carrie Lou! Carrie Lou! Answer me!" Impatient and annoyed, she looked around the dim attic.

Then she saw it. The shadow. The single bare light bulb hanging from the rafters made the slightly moving shadow look like a pendulum winding down. Alma slowly turned her head as her throat went dry and an icy chill hit her spine. She gasped and fell backwards against the wall. Alma covered her face with her hands and peeked out between her fingers. She tried to scream but could only croak. There, hanging from the rafters with a long-forgotten jump rope knotted tight around her neck was Carrie Lou.

★   ★   ★

They buried Carrie Lou in Woodlawn Cemetery. No one attended the short graveside service but Alma and her parents, Mr. Buckingham, Aunt Euella, and a minister the funeral director had recommended. Uncle Darcas couldn't get off work and they couldn't get word to Jimmie Lee in time.

They saw that Carrie Lou was dressed in her favorite outfit, even though the woman at the funeral home had not thought red and pink were appropriate.

Her mother and father insisted on a proper burial. "Please, Ma, please let me at least pay for the funeral," Alma had begged. Her mother refused. They paid for it from the small savings they had begun to accumulate again for The Farm, and a loan from Household Finance.

Before the minister's few words, Mr. Buckingham read a poem by James Whitcomb Riley, altering some of the words:

> "I cannot say, and I will not say
> That she is dead. She is just away.
> With a cheery smile, and a wave of the hand,
> She has wandered into an unknown land
> And left us dreaming how very fair ..."

Alma tried to take comfort from the words and Mr. Buckingham's clear, calm voice, but her thoughts kept racing back to the scene in the attic. *Carrie Lou, oh Carrie Lou, you shouldn't have done it.*

Mr. Buckingham continued to read as Alma glanced at her father's drawn face, and squeezed his arm tighter. *Poor Pa. Would he ever get over this? Carrie Lou, Carrie Lou, how could you do this to Pa?*

She looked over at her mother, who had her father's other arm in hers. Her face was expressionless. Alma felt a tinge of anger at her mother for being so strong. Aunt Euella, who had her arm entwined in Alma's other one, was looking at the ground, her eyes partly closed behind a black veil.

> ... Think of her still as the same. I say,
> She is not dead--she is just away."

"Mr. Buckingham had finished the poem.

It's not really true, thought Alma. It's not really true. ... Is it my fault? What could I have done to stop you? What could I have done? ... *Come back, come back, little sister. I've just realized I've never once told you I love you. Oh, Carrie Lou, I love you.*

Chapter 29

"**B**e back directly, Alma May," Lizzie said before leaving for the A & P market. She closed the front door behind her. From where Alma sat curled in her father's chair, she watched her mother plod down the walk leading from the flat to the sidewalk. Alma doubted that her mother would be back "directly." Seldom had she done anything quickly. She saw her mother bend down, pick up a dandelion, and inspect it. Alma realized, then, that it must be early May, for the lawn was studded with the bright yellow weeds.

Alma was staying at her parents' home for a few days, but only because her father had begged her to. "Havin' you in the house makes it easier when I think about poor Carrie Lou," he'd said, his voice breaking. Certainly she was not here for her mother's sake. Her mother didn't need her. She was still a little angry with her mother for being so stoic. How could she always be so strong? And go about her daily work as if nothing had happened?

But secretly, Alma was glad she was here. She had come down with the flu yesterday, and didn't have the strength to care for herself. Sarah, who had grown more independent lately, and reluctant to take on any new task Alma ordered, would be no good as a nurse. And it was a comfort to be in her father's chair surrounded by familiar things.

Except that these familiar things reminded her of Carrie Lou. As a little girl, her sister had often sat on the couch, now threadbare, across from Alma. Carrie Lou would select the brightest Crayolas from a dog-eared yellow and green box by her side, and do page after page of unimaginative sketches. And on countless Saturday mornings, she'd sit cross-legged on the floor in front of the Detrola by her mother's chair, enraptured by the dramatized fairy tales on "Let's Pretend." Carrie Lou, Carrie Lou, Alma thought as she felt the heartache begin again, how could you have done this to us?

Alma's anger turned to guilt and sorrow as the music from "Oklahoma" began to fill the room. Lizzie had turned the radio on for Alma before she left. Carrie Lou would have loved the musical. Alma had sat through the production in New York last week, a smile frozen on her face while her mind wandered back to Carrie Lou and her father.

Had she really been to New York? It must be true, because there on the table beside her were souvenirs of her three-day, whirlwind trip: the book of matches from the Diamond Horseshoe night club with a picture of a dancer holding her petticoat up and kicking her leg; the zebra-striped necktie from El Morocco, which matched the upholstery on the nightclub's seat backs, and which she would give to Mr. Buckingham; and the scarf, also from El Morocco, which was intended for her father. The black ashtray with large white letters reading "Stork Club" from New York's most famous club was also for her father. In the kitchen was a sample pot of honey from the club's acclaimed chef, M. Gustave Reynaud. Lizzie had scoffed at it when Alma gave it to her. "Probly not nearly as good as A & P's. They had a big sale last week an' I bought us a mess a it."

A week before the trip, Lizzie had paused in her mending and given Alma her familiar disapproving look when Alma announced that she would be driving to New York City with Hunt Westlake, who had been visiting the Carlsons again. "Nice girls don't go on trips alone with boys, even if they got lots a money an' come from 'high society.'"

Chet had looked up from the farm catalog he was pretending to read. "Oh, Lizzie, you know Alma May ain't goin' to do nothin' wrong. An' Alma May needs a change a scenery, what with all the time thinkin' about Carrie L--" He stopped and blinked his eyes as they began to moisten.

Alma had rushed to him and put her arms around his shoulders. Her father was always standing up for her.

Before telling her mother about the trip, she had asked her father in private if he would mind that she'd be gone for a few days. "Hunt is pressuring me to go, and"--she had felt suddenly awkward saying this to even her father--"he misses me so much, Dad."

A smile had brightened her father's face for the first time since Carrie Lou was gone. "An' does my little girl miss him, too?"

"Yes, Dad, I do." Alma had realized then that she had been cramming her days with even more portrait sittings than usual to get her mind off Carrie Lou. And she did miss Hunt. She missed him very much. His bright good looks, cheerful smile, and love of good times brought light into her life. Hunt was like an Impressionist painting.

"This Hunt Westlake must be quite the feller. Else my Alma May wouldn't be goin' to visit his family. But you ain't goin' to go an' get yourself promised to him without we meet him first, are you, Alma May?"

Alma had hesitated. She wasn't sure yet she had the chance to get "promised". "Of course not, Dad." She had glanced around the living room. The Kresge dime store linoleum on the floor, like the others in the past, was wearing out. The stuffing was pushing through on the arms of the couch. The European invasion map looked downright tacky stuck on the wall. It belonged in a study or den. How could she ever invite Hunt here? He'd bolt from the house and she'd never see him again. She'd have to invite her parents over to her apartment to meet him. But even then, could she trust her mother not to say something to make him feel uncomfortable?

Even though her father had insisted she take the trip, Alma didn't feel right about leaving him so soon after Carrie Lou was gone. But if she stalled Hunt much longer, she was afraid she'd lose her chance with him.

Alma and Hunt had arrived in New York City twelve hours after a pleasant but uneventful drive. (Her mother had nothing to be concerned about--he pulled the car off the road only once to kiss her.) She'd looked out the window at the maze of skyscrapers as they drove through the city, headed for the Westlakes' Park Avenue apartment, and tried not to seem too awe-stricken. She felt the same excitement she'd felt long ago when, as a young girl, her father first approached Detroit in Uncle Darcas's Model T.

As he introduced her to Humphrey, the butler, she patted her hair in nervous anticipation of meeting Hunt's parents. *Another butler out of the Arthur Treacher mold,* Alma thought. *Tommie should be here to see this. Tall, bordering on skinny, cold clipped British voice, haughty stare. Is this a prerequisite for all butlers?*

She smoothed the skirt of her navy and green print silk dress.

"Don't worry. You look perfect." Hunt smiled down at her. "Perfectly beautiful."

Humphrey took Alma's short navy blue jacket and Hunt's tweed cap and said, "The master and mistress are in the study."

She cleared her throat quietly as Hunt led her there. Would they see through her? Could they tell from her accent (although by now it was almost gone) that she was from the hills of eastern Kentucky, and not Louisville, as she'd led all her Grosse Pointe friends to believe?

The room was tastefully done in traditional style with colors of cream and green. Mr. and Mrs. Westlake sat in matching wing chairs before a bay window overlooking a small fenced flower garden. They both gave Alma and Hunt delighted smiles when they entered, putting Alma almost at ease.

"Mom and Dad, this is Alma." The pride in Hunt's voice filled the room.

Mr. Westlake rose quickly from his chair, as did Hunt's mother. He extended his hand to Alma and said in a skinny, falsetto voice incongruous with his hulking size, "My, my, so this is Alma. I can see, Hunt, that you didn't exaggerate one bit." His hand felt big and smooth.

Unlike "West" Westlake, who was ruddy complectioned and whose dark graying hair waved extravagantly from a low forehead, Rose Westlake was fair skinned and blue-eyed like her son, with the same fine, sharp nose and golden hair (Did she help the color along? Alma wondered.). She smiled a white smile like Hunt's and said in a soft, youthful voice as she put her arm around Alma's shoulder, "So glad to meet you, Alma. Hunt's father is right, my dear." Then, smiling at her son, she said, "She's lovely, Hunt."

Alma and Hunt crammed so many sights and parties and lunches into three days that Alma barely had time to change outfits for each occasion. She was glad Felicia had coached her on what to take. The new red silk two-piece dress with the peplum jacket was perfect for lunch at the Waldorf. (Alma was impressed by the forty-seven-story-high building's bronze portals, rare marble, paintings and murals.) The long green silk gown was appropriate for the small dinner party given by the Westlakes in her honor. Alma was grateful that the guests were all so talkative, asking only briefly about her background. She was reminded, then, of the first dinner party she had ever attended, given that wintry night by the Van Delores. Was it really less than two years ago? So many wonderful things had happened to Alma since then, except, except … Alma had bit her trembling lip and tried not to think of Carrie Lou. She hoped she had pleased Hunt and his parents and charmed all of his friends.

Looking back now, she probably enjoyed going to the Stork Club more than anywhere. The crowd and the din around her had taken her mind off Carrie Lou for a short while. Meeting the genial owner, Sherman Billingsley, had been impressive, too. After seeing *Oklahoma!* at the St. James, the family chauffeur, Edmond, drove them to the Club on 53rd street. They walked under the canopy bearing the club's name as Alma lifted her long periwinkle blue gown slightly to avoid catching the hem in the heel of her silver sandals. The uniformed doorman opened the door for them, and they stepped into a foyer, which to Alma's surprise was only about half the size of Sarah's small bedroom. It was jammed with people, all well dressed, some fancier than others. A stern-faced employee stood behind a velvet rope, his expression daring any of the guests to try to sneak past it.

"How long you been waiting?" asked a man in front of Alma to the man next to him.

"Seems like hours."

"I hear it's worth it, though. This is really the place to go. I hope my wife and I don't get turned away again."

Hunt casually waved his hand until he caught the eye of the employee. "That's Joe Lopez," Hunt said in a low voice to Alma. "He's really not as grim as he looks."

Lopez gave Hunt and Alma a big smile from across the heads of the crowd. He motioned for them to come forward. As they pushed their way through, they were met with annoyed and envious looks.

"Good evening, Mr. Westlake. Will it be the Cub Room tonight or the main room?" Lopez opened the rope and quickly fastened it back again when they stepped to the other side.

"I think my friend would enjoy the main room more, Joe."

Lopez nodded. He signaled to another uniformed employee who Alma assumed was the headwaiter. The man led them down a narrow aisle alongside a rectangular bar knee-deep with talking and laughing customers. Alma pressed her gown close to prevent tripping on it, and clutched her silver evening bag tight against her fur stole. "What's the Cub Room, Hunt?" she asked lightly, hoping her nervousness didn't show.

"That's a special room for special guests. Not nearly as crowded as this. You can drink and play gin rummy there. But this is livelier."

The headwaiter led them to what Alma at first thought was a lamp stand, but which turned out to be a ringside table crammed close to others like it. She tried not to stare at the guests when the waiter seated her and Hunt and took her stole to be checked. Was that really Dorothy Lamour sitting in the far corner? And was that Jack Benny halfway across the room?

Alma looked around the large area. Mirrored walls. Postage stamp-sized dance floor jammed with dancers doing the rhumba to "Besame Mucho." Small trio of musicians consisting of a bass fiddler, an accordionist and a pretty young woman shaking castanets. The trio stood on a tiny raised platform before a background of draped curtains and valances.

"Mother and Dad like going to the El Morocco where the crowd's older, but I prefer it here, even though there's no stage show, no vocalist, no big name entertainment." Hunt signaled the waiter. "Oh, I take that back," he said, laughing. "The entertainment consists of the everyday people looking at the celebrities and the celebrities looking in the mirrors, and both groups sitting bug-eyed in admiration."

Half an hour later, while their Roast Pheasant en Cocotte Souvaroff lay cooling at their table, Hunt pressed her close to him as they danced to the beat of "Amor" (Alma was grateful to Felicia for teaching her the basic steps of the rhumba.) and whispered, "What are you waiting for, Alma? I know you love me. I can tell you do, even though you've never really said so."

Did she? Did she love him? She missed him when she didn't see him for days, and when she did see him again, she felt suddenly more alive. Life was more--more fun.

"Well, I guess the only way to get an answer out of you is to give you an ultimatum. One week. That's it. One week, my darling."

An ultimatum for what? Alma thought. To live with you?

Alma tightened her arm around his shoulder. "Hunt." She took a deep breath and began. Play your cards right, Felicia had advised. But still--"I--I don't think you really know me. You would marry me?" She paused before going on. "And you don't really know what's important to me. My painting--"

"Oh, you silly little goose. Your painting. Your painting. I told you, you wouldn't need to paint anymore. You wouldn't have much time to paint. We'll be too busy." He stopped and smiled at her indulgently. "Oh, now, Honey, don't give me that look like I'm taking candy from a baby. I'll let you dawdle in your paints once in a while, just to get your fingernails dirty."

He had ignored the part about marriage.

When they returned to their table, their pheasant was completely cold, but still delicious. Alma took Hunt's hand in hers. She was always a little surprised to feel how smooth it was, unlike her father's. "You never told me why you think you love me, Hunt. What is there about me?"

"Everything. Your hair, your face, you like going to the same places I do. Maybe it's because you're not like other girls. With you, every experience seems so new, so fresh to you. And so, it makes it seem new and fresh to me when I'm with you. And, and--oh, I don't know. Because you're you."

"What if, what if I told you I'm not the girl you think I am?"

Hunt smiled indulgently again. "What do you mean you're not the girl I think you are? Do you have some deep, dark past you're hiding?"

Alma hesitated. "Oh, of course not. I--"

Alma looked up to see a pleasant-looking man wearing a loud tie standing by their table. He gestured for Hunt to remain seated and said, "Good evening, Hunt. And who is this lovely young lady?"

Hunt pulled out an empty chair next to him and motioned for the man to sit down. "Alma, this is Sherman Billingsley. Sherman, this is Alma Combs, my special friend from Detroit.

Alma extended her hand to Billingsley, who appeared to be in his forties and was balding slightly. He had a quiet, cultured look (except for the tie). So this was Sherman Billingsley. The famous Sherman Billingsley, who was just as much a celebrity as the high society and the movie stars who came here to his club. Alma had been reading about him and his establishment in the "Chatterbox" column for years. She liked him immediately. He projected a sincere warmth.

Billingsley smiled at Alma. "Detroit? Wonderful town! I lived there when I was just a young man in my twenties. Prohibition days, it was. Now I can admit to all the cases of liquor I bought across the river in Canada, and had delivered at night at the back doors of well-respected churchgoers. ..." He spoke in a slight drawl. (Alma remembered reading that he was from Oklahoma.) There was a twinkle in his eyes. Alma was reminded of the Carlsons and the fact that they bootlegged, too. Were they and Billingsley competing with each other in those days?

"But this is my city now," he continued. "I never want to leave it. Where else could I spend all afternoon and evening hobnobbing with celebrities and make a living at it?" He glanced around the room and waved at a platinum blond woman in a gold lame' gown. She and her escort, a tall tuxedo-dressed young man, were being seated at a ringside table.

Alma was overwhelmed, but tried her best not to show it. "Is that really Ginger Rogers?"

"Yes. She comes here often. Nice girl. All my customers are nice, including those at this table." He gave Alma and Hunt another warm smile.

Alma did a double take when a young woman in a red strapless gown at the next table lit up a white pipe. Was that the latest fad, and would it soon be catching on in Detroit?

Billingsley was continuing, "Yes, I'm just as star-struck when I see these celebrities as a guy from Peoria is. There is lots of people (Alma noticed that his grammar slipped occasionally, but it did not detract from his charm.) that I'd pay to come here. The Roosevelt boys--they're regular customers here--I'm working on them to bring their mother in!"

Billingsley rose. "Would you excuse me now? I really should go and say hello to Ginger and her friend."

Hunt rose, also, and shook hands.

"You really should think about moving to New York, Miss Combs." Billingsly's tone was genuine. "You'd be a real asset to the city."

"I'm working on it, Sherman, I'm working on it," Hunt said.

Billingsley touched the handkerchief in his own breast pocket as he caught the waiter's attention. Hunt told Alma later that this was a signal that the check was on the house.

When they picked up Alma's coat at the checkroom on the way out, the girl gave Alma a bottle of perfume. "Compliments of Mr. Billingsley," she said.

Early the next morning, Alma and Rose Westlake stood in the foyer by Alma's packed suitcase. Hunt's father had already said goodbye before Edmond drove him to his office, and Hunt had gone upstairs to direct Humphrey on what he wanted packed.

"It's been delightful having you here, Alma." Rose Westlake leaned forward and gave Alma a quick peck on the cheek. She smelled of Chanel No. 5, as Felicia did. "Just look at Hunt. He hasn't been this happy in years." She paused. "How--how should I say this." She hesitated again. "The girl who marries Hunt must not have a profession of her own."

"But Hunt hasn't asked me yet," Alma said. She felt her face begin to redden--sbe should not have said "yet." Now Mrs. Westlake must think that Alma was scheming.

"Oh, I know. Hunt has always said he's not the marrying kind. His problem is, too many girls have been willing to go along with that. But what I'm trying to say is, whoever does succeed in getting engaged to Hunt should know what she's getting into. He's like his father. When we were first married, I naively thought I could continue with my career as an interior decorator. But I found out the Westlake men want their women to be just extensions of themselves. West's father was the same way with Hunt's grandmother. My ambition was causing a real rift. I decided to give it up." She looked around the apartment. "Now the only interior decorating I do is for our own home." Was that a slightly bitter tone Alma detected in her voice? "I fill my time now by helping on charities that West likes."

"Mrs. Westlake--"

"Say you were the one to marry him. You can see how Hunt is. He would want to be the center of your life. Oh, I don't suppose he would care if you did a portrait now and then, but even then he would be jealous of the time you spent at it."

"My painting," Alma said, choosing her words carefully, so as not to jeopardize her chances, "It means so much to me, and Hunt doesn't take it seriously. It's a big part of my life."

Rose Westlake put one soft hand on Alma's shoulder in a gesture of understanding. "Felicia has told me how good you are at painting. She says you're so busy you haven't even had time yet to schedule Martha Revere. A lovely, charming young lady, a real leader, by the way. Felicia introduced us." She smiled once more at Alma. "Give our love to the Carlsons, will you?"

Alma adjusted her position in her father's chair now. Even that slight action sapped her strength. She should go to bed where she could rest more comfortably. But the thought of seeing Carrie Lou's things in the bedroom she once shared with her depressed Alma. She decided to lie down on the couch.

Once there, she covered herself with a faded blue afghan her mother had crocheted. Her thoughts drifted once again to Hunt. As Felicia had repeated so often, she'd be a fool not to marry him if he asked her. She'd have the world at her feet. Not only would she be part of high society in New York, but when she returned for visits with her Grosse Pointe friends, she'd be looked upon with even more respect and admiration than she was now. If it were not for her painting ...

Alma was startled by the sound of the front door opening. Could her mother be back this soon? Not her pokey mother.

It was Uncle Darcas! Alma sprang from the couch, in spite of her weakened condition, and covered her nightgown with the afghan. *How repulsive he looks! Even more so than before, if that were possible. Fat before, he's huge now.*

"Well, well, if it ain't the Famous Arteest, Alma May Combs!" Uncle Darcas closed the door behind him. "Heard you been visitin' some high muckymuck famly in New York. Heard you finally got yourself a man." His bloated face twisted in a grin. Uncle Darcas took several steps toward her as she backed away.

He grinned wider. "Came to borry some bakin' sodie. Got me a little indigestion." He rubbed his belly and walked toward the kitchen, still grinning back at her.

Alma looked away in disgust. It had been a long time since she'd seen her uncle, but Alma remembered her father saying that Uncle

Darcas was eating way too much lately, so much that he was worried about his brother's health. She wished her mother would walk in the door now. Luckily, he probably couldn't stay too long because most likely he was on his way to the afternoon shift.

Uncle Darcas returned to the living room, wiping baking soda from his mouth with the sleeve of his grimy blue coveralls. He spotted the souvenirs on the table. "Well, well, what's these animal-lookin' things? Is these from New York? What you got for your ol' Uncle Darcas?" He picked up the zebra-striped necktie and held it to his neck. "This for me?" He put it back down on the table. "Naw, your ol' Uncle Darcas wouldn't want that. Reckon if'n I had my druthers, I'd take this." He held up the scarf and, as if an amusing thought had just struck him, grinned once more and said, "How does them harem dancers go?" He swiveled his hips and waved the scarf back and forth in front of his belly as he sang, "La la la la la, la la la la la la la."

Uncle Darcas put the scarf down and picked up the ashtray. "The Stork Club, The Stork Club. What's The Stork Club? Is that some club what's for gals that's expectin' babies? You tryin' to tell us somethin', Alma May? Is Alma May Combs, the Great Arteest, expectin' a young'n'? An' who's the pappy? What's his name, Hunter or somethin'? Bet you been more'n sparkin' with that rich feller." He slipped the ashtray into the pocket of his coveralls. "Naw. Changed my mind. 'Druther have this."

Alma reached toward his pocket with one hand as she tightened her grip on the afghan under her chin with the other. "Give me back my ashtray!"

Uncle Darcas grabbed her arm and leered down at her. "Reckon if that ain't the first thing you said to your ol' Uncle Darcas in years." He twisted Alma's arm back until it hurt. "Sure, Alma May, you'll get your precious ashtray back. After you an' me have a ball."

Alma felt a sudden rush of fear, like that time long ago when she was guarding her father's "burial place." Her voice sounded strange as she croaked, "Ma will be back soon. She just went to the store for a minute." Her heart began to beat faster.

"You an' me both knows your Ma never does things in a minute. Your Uncle Darcas's got plenty a time before leavin' for work."

Alma's throat went dry. She must keep her senses. Remain calm. Uncle Darcas would let go of her arm when he heard her mother coming up the walk.

"Think your uncle don't know why you never looked him in the eye all these years? Think he don't know you was ascared to look at him, ascared he'd see the wantin' in your eyes? Think he don't know that smooth young body a yours was just achin' for his?" He bent down and tried to kiss her, but Alma quickly turned her head away. "Still playin' the shy act, ain't ya? He inhaled noisily and rolled his eyes. "Yum, yum, reckon if you don't smell as sweet as a plumgranite!"

Alma's heart pounded.

A male voice on the radio was singing, "... people will say we're in love."

Uncle Darcas cocked one ear toward the Detrola. "Listen, Alma May. They're playin' our song!" He hummed along with the singer. "Know when I first knew you was cravin' my dork? When you first got too shy to look me in the eye, that's when. Way back when your little nubs was first a fillin' out. Right before you come to Detroit City. Yup, as I always say, 'Old enough to bleed, old enough to breed.'" He grinned down at Alma again.

Alma winced. She pulled her free hand back and punched him in the belly as hard as she could. Uncle Darcas staggered back, letting go of her arm, as the afghan fell to the floor.

"You li'l bitch," Uncle Darcas cried, partly winded. "You're finally goin' to git what you been wantin' all these years. Bet you been wond'rin' why I ain't took you before this, ain't ya? All the time you actin' cool an' hoity-toity to me. Well, I jus' been awaitin' till some fancy feller got sweet on you, an' then I'd spoil you for him. That's why!" He lunged toward her.

Alma looked around for something heavy to throw at him. The table lamp. She reached for it, but Uncle Darcus grabbed both of her wrists with one of his huge hands and squeezed them together. With his other hand, he tore open the snaps of his coveralls. He smelled of body odor and dirty underwear. Alma struggled to twist her wrists free as she turned her head away.

She looked out the window, straining to see if her mother was coming.

"Don't you be a frettin', Alma May. You're goin' to love it, just like Carrie Lou did."

Alma looked back at her uncle. "W--What did you say?"

Uncle Darcas gave her another lunatic grin. "You're goin' to love it, just like Carrie Lou did. Me an' Carrie Lou, we had lots a fun for years."

"You lie! Carrie Lou wouldn't do anything with you!" Alma spat on his face.

Uncle Darcas did not bother to wipe the saliva off, just grinned and pulled down his urine-spotted B.V.D.'s. He jerked his legs free of the underwear and coveralls and kicked them away.

How revolting his naked body was! Like in some of those grotesque Beardsley illustrations. Alma turned her head away again.

Uncle Darcas took his free hand and pushed her face down toward his crotch as Alma continued to struggle. "Lookit, Alma May. That big ol' thing's just for you. That's what you been wantin' all these years. Your Uncle Darcas's finally goin' to find out if you're as good as your li'l sister was."

Alma mustered all the strength she had and kicked him in the shin.

"Ow!" Uncle Darcas yelped, lifting his leg and bending over to rub it with his free hand.

Alma took advantage of the opportunity and kicked him hard in the chest. He reeled, but did not fall down. She bolted toward the door, but Uncle Darcas grasped for her as the lamp next to her mother's chair fell to the linoleum and smashed. He pinned her against the door and with one hand locked it. The smell of his breath ...

Alma began kicking again as hard as she could. Uncle Darcas staggered from the blows on his shins but still held her tight. Alma tried to scream, but could only croak.

Uncle Darcas dragged her to the couch. Alma, still kicking, knocked over the now bare lamp table, which made a loud thud as it crashed to the floor. Please, God, Alma thought, let the people in the downstairs flat hear the noise and come to my rescue.

He threw her down on the couch. She felt a sharp pain in the back of her head when it hit the bare wood poking through the stuffing on the arm. Her heart was pounding so loudly that she could almost hear it. Let me die before he does it, Alma thought. Let me die! Still writhing to free herself, she felt his sticky, smelly skin next to her thighs. His blotchy red face was above her now, the lips twisted in that lunatic grin. His graying hair had fallen into his eyes. The lust shining there burned holes through hers. Alma closed her own eyes as tightly as she could to shut out the sight as she continued to squirm. She clenched her teeth so hard her jaw hurt.

He groped for her panties and with one swift yank ripped them to her knees. "The Great Arteest's bloomers feel like silk. I might a guessed that."

Alma felt his hand, callused and sweaty, travel from her twisting knee up her thigh.

His hand stopped. The pressure of his other hand on her shoulder stopped. Alma slowly opened her eyes. Her uncle's face above her was contorted in pain. He sprang from on top of her and sank to his knees, clutching his chest with both hands. "Help!" he whispered.

Alma slid backward on the couch out from under his knees, which straddled her body. She stared at her uncle.

"Help, help, Alma May! Git a doctorman!" Uncle Darcas's face was a putrid shade of gray. Beads of sweat were forming on his forehead. His hair was soaking wet. Alma swung her legs to the floor, hindered by the panties, which were now at her ankles.

"Help me, help me, Alma May! I was only funnin' you. Your ol' Uncle Darcas didn't really mean it!" He clutched his left arm. "R..un an' g..it a doc..tor..man, Al..ma M..ay. Was on..ly funnin' y..o..u…" He grabbed at his throat. His face above it was maggot-white now, his eyes bulging. His breath came in short puffs. "He…lp," he sputtered, before falling face down on the couch. Alma heard a final muffled blubber: "On..ly fun..nin' …"

The radio began to play, "Oh, what a beautiful mornin" …"

She stood looking dumbly down at him. Was he, was he … ? She looked at his back, the hairs on it curly and wet. His back was not going up and down. That must mean that, that …"

Alma felt a sudden chill. She reached down absently and gathered up the afghan. She draped it around her shoulders and stared in fascinated repulsion at Uncle Darcas's bare buttocks. She began to laugh softly. They reminded her of her mother's unbaked loaves of bread. She often made two loaves at a time. But these had curly black hairs on them. Her mother's loaves of bread didn't have curly black hairs on them. And her mother's loaves would rise. Uncle Darcas's loaves would never rise again. Never, ever. She pointed at her uncle's buttocks. "Uncle Darcas, your loaves will never rise, your loaves will never rise." She began to laugh louder.

Alma had stepped out of her underpants and was walking in circles around the room now. "Uncle Darcas, your loaves will never rise!" she shouted between gales of laughter, hysterical now. Alma held her stomach. It ached from laughing, but still she continued.

Her mother was suddenly in front of her, holding her by the shoulders and shaking her. "Alma May, Alma May, what's got into you? Why you laughin' like that?"

Alma gradually stopped laughing and stared blankly at her mother.

"What you doin' out a your Pa's chair! You promised me you'd stay there." Lizzie frowned. "They was such a big crowd a people at the A & P, an' they had a mess a sales, an'--" Lizzie stopped, noticing the broken table on its side on the floor and the smashed lamp. "What ...?" Then she turned and saw Uncle Darcas's naked body on the couch. She stepped back in horror as her hand flew to her mouth. "Is that--is that Darcas?"

Alma slowly nodded her head.

"Is he--is he--dead?"

Alma nodded again. "He must be."

"What, what happened? He didn't--he didn't ...

Again Alma nodded. Her voice sounded so far away, and like a stranger's when she said, "He tried to--to rape me, Ma."

Anger filled her mother's eyes. "Oh, Alma May, Alma May!" She took Alma in her arms.

It felt strange having her mother's arms around her. It had been so long.

Lizzie rocked Alma back and forth as they stood. "Oh, Alma May, Alma May."

Alma felt calm now. Her voice was muffled against her mother's shoulder. "But he didn't really do it, Ma. He, he must have had a heart attack before he could."

Lizzie released her from her embrace. "You goin' to be all right?"

Alma nodded.

"You go to your bedroom, Alma May. We mustn't tell anyone about this. I'll put your Uncle Darcas's clothes back on him an' you go to bed. I'll go an' call a doctorman. I'll have to think up a story. Mustn't tell anyone about this--"

"But, Ma! He tried to rape me!"

Lizzie put her finger to her lips. "Hush, child. That'll have to be our secret, Alma May. Yours an' mine. You know it would kill your Pa if he knew. An' your Aunt Euelly, too." Her eyes pleaded with Alma's. "Go to your bed an' try to rest. Your Pa will be home any minute an' we don't want him to see his brother like this."

"But--" Alma stopped. Her mother was right, of course. It would kill Pa if he knew.

She did not go to bed as her mother instructed. She walked slowly into the bathroom and locked the door behind her. She let the afghan fall to the floor, took off her nightgown, and sat down in the icy-cold porcelain tub. She adjusted the faucets until the water temperature was the hottest her body could bear. Then she picked up the bar of Fels-Naptha soap her mother kept at the back of the tub for washing clothes and rubbed it over her thighs until they were red and raw.

Yes, it would kill Pa if he knew.

★　★　★

Two days later Alma stood at the living room window and watched Jimmie Lee's Terraplane as it drove away, her father at the wheel. Her father had it fixed and polished for the funeral. Her mother would not hear of using Alma's Cadillac, of course.

Uncle Darcas would have even fewer people at his funeral than Carrie Lou had at hers, since Alma was not attending. He'd made no friends the many years he'd lived here. She overheard her father say yesterday when he and her mother thought she was sleeping, the hurt in his voice thick, "You mean Alma May ain't goin' to her uncle's funeral? Darcas thought the world a Alma May an' Carrie Lou. Remember all those treats he bought for Carrie Lou? Oh, I know he'd say some teasin' things to Alma May, an' maybe he went a little too far sometimes, but he was just funnin' her. He didn't mean nothin'.'"

"Chet, honey," her mother had replied, "I know Alma May wants to go more'n anythin', but--but you know she ain't over the flu yet. Just look how she's mopin' around with the punies. An' she ain't even over Carrie Lou's funeral yet."

There was a pause. Then her father said, his voice choking, "You're right, Lizzie. Carrie Lou's--funeral."

Alma had wanted to run and put her arms around him, but instead buried her face in Carrie Lou's pillow.

Now she watched the Terraplane disappear around the corner as it dawned on her that her mother had been telling lies these past two days. Lots of them. About Uncle Darcas's death. Her mother, of all people, who was always preaching to never lie, cheat, or steal.

She wondered what poem Mr. Buckingham had selected to read at the graveside. *What poem could possibly be appropriate for someone like Uncle Darcas?* She looked over at the couch and a chill came over her. She shuddered, remembering. The back of her head still hurt. Alma turned her face back quickly. She would push away the memory of what had happened. She would blank out the memory of Uncle Darcas forever.

Still, there was something weighing on her mind that could not be shaken off. Something that had followed her these past two days as she moved from her father's chair, to the tub, to her and Carrie Lou's room, and back again to her father's chair.

She looked down at her gold wristwatch. She must go someplace now. If she hurried, she'd be back before they knew she'd left the house. Alma ran to her bedroom. She grabbed some clothes from the closet, for once not caring what they were, and dressed. She glanced at her watch again.

Fifteen minutes later she reached her destination. She parked the car on the asphalt drive and walked over to an area where the ground looked as if it had been disturbed and then smoothed over. Little patches of grass had already pushed through. Yes, this must be it. There was a marker here, but no headstone yet. Her mother and father were saving for one. She was glad that Uncle Darcas wouldn't be buried in this same cemetery. He was not worthy to be in the same cemetery as Carrie Lou. Aunt Euella had selected a different one. A feeling of rage overwhelmed Alma. She stood there, shaking, until it subsided.

She knelt at the foot of the little grave, unmindful that she was getting her pink linen skirt and red blouse grass stained. Pictures of Carrie Lou flashed in her memory: Two-year-old Carrie Lou patting and smiling at her own reflection in the shiny wood floor of the house for sale that Sunday long ago. Carrie Lou running down from the front porch to greet her, a look of pleasure on her face in anticipation of a car ride. A delighted Carrie Lou pointing at a Snow White float moving down Woodward Avenue in the annual Hudson's Thanksgiving Day Parade. Carrie Lou ...

Alma fell forward on the ground, across her sister's grave. *Carrie Lou, Carrie Lou. Tell me it didn't happen. Did he do that to you? Did he do that to you?*

Chapter 30

Alma sat at her parents' dining room table, her back to the living room couch. Above her were a cluster of gayly colored balloons and spiraled fuchsia crepe paper. A small Salvation Army fan on the table was aimed her way, but it did little to thwart the heat and humidity of the June late afternoon. Her dress, of a thin voile material, also fuchsia, stuck to the back of her imitation leather chair. It seemed as though everything was warm today. Even the mellow voice of the new singer, Dinah Shore, singing "One Dozen Roses," which came from the Detrola in the living room. The beef (Her parents must have squandered their last red ration points on it) roasting in the adjacent kitchen added to the discomfort.

Her mother, sitting opposite Alma at the table, began to chuckle. She stopped reading the *Reader's Digest* long enough to say: "Says here--an' it's a true story--says here there's a lady hoarder who filled her cellar with canned goods. A rainstorm flooded the cellar an' washed all the labels off the cans." Lizzie chuckled again. "Serves her right!"

To Alma's relief, her mother didn't mention Felicia Carlson's hoarding.

Alma looked up at the crepe paper again, four streams of which started from each corner of the small room and met in the center at the chandelier. They were tied by the string that also held the balloons. In spite of the clumsiness of the decorations, Alma was touched by the thought of them, because they were probably her father's idea. He knew that the new fuchsia color was her current favorite. And maybe this little celebration for Alma's birthday was a sign that he was feeling better. These past few months, he seemed to have retreated even more to some unreachable place deep inside himself. If only she could ease the pain he was feeling.

Alma looked at the clock on the buffet. "Dad's a little late coming home from work, isn't he?"

Lizzie squinted her eyes toward the clock. "Reckon you're right, Alma May--"

"He doesn't have to go near where they're rioting, does he?" Alma asked, suddenly concerned.

Lizzie hesitated. "Oh, no, Alma May. He probably must a missed the second streetcar he has to take."

To pass the minutes, Alma looked down and admired again the new diamond shoe clips she was wearing for the first time that day. Alma was proud that she'd arrived at a point in her life where she could afford real diamonds. And to think, up until now, she'd been happy to have rhinestone costume jewelry.

After a moment, she looked at the clock again. Surely her father would be here soon. Alma couldn't remain at her parents' home too much longer, because Felicia had planned a celebration for her, too. Tommie would be there (What male "friend" would he bring this time?) along with the Van Delores and a special mystery guest. Tommie had confided to Alma who the mystery guest would be. None other than Martha Templeton Revere! Apparently Felicia was taking things into her own hands and arranging for Alma to finally meet the great Martha. "I don't know why in the world you have never answered her notes and phone calls in all this time, Alma. You know how much it would do for your reputation if everyone knew you've done a portrait of Martha."

Alma knew. But it was so enjoyable to continue savoring the small power she had over Martha Templeton Revere. Alma May Combs had something that Martha Templeton Revere wanted.

Would Felicia be giving a birthday celebration for her if she knew about her and Hunt? Alma had been putting off telling her.

She felt a lump forming in her throat as she recalled the last time she'd seen Hunt. He'd been firm about his ultimatum of having her decision within one week, and had arrived unannounced three weeks ago at her apartment door. He probably knew she'd try to stall him once more if she was aware he was coming. Alma had been painting and was dressed in a smock. She'd felt a rush of tenderness when she opened the door and saw him. Hunt was carrying a big bouquet of red roses and an enormous white teddy bear. He was an appealing contradiction--the look of a king with the charm of a boy. "Hunt! When did you get back in town?"

He walked to the white couch by the living room window and placed the bear on it. "I knew it was the same shade of white!" he said. He grinned, then plopped down next to the bear and motioned for her to join him.

Alma laid the flowers down carefully on the coffee table and sat down next to him. It was so good being close to him again. She realized once more how much she'd missed him. He pulled her to him and as his arms encircled her, she felt his lips move tenderly on her forehead, then to each cheek and finally to her mouth. She fought the desire to return his kiss until she could resist no longer.

"Alma, oh, Alma." His arms tightened around her. Finally, after a long moment he released her. "Well?" he began.

"Well what?"

"Well what's your answer?"

Alma hesitated. "Oh, that."

"Yes, 'that,'" he said. "And 'that' has grown into something more."

Alma felt her pulse quicken even more. "Something more?" Should she dare to hope--?

"'That' now means I want you to marry me." Hunt grinned. "Yes. It's true. I'm really saying it. I never thought I'd be saying that to anyone, but here I am." He confidently pulled her to him again.

Alma pushed him gently away and stood up. She gazed out the window.

Below, soft waves, sparkling in the noonday sun, were lapping against the dock, where a man and woman were hoisting the sails on their boat. Alma's heart beat wildly. Hunt had said what she'd hoped all these weeks he'd say. She had played her role right. But now, before it was too late, she must speak: "You--You don't even know me, Hunt. You don't know anything about me. I'm--I'm not what you probably think. What your family probably thinks. I came from the poorest part of Kentucky. I came from nothing. Nothing." She paused to gather courage to continue. "All the social graces, all the social connections, I've acquired since I moved up here with my family when I was a young girl. And you know how I got them? With my artistic talent, that's how. Felicia got me started, but now I've grown beyond painting her and her friends. I have my own business now. I'm making it on my own. And I love it!"

Hunt started to rise from the couch but Alma motioned him down tenderly with one hand.

"You silly girl," Hunt said, shaking his head, an amused expression in his eyes. "Do you think I care where you came from? All I care about is what I see now. And what I see is a lovely, unspoiled, intelligent young lady who loves doing the same things I do. Who I missed desperately for the past seven days. Who, when she marries me, won't have to even think about her own business." He gave her a confident smile. "I know you love me."

She studied his face carefully so as to remember every feature--the broad, high forehead, the soft clear blue of his eyes behind the fringe of thick black lashes, the Romanesque bridge of his nose, the gleaming teeth behind the full lips. The lips. She would not forget his lips.

"Hunt. Dear Hunt." Would she regret for the rest of her life what she was about to say? No. It had to be this way. "It wouldn't work. Even if you can accept my background, it wouldn't work because of my love of painting. Oh, it would be fun for a few months. Maybe a few years--"

Hunt jumped up from the couch as an expression of shock and hurt crossed his face. "Alma, you can't be serious!" He reached for her, but Alma stepped back. If he touched her again she could never say what she must. "You mean a lot to me, an awful lot. But, oh, sweet Hunt, don't be hurt. Right now my painting means more. Oh, please don't look that way--"

"You can still paint. I'll give you permission to paint. I've already told you--"

"Permission? You'll give me permission?" His mother was right. "You shouldn't have to 'give me permission.' If you loved me as you say, you should encourage me to pursue what work I want, to be the best I can possibly be at it. Not just 'permit' me to dawdle at painting in between cruises and holidays--"

"I'll give you permis--I'll see that you paint on our cruises and holidays." His eyes began to mist.

Alma looked away from him and out the window once more. The man and woman's boat was getting steadily smaller, its sails crisp white against the blue-green water. *Between our cruises and holidays. Between our cruises and holidays.* If Hunt had a goal other than her and their cruises and holidays. … If he had a burning desire to be good at something, be it the best stock boy or the best judge in the world--would she marry him then? Was his lack of ambition the reason she was refusing him? No, that was not it. Even if Hunt had an overwhelming desire to become President of the United States, and was striving to reach his goal, he would never understand that she had the right to have her own work, which did not include him. As his mother lived in his father's shadow, Hunt would want her to live in his.

Alma still dared not look at him: She would not be charmed into changing her mind. She took a deep breath and said firmly to a freighter that was heading slowly northward, "After a while you would begin to hate my ambition when it came between us, Hunt. And then, eventually you would begin to hate me. I couldn't bear that to happen, --"

"Me, hate you? Never!" His voice began to crack.

She must make him leave. Now. She could not bear to prolong his hurt. "Hunt, I know I'm being a fool letting you go, but I'd be more of a fool to marry you." Alma paused and brushed her eyes with the back of her hand. "Please go, Hunt. Now."

"Alma, Alma--"

"Right now, dear Hunt."

He turned and walked slowly to the door. He looked back at her and gave her a long pleading look. "If you need more time--"

"Goodbye, Hunt."

Now Alma rose from her parents' chair and fanned her perspiring legs with the hem of her dress. She still missed Hunt, but her days were filled again with what she loved most. She was booked solid with appointments for the next three weeks, except for this afternoon and evening.

Alma's thoughts were interrupted by the sound of the front door opening. She was relieved. It must be her father at last.

But it was Aunt Euella, carrying a cake box in one hand. Alma was astounded. She had never seen Aunt Euella like this before. She was actually--pretty!

"Hi, Lizzie! Hi, Alma May! Happy Birthday! Sorry I can't stay for your little party. Gotta go meet this lady who wants a roomer. Can't afford to stay in the flat no longer since Darcas's--gone. Me an' this lady, we're gonna be workin' together, too. Did you know I got me a job at N. A. Woodworth's in Ferndale? Be makin' big money workin' on a thing-a-ma-jig--a thread grinder thing, for the war. They got a bus goin' from John R Street right to the main gate. Already got me a couple a outfits for it. Gotta wear coveralls an' one a these"--Aunt Euella patted the red loosely knit net that covered her shoulder-length dark hair--"what you call 'em--snoods. How you like my new outfit? Got it with Darcas's final check." Aunt Euella twirled unsteadily in her red patent leather platform shoes. "Never had no high heels before. An' don't you think they just 'xactly match my new dress?" She stopped spinning and smoothed her red and white polka dotted rayon dress. "A course, the leg makeup ain't too good yet, it's kinda streaked, but I'll get the hang of it before you know it."

Alma smiled and hugged Aunt Euella in spite of the cake box between them. "You look absolutely beautiful, Aunt Euella." Alma gave her a kiss on the cheek, being careful not to smear Aunt Euella's thick pancake makeup or bright red lipstick. Aunt Euella smelled of Blue Waltz perfume.

"Almost forgot," Aunt Euella said. She placed the cake box on the dining room table. "Couldn't think a nothin' you ain't already got, Alma May, so I told your ma I'd bring you a cake. A real, store-bought one. Ain't no day-old one, neither. Got it from A & P's." She looked at the clock. "Ain't Chet here yet?"

"He should be here soon, and Mr. Buckingham, too." Alma said.

"Well, say 'Hi' to both of 'em for me," Aunt Euella said, her hand on the doorknob. "Gotta go now an' meet my lady. Glad she don't live where they's riotin'. Did you hear that the whites threw a colored woman an' her baby off the Belle Isle Bridge last night?"

"Yes," Lizzie replied, "but I don't believe it, no more'n I believe the coloreds killed seventeen whites in Paradise Valley last night."

Alma looked out the window at her departing aunt. Never before had she seen Aunt Euella walk with a bounce in her step. "What's happened to Aunt Euella?" she asked. "She's like a new person. I've never seen her look so good. Or talk so much. She said more in the last five minutes than she's said in the last twenty years. It's like someone opened a valve and out gushes all these words that were just waiting to get out. It's amazing!"

"No, it ain't so amazin', Alma May. You ain't seen her these past few weeks. It's just the old Euelly back, the way she was before marryin' your Uncle Dar--" Lizzie stopped talking and looked quickly away.

Alma and her mother sat down again at the table. "Aunt Euella looks twenty years younger," Alma said. "And--hey, I just realized. For the first time I can remember, she didn't have any black and blue marks on her face! Maybe she hasn't fallen down lately. Has she given up drinking?"

"Your Aunt Euelly never drunk that much, Alma May. She never wanted no one to know--guess she was ashamed a the fact--your Aunt Euelly never wanted no one to know Darcas beat her up bad. Don't tell your Pa! Sometimes she never got out a bed for days. You's too young to remember, maybe, but right before we come to Detroit City, she lost a baby because a your Uncle Darcas's beatin's."

"Oh, my god! Poor Aunt Euella. That's why all those black and blue marks! Why did she stay with him?" Alma wondered how she, Alma, could have been so naïve all these years. "What made Uncle Darcas the way he was? You'd never know he was related to Dad."

"Always wondered that, too, Alma May. Way I figure it, he felt, deep down inside, but never let on, a course--way I figure it he felt like he was no good hisself, an' tried his best to bring everyone else down lower than he was, so he could feel better'n them."

Alma shook her head in disgust. And wondered again how *she herself* could not have suspected. "Why did we put up with him for so long?"

Lizzie thought for a moment. "Way I figure it, because he was famly."

★   ★   ★

Chet stood hanging onto the swinging streetcar strap. He was part of what he and his fellow war workers jokingly referred to as the "strap hangers brigade." There were no seats left, but for some odd reason this streetcar was less jammed than the others he usually rode to and from work. Normally he would have stayed on the Grand Belt line, but this afternoon he got off at Woodward and transferred to this southbound streetcar. He would get off at Charlotte Avenue where Lyman's Jewelers was holding the rhinestone bracelet for his final payment of four dollars. Chet smiled when he visualized how Alma May's eyes would light up when she opened her birthday present. Just like his did when he first saw it in the window of the store. The bracelet had glittered on the dark velvet like--like a constellation of stars in the midnight sky. Chet smiled again, pleased with his analogy. He knew she would be thrilled. Didn't she wear a lot of rhinestone jewelry?

Chet removed his cap with his free hand and fanned his face. It must be in the high nineties in here, he thought.

He liked thinking about the bracelet. When he was thinking about the bracelet, he wasn't thinking about Carrie Lou and Darcas. Darcas, his little brother Darcas. It was all that stuffing himself with food. Too much weight to carry around, just like Chet had warned him. And now he was gone. Gone. Like his baby Carrie Lou, he was gone. Chet felt his throat tighten and his eyes begin to mist. He had failed his little brother, too. He should've insisted Darcas go to a doctor. Just like he should've insisted Carrie Lou stay home. He should've locked her in her room, should've locked her bedroom window. Should've seen that she had so much fun at home that she would not have to seek outside pleasures. Should've ...

Oh, it was no use going over and over all the should'ves. It was too late for poor Darcas and Carrie Lou. Now he would throw all of his energies into being the best man possible to Lizzie and the best Pa possible to Alma May and Jimmie Lee. That's why when Lizzie suggested they have a little celebration for Alma May's birthday, Chet had agreed.

This war couldn't last much longer, and before they knew it, their boy would be back home. And don't think for a minute that he and Lizzie had forgotten about The Farm. Didn't they already have a little nest egg started again for it? And after the war, when he and Lizzie are settled back home on The Farm, and Alma May and Jimmie Lee visit them, they'll see how wonderful their Ma's and Pa's life is, and how good it is being back in their mountains, and they'll want to live there, too, and ...

Chet became aware for the first time now of the whispering around him:

"I just hope I get home safe and sound."

"Me, too. My old lady and kids must be really worried about me."

"Didn't see many niggers at work today. Most of 'em are probably at home with their doors locked."

"Notice how the few niggers in here are all sittin' together in the back? Can't say as I blame 'em."

Chet looked around. Sure enough, except for the middle-aged motorman up front and the older conductor in the middle, what few colored people remaining were the men sitting together in the rear, their faces anxious.

Chet leaned over to the passenger standing next to him, a whiskered, knife-faced worker of about fifty with a gray-billed cap. "What's goin' on?" he whispered.

"There's rioting going on down here between the niggers and the whites," the man whispered back, "And I just heard that the niggers killed twenty-five whites over in Paradise Valley--

"Riotin'? I never heard about no riotin'." He and Lizzie hadn't had the radio on that morning.

"Me, neither, until I got off work and onto my other streetcar. If I'd known about it, I'd've taken a different route. I hear it all started on Belle Isle late last night." He leaned closer to Chet and made his voice even lower. "About time we put them goddam niggers in their place. They're getting too bold for their britches."

Chet looked at the man and felt pity for him.

"My god! Look at all the cops out there!" the man said. He bent over and peered out a side window.

Chet joined the other passengers as they stopped talking and looked, too. Never before had he seen so many policemen in one place.

The streetcar suddenly screeched to a stop, causing Chet and the others to lurch forward. He bumped his head on the man's shoulder.

"What the hell!" exclaimed the man as others shouted and several women screamed. Everyone looked out the front window. Apparently the motorman had wanted to avoid hitting a group of five or six young white men standing on the tracks several yards in front of them.

The motorman turned around and called, "You folks aw right back there?" He opened the front door from his stool, and stood up. He started toward the door just as the young men, armed with pieces of lead pipe, jumped up the steps of the streetcar and dragged him down to the pavement. Chet looked out the window in horror as two of them began beating the motorman with the pipes, while the remaining men rushed up the aisle, bumping into the standing passengers and looking from side to side. "Gotta find us some more niggers!" they shouted. "Gotta find us some more niggers!" Two of them grabbed the startled conductor in the middle of the vehicle and pulled him out from behind his metal rail and to the floor. One of the men held him down as the other began to hit him with his pipe.

Meanwhile, the other passengers, screaming and yelling, tumbled over each other in an effort to flee the car by the open front door. Chet rushed to pull the men off the conductor, but by the time he reached him, the conductor was lying on the floor, either unconscious or dead, and the mob of men had spotted the group of Negroes who had been sitting in back. The panic-stricken Negroes were trying in vain to get the conductor's middle door open as the men overpowered them and dragged them up the aisle past the protesting Chet. "Too hot in here to finish 'em off," one of the white men shouted. "We'll do it outside."

Chet ran up the empty aisle after them as the men dragged the Negroes down the steps and onto the pavement. One of the Negroes had escaped, but the other three were kicking their feet and flailing their arms as the men pulled them down to the pavement beside the still motorman.

"Stop it! Stop it!" Chet shouted. "They ain't done nothin' to you! Stop it! Stop it!"

The attackers were too intent on their mission to hear him.

He spotted a group of three policemen standing together and ran to them. "Help! Help those poor men!" He pointed in the direction from which he had run. The officers began to walk there. "Hurry, hurry!" Why didn't they move faster? "Hurry! Hurry! Before it's too late!" Chet almost lost his balance when another mob of young white men bumped into him as they ran past. Chet looked after them. He could not believe this. The country was at war and its races were fighting each other!

He looked up and read the street sign to get his bearings. Davenport. The jewelry store was two or three blocks south. He must hurry there, pick up Alma May's present, and slip onto a side street to get home. He would walk. Better not risk taking a streetcar or bus back north.

He glanced around as he walked. The area was a scene of shouting crowds and noises and smoke. Mobs of white men were chasing Negroes north and south on Woodward in frantic, violent madness. Just look at their faces, thought Chet. They're like wild animals, hunting prey without rhyme or reason.

To his left were the charred remains of what was once a car, maybe a Chrysler product. An orange handbill, miraculously untouched by fire, which lay in the back seat, caught his eye: "Let Us Repaint Your Car. Excellent Work. Reasonable." Across the street a group of policemen were trying to drive a white mob back to the curb with tear gas bombs. "Just like Germany!" yelled the mob. "You're just like Hitler! Hitler!"

Chet felt a tap on his shoulder. He looked around and saw a uniformed officer. "Better get on home, mister, before you get hurt."

"But I can't go home without I get my little girl her birthday present first."

"You crazy? You risk coming down here just to get your daughter a birthday present? Go home! The stores're probably closed, anyway."

"Oh, no," Chet said, "He wouldn't close. He's open till nine on Monday night. Besides, he wouldn't close when he knows how much I want that bracelet tonight."

The officer shook his head. "Don't say I didn't warn you."

Chet hurried south again, skirting a group of fifty or more white men marching in his direction, two abreast, bearing an American flag that they had apparently pulled from a sidewalk standard.

If only he could've gotten the bracelet last Saturday as planned, but he was ordered to work overtime that day, and the store closed early.

Two officers on his right were holding back a young Negro's arms while a young white man wearing brass knuckles made a pulp of his face. Chet overheard one of the officers say to the other, "The only good nigger is a dead nigger."

"Stop it! Stop it! You're supposed to be breaking up the fighting!" Chet cried.

The officers looked at Chet and grinned.

Chet ran faster. He would report them to the next policeman he saw. But his plan was interrupted by another group of fifty to sixty whites who ran in front of him and to the curb, where they pounced on a parked blue Ford. They began overturning it, as a Negro youth fled from the driver's side and started running across the street. Half of the mob of whites ran after him, lifted him up, and began pulling his limbs. The young man let out a cry like a trapped animal as they ran with him and disappeared behind a billboard. The remaining members of the group had the car upside down now. One of them screwed off the gas tank cover. The gas flowed onto the pavement. Another threw a lighted match into the pool of gas and in an instant the car was wrapped in twenty-foot high flames.

Chet continued on in the midst of police whistles. He barely heard the voice of a white man who walked past him, his eyes glazed and his shirt in shreds, who boasted, "I killed one of them at two this morning. I killed one of them at two this morning. I killed …"

On his left walked another group of whites, their knuckles wrapped in electrical tape, their heads turning from right to left, looking for more potential victims. Two young white bobbysoxers standing against the window of a clothing store shouted at the men and pointed southward. "Here comes one! Here comes one! Here comes another nigger!"

Chet almost tripped over a kneeling white priest praying over an old Negro man with blood streaming from a chest wound. An ambulance siren sounded in the distance.

At the next corner Chet saw a Negro youth slash a white man across the arm and back, before being arrested and handcuffed by an officer.

Several yards farther down, a small group of white youths began to surround a Negro waiting for a bus. Three young white soldiers stepped in and broke it up.

Chet stepped back as a white youth of maybe sixteen or seventeen ran in front of him. The boy swung his arm back and threw a rock the size of three briquets of coal at a southbound bus with one passenger, a Negro man. A police cruiser with several officers pulled up to the curb. Two of the officers got out, seized the youth, and put him in the back seat of the car, next to another officer. The car began moving away while a mob of whites surrounded it and shouted, "Let him go! Let him go!" The car tried to inch away from the curb again. Even more whites packed against it and began to rock it as they continued to shout, "Let him go! Let him go!" The door of the car opened. The officers released the youth and the mob stepped back and let the car drive away.

Several steps farther, Chet felt his feet stick to something. He looked down and discovered it was a clotting pool of blood. "Oh, my god!" he gasped. He glanced around, but could see no one bleeding nearby.

He was almost to Lyman Jewelers now. *It had to be open!* Chet felt his shoulder brushed as a Negro youth ran past him from behind. He glanced down just in time to avoid stepping into an open manhole. When he looked up, he saw the young Negro who had run past him now running back toward him. The boy was being chased by a group of rock-carrying whites in their mid-twenties. One of them was yelling, "Gonna git me a nigger! Gonna git me a nigger!" Another was giggling, a high, girlish giggle. Somehow, their voices sounded familiar to Chet. From long ago.

The Negro was almost up to Chet now. Chet stopped and stepped aside to let him pass. The youth suddenly turned his head back toward the approaching mob and then ducked. Chet saw the rock intended for the Negro coming, but even as Chet ducked he felt it hit his temple. He was aware of an agonizing pain as be fell to the pavement and rolled backwards. There was a sense of falling, falling. And then--darkness.

★   ★   ★

"What in the world is keeping him?" Alma asked. She looked at the clock again. *Almost six o'clock!* "Even if he missed his second streetcar, he should've been here way before this." She rose from the dining room chair again and fanned her legs with the hem of her dress once more.

"I--I don't know, Alma May." Lizzie looked anxiously at the clock, too, as she fanned her face with a folded copy of the *Free Press*.

Harry Buckingham paced the floor in front of the table. He lit another Lucky, his third in the past fifteen minutes. "You're right, Alma. He should've been home long ago. I'm glad he didn't have to go near where they're rioting. What fools--killing each other that way!" Mr. Buckingham took another drag on his cigarette. Alma noticed that the perspiration on the back of his white silk shirt was taking on the shape of a flying eagle. "I hear it all started out as a brawl on Belle Isle last night," Buckingham continued. "Probably too many people and not enough picnic tables and everything. It must be the heat and being tired and overworked because of the war that're getting to them. Maybe if those two hundred sailors from the naval armory hadn't rushed out and joined the whites, the police could have squelched it. You know the Navy is notorious for its anti-Negro prejudices."

Alma had heard about the sailors. She also had heard about the friction between several white and Negro students at her old high school a few days ago. And for years there had also been rumors of a "bump club," an organization that enrolled Negroes to shove or push the whites. But she never knew whether to believe it.

Her mother turned the radio on. The familiar voice of the popular newscaster, Harold True, filled the room. "And the crowd of Negroes stoned and broke into white-owned stores along Hastings Street in the Negro ghetto district known as Paradise Valley, looting merchandise, including guns and ammunition, from pawn shops. All white-owned stores are gutted. Patients are arriving at Receiving Hospital at the rate of one every two minutes. ..." Alma exchanged worried glances with her mother and Mr. Buckingham. The newscaster continued: "State police have been warned to watch out for carloads of armed Negroes coming to the city from Chicago--"

"Now, that last sentence is irresponsible reporting," Buckingham said. He ground his cigarette in the chipped ashtray on the table. "It will only cause more hysteria in the city. I don't know whether to believe half of what I hear."

Lizzie rose. "Sit down, Harry, an' I'll make us some coffee."

"Too hot for coffee, Lizzie."

Another voice was coming over the Detrola now. They listened as Governor Kelly announced: "And a state of emergency exists in the counties of Wayne, Oakland and Macomb. Stores are now closed at the request of Mayor Jeffries. Motion picture houses, theaters and other places of amusement are ordered closed until further notice. The sale of all alcoholic beverages is indefinitely suspended. A curfew is imposed between ten p.m. and six a.m. except for those citizens going to and from their jobs in war plants. I am requesting the full cooperation of all other citizens to remain off the streets and in their homes. ...."

Alma rose from her chair and picked up her purse. "I'm going to hunt for Dad. Something must be wrong--"

"No, you stay here, Alma, with your mother," Mr. Buckingham said. "The situation is getting worse out there. I'm going to try to find him--"

"Harry," Lizzie said, "I, I think I know where he might a went. But I don't know just where it's at. Me and Chet--we didn't know about no riot when he left this morning."

Had her mother been lying again? wondered Alma. Her mother? If so, that was twice--

There was a knock on the door and again they exchanged fearful glances. Mr. Buckingham, who was closest to the door, yanked it open as Alma and her mother rushed there. It was a police officer. Alma's heart began to pound wildly as the grim-faced officer removed his hat and gave them an empty, slight smile.

The officer looked at her mother. "You Missus Combs?" He looked down at a printed form in his hand. "Missus Chester Combs?"

Her mother stared speechless at the officer. Her lips turned white. Mr. Buckingham answered for her mother. "Y--Yes."

The officer took a deep breath and continued. "I'm terribly sorry to have to tell you this--"

Alma felt her legs growing weak.

"There's been a terrible accident. It's your husband, Missus Combs. The rioting on Woodward. There was an open manhole, and--" The officer hesitated. "I'll need you to go with me to identify the body."

Her mother found her voice. "Ident--Identify the body? Identify the body? You--You mean my man is--is ...."

"I'm afraid so, Missus Combs. I'm sorry."

Alma's knees buckled under her. The balloons and fuchsia crepe paper made a riot of swirling color as she fell into the arms of Mr. Buckingham.

Chapter 31

H er father was returning to his beloved mountains.
The rumble of the tracks below competed with the din of the passengers' voices in the crowded southeast-bound Louisville and Nashville Railway coach. Alma and her mother sat next to a window, opposite each other. Outside, Alma could see yellow poplars with their orange-tinted green blossoms race by. Down below in the distance, rose-purple great laurel in full bloom grew alongside the ravines.

It was not true. Her father was not in that wooden box in the railway car behind them. It was all a nightmare that she was observing. Her father would never leave them.

Even as she and her mother had sent a message through the Red Cross to Jimmie Lee, had tended to the funeral arrangements, and had thanked sympathizers, Alma thought it was someone else, not herself, doing those things.

Alma and her mother had pushed their way through the crowds at Detroit's Union Depot yesterday to board the jammed Chesapeake and Ohio train to Winchester, Kentucky. Alma had been hardly aware of the platform filled with uniformed servicemen kissing their clinging wives and sweethearts goodbye, of anxious parents and crying babies, of frazzled-looking businessmen, of posters tacked on walls asking, "Is This Trip Necessary? Our Brave Servicemen Have First Priority." Her mind had been on the long wooden box being lifted into a rear railway car along with packages and crates of freight. She tried to climb the steps to the car and ride alongside it, but a kindly Negro porter stopped her: "You can't get on that car, Miss. You belong up front."

Once on the train, they and other passengers had to stand up or sit on their luggage in the aisle. Luckier passengers sat in seats or grabbed auxiliary folding chairs and set them in the aisle.

After reaching Winchester, they transferred to this, the L & N No. 2. Again, Alma had tried to ride with her father, but Lizzie shook her head and pulled her firmly toward the passenger coaches. This train was less crowded and they were able to find a seat.

Even now, as she recalled the words about her father from newspaper accounts of the riot--the words in the *Free Press* would be etched in her mind forever--she refused to believe it had happened. The paragraph about her father, under a twenty-year-old photograph from a snapshot her mother had saved, and in a list with the other victims along with their photographs, contained only a few words:

> "Chester Combs, 51, (W), 2806 McGraw, died from drowning after a fall down an open manhole on Woodward Ave. near Charlotte. Police surmise fall caused by a blow to his head, probably from a rock thrown by an unknown assailant."

Her thoughts were interrupted by her mother's words: "Alma May, please. Have some beans an' bread. You know they let civilians in the dining car only once a day. You ain't ate nothin' since--since ..." Her voice trailed off. Her mother licked her spoon and put it and the small bowl that had contained her portion of the beans back into a frayed wicker basket. She started to fill another bowl with beans for Alma.

"No. I told you I'm not hungry," Alma said. She had forgotten all about eating. How could she possibly be hungry at a time like this? She looked across at her mother. *How could her mother feel like eating, either? How could she carry on so calmly? Just like she did after Carrie Lou died.*

She gazed out the window again. The late afternoon sun cast purple shadows on the mountains' flat-topped ridges and on the steep-walled valleys of dense pines. They would be in Whitesburg soon, where Ruby Young would be waiting to drive them the twenty or so miles south to Mountainview.

She hoped that Jimmie Lee had received the Red Cross message. Was he still in North Africa (if in truth he ever had been there, as her mother was certain he had), even though the fighting there was over? Had he been ordered to Italy? Mr. Buckingham and Aunt Euella couldn't get off work. Felicia had been sympathetic, but left on a New York shopping spree with Martha Templeton Revere. The thought of Felicia in Mountainview was absurd, even if she had offered to come. Felicia in Mountainview, when Alma had let her think she was from a genteel background in Louisville? Tommie had left a message of condolences with Sarah. She had received messages from the Van Delores and many others, but had pushed them from her mind. She could not deal with well-meaning friends just yet.

She heard the conductor's call behind her now. "Whitesburg. Whitesburg. Next stop Whitesburg." Her mother, who had sat with her eyes closed for the past few minutes, sat up erect and looked out the window. "I'd almost forgot how beautiful them hills an' mountains is, Alma May."

A moment later, the train hissed to a smooth stop. Alma stood up quickly and preceded her mother up the aisle. She was eager to be near her father again. She was the first passenger down the steps and rushed to the rear of the train, threading her way around groups waiting for other passengers. Her glance fell upon the familiar figures of a young soldier and a smiling, plump little woman. When they moved toward her she recognized them. "Jimmie Lee!" she cried. She ran forward and embraced him, her face pressed against the rough khaki breast of his jacket.

He hugged her tightly, almost smothering her, and said in a choking voice, "Oh, Alma May! Alma May!" Then, releasing her, he hugged her mother, who was behind her now. "Ma!"

After a moment, her mother stood back and cried, "Let me look at my young'n." She squinted up at him. "Oh, Jimmie Lee! You've put some weight on them bones a yours." She hugged him again and Alma heard her muffled words, "Oh, Jimmie Lee. Your poor Pa. We been dreamin' an' imaginin' your homecomin' all these months. It wasn't supposed to be like this."

"I know, Ma. I finally got me a thirty-day furlough. Was on my way home on the troop ship from Africa when the Red Cross reached me about--about Pa. Just landed in New York yesterday and there

wasn't time to come with you. Hitchhiked straight to Mountainview."
He hugged her again. "Oh, Ma. I can't believe it. Poor Pa. Poor Pa."

Alma finally looked at the woman who had been standing with
Jimmie Lee. Ruby Young looked almost the same as Alma remembered.
But her face was more lined and her dark hair mostly gray now. Her
voice was the same, though, when she spoke and reached for Alma's
hand: "Oh, Alma May. I'm so sorry about your Pa. We all couldn't
believe it. Not Chet. Dead. Not Chet!"

Alma took her hand and shook her head slightly. He's not dead, she
thought. I don't want anyone to say he's dead! My father wouldn't leave
us. "Thank you, Mrs. Young." She attempted a smile, and then hurried
to the rear of the train.

★   ★   ★

Later, at the Collins Funeral Home, Alma stood the entire evening
of visitation hours by her father's casket, barely hearing the words of
sympathy conveyed by the visitors. She wished they would go away
and leave her alone with her father. She wished Jimmie Lee and her
mother would go away, too. They didn't seem to feel as desolate as she
felt. They didn't love him as she did. Her brother, so tall and erect and
mature now, and strong. Her mother, so talkative (How could she feel
like talking at a time like this?) and in control. She wanted to see only
one person. Mr. McAllister would understand how she felt.

That was not her father's dear face, the skin so ashen, the cheeks so
puffed, the mouth so like a straight slash. Dressed in a dark Sam's Cut-
Rate suit her mother had hastily bought. Alma's gaze kept moving over
her father's small frame, from his head to his feet and back again, resting
mostly on his folded hands, so calm and cold. Those hands, small but
strong, had earned her first paintbrush, her first sketchbook. Those hands
had strummed his guitar, playing the first lullaby she could remember,
had lifted her up to pick her first leaf from the maple in their secret place,
had packed her first Detroit school lunch that day long ago. ...

She looked at the bouquet of wild flowers resting on a pedestal by
her father's head--white dogwood, lavender sweet williams, yellow lady
slippers--that her mother and Jimmie Lee had picked from a nearby
slope early that evening. And her own bouquet next to it, consisting

of just mountain rosebay. Only she knew the bell-shaped rose-purple flowers were her father's very favorite. Already they were beginning to wilt. She should go pick more, but she did not want to leave his side.

Finally, they all had left but her mother and Jimmie Lee and Ruby Young. The funeral director, Odell Collins, touched her arm and said softly, "Better go on over to Ruby's now, Alma May, an' get yourself some rest. You ain't doin' your Pa no good standin' here all night."

"But I can't leave Pa."

"Come on home with us, child," Ruby said. "Your Ma tells me you ain't had no food in three days. Your poor Pa would a wanted you to eat. You know that."

"I can't--"

"Odell here, he's got to close up, child." She put an ample arm gently around Alma and led her out, even as Alma protested again and looked back at her father.

★　★　★

Ruby and Buford Young no longer lived in a company-owned row house. Their clean and tidy three-room home was situated off the main road and actually had a small yard surrounding it, profuse with pink and white rhododendrons. "Since we got the union here now, we're the boss of our own money," Buford said. "Not that we git all that much, but leastaways we don't owe most of our earnin's to the company store. Ain't no more scrip, neither, like when Chet"--his voice got softer when he looked at Alma--"worked here," he finished lamely. He resumed setting up the chairs brought by neighbors.

The Youngs' oilcloth-covered table was laden with food prepared by Ruby and friends and neighbors who had known Chet. And others not at all familiar-looking to Alma, who she thought probably looked upon this gathering as a big social event.

Alma sat in a lumpy frieze chair with crocheted doilies on its arms. She had selected this seat so that she could look out the window and see the foothills and Big Black Mountain, but it was getting dark now. Two little girls in overalls were fighting over a rag doll in the corner of the room. Ruby had set a plate in Alma's lap, filled with a hearty portion of everything from the table, including beans, gritter bread, and wild strawberry preserves. "Eat, child," she said kindly, before she took a dish from the latest guest to arrive and attempted to find a spot for it on the already groaning table.

Alma smiled dutifully as the visitors praised her father, all the while feeling as though she were someone else viewing the scene:

"Your Pa," said Joseph Kazmarick, who Alma remembered vaguely as being small and dark and who was even more so now, "reckon he was one a the hardest workers we had in the old days. ..."

"Alma May, you probably don't remember me," a withered mushroom of a man said. He stood before her with his arm around a stooped, graying woman. "Howard. Greenberry Howard. Worked right 'longside your Pa all them years. An' this here's my woman, Ellie May. Just want to say, Alma May, I never knew no finer person than your Pa. 'Pon my honor. ..."

When they walked away, she remembered, then, that he had once been tall and gaunt, and Ellie May Howard had been young and plump and pretty.

"I'm Opal Miller," said an older, stern-featured woman, who reminded Alma of the woman in Grant Wood's *American Gothic* (just as her friend, the guard at the art institute, reminded Alma of the man in that same painting). But her hand was surprisingly gentle as she squeezed Alma's arm. "My man--maybe you remember J. T.--my man, he died in that methane explosion right before you an' your folks left for Detroit City. Me an' my boy, Rader, we been thinkin' all these years mebbee we should come to Detroit City, too. Rader's been workin' the mines, too, but the workers been on strike all these months--'course you know that, been in all the papers--we been thinkin' mebbee we'd come up north. You know they's been beggin' for war workers. But we wouldn't go without we got a place to live first. Do you think mebbee you could help us find us a place to stay?"

"Of course," Alma said absently. She did not remember the woman at all.

Alma rose from the chair and looked for a place where she could stash her untouched plate. While she walked to the kitchen, she overheard the voices around her:

"Lizzie, you must be proud a your young'n's. That Alma May, if she ain't the prettiest thing. An' wears such fine clothes. Does she still draw them pretty pitchures like she used to? An' Jimmie Lee. So tall an' good lookin'. How come they ain't got themselves wedded to some lucky man an' woman?"

"Enrico Pignatelli? Oh, he left Mountainview an' went to work the Harlan mines. Got killed in the bloody Harlan strike back in thirty an' four."

Alma heard Jimmie Lee's voice: "Yes, we did find Mister McLaughlin once years ago, but lost track of him again."

"Ruby Young, ain't nobody 'round these parts can bake a blueberry pie good as you. You bringin' one to the quiltin' bee Tuesday?"

She recognized her mother's voice: "Still have that pie tin you gave me the day we left, Ruby. Been usin' it all these years."

"Lizzie, we was all so sorry to hear about your littl'n. What was her name?"

"Carrie Lou."

"Carrie Lou. So sorry to hear about Carrie Lou an', a course, Darcas."

"We finally got us 'lectricity 'round these parts, Jimmie Lee."

Alma looked around. She didn't see him in the crowd. Had he changed so much that she didn't recognize him? After finding a place, finally, to hide the plate, she tapped Ruby on the arm and, getting her attention, asked, "Where's Mr. McAllister? When will he be here?"

Ruby looked up at Alma and put an arm around her. "Oh, Alma May. Poor child. Ain't nobody told you yet? Ian McAllister died over a year ago. It was consumption that got him. They call it T.B. now."

★　★　★

The day had no right to be so beautiful. The robins and Carolina chickadees had no right to chirp so sweetly, the wild asters that grew by Knee High Creek no right to be so blue, the sun no right to shine so brightly here in the hollow and on Big Black Mountain in the distance. Alma felt the day to be ludicrously, cruelly out of keeping. It was almost as if it were taking the solemnity of what was happening lightly.

Finally, they were by the gravesite. She and her family had selected a plot on the highest section of the flat. Her father would be facing Big Black Mountain.

She had not slept at all the night before. The visitors had stayed the entire evening. Alma was vaguely aware that a large crowd had gathered now, but her attention was riveted on her father. A few more minutes were all she had. Only a few more minutes. But this was only a cruel joke. Only a nightmare from which she was about to awaken.

The crowd began to sing, shyly at first, and then with confidence. Ruby Young, standing somewhere on Alma's left, was singing harmony, her voice sweet and clear.

> "Amazing Grace, how sweet the sound,
> That saved a wretch like me.
> I once was lost, but now I'm found,

(Oh, Pa, Pa, Alma thought. I'm the one who's lost.)

> Was blind, but now I see.

She was conscious of Jimmie Lee's arms pressing tighter around her and her mother. Of her mother, who stood stoically on Jimmie Lee's left. *They will not be as lost as I will be without you, Pa.*

> "Through many dangers, toils and snares,
> I have already come.

The sun moved over the open casket. Over her father's face, over his hands. She had been wrong. It was right that the day be beautiful, that the sun shine brightly on her father, on this, his last day--

> 'Tis Grace that brought me safe thus far,
> And Grace will lead me home."

The crowd had finished singing. The minister from the Baptist church, who had been unknown to Alma and her family, but who was recommended by Ruby, spoke from across the open grave: "I have here something to read that Missus Combs brought. It's from her husband's good friend. A good family friend. A verse from a poem by William Cullen Bryant." He opened a folded sheet of paper and began to read the words sent by Mr. Buckingham:

"I gazed upon the glorious sky
And the green mountains round,
And thought that when I come to lie
At rest within the ground,
'Twere pleasant that, in flowery June,
When brooks send up a cheerful tune,
And groves a joyous sound,
The sexton's hand, my grave to make,
The rich, green mountain-turf should break."

The minister was silent for a few moments, and then said, "Is there anyone who has anything to say about our dear, departed brother?"

"Chet loved the mountains," a man in back of Alma said.

"Amen. Amen." the crowd said.

"Weren't a finer man than Chet Combs. 'course, everybody knows that."

"Honest as the day is long. ..."

"Good man to Lizzie. Good pa to Alma May an' Jimmie Lee here. Sorry ain't none o' us got to know his littl'n, Carrie Lou, but we're sure he was a good pa to her, too. An' everybody knows he was the best brother Darcas could have."

"Chet liked a good story. An' could tell a few, too."

"Amen. Amen. ..."

The tributes to her father went on and on. Finally, it was time for the minister to say a few words. He cleared his throat and began:

"Lord, from all I've heard from these fine friends here, and from his family this morning, Chet Combs was a good man. I wish I had had the privilege of knowing him. ..."

Alma tried to listen, but as he spoke, remembrances of her and her father filled her thoughts: *Oh, Pa, why was I embarrassed for my classmates to see you when you drove me to the dance that time long ago?*

"We know that if ever anyone is deserving of a special place in your Kingdom, it is Chet Combs here..."

Why did I blame you at first when you couldn't find a job for so long? Why ...

"We don't know if Chet received you, Jesus, as his personal Saviour. We don't know what was truly in his heart. We don't ..."

And why didn't I spend more time with you these past few weeks. Why did I run off to New York with Hunt? If only I had known ...

"And, Lord, if there is any one of your children gathered here now, any poor soul here who is lost. Any poor man or woman who is a doubter, let these words enter their heart. Let them repeat after me this prayer:

> "Dear Lord Jesus, ...
> "I really know I'm a sinner and need your forgiveness. I really think you died for my sins. I want to turn away from all my sins. Please, Dear Lord Jesus, come into my heart and life. I truly want to trust you as Saviour and follow you as Lord. Amen."

There were a few moments of silence. Alma looked once more at her father. But it was not really her father. It was an empty shell. Her father was gone. Her gaze rested for a final time upon his hands. Then, she turned her head. She could not watch as the lid was closed and the coffin lowered.

"I have to go someplace now," she said to her mother.

Lizzie stood expressionless. "Alma May, you shouldn't leave without it's--it's over."

Jimmie Lee took Alma's hand. "Where you goin'? Do you want me to go with you?"

Alma shook her head.

★　★　★

The main road was still paved with coal slag, although the walk in front of the store was of concrete now. The store no longer bore the Independent Mining Co.'s name, but it looked much the same as before. Only smaller. Strange how she remembered it as being really large. Alma crossed the road and angled right. The faint sound of singing voices coming from the cemetery floated through the air:

> "In the sweet by and by
> We shall meet on that beautiful shore. ..."

The steep path was barely discernible now. Alma threaded her way around the ferns and azaleas growing in great profusion over it. She used to like walking up this path, she remembered, because the yellow poplar and sourwood trees grew on either side and formed a canopy that made her feel secure for a moment from the outside world.

She at last came to it. It looked smaller, too. The one-room school house in which she'd spent so many days. Someone had told her--was that yesterday?--that a new brick school was built last year on the edge of town.

When she drew closer, she noticed that the windows were broken and the door ajar. She pushed the door open farther and entered. It was devoid of furnishings. Except for the blackboard on which vandals had scrawled vulgar words.

Alma looked at the spot where Mr. McAllister's desk used to be. How many times had she come here from her seat and asked him to explain math problems? How many times had she asked him about points of history? How many times had she proudly shown him her latest drawing? So long ago that was. How young she was. Even though she hadn't written him for a long time and hadn't received a letter from him, either, somehow she imagined Mr. McAllister as always here. Waiting for her questions. Waiting to encourage her artistic development.

What was it he'd said the last time she saw him? She recalled how shy she'd been then, how she'd blushed when he told her she had a special talent, a--a feeling for capturing beauty. He'd said something else, too, but Alma couldn't recall what it was.

Now he was gone. Mr. McAllister had abandoned her, too. She turned her head from where his desk had been and walked outside.

Next to the schoolhouse was the yard, overgrown with weeds now, where Mr. McAllister led them in youthful games, such as "The Needle's Eye." She could still hear the childish chants.

She took one last look at the schoolhouse and then headed back down the path. Before reaching the main road, she turned left and began to climb another steep slope. The wild grapevines and saw briars were even thicker than she remembered and tore at her nylons and black silk dress. She paused for a moment and looked around. Would she be able to find it after all these years? She skirted the low-growing redbud, huckleberry, and poison ivy until she saw the familiar cluster of pines. They were taller now. Yes, she was heading in the right direction.

The sumac and ear-leafed magnolias on either side were even more abundant now.

After a few minutes, she reached it. Her maple tree near the edge of the ridge. Her and her father's secret place.

She looked down at the spot where they used to lie and daydream about The Farm. It was completely overgrown with coarse fescue grass now. She kneeled down and patted the ground. Her father would lie here. She would lie next to him there. How hopeful they both had been. How happy he had made her feel when he praised her sketches. "Some day, Miss Alma May Combs, you're goin' to be a famous artist," he'd say.

She ran her hand across the rough trunk of the tree. *Here. Here was where his back would rest as he played his guitar and sang those old ballads.*

Alma rose slowly. She stood and gazed for a moment at the surrounding purple and green foothills, struck by the sight of them. They were the same as before, only somehow greater. She turned her head until she faced south. There it was. Big Black Mountain. Looking even taller and more majestic than she remembered, if that were possible. Several lines from a poem she'd long forgotten that Mr. McAllister had read returned now. It was by Emily Dickinson:

> The mountains grow unnoticed,
> Their purple figures rise
> Without attempt, exhaustion,
> Assistance or applause. …

Oh, Pa, she thought, no wonder you wanted to return to your mountains. I'd almost forgotten how beautiful they are.

She looked around once more and breathed deeply of the pure, sweet air. "Pa! Pa!" she cried. "It's not fair. It's not fair what happened. You should not be returning to your mountains like this. Not this way!" Alma fell slowly to the ground. To the spot where they used to lay. "Oh, Pa. Pa. I love you so much, Pa. I'll make you so proud of me. You'll see. I'll be that famous artist someday. Don't I already have a start?"

Finally, the tears came.

Chapter 32

F elicia extinguished her cigarette in the ashtray on the coffee table before her. "Alma Combs, look at you! You look almost gaunt. How much weight have you lost?"

"I, I don't know. I haven't weighed myself in a long time."

"Well, what you need is to get out and socialize again. And the Grand Opera is a good start."

"Grand Opera? What Grand Opera?" Alma wanted so much to lean back in her chair next to the couch on which Felicia and Tommie were sitting. But that might encourage them to sit back, too, and visit longer. She appreciated their concern, but right now she wanted to be alone with her thoughts.

"You mean to tell me you don't know that the Philadelphia La Scala Opera is coming to Detroit? Performing 'Aida' at the Masonic Temple?" Felicia asked. "Oh, Alma, Alma, you've got to get back into the real world."

Tommie looked over at the easel on which the beginning of a portrait rested. "Felicia's right, Alma. You haven't painted a stroke since the last time we were here. Is the dowager Gilden going to live out the rest of her days with only one eye?"

"If you don't finish that portrait, Alma dear, and start work on all those others you've promised, the word is going to get around that you're through. Dried up," Felicia said.

"Oh, I know. I know," Alma said. "I'll ask Mrs. Gilden to come by tomorrow. I promise." But would Alma really do that? She had no energy to resume painting. To resume anything. Truth was, she had not been satisfied with the way the portrait was going. Though she realized it only now, she hadn't been satisfied with her painting even before--before what had happened to Pa and Carrie Lou.

"Oh, I almost forgot," Felicia said. She rose from the couch and walked to the foyer, returning with a large silver box. "I want your opinion on the gown I'm wearing to the opera." Felicia opened the box and held a black satin creation up to herself. It had a perky velvet peplum, and dainty pearls covered the bodice and padded shoulders.

"Glamorous. Very glamorous," Alma said. The design was exciting, in good taste.

"It's a 'Tommie Original,' of course," Tommie said. He rolled his eyes in an exaggerated manner. "I'm getting so well known, I don't have to use my last name anymore. And note the new street length. Saving material for the war effort, you know."

"Oh, Alma, do say you'll come with us," Felicia said. "We're going with the Reveres, of course, and we're meeting Tommie and Richard for dinner at the Detroit Club first."

"Richard is just dying to hear the La Scala, so I invited him to stay the weekend," Tommie said. Richard was Tommie's latest "friend."

Alma looked at Felicia, but Felicia's face was inscrutable.

"I could whip you up a Tommie Original. The opera is still two weeks away," Tommie said.

"We'll see," Alma said.

Finally, they and their advice were gone. Alma sat down in one of the chairs by the living room's big window and settled back. Why was it that after all of her friends once gave her their hasty and awkward condolences, no one mentioned her father to her again?

Except for Mr. Buckingham. He had come by often these past few weeks. But he, too, was full of advice. Only yesterday he sat across from her and said, "Alma, you must take care of yourself. Look how thin you are. You know your father wouldn't like that. As your mother says, you're 'fallin' off.' And speaking of Lizzie, why don't you go see her? You know she misses you."

"She's doing fine, Mister Buckingham. She always does fine. She doesn't miss me. And she's not lonely, because she's got Aunt Euella and her girlfriend living there now. Of course, she won't accept any money from me for her living expenses."

Then, changing the subject, Alma had said, "Mister Buckingham,
I've been wondering. Why--Why didn't Pa come straight home the
night that he ..." Alma looked away as her eyes got misty. "Why did he
go downtown? Was he going downtown to get me a birthday present?"

Mr. Buckingham had hesitated for an instant. "I, I don't know,
Alma. But why are you torturing yourself wondering?"

"Because I have to know if it was all my fault!"

Mr. Buckingham still said nothing, but took her hand in his.

No, no. She didn't want to know. She hoped she would never find
out. "Oh, why, why did it have to happen? Pa was so good. He never
hurt anyone in his whole life. If that Scatelli hadn't been there right
then--but I'll never know if he really was there. If Mayor Jeffries and
Governor Kelly hadn't dilly-dallied around for so long and had asked for
federal troops sooner, they would have stopped the rioting right away."

"Alma, dear Alma, stop torturing yourself like this. If, if, if. Iffing
won't bring back your father. I know, it seems that you'll never feel
whole again, that you'll never have any joy again. But life must go on.
Your father wouldn't want you to be grieving so long."

"I know, I know, Mr. Buckingham."

"Don't you think it's about time you called me Harry? After all,
we've been through so much together."

"So much together? What have you been through--?" Alma stopped,
suddenly ashamed. "Oh, I'm sorry. I'm sorry. You loved him, too."

"He was the dearest friend I ever had," Mr. Buckingham said, his
voice choking.

Alma patted his hand with her free one. Then, changing the subject
again, she said, "Mr. Bucking--Harry, (She felt strange calling him that
after all these years)--I'm sorry that I didn't feel like spending much
time with Jimmie Lee. I always had thought I'd take him out on the
town and spoil him rotten the first long furlough he got."

"Don't feel bad about that, Alma. Jimmie Lee didn't really feel much
like going out, either. Don't be so hard on yourself. Be very gentle with
yourself. Treat yourself with the same care and love that you'd treat a
good friend if this happened to her."

There was a moment of silence. Then Harry continued, "You
know, the Army has really changed that brother of yours. He was a kid

when he left. Now he's talking like a man. By the way, your mother has pinpointed on the map where she thinks he might be. Salerno."

"Salerno?" Alma hadn't been keeping up with the news.

"Salerno's in southern Italy. And, you know, your mother might be right. She was right about Jimmie Lee being in that news photo taken at the Kasserine Pass."

Salerno. Italy. Her little brother was probably in Italy and she hadn't even wondered lately where he might be.

Harry was right, Alma thought, as she settled back into her chair now. Jimmie Lee had changed. Alma recalled the last time she'd seen him. It was at her mother's house. Her mother had prepared a farewell supper of her brother's favorite meal--beans and cornbread. Harry had been there, of course. And Aunt Euella and her friend, Lillian Pickford Marsh, who both shared Alma's and Carrie Lou's old bedroom. They had vacated their own apartment and moved in with Lizzie to assist her with living expenses and to do their bit to help ease the extreme apartment shortage. "Lil" had been named after her mother's favorite screen stars at the time she was born, Lillian Gish and Mary Pickford. She looked like neither. Lil, a tall, big-boned woman of about thirty-five, looked as though she might have just gotten off a Greyhound from Appalachia, but she had lived in Detroit all her life.

"I love men," Lil had said as they all sat at the dining room table. "Any and all men. Can't resist 'em. Married three of 'em, didn't I? That's one reason why I go to the USO with Euella. Men coming out of the woodwork there." Her merry brown eyes focused on Alma. "Say, Alma May, why don't you come with Euella and me tonight? You'd have a ball, I guarantee. Good, clean fun. Dancing to the jukebox, bowling, playing ping-pong, passing out Cokes and coffee. You can even hear the stars on the USO Service Serenade broadcast--sometimes Wee Bonnie Baker, or Guy Lombardo, or Perry Como."

"Lil's right," Aunt Euella said. "An' you'd be helpin' keep up the morale of our boys." Aunt Euella was all dressed up in a frilly white blouse and black flared skirt.

"Oh, maybe sometime," Alma said. She had no intention of ever doing so, but didn't say this to Lil. She couldn't help liking the woman because of her disarming frankness.

"It'd be good for you, Alma," Jimmie Lee agreed. "I know--"

Jimmie Lee was interrupted by a knock at the door. Alma, who was closest, excused herself to answer.

To her surprise, a Negro, a withered shadow of a man whom Alma guessed to be in his sixties or seventies, stood with his hat in his hand. "This where the Combses live?" His voice was frail and shy.

"Y--Yes," Alma replied. What now? What else could happen? She knew her remaining family to be safe inside.

You must be Chester Combs's daughter."

"Yes. Chester Combs's daughter." Her father's complete name always sounded so formal.

"Sorry to read about your poor pa, ma'am. He reached into a pocket of his baggy pants and pulled out something shiny. "Been hangin' onto this here spoon for all these years, keepin' good care of it. Hopin' to somehow run into your pa an' give it back. Never knew his name, but when I seen his picture in the paper, I jus' knew it was him."

Alma stared dumbly at the gleaming silver-plated utensil, which the man put into her hand. Its familiar pattern matched the one on the spoons being used at that very moment.

"Your Pa--bless'm an' God rest his soul--your Pa befriended me one day years an' years ago when no one else did. I was sittin' on a bench in Cad'llac Square an' your Pa came 'long an' insisted I finish his lunch. Beans an' cornbread. Remember it like it was only yesterday. Best beans I ever ate." He cleared his throat in embarrassment and looked down at his shoes. They appeared as though he'd spent half a day polishing them. "Jus' wanted you an' your folks to know your pa was one of the kindest g'men I ever met."

"Thank you," Alma said, beginning to collect her wits. "Would you like to come in and join us for supper?" She could not believe what she was saying. "As a matter of fact, we're having beans and cornbread right now."

"Oh, no, ma'am, thank you kindly." He began to turn his hat in his hands. "Me an' the missus, we're goin' to see our daughter an' her kids now."

Alma looked out to the street and noticed for the first time a clean but beat-up sedan, the door on the passenger side fastened to the frame with a rope. Inside, a Negro woman of about the man's age smiled shyly at her.

The man smiled once more, then left and drove off before Alma realized that she didn't even know his name.

She clutched the spoon and, returning to the table, related to the astonished others what had happened. To think that he had kept the spoon all these years. A long, emotional silence followed, after which Alma asked her mother if she could keep the spoon.

"A course, Alma May."

Alma fingered the spoon as Jimmie Lee broke another stillness. "I hope I can be just like Pa. You know, when I first joined the Army, I was ashamed to tell them where I was born, because they'd razz me. But they could tell from my drawl, of course. Then they started callin' me Hillbilly, just like they did Pa. But now I don't care anymore. When I was in them foxholes an' wonderin' if I'd even see the next day's dawnin', sometimes I had plenty of time to think." (This was the first time Jimmie Lee had wanted to talk about his part in the war, Alma had realized.) "...I got to figurin' what's really important. I was just a green kid. I thought I was joinin' the Army to beat them Japs single-handed. Shoot. I ain't even seen one Jap. Got sent to kill the Germans. Now, when I hear what the government's doin' to them Japanese-Americans, I'm ashamed, just like Pa would've been. Sendin' them to those interment camps. The Japanese-Americans are innocent. Pa'd say they can't help it that they're part Japanese and that their relatives are fightin' us, any more'n we can help it that we're hillbillies an' happen to be born in Appalachia. Well, now I realize what's important is to get this war over soon so's we all can go back to our own way of livin'." He sat back in his chair, his speech over.

"Are you going to start saving for The Farm again, now, Lizzie?" Harry asked.

Her mother hesitated for a moment while she considered. "My dream a The Farm died with Chet. I'm a Detroiter. I belong in Detroit City."

Now, still thinking about that evening, the last time she'd seen Jimmie Lee, Alma settled back in her chair again. Her thoughts were interrupted now by the phone ringing. Since Sarah had Sundays off, Alma walked to her studio to answer it.

Miss Galbraith's voice was cheerful and effervescent, as always. She had been keeping up on Alma's progress all these years. Alma could picture her former art teacher's round, smiling face as she talked:

"... And Alma, I hope you've started painting again, like you promised. The sooner you get back to work, the sooner you'll feel better."

"I know."

"Well, just checking up on you, dear. And, oh, by the way, I have a brilliant idea."

"What?" More well intended advice, no doubt.

"How would you like it if I could arrange to have an exhibit of your and Purlie Washington's work at the Summit Club gallery? Of course, Purlie couldn't attend the opening, because it wouldn't do to let the members know she's colored. They'd never agree to her exhibiting there if they knew. But don't you think it's a great idea? It would give you some goal to work toward."

"Oh, I don't know, Miss Galbraith. I'm flattered that you want to do this, but--but the thought of having an exhibit right now--"

"But it doesn't have to be right away, dear. Just promise me you'll think about it.

Alma exhaled. "Oh, all right, Miss Galbraith. I'll think about it," she lied. She was glad when Miss Galbraith hung up.

She turned on the Stromberg-Carlson. The rich baritone of the newly popular singer, Frank Sinatra, filled the apartment as Alma walked absently from room to room:

> "Won't you tell me when
> We will meet again.
> Sunday, Monday, or always. ..."

She looked at the portrait of Mrs. Gilden. Oh, Pa, Alma thought, I know I promised you I'd be a famous artist and make you proud of me, but I can't help it. I just don't have the energy to start painting again.

The confines of her apartment became intolerable. Alma rushed out the door and locked it behind her. Not until she was in the elevator did she remember she'd forgotten to turn the radio off. It seemed as though she was forgetting to do a lot of things lately.

The pavement was damp in spots. Alma was unaware that it had rained. She strolled aimlessly down to the river's edge, the air around her a mixture of fish and water smells and wet wood of the dock. It was not unpleasant. The sound of the water lapping against the dock caused her to look down. How deep was the water? she wondered. She noticed that no one was on any of the sailboats anchored nearby or on the power boats along the dock in the distance. There were only a few people strolling here and there. No one was looking. She leaned over the edge of the dock and peered deep, deep into the gray-green water. If she should accidentally "fall" into the water, no one would notice. No one at all. She glanced downriver to the Ambassador Bridge in the distance, spanning the river from Detroit to Canada. How easy it would be to walk to the bridge, climb on top of its girders, and jump. So simple. No one would miss her for days. ...

A sudden gust of wind blew her curls forward onto her face, and caused her to shiver. She turned from the water and walked inland.

Several minutes later she arrived at a small public park. When she passed the metal stands holding the city's three newspapers, one of the headlines caught her eye: "YANKS WIN SALERNO IN TANK BATTLE" If Jimmie Lee were really there, would he stay in Italy and fight another battle?

Jimmie Lee. She wished he were here. She looked at the date of the paper. Sunday, September 12, 1943. *September twelfth. It was not possible. Where had the weeks gone?*

Some of the trees in the little park were beginning to shed their leaves. A few stubborn shriveled rose petals still clung to the nearby bushes. The fallen petals blended with the leaves scattered on the ground. The chrysanthemums were in full bloom along the walkway. Pa used to take pride in the chrysanthemums he tended at their flat years ago. A flock of red-winged blackbirds made a loud sound above her as they took wing and headed for a distant tree, a sure sign of fall.

A few yards away, a father was pushing a young girl of five or six on a swing. The girl squealed with delight as the swing climbed higher, higher. Alma passed another father who lay on his back under a tree, a young girl of maybe nine or ten beside him. They were intent on looking at the sky. First the man would point up at the sky and say something that Alma could not make out. Then, the girl would smile and point up, too, and say something.

Alma rushed past them. Her throat hurt as she held back the tears. She saw a bench under a tree a few yards ahead, hurried to it and sat down. A chill passed over her and she realized she hadn't thought to put a jacket on. If her father were here, he would give her his.

"Oh, Pa, Pa," Alma whispered, "I don't want to go on without you."

The ache in her throat became unbearable.

Chapter 33

Alma wove in and out of the heavy flow of Saturday evening traffic going southeast on Grand River Avenue. Beside her sat Aunt Euella, who was applying Tangee Natural lipstick for the third time since leaving the house. Lil sat in the back seat. With her green Chesterfield coat over her bright red dress, she looked like a huge, bumpy, Christmas package wrapped by a four-year-old.

As usual, Lil did most of the talking. "And if this isn't the cat's meow. You must've paid a pretty penny for this, Alma. My second husband--George was his name--always wanted a Cadillac just like this. ..." The deep, mellow voice of Bing Crosby singing last year's hit, "White Christmas," came from the radio. It muffled some of what Lil was saying.

The red and green decorations on the streetlights and storefronts depressed Alma. Thanksgiving, a dismal day spent at her mother's house, was just over, and now the merchants were rushing Christmas. It would be a miserable Christmas without Pa and Carrie Lou and Jimmie Lee.

"... and next to payday, the average soldier likes most to dance, and I aim to accommodate his wish," Lil was saying now. Alma tried to listen, but she was thinking of what Miss Fairbanks, the USO director, had told her: "Alma, the chief function of the United Service Organizations is to provide opportunities for servicemen and women to follow leisure-time interests outside of military reservations. Interests like they knew at home. You're part of twelve thousand USO volunteers in the Metropolitan Detroit area. It will be your duty not only to be a dance partner, but also if the need arises, to be a waitress, or write letters home for servicemen, or type, and sometimes even mend socks and sew on rank insignia. But your most important duty is to be a friendly, intelligent, wholesome, feminine companion to lonely servicemen far from home. The most popular hostesses remind them of the girls back home." Alma's background had been carefully checked, and then she'd been quizzed on her interests and talents. She wondered if the director knew about Lil's three marriages.

It felt strange going someplace with her Aunt Euella, who seemed like a different person now. And Lil. Lil was someone Alma never would've sought out for a social companion. But it was true what Harry had said several weeks ago. Alma must not be so hard on herself. She must go on with her life and get away from her thoughts.

Harry had said it again just a few days ago when he returned from a weekend in Chicago, where he'd gone to ride on the city's new subway system. Alma was folding and sealing a letter to Jimmie Lee, written on the new lightweight V-mail stationery. She'd wondered exactly where he was. The Allies were firmly ashore at three points in southern Italy; Italy was an ally now. Naples was allied occupied. Was Jimmie Lee moving east toward Germany's Gustav Line, as her mother thought? Alma was glad he wasn't part of the blood bath battle against the Japanese at Tarawa in the Central Pacific.

"You must get out of yourself," Harry had said. "Do something different that you've never done before that'll keep your mind occupied, even if it's only for a few hours. Do something for someone. Why not go with Euella and Lil to the USO, like they've been asking? Try it. What have you got to lose?"

"It won't work. I think about Pa wherever I go."

"Sure you do. It's only normal. You need some new challenging experience that will take all your concentration. Your father would want you to do something besides grieve over him.

"Though nothing
Can bring back the hour
Of glory in the flower,
We will grieve not, rather find
Strength in what
Remains behind"

Harry smiled. "As you've noticed, I take comfort in the words of wise poets. Those are by Wordsworth."

Alma attempted a smile. "Why is it, Harry, that all my friends, except for you, never mention Pa anymore? It's like he never existed, like his life had no meaning. And it's as though my pain is inappropriate or inconvenient for them."

"People feel uncomfortable around the subject of death, Alma. I don't know how we ever got the idea, but we think life should never hurt. If we do feel heartache, we shouldn't let it get us down too long. We should repress it. They want you to be the same old Alma now."

"I'll never be the same old Alma, Harry."

★　★　★

The USO dance hall was a sea of olive drab and Navy blue, sprinkled with bright colors of the dresses on the chaperones and volunteers. Miss Fairbanks, a tall, blue-haired woman with parentheses around her mouth even when she wasn't smiling, greeted them. "Now, Alma, I know you're going to do just fine. This is your first time, I know. Just be your own sweet self. I'll have you do something easy to start off. Lil and Euella, show Alma where the coat room is."

They threaded their way through the crowd toward the coatroom, and Alma glanced around. So this was what Carrie Lou had seen. Large, high-ceilinged room. Refreshment counters against all four walls. A juke box in the corner, silent tonight because a live band had been scheduled for a special dance. The musicians were warming up, each practicing his own part of the evening's planned music. The discord was too much, along with the din of voices. Alma wished she hadn't come. In her frame of mind, she'd be no good to any lonely serviceman. She wished she were at home in her quiet apartment. Or at her mother's house, curled up in her father's chair. She wished she could curl up so tightly in it, and make herself so small, that she would disappear into herself.

They hung their coats in the coatroom and went down the hall to the ladies' lounge. Alma looked at Aunt Euella in the mirror as they put their name tags on. She was applying lipstick again and refreshing her Blue Waltz perfume. "You look very nice, Aunt Euella."

"Thank you, Alma May," Aunt Euella said. She patted her pageboy and fluffed the ruffles on her white blouse. "Oh, Alma May, it's--it's like I was sixteen again an' all dressed up for the dance at the Letcher County Fair before I met--Darcas. Poor Darcas. I'm sorry he died, but it's like I got me another chance in life. A chance to make somethin' a myself an' have a little fun, too. A course I ain't expectin' to meet nobody here to marry or nothin' like that--most a them's too young for me--but it makes me feel good to just listen while they talk their poor li'l hearts out. I'm doin' somethin' for the war effort. Do you think I'm such an awful person 'cause I ain't home cryin' my eyes out over your Uncle Darcas?"

"Of course not, Aunt Euella." Alma freshened her own lipstick. She hesitated as she thought how she should phrase the question she'd been wanting to ask. "Aunt Euella, why--why did you stay with Uncle Darcas so long, when he was so--so--my mother told me he beat you."

Aunt Euella blinked her eyes to hold back glistening tears. She reached for her purse, but Alma handed her one of her handkerchiefs. "Oh, Alma May, I felt so low about myself then. He kept tellin' me I was such a dumb, stupid woman that I deserved to be beat regularly. An' after a while, I began to believe him. I thought I was too stupid to make it on my own. Oh, your Ma kept tellin' me I should come an' live with you all, but that wouldn't a done no good. He still wouldn't a left me alone, an' besides, I didn't want your poor Pa to know. It would a hurt your Pa so much."

"Besides," Lil said, "she kept hoping he'd change. Kept hoping for a happily ever after. Well, take it from me--Ol' Lil's an expert at it. You can't make a man change." Lil leaned closer to the mirror and inspected the black showing at the roots of her bleached blond hair, which was done in an upsweep. "Got to get me a touch-up, and real soon." She stood up tall, adjusted her shoulder pads, and took a deep breath. "Ready, girls? All them men are waiting impatiently for us!"

Alma's first duty was behind one of the refreshment counters, jammed with servicemen and service women anxious to be waited on. She put on a white frilly apron and joined two other young women volunteers. They were too busy to explain much about the routine. Alma had never before worked serving food or drink. At first she felt as though she were all thumbs, and made a few mistakes. Once she served soda water when a sailor had requested coffee. Another time she handed out a donut to a WAVE who'd asked for a tuna sandwich. But the guests took it all in good humor, and soon she began to relax and feel adequate. She could even listen with one ear to the music of the band, which seemed to be playing a lot of swing. And she overheard snatches of the conversations around her:

"Got me two free tickets from the USO at the YMCA to see Alan Ladd in *China*. Wanna go?"

"Why would I want to go to *China*? I've had enough of Orientals. Just got back from fighting the Japs in the Solomons."

"Very funny. You're even funnier than Abbott and Costello."

From the other end of the bar, a soldier said, "Yep. When I get stateside for good, I'm going to get me a little house."

"Not me. I'm gonna get a trailer--an Airstream, no less--and see this country of ours. Never appreciated it till I was fightin' in New Guinea."

From a nearby Marine: "Been awake for two days. Don't want to miss anything. Why should I sleep my pass away?"

"Betty Grable ain't got nothing on you, Sweetie," said a sailor to a WAC who stood near where Alma was filling a glass with Coca-Cola. "Don't call me 'Sweetie'. I'm 'Sergeant' to you, sailor."

Alma felt a tap on her shoulder. She looked up to see a blond woman of about forty smiling at her. "Miss Fairbanks says I'm supposed to take over for you. You've been here an hour. You're supposed to go ask someone to dance now."

An hour. She'd been here an hour already? Alma untied her apron and handed it to the woman.

Alma joined the other hostesses standing along the wall. She should go to the ladies room again and freshen her makeup, but she didn't want to fight the crowd. She felt awkward standing here. It had been so long since she danced. Would she remember any of the steps?

The music started again. A hulking gap-toothed sailor immediately pulled her onto the dance floor and clutched her close to him. "Name's Hector," he said, grinning down at her from what seemed like three feet above. "What's yours?" He squinted as he bent over and read her name tag.

"Alma."

"Alma. That's real pretty. Never knew anyone named Alma before. My friends call me Heck. Sometimes when they want my attention they call, 'Oh, Heck!' I'm glad they don't call, 'Oh, Hell!' Wouldn't that be funny if they did that?"

"Very."

He pushed her backwards unexpectedly with his hand on her waist and spun her fast several times. Alma looked around at the other dancers. No one else was twirling. The music was a slow piece: "A Lovely Way to Spend an Evening."

He clutched her to him again and continued stepping offbeat to the music. "Love to dance. *Love* to dance." He inhaled deeply. "Hey. Your perfume sure smells yummy. What's it called? Never was too good at sports. You'd think I'd be a linebacker with this body of mine, wouldn't you?" He pushed her away and spun her even faster this time. "Never was too good in academics, either. But they say if you try hard enough, you'll find something you're good at." He pressed her to him again. "Mine's dancing," he continued, stepping on her foot. "*Love* to dance!"

Alma winced. What had possessed her to wear open-toed sandals? She looked around for someone to rescue her, and noticed that the other dancers and the crowd ringing the floor were looking at her and her partner and smiling in amusement. But Alma was not amused. She couldn't decide which hurt the most--her bruised toes or her neck, which she was forced to crane backward as she looked up at her partner.

Mercifully, the music ended. "I think I'll just keep you all to myself tonight, Alma. Won't that be fun, just dancing with me all night, now that you've gotten used to my fancy steps?"

"That would be a lot of fun, Heck, but one of the rules says I can't dance more than one dance in a row with anyone."

"Oh, the Heck with the rule! Get it? Get it? *Heck* with the rule? You can break the rule just one little time. You and me--we're dynamite together. Just wait 'til I show you what I can do with a waltz!"

The music started again, another slow piece. The other dancers were switching partners, but Hector held her tightly. "You're not getting away from me, little girl."

Alma looked around for a chaperone and tried to free herself graciously. Oh, Harry, she thought, why did I let you talk me into coming here tonight? I--"

"My turn, sailor," a voice next to her said. Alma looked up to see a soldier tapping Hector on the shoulder. "I've been waiting eleven years to dance with this young lady."

"Get lost, private," Hector said. He put his arm possessively around Alma's waist.

"Please. No hard feelings. I'll dance with you again later, Hector," Alma said. She was glad when she saw Miss Fairbanks approaching.

Hector noticed the director approaching, too. "Well, okay. But don't forget." He stumbled away and Alma saw him pull another hostess onto the dance floor. Miss Fairbanks disappeared.

"Poor Hector," the soldier said. He took Alma in his arms.

"What do you mean, 'poor Hector'? I feel sorrier for my poor toes," Alma said, with a laugh.

"Do your toes hurt too much to dance?" His voice was slow and easy, verging on a drawl.

Alma looked up at him and smiled. "I've forgotten about them already."

"Good. Like I said, I've been waiting eleven years to dance with Alma Combs."

"Eleven years. What are you talking about?" She looked closely at his face for the first time. Nice looking, but not a face that would be noticed. Smooth, clean complexion. Clear blue eyes. Medium brown hair cut in an Army regulation brush. No outstanding feature that triggered memories. Still--there was something vaguely familiar about it.

The soldier glided her around the floor. "I like your dress, Alma Combs."

"Thank you," Alma said absently, still trying to place his face.

"It's almost the same color as the little flowers in the dress you wore to the dance."

"Dance? What dance?"

"The Autumn Fantasy. You were beautiful in that dress. The most beautiful one there."

Autumn Fantasy. Autumn Fantasy. That sounded familiar. Alma thought hard for a moment. Yes--*Autumn Fantasy*, a name that she'd buried long ago. And now, hearing it again began to bring back sad memories. Memories of disappointment, of failure. She looked even closer at the soldier's face. *No, it couldn't be Albert—Albert Salvatore. ...*

She'd buried that name, too, along with memories of other failures. Failures of Alma May Combs, the little hillbilly girl from Mountainview near Harlan.

"I'll make it easy for you. I'm Joe. Joe Smith. Your old classmate. The skinny little twerp who asked you to dance that night and who you turned down. I don't know what I would've done if Gladys Polaski hadn't been there to bail me out of my embarrassment and dance with me."

She continued to scrutinize his face. *Of course.* She remembered now. *Joe Smith. The kid with the Adam's apple and, and …*

Alma started to giggle. She looked up at the top of his head. "Thank heaven for brushes."

Joe's eyebrows rose. "Brushes? What're you talking about?"

"Brushes. Brush haircuts. Your cowlick doesn't stand at attention anymore, and you don't have to douse your hair with Brilliantine."

They both laughed, remembering, and continued to move around the floor. Alma felt at ease with this soldier, her old classmate. More at ease than she'd felt all night. She was sorry when the music ended.

"Aw, shucks! Foiled again!" Joe said. "What would happen if we danced the next one, too?"

Alma looked around. Neither Miss Fairbanks nor a chaperone nor Hector were looking their way. "Nothing. Nothing at all."

The music started again, and Alma became more aware of his arm on her waist, of her hand on his shoulder. It felt natural when he pressed her closer to him.

"I was so sorry to hear about your father, Alma. He seemed like a very nice man."

"Thank you." *Pa, forgive me,* she thought. *I haven't thought about you once in ten minutes.* "How did you know? Were you around then?"

"I was at camp. But my mother forwarded the *Detroit Times* to me–"

"By the way, what are you doing here? Usually guys who come here are strangers in town."

"All my buddies are overseas. And it seems like all the girls I know are married."

Lucky for me, Alma thought. She pressed her cheek against his. She smelled the familiar scent of Williams shaving soap. Her father used that.

The trumpet soloist was doing a remarkably good imitation of the late Bunny Berigan playing "I Can't Get Started with You." The style, distinctive and uninhibited, was a pleasure to dance to. He played through the wide range of notes, the tone gutty and sometimes growly, pausing on a high note for a lip trill. Alma nestled closer in Joe's arms. She felt comfortable, secure. She had come home again.

The music ended once more, and Alma didn't look around this time to see whether a chaperone was checking on them. The lights dimmed again and the band began playing another slow piece. The mirrored ball above the dance floor made swirling reflections around them while she and Joe danced. Alma became unaware of the other dancers. The only things existing were herself and Joe and the music. And the lyrics of the female vocalist, singing to them alone:

> "My heart tells me this is just a fling,
> Yet you say our love means everything. ..."

Oh, Pa, Alma thought, *am I falling for this boy?*

"Alma," Joe said. "You're going to think I'm loco or something, but I've been dreaming of this moment for years. Holding you in my arms, dancing to a romantic number. Whoever thought I'd see you here tonight?"

Alma smiled up at him. She hadn't noticed before how perfectly shaped his eyebrows were. "Yes. Whoever thought you'd see me here tonight." She pressed her cheek against his again and asked, "Why didn't you call me all these years?"

"Afraid. Afraid you'd turn me down like you did at the dance. I kept following your progress in the society pages, your name linked with this and that society person. And all those portraits you've done. I knew you must've made a fortune from them. With all that, why in the world would you want to be seen with a common guy like me?"

"Why indeed?" she said, her tone teasing. The vocalist repeated:

> "Do you mean what you are saying,
> Or is this just a little game you're playing. ..."

The music would end soon. Alma clung a little tighter. "A common guy like you. What's so common about you?"

"No big ambitions. Just waiting for the war to be over so I can come back home and get started in life."

"And how would you get started?"

"Oh, I don't know. Probably save for a farm."

"A farm! You're kidding!" Alma's eyes widened.

"What's wrong with wanting a farm?" Joe's tone was defensive.

"Nothing. Nothing at all. I think a farm is a great idea."

"Of course, it'd have to be a small one at first. But I know I'd be good at farming, especially after I went to agricultural college. I hear they're working on a bill that'll pay for veterans' tuition at most colleges."

She loved the way his eyebrows rose when he talked. "And where would this little farm be?"

"Oh, I don't care. Here or in northern Michigan. Or even another state."

"How about Kentucky?"

"That'd be all right, too. Or West Virginia. My family's from West Virginia."

"So that's why you have a slight drawl. I never thought of you as being from West Virginia."

Joe grinned. "That's because you never thought of me at all."

It's true, Pa, Alma thought. *I think I'm beginning to fall for this boy.*

The song ended. The band began to play a fast number. Joe looked at the other dancers going through their gyrations, and shook his head. "I'm no good at jitterbugging. Let's go to the lounge where it's quiet."

The lounge was a large room at the end of the hall. It was furnished with comfortable leatherette couches and chairs, table tennis, and several card tables. A one-armed soldier sat alone in a corner patiently trying to shuffle a deck of cards. In another corner, a Marine was engrossed in a jigsaw puzzle, his elbows resting on the table, his hands holding his head. Every available seat was taken by servicemen and service women and hostesses. Alma wondered where Aunt Euella and Lil were. She hadn't thought about them since they all parted outside the ladies room.

"I know a nice little bar," Joe said. "It's right across the street."

Alma put her finger to her lips. "I'm not supposed to leave here with anyone," she whispered.

"You won't be leaving with me," Joe whispered back. "I'll go first and wait in front of DeLong's Lounge for you."

"But I'm not off until midnight. And my aunt and her friend are depending on me to take them home."

Joe reached into his wallet and handed her two dollars. "Here. This'll be plenty for them to take a taxi home."

"But--"

He took her hand and squeezed it gently. "Please. There's no privacy around here. And this is my last night home--"

"Your last night! Where are you going?"

"Hard telling. I have to catch the train tomorrow afternoon for New York. I'll be shipped out from there."

A sinking sensation hit her. Shipped out. What if she never saw him again? "All right. Wait for me in front of DeLong's."

His look held hers for a moment. Then he was gone.

She circled the dance floor several times looking for Aunt Euella or Lil, but found neither. Finally, she caught up with Aunt Euella washing her hands in the ladies room.

"Aunt Euella. I--I met a soldier, an old classmate, who needs a ride home. He's not feeling well, see, and asked me for a ride."

"Why, that's fine, Alma May. I'll go fetch Lil an' we'll all ask Miss Fairbanks if it's all right to leave now--"

"But he wants to be alone with me. You know, he wants to talk about old times, and ..."

Aunt Euella looked hard at Alma's face and then hugged her. "You go along then, Alma May. I'll tell Miss Fairbanks you got sick."

"Here's money for a taxi," Alma said. She handed Aunt Euella Joe's money.

Aunt Euella pushed it away. "Oh, pshaw! I got me more money'n I can shake a stick at, what with workin' overtime an' all."

Alma spotted Joe's tall, erect figure waiting for her in front of DeLong's. He looked very handsome in his uniform.

Joe took both her hands and kissed her on the forehead. "Missed you," he said, smiling down at her.

DeLong's was crowded with civilians and servicemen. A balding, harried waiter, balancing a drink-laden tray on each shoulder, motioned them with his chin in the direction of the only empty booth. They sat down and Alma looked around. It was noisy, and cigarette smoke hung in the air. On the wall next to her was thumbtacked a poster with a drawing of a large human ear and the words:

The Enemy Is
Always Listening
So Keep Your
Mouth Shut!
This Bar Discourages Loose Talk

Four sailors were drinking and laughing loudly in the booth in front of them. A young corporal and his even younger girlfriend held hands at the table across the aisle.

"I'm sorry," Joe said. "I remember this place as being quiet and intimate."

"The war's changed a lot of things," Alma replied. She tried to make herself heard above the din.

The juke box was booming out "Praise the Lord and Pass the Ammunition," fighting with the voices of the customers and the rattling of the glasses.

Joe ordered a rum and Coke for Alma and a Stroh's for himself. The Stroh's reminded her of Uncle Darcas, but she pushed him quickly from her thoughts.

Alma glanced in amusement at the corporal and his girlfriend. It was obvious they were very much in love. He couldn't keep his eyes off the girl, and she clung to his every word.

"Isn't love grand?" Joe asked as he glanced at the couple, too, and looked into Alma's eyes.

Alma looked away, feeling suddenly shy, "Yes. I guess it probably is."

Joe reached across the booth and took Alma's hand. "The hand of an artist," he said. He rubbed it gently across his cheek. "I used to wonder how it would be to hold your hand and--and kiss your lips. I used to walk back and forth past Miss Galbraith's art room and look at you while you worked. The sunlight coming in from the window catching your hair, making it glow like a reddish gold halo." He pressed his lips to the palm of her hand and kissed it. "And now. I can't believe it. Here we are. I'm so glad I went to the dance tonight. Are you?" His voice had grown husky.

Alma looked steadily into his eyes now. "Yes. Oh, yes." How good he made her feel! She hadn't felt this good since--

Pa, Pa. Is it possible to fall in love so suddenly, Pa? I think you would love him, too--

"Look at them," Joe said, his focus shifting to the young couple again. "They probably have only a few hours left together. He's probably being shipped out tomorrow, like me. He's desperately in love with her, like--like I am with you. He's probably trying to convince her that they should spend every available minute together. Alone. She's wondering if she does that what he'll think of her after he's gone. What she'll think of herself. What her family would think of her if they knew. She's wondering what would happen to her if she got--pregnant."

The music from the juke box ended abruptly. The girl, who had been shouting over the noise in order to be heard, finished her sentence: "... and what if I get pregnant?"

The customers looked her way and laughed. When she realized that they had heard what she said, the girl's face turned red. She jumped up and fled out the door, the corporal fast behind her, carrying her purse.

After the laughter died down, Joe continued: "She'll get over her embarrassment. Then she'll realize that he truly loves her and that she thinks she's fallen in love with him, too. And that the only thing that really matters is their being together. They'll have those few hours to remember. It would be a sin not to be together, not to grab what happiness they can."

Yes, to grab what happiness they can, Alma thought.

"Oh, Alma," Joe said, "do I--do I dare to think you're thinking what that girl will be thinking? That the only thing that matters is the moment. To make each other happy?"

Alma turned her face away. The raw emotion in his eyes was too much to bear.

Joe reached across the booth and moved her face gently back. "Look at me, Alma. I have a feeling you're beginning to care for me. Do I dare to hope you're thinking what that girl is thinking?"

Pa, I love him. I know you'll understand what I'm about to say. "Yes," she replied, surprised at the emotion in her own voice, "you dare to hope." Joe kissed her hand again. He motioned for the check. "Let's go."

★　★　★

They made a quick stop in front of a Cunningham drug store where Joe visited the pharmacy counter, and Alma waited in the car with her head turned away.

They couldn't go to her apartment because Sarah was there on Saturday evenings. They couldn't go to his house because his widowed mother was at home. After searching for several hours, they finally found the only room available, in a downtown hotel on Woodward Avenue.

Alma felt uncomfortable as they approached the desk. She looked around to make sure no one she knew could see her. That was silly, though: No one she knew would be in a place like this.

The clerk was annoyed that they were interrupting his game of solitaire. "I just called. You said there was one room left," Joe said.

The clerk barely looked up from where he sat in his chair behind the scarred wooden counter. He motioned for Joe to sign the register. Alma watched over Joe's shoulder while he wrote "Pvt. & Mrs. Joseph Smith." She shoved her ringless left hand into her coat pocket.

After a long moment more of ignoring them while he continued to deal his cards, the clerk stood and turned the register so that he could read it. He squinted at the signature through cracked spectacle lenses held together by stained adhesive tape, looked up at Joe and raised one bushy brow. "Private and Mrs. Joseph Smith, eh?" he asked with a smirk.

Flustered, Joe replied, "That's my real name. Honest. Here--I'll prove it." He started to open his wallet to show his Army identification, but the clerk motioned it away with one white hand. "It don't matter one whit to me what you sign. You could sign General and Missus Dwight D. Eisenhower, for all I care. All I care is you got eight dollars for the room and you don't break the plaster off the walls." He raised his arm up to his nose and wiped his nostrils and the tufts of hair growing out of them with his shirtsleeve. Joe placed a five and three singles on the counter.

The man reached behind him and pulled out a key from a pigeon hole numbered three-oh-four. He handed it to Joe. Joe took Alma by the arm and led her toward the stairway.

"Where's your luggage, Private and Missus Smith?" the clerk asked. He laughed as he sat down and resumed his card game.

The room was small and stifling hot. Joe locked the door behind them. It was furnished with an iron double bed with a torn and stained chenille spread sloppily thrown across it, a padded straight-backed chair with stuffing sticking out of its sides, a metal clothing rack, and a rusty tin wastebasket Alma recognized as being from the Statler, one of Detroit's finest hotels.

"I'm sorry," Joe said, "This is awful. Let's go. If I'd known it was this bad …" The sound of the hissing radiator under the double window drowned out the rest of what he was saying.

Alma shook her head. "No. It's all right." She tried, but her voice failed to hide the repulsion she felt. This was not the way she had always imagined it would be for her first time. She would be staying at a country inn. There would be a large room filled with fresh flowers, a fire crackling in the fireplace, champagne chilling next to the bed, which was covered with the finest pink silk sheets and comforter, and …

Alma sighed and walked over to the window. The cold air seeping in where the putty was missing didn't help the room's uncomfortable temperature. She wiped a patch of grime from the window with her hand and looked down. Across Woodward a line of swingshifters was forming to buy tickets at an all-night movie theater advertising *So Proudly We Hail!*, and two other movies, probably grade B, that Alma hadn't heard of. On a corner, a group of young men wearing zoot suits were gathered near a traffic light post trimmed with holiday decorations. Farther south, a huge pink and green neon cocktail glass above a bar kept filling and emptying. She glanced at Joe.

"What a moron," he said. "I even forgot the champagne. I'll hurry down and get some. It'll chill in no time--"

"No. It's all right." Alma knew if he left her alone for a minute she'd lose her nerve and flee.

Joe walked over and gently helped her take off her coat. He hung it on the rack in the corner, took off his wool jacket and hung it beside it. Returning, he took her hand in his. He looked out the window. "I haven't seen any of those movies, have you?"

"No."

"But I hear *So Proudly We Hail!* is pretty good."

"Yes."

"Do you like going to the movies?"

"Yes."

"It's a little early for Christmas decorations, isn't it?"

"Yes."

"Is that all you can say--'yes' or 'no?'"

Joe laughed and looked at her. She laughed, a nervous, high-pitched laugh that sounded unlike her own. What was she supposed to do now? Was she supposed to start taking off her clothes? Joe unzipped the back of her dress. It fell to the floor in a shiny blue heap. Alma thought it looked pretty against the green threadbare rug. She felt strange having a man see her in her underslip and brassiere. She wished she had a robe to cover herself.

"Don't be embarrassed. You're beautiful. Just beautiful." Joe's voice was cracking again. He began to unbutton his shirt and pants.

Alma turned her head away, thinking of Uncle Darcas once more. She'd pushed the memory of what had happened from her mind these past weeks, but now it was returning--

No! She would not let it return! She pulled the bedspread down, jumped into bed, and covered herself with it.

"You silly little girl," Joe said. "Are you that shy?"

Alma didn't reply. She kept her head turned away.

"Okay. I'll make it easy for you. I'll undress in the bathroom."

Alma heard him walk over to the bathroom and close the door. She peeked out from under the spread to make sure she was alone. At that moment, she hated her mother for not telling her anything about what goes on between men and women. She sat up on the edge of the bed. What was she doing here? How did she know he really loved her? How did she know she really loved him? Should she grab her coat and leave, and--?"

The bathroom door opened. Joe was carrying his clothes and was naked, except for a towel around his waist and a dog tag around his neck.

She stood up abruptly and looked out the window.

Joe came and stood beside her. "You must know every inch of that street down there by now," he said. He put his arms around her and pressed her to his body. His towel fell to the floor.

This was the first time she'd ever seen a man entirely naked (other than Uncle Darcas). Except for statues and in art books, of course. It felt strange being next to a naked man's body. Alma's heart began to hammer. Could he hear it? His lips moved over her forehead, down her cheek, and found her mouth. Alma began to kiss him in return. Her heart pounded even harder. There were only a few precious hours left. How could she have thought she could leave? She did not resist when he unfastened her brassiere. She helped him pull her slip up over her head. It and the brassiere joined the dress on the floor. Alma sat down on the bed and unfastened her garter belt, took it and her stockings and shoes off, and got under the bedspread once more.

Joe lay down beside her. It felt both strange and natural that he should be there.

"Your skin is so smooth, Alma."

"So is yours."

"Are you afraid?"

"Not anymore."

"I'm the luckiest guy in the world."

"I never thought I could feel this way about someone."

"Oh, Alma, Alma. I love you so much."

"I love you, too."

Joe reached down to the floor and groped for something in his pants pockets. He pulled his wallet out and fumbled through it.

Alma averted her eyes to the window.

"Just to be safe," Joe said, his voice cracking with emotion.

He was on top of her now. His buttocks were smooth and firm, the muscles of his thighs hard. He kissed her softly at first, and then his lips became harder as he spread her legs apart with his hand. "I'll be very gentle," he whispered.

Afterwards, Joe sat up and lit a Camel from a pack in his pants pocket. "I knew you'd be a virgin," he said, smiling at her. "I have a confession to make. I know you won't believe this. I was one until just now, too. I just couldn't do it with someone I didn't love."

Alma sat up, too, and pulled the spread close under her chin.

Joe drew her to him with his free arm. "That's one of the many things I love about you--your modesty. He kissed her face with soft light kisses and ran his hand through her tangled curls. "I'm a lucky guy," he said. "I still can't believe I'm here with you."

Later, as Joe lay in bed, Alma closed the bathroom door behind her and looked at her face in the mirror. She looked the same as she always had. Could her mother tell what had happened? Her mother would never understand. After all these months, she still brought up the fact that Alma had traveled to New York with "that Hunt feller". No, her mother would not understand. Not like her father would. *I belong to someone now, Pa. And he belongs to me.*

Alma lay down gingerly in the cold and gritty porcelain tub and rinsed herself off as best she could. Wheat germ, that's what it smelled like. Wheat germ.

★ ★ ★

Late the following morning, Alma and Joe waved hello to Max as she drove past the entrance to the grounds of her apartment building. She had nothing to worry about. Sarah had Sundays off. And they would be leaving for the train in a few hours. She looked over at Joe. She had someone to love. And he loved her, too.

Joe was feeling the leather upholstery on the dashboard and seats. "Out of my league," he said.

"You can drive it when you get back," Alma said. She didn't want to think of him going away.

Joe whistled softly in admiration when he entered her bedroom. He took off his boots and socks and wriggled his toes in the long white fibers of the rug. "I don't think I've ever walked on a rug so thick. This is sure a lot different from our barracks floors. And look at that bed. This must be what Heaven's like!" He walked over and felt the sheer silk bedspread. His face clouded a little. "I'll never be able to afford this kind of life for you."

"I'll make enough for both of us."

"No," Joe said firmly. "You'll keep what you make and we'll live on what the farm brings in."

He thinks that now, Alma thought, but wait until he gets a taste of real luxury. I could never give it up. "And I'll still do my painting every day," she said, testing him.

"Of course. Think I'd ask you to give it up? You'll be the best artist in the world and I'll be the best farmer."

Alma looked at him and smiled, remembering her last conversation with Hunt. How long ago that seemed now! "You're wonderful," she whispered.

He pulled her to him and kissed her eagerly as he unbuttoned the back of her blouse. His lips were warm and soft and then became firm as she removed his jacket.

A moment later, they were between Alma's silk sheets. Their lovemaking was becoming better now. She'd gotten over some of her modesty, her inhibitions. She was beginning to be familiar with every plane, every muscle of his body.

"You're beautiful, Alma."

"I never dreamed it could be this wonderful being so close with someone. ..."

"Not in my wildest fantasies, either. Oh, Alma, Alma, I love you so much."

A few minutes more, and their lovemaking became intense. It was almost more than Alma could bear. She accepted him eagerly, impatiently, her body in tune with his body, her rhythm in tune with his rhythm. "Joe, I love you so much. ..."

★　★　★

Alma was awed, as usual, by the size and beauty of Michigan Central Station: a sixteen-story neoclassical limestone and tan brick structure with Corinthian columns and tall, graceful Romanesque exterior and interior arches. This afternoon, it was a swarm of humanity.

Alma hoped she wouldn't see anyone she knew. She didn't want to share her and Joe's few remaining minutes together with anyone else. They had lingered at her apartment until the very last minute, and now Joe's train was almost departing. They pushed their way through the crush of travelers. Alma glanced out of the corner of her eye at the USO-Travelers Aid Society counter. "If you don't know the number of your husband's division," a patient woman volunteer asked a pretty young woman who was almost in tears, "do you know the number of his regiment or battalion, or anything? No? Well, don't you worry, dear. We'll locate him for you."

Several of Alma's friends, volunteers from the Women's Ad Club, staffed the USO counter here on weekends. She was relieved to see none of them here today.

At last they were at the departure gate. Joe leaned against a roof support with a poster attached. The poster showed an Army private with a duffle bag on his back and a rifle resting in his hands. Below his picture were the words:

THINK BEFORE YOU TRAVEL
Association of American Railroads

"Well, I'm thinking before _I_ travel," Joe said, embracing her. "I'm thinking I'm the luckiest man in the world. I've been in love with you since the Autumn Fantasy, Alma Combs, and to think, wonder of wonders, you love me, too."

"I'm the lucky one," Alma said, her voice choking. Her arms tightened around him. His jacket against her cheek felt warm and rough and secure. Now that she'd found him, how could she let him go?

Alma glanced around. She was just one of many young women gathered here saying goodbye to their men. Somehow, being a part of this group of women was a little comforting. She kissed him for the final time, then clung to him. "I love you, Alma," he whispered.

A moment later, Alma spied his face as he waved from a window of the departing train. She ran alongside his car. The engine picked up speed. She almost collided with several porters and groups of people waving goodbye, but kept her gaze fixed on his.

Then, he was gone.

★　★　★

Late that evening, Alma lay in bed. She caressed the sheet where Joe had lain. She picked up his pillow and hugged it tightly against her breasts, remembering their time together. It had all happened so fast. Was she sure she'd marry him? Had he actually asked her?

A nagging thought kept creeping into her head. A disturbing thought. Joe had been right, what he'd said last night (Was it only last night?): "She's wondering if she does that, what he'll think of her after he's gone. What she'll think of herself. She's wondering ..."

Oh, she had been so easy!

The phone rang. Alma picked it up and held the receiver to her ear. "Hello?"

The operator's voice said, "I have a call from New York for Alma Combs."

"This, this is Alma Combs."

"Go ahead."

Joe's voice said, "Just wanted you to know I still love you after all this time. And that you're wonderful. And--and there's something I don't remember you actually saying you'll do. You will marry me, won't you? Soon as I get back?"

Alma felt her heart beat faster and a loaded feeling in her throat.

"Oh, Joe! Joe! Of course. Oh, I love you, Joe!"

Chapter 34

Alma sat on a small couch with a group of fellow workers in the corner of the women's lounge. This room and most of the factory were now so familiar to her, it was hard to believe she had been working here at Blakely Ball Bearings for only two weeks. In front of the dingy tan wall to her right was a table with two large coffee urns, and a long leatherette couch crowded with employees. Above the couch was a sign:

STOP LOOSE TALK CAMPAIGN:

1. Keep military information out of your conversation at all times.
2. Do not discuss the movements, training, or equipment of any member of the armed forces.
3. Do not discuss anything which might disclose the arrival or departure of troops or ships.
4. Do not discuss anything related to war production, the character of war equipment or the shipment of war supplies.
5. Warn others who are careless.

To her left, above another couch also crowded with employees, was a poster showing a glamorous young woman dressed in blue coveralls. A red and white polka dotted bandanna covered her hair. She was making a tight fist and pulling up her sleeve to show her bicep. "WE CAN DO IT!" she said.

The workers had just returned from an assembly where they were awarded the armed forces "E" flag for production excellence. Alma felt proud to be a part of that excellence.

Alma finished the sandwich she had brought from home, stuffed the waxed paper and brown bag into the wastebasket, and glanced at her watch. Eight more minutes remained of their lunch hour.

"Wasn't that something? The military band playing for us and everything," said Mabel O'Leary, a worker in her mid-forties who sat next to Alma. Her voice sounded scratchy and deep, as if she had spent too many years smoking too many cigarettes and drinking too much booze. Mabel had short, see-through permed hair the color of twice-used dishwater, and her pale skin stretched like parchment over her narrow face.

"Oh, it's all right, I guess. But I'd rather have a raise, not a flag," said little Ann Snycerski, who sat by Alma's feet on the asphalt floor. She was dark-haired and pretty, and looked older than her thirty-five years.

"Oh, you sound so mercenary and unpatriotic," Mabel said.

Alma smiled. "What made you all decide to work here?" she asked.

"Well, if we would all admit it, most of us are here mainly for the money," Ann said. "This is the first time in years I've had three square meals a day, decent clothes on my back, and shoes without holes. And my husband and kids have them, too. I haven't forgotten how it was during the Depression, you know."

"I'm in it for the money, too, Alma," said Gloria Knapp, a matronly gray-haired woman with grown children and a stingy husband. "But another reason is that for the first time in my life I feel like I'm doing something important. This is the first time I've ever worked outside of the house. I'm finding out I can do something more than scrub the floor or clean the toilet or cook the meals. And you know what? I'm doing a great job of it, too. And for the first time since I got married, I have my own spending money jingling in my pocket."

"There's one drawback, though," Ann said. "On the one hand I get praised for doing war work, and on the other I get condemned by the editorial writers for not being home with the kids. There's a rise in juvenile delinquency, and supposedly I'm to blame." The others nodded their heads in empathy.

"There's another thing, too," Ann continued. "I still have my job to do when I get home. Do you think it would ever occur to Pete to start supper? Hell, no. He'd sit there till hell freezes over drinking his Stroh's until I got home."

"You ought to go on strike," Mabel said. Everyone laughed.

"And sometimes I don't get home for hours, what with doing the shopping--"

"If you're lucky enough to have any ration stamps left," Gloria said.

"And on the weekends there's laundry and house work, and other crap."

Mabel looked at Alma and smiled. "Why you working, Alma?"

Alma had been amused by and interested in the conversation. Now she thought for a moment. "Well, I guess you could really call me 'The Girl Behind the Man Behind the Gun,' as the slogan goes."

"No kidding!" Ann said.

"Are you real?" Gloria asked. She reached one chubby finger up and felt Alma's shoulder. "You mean all that propaganda they're trying to feed the American public isn't entirely propaganda?"

"Aw, c'mon, girls. Leave Alma alone," Mabel said. "I think Alma's really serious."

Alma smiled. Nothing bothered her these days. Not since she met Joe. "Of course I'm serious. Maybe one of those ball bearings I checked will be used in the jeep my brother drives. Maybe the next one will go into the plane protecting my--fiance." The word, "fiance," sounded strange but nice to Alma. This was the first time she had actually said it out loud.

"Now ain't that noble," Ann said.

"The only thing I don't like, though," Alma said, "is the way that Steve guy tries to rub against me when he's standing behind me and puts a new tray of bearings in front of me."

"I told you what you should do the next time you need more bearings," Mabel said.

Ann and Gloria nodded their heads in agreement as everyone laughed.

"I haven't forgotten," Alma said.

"These men," Gloria said. "It's so obvious they resent our being here. They still think we should be back home, dependent and helpless. But they're finding out we can do just as good or better a job than they can. And they damn well better get used to it, because we're here to stay. This ol' world will never be the same again!"

"Amen," Mabel said.

The whistle blew. The women rose as Ann said, "Well, I sure hope the war doesn't end before I get my stove paid for."

They had to pass all the male workers on the way back to their jobs. Management kept the men and women separated because the men couldn't keep their minds on their jobs if the women worked alongside of them, and that affected production. They passed one group of men as one of the male workers shouted, "There she goes, the gal with the streamlined hips!"

"Who's he referring to?" Ann asked. She had to shout to be heard over the noise of the machinery.

"It must be Alma," Mabel shouted. "I don't think it's either one of you and it certainly ain't me." The women laughed.

When they passed the next group, another worker gave a loud, admiring whistle. Ann stopped walking, looked him in the eye, and whistled back. "Look at the look on his face. He doesn't know what to do now. It works every time!"

Back at their stations now, Alma was always surprised by how grimy and dark it was. Like working in a dirty cave. Oil on the floor. Almost every inch of the entire plant taken up by machinery for war production. Alma's job was simple: inspecting rough ball bearings. But it was formerly a man's job; some of the bearings were so heavy it was difficult for her to lift them. She put on her gloves. The foreman would have to give her new ones soon. They were almost in shreds. The gloves didn't last long, because the bearings were of rough steel and tore them. The palms of Alma's hands were almost covered with small cuts from where the bearings had ripped through. Her hands had become hardened, though, and did not hurt as much as before. She smiled now as she recalled how shocked Felicia Carlson had been when she saw them. Felicia had dropped by unexpectedly last Sunday to lend Alma her copy of *Forever Amber*, the risque new historical novel that all of Felicia's friends were reading. Felicia had marked all the "good" parts. Alma graciously declined the loan, saying that she was too busy.

"Alma, dear! Look at your hands! What on earth are you busy at? Don't tell me painting would do that to your hands."

Alma had laughed. She couldn't tell Felicia the truth, that she was working in a factory, of all places. Felicia wouldn't understand. Alma would have to come up with some explanation. "I'll tell you some day soon," Alma promised.

"Now you've got me really curious," Felicia said. She glanced at her image in the ornate mirror above the hall console and patted the flesh under her chin. "Does it involve a man? You certainly are a changed person. I've never seen you this happy. You're positively glowing!"

Yes, Alma thought, as she lifted a heavy bearing now onto the gauge to see whether it met specifications. I am a changed person. I love Joe and he loves me in return. It's like the old cliche. Since loving Joe, I'm in tune with myself and the world around me. I'm a whole person now. I can do anything I set my mind to. Oh, Pa, I wish you were still here to know Joe, too.

Harry Buckingham had noticed the change in Alma, too. Last week while they sat drinking coffee in Alma's kitchen, Harry grinned at her, and said, "'Love comforteth like sunshine after rain'."

"Oh, Harry, you and your poetry," Alma had said, her voice affectionate and teasing.

"That's not mine. That's Shakespeare's," Harry said. After a moment during which he studied her face, he smiled and continued, "You're bubbling over with happiness. Tell me more about this Joe fellow."

"I've told you just about everything I know, Harry. All I know is I've never felt this way before. I've finally found something that I've never found before. I guess I didn't know what I was missing until it came to me."

Alma looked at herself now. If anyone had told her a month ago that she would be wearing these coveralls and have her hair tucked into a snood to work in a filthy, noisy place like this doing heavy manual labor, she would have told them they were out of their minds. But she had found that just doing her painting and volunteering at the USO, and waiting for Joe's letters, were not enough. She had to get out and DO something to bring Joe back home to her sooner. Maybe her new fellow workers were right. Maybe she did fall for that propaganda. Maybe that poster was the final factor that led to this decision. That poster of the young woman clutching letters from her sweetheart, with a faraway, longing look in her eyes: "Longing Won't Bring Him Back Sooner. ... Get a War Job!"

Then, too, she was here for her father. He had done a job for the war effort, so she was doing one, too. Somehow, that was comforting. The only thing she regretted was that, after putting in a long day here, she was too tired to lift a paintbrush when she got home. Her painting would have to wait.

And while the war had been more or less a remote, uninteresting activity to her before--except for wondering about Jimmie Lee, of course--suddenly the war filled her thoughts when she was not thinking of Joe: She gave all her earnings from this job to the 4th War Loan Drive; she drove her car as little as possible to save on gas and tires; she strained her used cooking fat (which she heard was needed for glycerin in explosives and other war materials) into an empty tin can and took it to her meat dealer, who in return offered her two brown ration points and four cents for each pound, which she never accepted. And the last time Sarah threatened to get a war job if Alma did not give her another hefty raise, to Sarah's surprise, Alma discharged her and encouraged her to get one.

Alma felt very American.

Mabel, who stood next to Alma at the bench, pointed to her supply of bearings now, indicating that Alma was almost out of them. Alma nodded and caught the attention of Gloria and Ann, who worked across from them. She left her station and walked to the table behind her where trays of the heavy bearings were filled. There she waited for Steve, the foreman, who would take filled new trays to the women workers when their supply was almost depleted. The women were never supposed to lift the trays because of the weight.

Alma selected a tray that appeared to have more bearings than the others. She tried to lift it, but could not make it budge. She then chose a tray with fewer bearings in it, and after several attempts, succeeded in at least tilting it to one side. The bearings crashed to the floor, making a sound so loud it was heard over the usual noise. Mabel and the rest of the women had been watching, and stepped out of the way before any of the bearings could hit them on their ankles.

The women struggled to keep a straight face as Steve hurried up the aisle, his face red under his graying brush. "What the hell you tryin' to do? You know you're not supposed to lift those trays!" he shouted at

Alma. He grabbed the empty tray, squatted down on his stubby legs, and began filling it with the scattered bearings. Alma started to squat down and help fill the tray, too, but Mabel tapped her on the arm and shook her head. After Steve had refilled the tray, placed it on Alma's bench and left, still furious, Mabel shouted to Alma: "Do that a couple of times, and the big boss will be over here, raising hell with him for letting you lift your own trays. Soon the Friendly Foreman will catch on. He'll never try to rub against you again. That spill worked for all of us." The other workers were still grinning.

Later, as she punched out at the time clock under the sign reading "Don't Let Them Catch Us With Our Plants Down!" Alma realized how much her arms ached and her hands hurt. She was tired, but it was a healthy, satisfying tired.

"Oh, no! Snowing again!" Mabel said. She hurried toward her bus stop and waved good night to Alma and the crowd of workers. Alma waved back as snowflakes fell, fat and flat, on her face. The snow--it was beautiful! She hadn't seen a snowfall this beautiful in years. She wished Joe were here to share it with her. She adjusted the string of her parka tightly around her face and pulled on her gloves. Alma breathed deeply of the fresh, wet air and felt the fatigue leave her. Maybe she'd walk home. ... Anxious to get home to Joe's letter, though, she decided to take the bus.

It did not bother her that the DSR bus driver bawled her out when she mistook one of the new zinc-coated steel pennies for a dime and dropped it in the fare box. It did not annoy her to be stuffed like a pickle in a jar along with other passengers standing in the aisle because all the seats were taken. It did not faze her when a middle-aged woman passenger gave her a disgusted look because Alma fell into her package-filled lap when the driver made a sudden stop. Her mind was on Joe's letter.

"Wonderful day, isn't it, Max!" Alma called through the open slot of the guard's glass-enclosed gatehouse. Max smiled and nodded. She looked around at the tall pines and low shrubs, their branches drooping from the weight of the snow. It was like a scene from a Currier and Ives painting, Alma thought. She glanced to see if any of the other residents were there to notice her. If they were, no doubt they would complain to the management that someone employed in a common, dirty laboring job was living among them. Alma smiled at the thought of that.

There were two letters from Joe and one from Jimmie Lee in her mailbox. At times she did not receive a letter from Joe for several days, and the next day there would be a pile of them delivered.

Alma subscribed to the three Detroit newspapers now, so she could keep up better with news of the war. They were waiting in a heap at her apartment door. She scanned the front pages. For the past several days, news of the Bataan Death March was starting to be disclosed, overshadowing news of the Italian front. Today, one of the headlines read:

JAPS TORTURE YANKS
Escaped Americans Tell of Shocking Prison Camp Atrocities

Alma shook her head. *How horrible.* She didn't take time to remove her parka and boots, but walked straight to her studio, where she always read her letters from Joe and Jimmie Lee. She kept a map of the European front tacked on one wall there. She would read the letters and try to visualize where they might be fighting (to think--she used to be amused by her mother's war maps!) The blue pins represented Joe, the red ones Jimmie Lee. The way she could best figure it, they were both in Italy. Joe might be in Anzio and Jimmie Lee might still be fighting in Cassino. If this were true, they would be fairly close to each other.

She picked up one of Joe's letters first. His handwriting was clear and confident--like he himself was. She pressed her lips to the back of the envelope where his lips had sealed it. When she opened it, a cartoon by Bill Mauldin fell into her lap. It pictured the famous dogface "Joe" sitting on the ground, trying to dig a foxhole in Italian rock. Alma smiled. Was Joe trying to give her a clue to where he was?

She read the closing of his letter first, as she always did. Yes, it was there as usual: "I love you with all my heart. Your Joe."

Then she read his letter quickly. Later, she would read it again and again, and memorize her favorite passages.

> My Dearest Alma,
>   I am in my dugout I share with David Peterson. We have become good friends. He's from Ohio and a real sharp guy. The flame from a candle stuck in an empty cognac bottle gives enough light to write. Because of the constant shelling

by the xxxxxxx, most of the army has moved under-ground. There are thousands of dugouts here. The xxxxx beachhead is flat, and there is no other place to take cover.

Sweetheart (Alma was not yet used to that wonderful word), it would break your heart, especially you being an artist, to see the city of xxxxx and all the destruction the xxxxxxx have done. You would die if you saw the marble statues crumbled in the patios. Lots of trees are uprooted. Many of the wonderful old buildings are either destroyed or damaged. Tons of wreckage is washed xxxxxx. ("Ashore" is probably the censored word, Alma thught.) Everywhere there are mud and rubble and mud and broken electrical wiring and more mud.

But enough of that. Do not worry about me. I am not in great danger. As long as I have you waiting for me, I know I can live through anything. And, actually, one day of bad rainy weather (and there have been many days of it!) does more to slow our progress than a month of xxxxxx shelling.

Our staticy radio is playing wonderful love songs. Right now they're playing "I'll Be Seeing You." I know they're playing it just for us, Sweetheart.

My world is very small. Yours is probably much bigger than mine. (Alma wondered whether he'd gotten her letter yet telling him she had a war job.) It consists of this dugout or a foxhole or running between both. And the letters from you and Mom. I have your picture tacked up alongside my pallet. It is the last thing I see before closing my eyes.

I cannot imagine a future without you now. You are the reason for what I'm doing.

Will write more later tonight.

I love you with all my heart,
Your Joe

P.S. Can you believe this? Uncle is telling us to put brushless shaving cream on our feet so we won't get trench foot.

To have something to look forward to, she would read Joe's second letter after Jimmie Lee's. Alma opened her brother's letter with apprehension. Lately, his letters had taken on a pessimistic tone. Alma scanned it first. She would read it, too, more thoroughly later.

... "If it would only stop raining. We havent been dry in weeks. Water comes seeping up from the bottom of our foxholes. Us guys are laying right in it! And its raining on us from above, to. And its so cold. Most of the time us guys are knee deep in mud. I got trench foot so bad. The turane of this part of the country is so hard to fight on. Im so tired. (*How did this letter get by the censor?* Alma wondered.)

Alma you cant get a real impreshun of war until you smelled death. I been smelling a lot of death lately. Early this morning they brought down ten bodies from our platoon from the mountain (*Is that mountain Mt. Cassino?* Alma wondered.) Three of them were my good buddies. They even brought down our captain. And there isnt a better guy than our captain. They had to bring there bodies tied on the top of mules. Nobody wanted to lift off these poor guys from on top of the mules so the sargent told me and these two other guys we had to do it. It was awful. We layed them against a building and there waiting for somebody too come and get them.

Im living in a captured dugout. Theres olive trees all around. To bad I hate olives. ...Im so sick of the sound of artilury and the English spitfire planes that are protecting us up in the sky. But we got to finish this job. ...I use to think the most important thing in the world was too be rich like you Alma but now Id give my right arm just too be home and sitting in Ma's shabby little flat and eating a big mess of her beans and a big chunk of her corn bread. Im so sick of eating C rashuns and D rashuns... These hungry little kids watch me when I eat and it makes me lose my appatight so I end up giving it to them. ...

Alma could take no more of Jimmie Lee's letter right then. She would finish it after dinner. Alma picked up the second letter from Joe. Her spirits began to lift.

A faint, timid knock on her door interrupted her and she frowned in annoyance. *Who could have gotten upstairs without first sounding the lobby buzzer? And who would drop by at this time of day? And in weather like this.*

She opened the door, the letter still in her hand. A woman, small and middle-aged, slightly stooped, and dressed in black, stood there.

"You--You Alma Combs?" Her voice was soft, with a hint of a southern drawl.

Alma nodded yes. The hall light from above made the woman's dark, inexpensive coat, wet with snow, glisten.

"I--I'm Emma Smith." The woman cleared her throat nervously. "Joe's mother."

"Joe's mother," Alma repeated, without comprehension.

The woman nodded.

"Joe's mother. Oh, Joe's mother! Well, how do you do? I've been meaning to call you soon."

"You going somewhere?"

"Going somewhere?"

"You got your coat on."

Alma looked down at herself. She smiled. "Oh, no. I just got home. I always read Joe's letters first thing. But I'm forgetting my manners. Won't you come in?" Alma opened the door wider. When Mrs. Smith stepped inside, Alma noticed she had the same perfectly shaped eyebrows as Joe.

"I--I thought it best I come and tell you in person. Instead of on the phone."

Alma felt her heart sink. "Tell me what?" she asked. She closed the door behind them.

Alma gestured toward the chairs in front of the window. "Won't, won't you have a seat?" Her voice sounded high and not her own, like when Pa ... "But let me take your coat first. And will you have something to drink? A glass of sherry. Or tea or coffee?"

"No thank you, Alma. I can't stay long. But you can take my coat. I don't want to get your beautiful chair all wet."

Alma took her coat, which smelled of wet wool, and hung it in the closet. She followed Mrs. Smith over to the pair of chairs near the window and sat down in the chair opposite her.

"My son's been writing such wonderful things about you. Now, meeting you, I can understand why. Fact is, I've been meaning to call you up and invite you over, but--well, I guess I've been too shy. But now, meeting you, I can't understand why I hesitated."

Alma put Joe's letter down on the end table. She sat there, staring at his mother, too afraid to say anything, to ask why she had come.

"I've been thinking and thinking how I should tell you, Alma." Mrs. Smith reached into her purse and pulled out a folded piece of yellow paper. "And I finally decided there is no good way." She hesitated and then handed the paper to Alma.

Alma took it between two fingers. It was smudged and obviously had been folded and refolded many times. She opened it slowly, reluctantly, afraid to read it, but knowing she must. Her hand began to shake.

At the top of the paper were the words *Western Union*, and a sentence below that stating it was from the War Department. And then:

WE REGRET TO INFORM YOU THAT YOUR SON
PFC JOSEPH SMITH WAS KILLED IN ACTION 30
OCT AT...

She stared at the words and then read them again. "Joe? Killed?" she croaked. "There must be some mistake. Joe's not killed. I just read a letter from him. And here's another--"

"I know, I know, dear. I felt the same way. It just doesn't seem true. It doesn't seem true." Mrs. Smith rose from her chair. She stood by Alma and put her arm around her shoulder.

Alma continued to stare at the words. Some of what Joe's mother was saying floated down to her from what seemed like far away: "Think it happened at Anzio from what I can tell. ... My poor boy, my poor boy! Probably be awarded the Purple Heart. But what good'll that do now. ... My poor Joe ..."

★　　★　　★

Alma stirred in her chair. She looked over at the chair opposite hers. It was empty. Joe's mother had let herself out. How long ago had that been? What did it matter? Nothing mattered now.

She glanced at Joe's unopened letter on the table. She could not bring herself to read it now. Maybe some day she could. But not for a long, long time.

They were all gone now. All the people who meant the most to her. Her father. Carrie Lou. Even Mr. McAllister. And now Joe.

She looked absently out the window. The blackness was broken only by a light from the wharf in the distance. She sat there, for how long she did not know. Try as she might, she could not block the words that kept returning: *Do not worry about me. I am not in great danger. As long as I have you waiting for me, I know I can live through anything. Do not worry about me. I am not in great danger. As long as I have you ...*

She had only one thing left now. One thing that had never deserted her.

She rose from the chair. On the way to her study, she caught a glimpse of herself in the full-length mirror hanging in the hall. She still had her parka and boots on.

She picked up the phone on her desk and held the receiver to her ear. The operator's voice was cool, crisp. "Number, please."

"Townsend eight three nine four two."

"Thank you."

The number rang for a long time, and finally a sleepy voice answered. "Hello?"

"Miss Galbraith? I'm ready to talk about having that exhibit now." There was a pause. "What? What? Who is this?" Then another pause. "Alma, is that you?" Still another pause. "Alma, dear, is that you? Is something wrong? It's four-thirty in the morning."

"Four-thirty? Four-thirty in the morning? Oh, I'm so sorry. I didn't realize--"

"That's okay, dear. I'm delighted you finally made up your mind to exhibit. I'll get hold of Purlie today. But, Alma, are you sure you're all right? Your voice sounds strange. Have you been crying?"

There was a pause, and then Miss Galbraith repeated, "Alma, are you all right?"

"I'm fine. Just fine. 'Bye, Miss Galbraith." Alma hung up.

She fell into the swivel chair and rested her head on the desk in her folded arms. "Oh, Joe, I love you so. I love you so."

Chapter 35

"I'm certainly impressed with the amount of work you've done these past few years," Miss Galbraith said as she moved around Alma's studio and looked at the piles of portraits stacked against the walls. So eager had Alma's clients been to have their portraits exhibited at the prestigious Summit Club gallery, they had either hand-delivered them themselves to Alma's apartment or had their chauffeur bring them. Miss Galbraith pointed a plump finger at each portrait and made a silent rough count. "You must have at least a hundred here."

"Yes, I've done a lot of portraits these past few years, except lately, I …" Alma looked over at the portrait of Mrs. Gilden, still not any more finished than it had been months ago. Even if Joe hadn't-- hadn't died, Alma would still not have had the enthusiasm to finish it.

Miss Galbraith looked up at Alma, concern wrinkling her face. "Alma, dear, you don't look very well. Not like the old Alma. What's wrong?"

Alma just this moment realized that Miss Galbraith was no longer young. Her face was that of a middle-aged cherub, if there were such a thing, with fine wrinkles around the corners of her eyes and mouth, probably caused by all the smiling she had done throughout the years. "I'm fine. Really. I think I had a touch of the flu a few days ago, and I haven't had much sleep, either, thinking about the exhibit. I've been to the doctor, and I have another appointment tomorrow. He'll probably give me something to make me sleep." Alma hadn't told Miss Galbraith about Joe. His death was still too new and painful to talk about.

"Well, good. He'll fix you up." She scanned the paintings again. "I wish Purlie had more paintings. She'll only allow me to have what she considers her ten best. The exhibit will be a little lopsided, but what can I do?"

Alma had not seen Purlie in years. "Is Purlie still living in the Sojouner Truth Housing Project?"

"Yes, and she's commuting to Willow Run five days a week. She's a real Rosie the Riveter. And she volunteers at the new USO for Negroes on John R. Too bad Purlie and her family can't be at the opening Saturday night. You know there's an unspoken law that Negroes aren't allowed to exhibit at the Summit Club. And they're not even allowed in the place to see the paintings. Purlie understands this. Maybe someday it'll be different. Oh, I almost forgot to tell you. The regular critic for the *Times* is out of the country for a few weeks, so they've hired a New York critic to do the reviews temporarily. His name's Julian Nichols, and I hear he's really tough, but you and Purlie certainly don't have anything to worry about--"

The phone rang. Alma excused herself as Miss Galbraith waved goodbye.

It was Felicia. "Oh, Alma, it'll be so FUN Saturday night. All our friends will be there. Too bad Martha will be out of town. It would have been a really good chance for her to see your work all in one place. What are you serving? Let me tell you about the champagne I tried the other night at Martha's. ..."

★   ★   ★

Somehow, Alma found her way out of the doctor's office, paid the receptionist, and headed toward the door leading to the elevators. *It couldn't be true. The doctor must be mistaken.*

"Oh, Miss Combs, you forgot your pocketbook!"

He has to be mistaken—

"Miss Combs! Miss Combs! Come back! You forgot your pocketbook!"

Alma felt a tap on her shoulder. She turned around and saw the receptionist holding her brown alligator purse. "Oh, sorry," Alma said. "Thank you."

She drove home in heavy noon traffic, Dr. Huebner's words echoing in her ears: "You seem very distressed, Miss Combs." The gray-bearded doctor had rested back in his chair, and peered across his wide desk at her over thick, black-rimmed glasses that kept sliding down his narrow nose. "But it's not the end of the world. Is there someone you can confide in? Your mother? A close girlfriend? Will your young man marry you?"

Alma had sat there, her heart beating faster, her hands growing clammy as she gripped the arms of her chair. *Young man marry you. Young man marry you.*

Dr. Huebner pushed his glasses back up his nose. "Well, from what I can tell, there's no reason why your baby won't be born healthy and normal--"

Healthy and normal. My baby born healthy and normal--

"And if you decide not to keep it, and I strongly urge you not to in your situation, there are plenty of couples--wealthy, kind couples who have been waiting for years to adopt a healthy, normal, white baby." Dr. Huebner leaned forward on his elbows and lowered his voice, as if someone might be listening, even though he and Alma were the only ones in his office. "Well, go home and think about it. And--" He paused for a long moment while Alma's heart beat even faster. "if you decide not to have the baby, come and see me again. Don't talk with my nurse or receptionist. And don't call me on the phone. I'll give you the name of a doctor who'll--who'll fix you up."

Fix me up. Fix me up. He couldn't mean--

She slammed on the brakes. Her tires squealed as she almost crashed into the De Soto in front of her. The middle-aged driver stuck his head out the window, looked back and shook his fist at her.

A few minutes later she stood in front of the full-length mirror in her apartment. She scrutinized her body. No, as far as she could see, there were no telltale signs yet. Had anyone noticed?

I thought the doctor would say all that vomiting I did was from a bad case of the flu. What was she going to do?

Alma found herself in the living room. She fell into one of the chairs by the window overlooking the river. She must get through the opening Saturday evening. She must pretend that nothing was wrong. Then, Monday morning she would go to the personnel office and quit her job. She would decide what to do after that.

Alma felt cold and alone. *An illegitimate child. A horrendous handicap.* She would be ostracized.

She leaned forward with her elbows resting on her knees. "Oh, Joe," she whispered, "This can't be happening. Not from just those few short hours of happiness together. We were so careful. Pa. Pa. What am I going to do?"

★ ★ ★

"How strange to be in the same room with all our friends and see pictures of them on the wall, too," Clara Van Delore said. She puffed on her silver cigarette holder and looked around the large, crowded gallery.

The cigarette smoke was making Alma nauseated, but she smiled at Clara and said, "It's strange for me to see all the work I've done these past few years displayed in one room, too."

"And beautiful work, too, I might add," Percy Van DeLore added with a charming smile.

Alma smiled her thanks at Van Delore as Felicia whispered, "Who in the world is P. Washington? His work is terrible!"

"I agree," Colonel McIntosh said in his booming voice. "I never did think starving poor people and Negroes and war workers were fit subjects for art."

Alma noticed the frowns on the faces of several visitors, including Tommie, as they looked over at the Colonel. "Excuse me," Alma said. She left the group and walked toward Tommie, who stood with a young man several yards away. He was viewing a painting by Purlie. It was of a depressing subject, a young Negro woman waiting in a long line-- probably a relief line--holding a malnourished infant.

"Who is P. Washington?" Tommie asked. "Is he from Detroit?" Tommie stepped back several feet to view the painting better.

"I, I don't know," Alma said. Miss Galbraith had sworn her to secrecy. She and Alma had carefully worded the invitations and publicity, using only Purlie's first initial. The name "Purlie" would have been a dead giveaway that the artist was a Negro.

"Why?" Alma asked Tommie now.

"Because he really seems to know his subject."

"Yes. Too bad he didn't have more work to show. I feel as though I've hogged almost all the space."

"Well, it's not your fault." Tommie's tone was reassuring. "And I must say you've done a lot more paintings since I've known you than

I realized. And that one of old flour-face is certainly a miracle!" He pointed to the portrait of Mrs. McIntosh that hung on the far wall. "Somehow you've managed to flatter her incredibly, but still we all know it's her. No wonder she likes it so much." Tommie looked at his companion and then at Alma. "Oh, I'm sorry. Alma Combs, this is Bobbie Wentworth."

Alma shook Bobbie's hand. It was smooth and lax. His face had a delicate, rosy glow like the faces of the female subjects in the paintings of Raphael. Alma wondered how long Tommie had known this one.

She motioned to the serving girl to replace their empty champagne glasses and to bring more hors d'ouevres. Then Alma noticed Aunt Euella and Lil standing together in a corner, looking ill at ease. She excused herself and walked over to them.

"Oh, Alma May," Aunt Euella said, "I feel so out a place. I ain't been to no art place before. But I wanted to come and see your purty pitchures." Aunt Euella grasped her glass of champagne awkwardly with both bands. Probably one hand was steadying the other, Alma thought. She patted Aunt Euella on the arm of her Woolworth's red rayon dress and whispered, "You're doing just fine, Aunt Euella."

Aunt Euella smiled in relief. "You really think so, Alma May?" She smoothed her hair, which she obviously had had done in a beauty shop after work. It was styled with a high pompadour in front and a pageboy in back. Like Carrie Lou used to try to style hers. Alma felt a pang of heartache, remembering. Aunt Euella had stuck a red rayon rose, which clashed with the red of her dress, over one ear. "Mister Bucking--Harry thinks I look real purty-like tonight."

"Harry?" Alma asked.

"Might as well tell her, Euella," Lil said.

"Tell me what?" Alma asked.

Aunt Euella hesitated. She glanced over at Harry Buckingham, who stood by himself, viewing one of Purlie's paintings. "Oh, Alma May, you won't believe this." Aunt Euella hesitated again. "Me an' Harry--we been datin'. He's been treatin' me like I was a real queen. He says I deserve it after all them years with--with your poor Uncle Darcas. An'--An' Alma May, he makes me feel just like I'm really somethin'. An' I'm already signed up for a grammar class, at that adult night school, you know, so's I can learn to speak real good like he does. An' one a them—" She looked at Lil.

"Literature," Lil prompted.

"Litachure classes," Aunt Euella continued, "so's I can talk about them high muckymuck books an' pomes with him that he's always talkin' about, him bein' a English teacher an' all before workin' in the factry."

Aunt Euella dating Harry? Why would Harry--?

"But Lil's got some good news, too," Aunt Euella said. "Ain't you, Lil?" She looked at Lil with eyes as excited as a little girl's just bursting to tell something.

Lil giggled. "Guess what, Alma? I'm getting married again. Met him at the USO. Sailor named Robert Szymanski. We're getting married next weekend on his last leave before he ships out." Lil looked at Aunt Euella and then back at Alma. Her tone was defensive when she continued: "Well, he's dying to get married, so why shouldn't I marry him? Someone has to. He's going off to war to fight for our country. He might get killed and never come back--" Lil's hand flew to her mouth. "Oh, Alma! I'm so sorry! What a thoughtless ass I am!"

Alma felt as though she'd been hit in the stomach. "It's all right, Lil," she said, her voice breaking. She took a deep breath and looked around. She noticed Miss Galbraith talking with Gladys Polaski. Alma smiled at Lil and Aunt Euella. "Excuse me for a minute. ..."

Gladys had not been sent an invitation. She must have read about the opening in the paper. Gladys was dressed in a gray wool skirt (*versatile--it could be worn with many things*), a navy blue blouse, black galoshes, and a dark brown turban (*last year's style, but it covered her hair. Good.*). Alma could not believe she felt a tinge of envy upon seeing Gladys: Gladys was securely married, although her husband was in the Army.

Miss Galbraith's face was even more animated than usual as Alma approached. "This gallery is really great for showing off your work," she said. "Purlie's, too." She looked at Gladys, then back at Alma. "Gladys has promised not to mention that she knows who P. Washington is," she said, conspiratorially.

Alma looked around. Yes, it was ideal for exhibiting--spacious and plenty of light. And unique: All the furniture, lighting fixtures, doors, beams, woodwork, just about everything was handcrafted by Summit Club members.

"It's done in the Arts and Crafts style," Miss Galbraith said, seemingly reading Alma's mind. "It originated in Great Britain in the nineteenth century. They rejected anything machine-made."

"Just look at these high ceilings!" Gladys said. "They should lower them. Think of all the heat they're wasting!"

Miss Galbraith ignored Gladys's remark and continued, "Can you girls make out the signatures on those beams up there? All famous American artists, and Diego Rivera, who've visited here: Ben Shahn, Reginald Marsh, Norman Rockwell, and--oh, I forgot to tell you, Alma, the gallery director said the three newspaper critics were here yesterday. They probably had to turn in their reviews already."

Alma stole a glance at the one-of-a-kind clock. Still two hours to go. She smiled at Miss Galbraith and Gladys. "More champagne?" she asked, as she caught the attention of the serving girl.

Gladys nodded yes. "This is delicious, Alma. But think of the champagne that's wasted if the bottles are opened and nobody finishes them. Champagne gets flat so fast. You should have served wine. At least you can keep leftover wine a while."

Gladys is still a Cotton, Cotton, Cotton, thought Alma. She smiled at both of them and walked toward Harry Buckingham.

Harry was still viewing the same painting by Purlie! It was of three small Negro children huddled in a corner. The smallest of the three, even more raggedly dressed than the others, was sucking his thumb, and the other two children, girls, had their arms around him. Was this a scene from Purlie's childhood? Were they crowded together for warmth or out of fear?

"Tell me, Alma," Harry whispered, "is this 'P. Washington' the same Purlie Washington, one of your old classmates?"

Alma's eyes widened in surprise. "How did you know?"

"I just put two and two together. Most of the subjects are Negro. And it looks as if part of the signature on the paintings has been painted over. You said once that your art teacher had been trying for a long time to have you and Purlie Washington, her 'two all-time best students', exhibit together." Harry grinned. "But don't worry. My lips are sealed."

"Is it really true, Harry? About you and Aunt Euella?"

"Me and Aunt Euella what?"

"You know. Dating."

Harry hesitated. "Does it bother you?"

"Of course not. I'm happy for both of you."

Harry read her thoughts. "You say that, but you don't know if you really are happy about it, because the idea is too new, right?" He squeezed her arm gently. "I understand. Too many things have happened to you lately."

Alma stole a glance down to her waistline. She had selected a periwinkle blue loose-fitting dress for the opening. She folded her arms self-consciously over her stomach. Did Harry suspect?

"Your aunt, your aunt makes me feel ten years younger, Alma. It's been such a long time since I've known a woman who's so easy to please, so eager to learn. It's like she's a young girl just becoming aware what fun there can be in living. I ..." He paused and studied her face. "How are you really doing, Alma? You're amazing to pull this all together." He looked around again. "The show looks great. I only wish your father and Carrie Lou and Jimmie Lee could be here. ... And ... Joe."

A weak smile played across Alma's lips. "Thank you, Harry." She looked around, too. To her surprise, Tommie and Bobbie were engaged in a conversation with Aunt Euella and Lil.

Alma hesitated. "Why didn't she come, Harry?" Her voice quavered. "Who?"

"You know."

"Who? Your mother?"

Alma nodded.

"You know how busy she is, Alma, taking care of the flat all by herself and--"

"But she's not too busy to go to places she wants to go to. Aunt Euella says she went to Paradise Valley to hear Eleanor Roosevelt speak at an inter-racial forum. No, she still doesn't approve of Felicia, and Felicia's the one who first got me started painting all these people."

★　★　★

Alma was fully awake now after a night of fitful sleep and intermittent dreams. She slid her feet into her silk slippers, dragged to the bathroom, and splashed cold water on her face. She examined her body carefully in the hall mirror, as she'd done every morning since her visit to the doctor's office. *No signs yet.*

The headlines of the three Sunday newspapers said basically the same thing: "Yanks Seize Airbase Periling Truk/American Warships Bombard Rabaul And Karvieng." She felt again the pain of Joe's death as her glance fell upon the heading of a *Sunday Free Press* story about Anzio: "Nazi Dead Cover Beach Below Rome."

Alma sat up in her bed with two pillows plumped behind her, and the papers at her side. In the society pages, there was a picture of Felicia and Martha Templeton Revere sitting at a table during a recent Soroptomist luncheon. Mrs. Revere was being honored as "Woman of the Year," and Felicia, president of the organization, was presenting her with the award.

She'd saved the best till last. The exhibit reviews. She turned to the *Detroit Times* art section first. There were two photographs of Purlie's paintings included in a lengthy review that covered over half of one page. But--none of hers! She scanned the review.

> "P. Washington has wisely chosen to use only grays and whites and blacks to portray the grim, raw reality of his Depression-era scenes. ... Reminiscent of Dorothea Lange's famous 1936 gelatin-silver photographic print, *Migrant Mother*, done for the Farm Security Administration, P. Washington's *Mother and Children* evokes sympathy and heart-wrenching remembrances of America's not-too-distant past. Here we see not the plight of one family, but a shameful and pitiful universal human condition."

Alma could not believe this! So far, Julian Nichols had not mentioned her work once. She continued scanning:

> "In several scenes depicting war workers on the job, we are reminded of the series of frescoes by Mexican artist Diego Rivera at the Detroit Institute of Arts glorifying the worker on the automotive assembly line. Art is primarily a language of the emotions. P. Washington's paintings are filled with human emotions. Just as we can feel the despondency on the

faces and in the eyes of the subjects in *Mother and Children,* we can almost reach out and touch the pride in the actions of the bomber workers at Willow Run. ... The workers, really representing all of us, have found a cause to believe in. Once more we have come to believe in our nation and in ourselves. ... "

Julian Nichols went on and on about Purlie's work. Finally, in the second to last paragraph, there was mention of Alma's portraits:

"Also in the exhibit are numerous oil portraits of leading Detroit society figures by artist Alma Combs. The Combs paintings are decorative rather than substantial in nature, and the artist has learned the painterly tricks of vividly simulating materials and textures. The luminous skin of the female subjects shows a knowledge of paints which may someday approach that of the American painter, John Singer Sargent.

Alma read the final paragraph:

"The viewer will not forget the powerful paintings of P. Washington. The artist shows a genuine concern for people and sensitivity to their dignity. Run, don't walk, to the Summit Artists gallery to view his forceful work."

Alma tore the art page from the section, crumpled it in her hands and tossed it into the chrome wastebasket by her bed. "Decorative rather than substantial," he had called her work. That was an insult! And to think that he had devoted all that space to Purlie's work! Well, that was only one art critic's opinion!

She picked up the *Sunday Free Press* and opened it to the art section. Again, the review covered half the page. The heading read: "Expressive Paintings by New Artist Shine at Summit Artists Gallery". The sick feeling in the pit of her stomach grew as she scanned the review:

"What Dorothea Lange did in her Farm Security Administration photographs of the 1930's, what John Steinbeck did in his masterful novel, *The Grapes of Wrath,*

P. Washington does in his powerful paintings of Detroit's Depression-era desperate and downtrodden. ...

"Contrasting with this earlier work, the subjects of P. Washington's oil paintings depicting work in the Willow Run Bomber plant illustrate the simple dignity and worth in labor ... the fact that work makes ordinary people feel important. ...

"It takes a special vision to be an artist who stands out from the crowd. P. Washington has that special vision. ..."

Once again, there was not much mention of Alma's work:

"The artist's oil portraits show a refined sensuousness, reminiscent of the 18th century Rococo master, Fragonard. ..."

It can't be true! All this space devoted to Purlie's few paintings in the *Free Press*, too. With increasing apprehension that made her hands shake, she slowly opened *The Detroit News* to the art page. There must be a conspiracy against her, for once more, most of the words of the full-page story were devoted to Purlie. The opinion was basically the same as that of the other critics, and added that "P. Washington shows a real knowledge of his subject." Alma's work was "painterly," "fluid," "pleasant." The costumes on her female subjects were "opulent." Their flesh tones were "creamy white and smooth."

Alma ripped out the page, along with the one from the *Free Press*, and crumpled them both. She stuffed them into the wastebasket on top of the one from the *Times*. Alma's work was "pleasant". *Pleasant!* She hated that word when it described her work. He might just as well say it's boring!

The buzzer sounded. Who could that be so early in the morning? She was in no mood to be pleasant. She returned the buzz.

A moment later Tommie appeared at her door. Alma tried to hide her irritation. "Surprised you're up at this early hour," she greeted him.

"You're fuming inside, aren't you? Well, I can't say I blame you. It's not fair. This P. Washington guy gets most of the ink and he only has a few paintings in the show!"

"Oh, it doesn't really matter." Alma tried to make her choking voice even. She sat down opposite Tommie in one of the chairs by the window.

"Well, that's good."

There was an awkward silence after which Tommie made small talk and Alma wished he would leave.

"Well, I'll bet Mrs. Sycophant is calling my house right at this very moment," Tommie said. A grin lit his face.

"Why would Felicia be calling you so early on a Sunday morning? She always sleeps in on Sundays."

"She probably got up early to read the reviews to see if her portrait was mentioned. She'll see what a big splash this P. Washington made in the art world, and she'll want to meet him. She'll want to be seen with him and photographed with him. You know how Felicia is."

"True, but you can't introduce them. You don't know him." Alma fidgeted in her chair.

"Yes, but she probably thinks you do because you both know Galbraith. She'll probably see if I can wrangle some information about him out of you. Just you wait and see." Tommie grinned again.

Alma could not hide her annoyance much longer. She did not want to talk about Purlie Washington or even think about her. "Why did you come here, Tommie?"

"Just to cheer you, I guess."

"Well, you're not doing a very good job."

Tommie was silent for a moment. Finally, he said, "I'm sorry. I guess I really came here to give you advice."

"Advice? I don't need any advice!"

Tommie hesitated. "It's just that--it's just that I think you should be true to yourself. You should be painting about things you really feel. You don't really feel anything about the subjects you're painting. You--" He took a deep breath as if to gather courage to continue. "You shouldn't be phony and pretend you're something you're not. You're not really originally from a horse farm near Louisville. You're from one of the poorest hollows in Eastern Kentucky. You're a hillbilly, Alma. I suspected all along. And your aunt told me all about your background last night when we had a long conversation at the gallery."

It was finally out in the open. What Alma had suspected he knew all along. There was no denying it. "So?"

"*So* I think you shouldn't be phony and pretend--"

"I don't like to be called phony!"

"I'm sorry, Alma, I shouldn't have used that word. But I'm just trying to make you see. I'm just trying to help. 'To thine own self be true'."

Alma had just about enough of Tommie's "help." "'To thine own self be true'," she cried. "'To thine own self be true!'" Her voice rose. "I didn't ask for your advice! And talk about being phony! Who could be phonier than you?"

Tommie's lips parted in surprise. His cheeks grew pink below his usually penetrating brown eyes, which he now quickly averted from hers. "What, what do you mean?"

"You know what I mean."

Tommie began to shift uncomfortably in his chair. He glanced at his watch. "I didn't realize how late it's getting. I really should be going."

"Are you going home to your latest 'girlfriend'?"

"What do you mean 'girlfriend?'" He rose from his chair, still not looking at her.

"Oh, come on now, Tommie. Don't try to tell me you don't have a thing going with Bobbie. And before that it was Stevie, and before that--"

Tommie picked up his hat and gloves from the foyer console. "Bye, Alma," he said in a small voice. He closed the door behind him.

Good. It was finally out in the open, too. Tommie deserved that. She walked to the kitchen and poured herself a glass of water. She felt smug as she took a few swallows, and then an image of the crushed expression on Tommie's face flashed in her mind. How cruel she'd been to say that! She ran out of her apartment and down the hall. "Tommie! Tommie! I'm sorry!" she called. Too late. The elevator was already descending. She would phone him and apologize.

Alma returned to her chair and sat down. She thought about the reviews again, the pity for her they would cause among all her friends.

She sat there for a long time, losing all track of the hour. Maybe her work did *not* deserve any more mention than it got. Maybe she wasn't as good as she'd thought all these years. Maybe that Federal Art Project mural director--what was that greasy, cruel man's name? Alma could not remember. But maybe he was right all along. Maybe she wasn't a very good artist. Had she been fooling herself all this time? Had she been fooling her family and friends? Had she let Miss Galbraith down? She thought of her father. She was glad that he would never read those reviews.

For the first time in a long time, she thought of the choice she had made because of her painting. She had given up a life with Huntington Westlake III and everything that went with it because of what she thought was her gift for painting. She looked down at her stomach. If she had married Hunt, she never would have met Joe again, and this would not have happened. What a fool she had been to give up all that for a talent she never really had!

She rubbed her stomach gently with her hands. The seriousness of her situation enveloped her again. What was she going to do? She must make a decision. And quickly. Before anyone--

The buzzer sounded again. A minute later, she opened the door to Harry Buckingham. He handed her a pink corsage and said, "Just what a lovely young lady should wear when she goes out to lunch with her old friend, Harry Buckingham."

"Lunch? It's not lunch time yet."

Harry glanced at his watch. "It most certainly is. It's exactly twelve oh three and twenty seconds."

Alma looked down at herself. She was in her robe. She thought it was still early morning. Alma tried to return Harry's smile. "I don't feel like lunch, Harry."

Alma returned to her chair and gazed, unseeing, out the window. He followed and sat down across from her.

"You're taking it all too seriously, Alma."

"No, I'm not. Not when all three of them just about ignored my work and raved on and on about Purlie's."

"It's just that the subjects of Purlie's work are more, more--"

"Powerful," Alma finished for him.

"What's one exhibit? You'll have lots of exhibits."

"No," Alma said softly. After a moment she continued, as if she had just made the decision and was speaking to herself, "I don't have the heart to paint anymore. I'm finally realizing I don't have the gift I thought I had."

Harry's eyebrows raised in surprise. "Not paint! You can't be serious. You've lived your life for your painting."

"To think that I was concerned that Purlie had so few paintings in the show that they would hardly be noticed." Alma laughed ironically, feeling the swat of the critics' near-omission once more.

"But you should read the few lines they devoted to you more carefully. They mentioned you in the same breath as John Singer Sargent and Fragonard."

"Yes, and they also mentioned that my work was decorative and pleasant, rather than substantial."

"You should build on the good things they said."

They sat there silently for a few minutes. There was nothing more to say. Alma wanted to be alone with her thoughts.

Finally, Harry said. "Well, I don't consider your exhibit a failure. But even if it were, we all have our little failures, you know."

Alma looked at him. "Failures? What possible failure have you had?" She knew that he was trying to divert her thoughts from herself.

"Oh, I don't know," he said slowly. "A man always feels these days that he's not doing enough for his country."

"Not doing enough for his country? Look at all the hours you put in for war work."

"Yes, but--but if I didn't have these flat feet and was younger, I'd be in the service."

Alma looked at Harry closely. She had not noticed before that his blond hair was streaked with gray now, that the crow's feet around his eyes had grown deeper. But he was still a handsome man.

"Harry," Alma said, her tone soft. "I've been wondering. The Detroit schools are crying for teachers. There's such a shortage, you know. And they've raised the salaries to almost those paid to semi-skilled factory workers. And the juvenile delinquency problem is getting worse. Wouldn't it be just as patriotic for you to quit your factory job and go back to teaching English?"

Harry was silent for a moment. He pasted a Lucky Strike to his lower lip, lit it from Alma's table lighter, and took a deep drag. "Oh, Alma, I can't pretend to you any longer. I'm not a former English teacher. I never taught an English class in my life."

This *was* a day for surprises. "You're, you're not an English teacher? I don't believe it!"

"It's true."

"Why did you pretend you were?"

"Oh, I don't know. When I was young, I really intended to be an English teacher. And then the Depression came along. I didn't have the money for tuition. I barely had enough money for food. And then I found the job at Dodge Main. At first I thought I'd work for only a year and save enough to go back to school. But it got so secure and comfortable having a job when they were so scarce that I was afraid to leave. And soon I began to pretend that I really had been an English teacher. I suppose it was because I wanted my co-workers to think I was special. But probably it was because I myself wanted to feel I was. Soon I began to think I really *was* a former English teacher."

Alma sat there in disbelief. He had lied to them all these years! He had lied to her father!

"I guess," Harry said, "what you think you are, you are."

"What famous literary figure said that?" There was more than a tinge of sarcasm in Alma's voice.

"No one. I made that one up myself."

After he'd gone, Alma walked to her study. She selected an art reference book and thumbed the pages until she came to the name of Fragonard. Beside his name were the words: "Later 18th century Rococo master. Refined sensuousness, but lack of emotional depth; sophistication; young aristocrats amusing themselves." *Lack of emotional depth. Lack of emotional depth.*

Alma retrieved the crumpled reviews from the wastebasket in her bedroom. She smoothed them out as best she could, carried them to her chair by the living room window, and sat down. She began to read them again.

Chapter 36

E xcept for a quick trip to the Blakely Ball Bearings personnel office to sign separation papers, Alma remained in her apartment for a week following the disastrous reviews. She did not answer the phone when it rang. At times, she even took the receiver off the hook. She wanted to be alone to think. If Felicia or her other friends had phoned, she didn't know it.

She had entered through the rear door of Blakely to avoid walking past Mabel and her other co-workers. Most likely, none of them read art reviews, but in case someone did, she did not want to discuss hers.

Mr. Terrell, the assistant personnel manager, had sat and studied her through owly eyes below shaggy red brows. "You probably have an extremely important reason for quitting. Your job isn't frozen, but you must realize how vital our work is to the war effort."

"I wrote it on the form. I've got another factory job," Alma lied.

An I-don't-believe-you smile twisted his mouth to one side. "I've noticed that you don't look very well lately, Alma. And you've been absent for a week. Maybe you just need a leave of absence. We could even arrange to have it written up as though you were laid off. Then you would get unemployment compensation. The only time you couldn't is if you were pregnant. Michigan does not pay workers laid off because of pregnancy. But I guess we don't have to worry about that, do we?"

Alma felt her heart pound. "Of course not," she answered, her tone light. She managed a slight smile.

A moment later she had signed the necessary separation papers (Terrell must have really suspected her condition, or he would have questioned her more) and left quietly by the same door through which she'd entered. She felt guilty for not saying goodbye to her co-workers. Maybe someday she would look them up.

She glanced over at the phone on her study desk now, its receiver off the hook. Dr. Huebner's words returned to her, as they had over and over: "Don't call me on the phone. Don't talk with my nurse or receptionist. ... If you decide not to have the baby, come and see me. I'll give you the name of a doctor who'll fix you up."

It would be so easy. No one would ever know. She would pretend she had left for a vacation, and return in a few weeks.

Her glance fell upon the reviews again, which were spread on the desk. She felt the sting once more of the word, "pleasant." Her paintings were pleasant.

Seeing the reviews gave Alma the sudden desire to return to a place that she had frequented countless times. To see once more something that she had seen countless times.

On the way out of her apartment building, she passed a tall young woman in a fur coat who stood in the lobby. The woman was pushing a leather-gloved finger on a buzzer to one of the apartments. Alma stopped short. She recognized the profile under the mink turban, the dark, straight bangs peeking out smartly below the turban's top. Alma hurried toward the glass exterior doors. A shiny black limousine idled in the driveway. Alma would exit the building before the woman--

"Excuse me," Martha Templeton Revere said as she turned her head toward Alma. "Do you know Alma Combs?" Her voice was youthful, yet throaty and well modulated, as before. "I've been trying to call her every day for a week, and either there's no answer or a busy signal."

"Y-Yes," Alma replied, her own voice sounding cracked and common. "I'm Alma Combs."

Mrs. Revere looked at Alma more closely, with almond-shaped brown eyes behind curled black lashes. "But of course you're Alma Combs. I recognize you from the newspaper pictures with Felicia. I'm sorry we haven't made contact in all this time. And I'm sorry I couldn't attend the Summit Club opening. But I did get over to see the exhibit."

Alma's stomach began to knot. Of course, Martha Templeton Revere would be too gracious to mention the reviews. In an attempt to change the subject, Alma asked politely, "What did you want to see me about?"

Mrs. Revere smiled, revealing small, perfect teeth. "The invitation still stands. I'd like you to do my portrait."

"You, you still want me to do your portrait?" *Maybe Mrs. Revere hadn't read the reviews. Felicia had said she was out of town.*

"Of course," Mrs. Revere replied, smiling wider. "But I'd like you to do a very realistic painting. Don't flatter me at all. I'm not like Felicia and Colonel McIntosh and Clara Van Delore and all their friends. I've always wanted a very uncompromising portrait. One that shows all my flaws." She paused and waited for Alma to consider.

All her flaws? What flaws? How ridiculous. "I--I can't promise. I was thinking of going away for a while."

Disappointment puckered Mrs. Revere's smooth brow. "Well--I've waited this long. I guess I can wait a little longer."

How could Alma admit that she had lost her confidence? That she was afraid to pick up a paintbrush again? But was this the real reason she hesitated?

"The newspaper reviews were unfair," Mrs. Revere said. "Sure, this 'P. Washington' artist is good, his subjects are thought-provoking, but you're better with a paintbrush."

She was better with a paintbrush. Mrs. Revere thought she was better with a paintbrush. Did Alma dare ask what Felicia and her friends thought of the reviews? She cleared her throat.

"Ah--I haven't talked with hardly anyone since the reviews came out. What did Felicia and everyone say?"

Mrs. Revere hesitated. "Well--you know Felicia and all her friends. They're--I hate to say it--they're shallow as far as understanding art. They're each mostly insulted that their own portrait wasn't mentioned. And, and they don't understand that your work--your work has been mostly ignored. They're, they're pitying you because the other artist got all the attention."

Mrs. Revere patted Alma's arm gently. "What do you care? It's only one exhibit." She smiled and added, "Think seriously about doing my portrait. Felicia and her friends are like sheep. They'll see what a marvelous job you'll do with my portrait, and soon they'll all want a realistic, unflattering one of themselves. Maybe even Colonel McIntosh. It will start a trend in the crowd. Everyone will want their portrait redone by you." Her eyes danced merrily below perfectly arched black brows. "Let me know your decision when you get back."

She turned toward the door. "Oh, incidentally, Felicia asked me to find out if I can wrangle P. Washington's number from you. She called the Summit Club and they don't have it. Then she called Miss Galbraith and she said she doesn't have it, either. You know Felicia--she won't rest until she gets it." She raised her eyebrows and rolled her eyes knowingly. "She wants to be the first to be seen with P. Washington." Mrs. Revere giggled, the same old infectious giggle that Alma and her classmates used to try to emulate. "And she wants a new protege."

"I, I don't know P. Washington," Alma said, her tone even. "Sorry."

Mrs. Revere pushed the door open as Alma asked, "By the way, whatever happened to Albert Salvatore?" She was immediately sorry she had asked: She felt like an idiot.

"Albert Salvatore?"

"Yes. Albert Salvatore. He went to Northwestern High School, too."

Mrs. Revere thought for a moment. "I don't remember Albert Salvatore. But how would you know that name?"

"I--I went there, too."

"Oh, I forgot--Felicia did mention that. She wondered if I remembered you."

Alma looked through the entrance as the chauffeur opened the limousine door for Mrs. Revere. To her surprise and annoyance, she felt herself liking the young woman. She stood there for a moment and watched the vehicle make its way down the drive.

★　★　★

Alma nodded to the guard when she entered the art institute's Great Room.

"Well, well," he said in a hushed voice appropriate for an art museum. "We missed you around here, little lady. It's been a long time."

Alma returned his smile. He had changed little in all these years. He had looked old before, and barely older now. "I've been very busy," she said. She wondered if he had read last Sunday's art sections.

She continued walking through the huge room as there came into view what she had come to see, even before she passed through the archway leading into the vast Garden Court. The murals. The Rivera murals. Once inside the Garden Court, she turned slowly around, her eyes taking in all four walls. She began to see the murals as she had never seen them before. The greatness of them. The richness of the artist. The uniqueness of his perception. How man and nature and industry are mutually related. *Purlie had understood this that day long ago.* Miss Galbraith had tried to make Alma understand it, too. Why hadn't she cared to understand it then?

Rivera has a great feeling for his subjects, Alma thought. *He understands the dignity of the human being. Purlie understands this, too. But more important, Diego Rivera paints from his heart. Just as Purlie paints from hers.*

Alma sat down on the bench facing the large mural on the south wall. It depicted men working on a number of parts of an automobile assembly line. As in many times past, Alma saw several men working on a giant automobile body press. *But this was the first time she actually saw them.* Miss Galbraith's words from that time long ago came back to her now: "You must be very proud, Alma, that your father is part of such a huge industry that makes life easier for all of us."

Alma had been ashamed of the work her father did. To stand in one spot all day and do menial work. Day after day after day. She had not agreed with an artist who glorified the common worker, the common masses. She had not wanted to see then an artist's work that reminded her that her father was a common laborer.

When had she started to reject her background? When had her head started to fill with a desire to mingle with the wealthy and socially influential? When had she first experienced the consuming craving for luxuries? For big cars, expensive clothes, and high-rent apartments. For things. *Things.*

Had it all started by listening to the stories of Miss Di Inganno? (Alma would always think of her as Miss Di Inganno.) Stories of Hollywood glamour and parties and fancy clothes. Had Alma's cravings been fueled by Felicia? Felicia with her Grosse Pointe home, her cars and servants, her own nouveau richness, her own social climbing. Had it started as early as when she read the glowing letters of Mr. McLaughlin?

Somewhere along the path, she had lost her way. She had prostituted her gift, her talent, in exchange for material things and superficial relationships. Tommie was right. She had not cared about what she was painting. She had not been deeply moved by the subject, as Purlie was. Alma had painted only the surface, and she had even altered that to satisfy the ego of her clients. Purlie had painted the inner beauty. As Rivera did. As most artists who achieve greatness do.

Mr. McAllister's advice from long ago came back in a rush to her now, finally. "You are indeed fortunate. You have a special talent, a feeling for capturing beauty. Take the time to develop it, and you could very well be a successful artist someday. Maybe even a great one. But don't waste your gift. Learn to look deeper than what appears on the surface. It is the poet, the writer, the musician, the artist, who bring these feelings into focus, allowing all of us to have a deeper sense of what life is about. An artist has an inner eye to see things that have not yet been realized by other people. ..."

Learn to look deeper than what appears on the surface. Learn to look deeper. Now, at last, she understood.

And now, at last, she could admit what she had not wanted to admit all these years: She was envious of Purlie. And had no concept of her work as talent.

She continued to view the mural as a phrase from one of the reviews returned to her: "... the simple dignity and worth of labor." *Yes, Diego Rivera and Purlie understood.*

Just as Miss Di Inganno had been wearing a disguise, so had Alma been wearing one when with her Grosse Pointe friends. Feelings of peace and belonging came over her as she studied the murals. Feelings she had never gotten from living her pretense.

She rose from the bench and took one long, last look at the murals.

★   ★   ★

Alma picked up the newspapers that had been accumulating at her front door for a week and dumped them on the console in the foyer. She flipped through her mail, not caring what it contained. Among the usual statements there was also a letter from Martha Templeton Revere and one from Jimmie Lee. She ripped up the unopened letter from Mrs. Revere and threw it into the nearest wastebasket. Alma put Jimmie Lee's letter aside to read later when she felt better. Jimmie Lee's letters were getting even more depressing.

She threw her coat and hat onto the nearest sofa and took off her fur motor boots, then hurried to the desk in her study and opened a drawer. She pulled out the pile of letters and messages from Martha Templeton Revere, a pile that she had read and reread until they were almost falling apart.

Mrs. Revere was right: Doing a realistic, uncompromising portrait of her would certainly guarantee a trend. Soon the rest of the crowd would want one like that of them. Alma would be busy for years, and her business would continue to rake in huge profits. There were probably many struggling artists who would envy her position. But ...

Alma placed the phone receiver on its hook, picked it up again, and in a determined voice gave the operator the number that had been etched in her mind for a long, long time. To her surprise, Martha Templeton Revere answered the phone herself. "Mrs. Revere? This is Alma Combs--" Alma took a deep breath and plunged ahead, her tone unwavering. "I've been thinking about your offer, and--and I've decided to give up portrait painting." Alma listened to Mrs. Revere's surprised voice and then continued, "That's right--I won't be doing any more portraits. Nothing personal. Sorry if I've inconvenienced you. And thank you again."

Alma thumbed through her black appointment book until she found another number. She waited until the maid on the other end put Alma's client on the phone.

"Mrs. Gilden? This is Alma Combs. Sorry I haven't gotten back with you about another sitting for your portrait. I've been very busy. And I called to tell you that I'm not going to do portraits anymore. I'm so sorry if you're disappointed. And I really want to pay you for any inconvenience this may have caused you. You heard right. I won't be doing any more portraits. Give my regards to Mr. Gilden. Goodbye."

Alma looked in the book for other clients for whom she was to have made appointments, and gave them the same message.

Her calls finished, she left the receiver off the hook and again picked up the pile of letters from Mrs. Revere. She walked to the living room fireplace and tossed them onto the grate, took a match from the ornate brass matchbox on the mantle, and with great ceremony, struck the match and held it to the pile of letters. How lovely the blue and yellow flame looked. How quickly Mrs. Revere's elegant script curled and then disappeared into a black charred mess. Alma stood smiling at the smoking ashes for a long moment.

She hurried to the easel in her studio and yanked the uncompleted portrait of Mrs. Gilden from it, rushed to the fireplace, and threw it on the dying ashes. She lit another match and placed it on Mrs. Gilden's mouth. The flame quickly ate away a part of Mrs. Gilden's lips and distorted her mouth so that it curled up to meet her one completed eye. Alma clapped her hands and laughed out loud at the grotesque image. A carefree, relieved laugh. She was free of Mrs. Gilden, too.

She walked to the bedroom and lay down on the bed. Her laughter ceased: She must decide on a plan. She thought of Dr. Huebner and how easy--

No. She could not do that. She could not kill an innocent child. Especially her and Joe's child. Not her father's grandchild.

She would go away until after it was born. Pretend she was on a long cruise. She could live frugally for a while on the little bit of money she hadn't squandered. And she would find an agency that would arrange for a loving home for the baby. Hadn't Dr. Huebner said there were many couples eager to adopt? After it was all over, the memory of the child would fade. She would make it fade. She would *will* it to fade.

She rose from the bed and wandered around her apartment. She would leave everything here, just as it was. There was not time to store the furniture but she would sublet the apartment. Yes, that was what she must do.

But first, there was someplace she must see one more time. Just one more time she must sit in her father's chair, just one more time she must flip through his dog-eared farm catalogs, just one more time she must hold his guitar in her arms. After that, she would return to her apartment and pack a few clothes before leaving.

She replaced the phone receiver on the hook. On her way out the door, she noticed Jimmie Lee's letter on the console. She frowned and opened it. To her surprise, the tone of the letter was not sad:

"Oh, Alma, I'm just busting to tell you. I met this wonderful girl here. Shes a refugie from xxxxxx. I saw her once when we were there and cant beleive shes here now. It must be fate that we should meet again. She is still bitter about what those dam xxxxxxx did to her beautiful city. Her name is Sophia xxxxxxxx and shes a little bit younger than me. But she seems older because her life has been so hard. Shes got big brown eyes and long black hair and I know you and Ma will love her like I do. Im going to marry her if shell have me and bring her back home. But we wont be living in the city like you and Ma. I use to think I wanted to be rich like you Alma but ever since Pa died and we went back home to Mountainview I been thinking how I miss that place and how I want to get me a little farm by the mountains just like Pa always wanted and I don't care if I never get rich off it. I just want to make enough to get by just like Pa always said. I just want to be my own boss. Im so sick of taking orders from Uncle and every other guy above me. She says she wants to live on a farm too like she did before. Shes so all alone. She doesn't have any family left. They were all killed. I never thought Id feel this way about anybody Alma but I just want to take care of her the rest of my life. ..."

A trace of envy hit Alma, and then was quickly replaced by a feeling of gladness for her young brother as she read the letter again. *Jimmie Lee wants to get married? My little brother?* How could he be sure? She hoped that he had not fallen for this young woman just because he was vulnerable. Where was this Sophia What's-her-name from? Most likely Naples. So many things were happening so fast. It was hard to accept all the changes. Maybe Jimmie Lee was just infatuated. Maybe he would change his mind before he was shipped home.

Alma stuffed the letter into her purse. She would think about this later. The phone rang as she closed the door behind her.

Alma joined the heavy midafternoon traffic on northwest-bound Grand River Avenue. Now that she had made her decision, she must think of a place to live. She must think of a reason for leaving that her Grosse Pointe friends would believe. She turned right on Linwood Avenue as she was struck by the realization that she had not missed

Felicia or any of her crowd this past week. In fact, she hadn't cared much whether she had or had not seen them these past few months. And if she hadn't cared whether she saw them, then she didn't care what they thought of the reviews. She did not care that they were pitying her. And if it didn't matter what they thought of her, then why was she running away until after the …?

No, she would stay here. It was her life. She answered to no one.

But an image of her mother's disapproving face flashed before her. Aunt Euella had said only several weeks ago that her mother had mentioned again Alma's unchaperoned trip with Hunt. No, she could not stay here, as much as she desired it.

She would call Harry and say goodbye, of course, and leave word with her mother for Aunt Euella and Lil, since they would not be at home now. And she would call Tommie. She realized now that he had only meant well by saying those things.

Harry was right. How many other artists were mentioned in the same breath as Sargent? No, she could never give up her painting. It was so much a part of her. She would pack her easel and paints and brushes, as well as a few clothes. She would find a quiet spot far from here. And she would begin to paint again. Painting what, she did not know. But it would be something she was compelled to paint. Something she felt deeply about. And her paintings would be good. Very good. She knew it.

No, she did not care to do a portrait of Martha Templeton Revere. She had built her business on prostituting her talent for the vanity of others. The thought of pleasing their whims once more for money was repugnant.

Alma spotted a Kinsel drug store on her right. She parked the car, hurried inside, and walked directly to a phone booth where she looked up the number for the *Detroit Times* classified ads. Larger than the other two newspapers' classified sections, her ad would reach more people. A moment later, she was dictating to a clerk there: "For sale immediately. Entire quality contents of five-room luxury apartment. Very reasonable. Trinity 2-4389." She smiled with satisfaction. After visiting her father's place, she would go to her rental agent and get out of her lease.

Alma parked her car in front of her father's flat. She noticed that the walk leading to the porch was newly shoveled. A feeling of sadness hit her. Shoveling the snow had been one of her father's chores. Her mother must have done it.

When she reached to open the door to the flat, she glanced at the window and was distracted by a movement inside. She put her face to the glass and looked in. Alma squinted, straining to see beyond the stiff lace curtains. It was her mother. Sitting in her father's chair. Alma was surprised to see that she was holding her father's guitar in her arms and rubbing its fretted side against her cheek.

Alma opened the door. Her mother jumped from the chair and rested the guitar against it. "Alma May!"

Her mother's face and eyelids were red and puffy from crying. Her mother--crying! Embarrassed, Lizzie reached down and pulled up the hem of her plaid housedress and dabbed her eyes with it.

"Ma, that's the first time I've ever seen you cry! What's the matter?"

"Nothin', Alma May."

"Nothing?"

Her mother shook her head and looked down at the floor. "Sorry you had to see me like this, bawlin' an' everything."

"Sorry! Why should you be sorry?"

"I, I don't know, Alma May." Lizzie dabbed at her eyes with the hem of her dress again and looked up. "Oh, Alma May, I miss your Pa so much. Every day 'long 'bout this time, I still expect him to come in that door. I try to keep so busy so's I ain't got no time left to think a him, but most times it don't work. An' poor Carrie Lou. I miss her so much--"

"Oh, Ma--" Alma reached her arms out to her mother while Lizzie shyly extended her own.

Her mother's voice was muffled in Alma's embrace. "Oh, Alma May, sometimes I get so tired a bein' so strong. So tired."

"Ma, that's the best thing I've ever heard you say." Alma pressed her arms tighter around her mother, and realized for the first time how much her mother had loved her father. Why had she not known it before? And she realized now that this, being in her mother's arms, was the main reason she had come here today.

"Alma May, you ain't thinkin' a givin' up your baby, are you?"

Alma dropped her arms in surprise. "Wha-What baby? What are you talking about." She pushed her mother away gently.

"I ain't seen much a you lately, but I can tell you got that look. I seen lots a women back home get that look. Look like their breasts is fillin' out without their stomach ain't stickin' out yet."

There was no use in lying to her mother. "Ma. I'm so ashamed. I don't want to bring shame on you, too. I'm going away until after it's born, and--"

Her mother's mouth flew open. "Goin' away? You ain't doin' no such thing, Alma May. You're goin' to stay right here an' hold your head up high. You ain't the first girl got in a famly way without first she got a man. We ain't goin' to lie to nobody. An' I hope you ain't thinkin' a givin' that young'n' away. Think I'd let you give me an' your Pa's grandbaby away? An' what about your Joe's ma? Do you think she'd want you to give away her grandbaby, either?"

Joe's mother. It had not occurred to Alma to think about Joe's mother.

"Ashamed?" her mother continued. "I'm the one feels ashamed. Ashamed I ain't been a ma you could tell me right off you're in a famly way. I never been the kind a ma you could talk to."

"Oh, Ma--"

"We ain't got much family left, Alma May. We got to stick together. There's only you an' me an' Jimmie Lee. An' a course, your Aunt Euelly." Her mother began to smile, then, as if she remembered something. "Oh, Alma May, Jimmie Lee's got hisself an Italian girl. An' he's goin' to marry her an' bring her back home an' live on a farm, just like your Pa always wanted."

"I know, Ma."

"An' they're goin' to be real happy, I know they are."

Alma nodded her head in agreement.

"But I ain't never goin' back home to live no more, Alma May. My place is here now, because ... Well, I been thinkin', Alma May. They want volunteers to work at the Inter-Racial Committee office. I been thinkin' I'd call them up tomorrow an' see if there's anything I can do, even if it's just somethin' real simple. Your poor Pa died because a the racial prejudice in this town, an' maybe, maybe, Alma May, there's somethin' I can do to help the coloreds and whites get along better together."

Alma, surprised, stared at her mother. *Her mother, the stay-at-home, doing volunteer work?*

She looked at her mother's hair sticking out from its bun. When had it started to gray?

Her mother's smile grew wider. "Alma May, I want to show you somethin'," she said, her voice excited. She stepped into her bedroom and came out with something pale yellow in her hands. When her mother drew closer, Alma saw that it was a crocheted infant's sweater and matching booties. "They got such shoddy things in the stores these days, since the war. Don't want no grandbaby a your Pa's an' mine wearin' somethin' that'll take an' fall apart first time it's worn. I whipped these up quick as a jackrabbit. Course, couldn't make no pink or blue ones, bein' as we don't know yet if it's a boy or girl." She handed them to Alma.

They felt soft in her hands as Alma inspected them in the sudden ray of sunlight coming through the curtains. Dainty pearl buttons were sewn on the front of the sweater, and ribbons of white silk gathered its neckline and the tops of the booties. Speechless for a moment, Alma said, finally, her voice beginning to choke, "Ma. They're beautiful. Just beautiful."

The End

CPSIA information can be obtained at www.ICGtesting.com
Printed in the USA
BVOW05s0422180414

350985BV00002B/6/P